MY BLOOD IS ROYAL

('S rioghal mo dhream)
The Motto of the MacGregors

Joyce Milne D'Auria

ISBN: 1466394676
ISBN-13: 9781466394674
Library of Congress Control Number: 2011918008
CreateSpace, North Charleston, SC

Acknowledgments

My sincere thanks to:

The PINAWOR writers' group, in St. Petersburg, Florida for encouraging my earliest efforts, and to my teachers E. Rose Sabin for organizing my initial ramblings and Laurie Viera Rigler who tamed the original volume. The Dunedin writers' group, especially Mary T. Dresser and Ann O'Farrell, and to Barbara Schrefer, my guide to the museums and other delights of New York. We call them research trips! Kimen Mitchell, who read early and late drafts and to other readers including Lynn DiPier, Gabriel D'Auria, Nancy Dalton, George Felos, Susan Kelly and Gino Pullo who all provided sound advice, support, and encouragement.

My cousin Anne Shimmins who bravely escorted me into Rannoch on several occasions and climbed over the walls of old cemeteries. Together we visited the Old Monkland Cemetery in Coatbridge to lay flowers on the graves of our ancestors, and marvelled at the dates on the headstones of the young children and babies, sons and daughter of the great-grandmothers. We spent days at the Monkland library in Airdrie and Anne even went with me on a clandestine visit to the Big Tree Bar in Whifflet, a place women rarely dared to go when we were young in that town. My cousin, Jim Shimmins, who offered valuable historical information, critiqued my research, and made a cosy room for me to stay on my visits to Scotland. We spent hours remembering family stories...some of them true.

To Linda Frame, editor extraordinaire, who also happens to be my daughter, for copy-editing and making insightful suggestions.

And, finally, to Paul who keeps everything running.

To the grandmothers for their courage, constancy and faith

Also by Joyce Milne D'Auria
Lumpy Porridge and other Scottish Memories
Available at www.JoycetheScottishWriter.com

Part One

Rannoch

CHAPTER ONE

Hogmanay

Rannoch December 31, 1859

I come to wish you all a good New-Year
Old Father Time deputes me here before ye,
Not for to preach, but tell his simple story

—Robert Burns

Lizzie awoke sobbing. The same nightmare that had plagued her since she could remember lit the hours of darkness. Orange, yellow, red flames leapt from the windows and thatched roof of the stone cottage; the trapped animals inside the attached barn bellowed. She looked around to count the members of her family. Everyone was there except Gregor. He must be trapped inside the house. She started to scream, then felt the shawl around her shoulders weighted down like a sling against her rump. The small body inside it was clinging to her. In her dream she knew it was the sickly lad, her favourite wee brother, out of harm's way and by her side. She felt great relief.

"Sssh, sssh, it's all right lass. Don't wake the others. You're home here, safe in your own house." Her mother's voice carried the melody of her home town of Stornoway on the Isle of Lewis, the Hebridean island where she had been raised; it soothed Lizzie like the sound of the waves lapping on the shores of Loch Rannoch. Ma lightly touched her on the forehead, then moved the auburn curls, heavy with sweat, away from Lizzie's burning cheeks and turned the pillow to the dryer side. Lizzie felt the chill December air in the stone croft cooling her brow.

By now everyone was rousing in the only bedroom. Lizzie's thrashing had pulled the covers off her fourteen-year-old sister Annie and wee Gregor, who had been wrapped in the blanket at Lizzie side, the weight she felt in her dream. The four-year-old sighed deeply, shuddered, and snuggled closer to Lizzie, accidentally kicking Annie, who groaned and tried to kick back but instead hit the rear of the box-bed with her big toe and awoke howling. Charlie and the twins, about four feet away on a pallet, mumbled variations of "Shut-up, Annie" from the other wall in the cramped quarters of the sleeping room.

Annie angrily grabbed more than her share of the patchwork quilt and buried her head into it, muttering words Lizzie hoped her mother did not hear.

"These dreams, lass, you're just overtired from all the help you've been giving me to get ready for the big party tonight. Don't you know you're safe...?" Her mother's whispered reassurances were interrupted as the room came alive with morning grumbling.

"C'mon, you lot. Don't ye know that however ye act on Hogmanay will set your luck for the New Year?" her father called from the main room where he and Ma had a hole-in-the-wall bed they shared with the youngest, Kate.

"Jamie, tonight's the party." Donald, the twelve-year-old, swung a chaff-filled pillow at his twin's head.

Charlie dangled his legs over the edge of the bed he shared with the younger twins. He tried to smile through sleepy eyes at his sister. "There's still plenty to do before tonight, Lizzie. Oh, and thanks a lot for getting us up early."

"I'm sorry. It's just...."

"I know, I know, the bad dreams," said Lizzie's twin, Charlie, sixteen this coming year. He always had the ability to read her mind and kindly too.

CHAPTER TWO

Ne'erday
The Best Holiday

Should auld acquaintance be forgot,
And never brought to mind?
Should auld acquaintance be forgot
And auld lang syne.

For Lizzie the best thing about winter was the celebration that started on Hogmanay, New Year's Eve, and lasted all night till New Year's Day. Hog-ma-NAY! She said it over and over again to herself. On other years the MacGregors had gone out calling on all their neighbours in the tiny hamlet but, this year, because of the wee ones and Ma's delicate condition, they would stay home and wait for the first-footer. The first one to step over the threshold after midnight must be tall and dark-haired and carry a gift. The old Scottish tradition would bring luck to the host all year.

Lizzie thought about what "good luck" might look like for 1860. Ma delivering this next bairn without serious problems would be a fine start. Wee Gregor getting some strength back made the list. Jock Campbell talking to her again was a wish close to her heart. She thought about him day and night. Otherwise she felt her life was fulfilled and satisfying. She did pray they'd never have to leave their croft but Pa always assured her that the days of the Highland clearances were over even when a lassie in school didn't come back after the summer holidays. It was whispered among her classmates in the playground that the landlord had evicted her family. Though the clearance happened in another parish Lizzie couldn't get it out of her mind.

Lizzie, her sister Annie and her mother Flora had been baking and cleaning for weeks, tripping over the twins and wee Gregor in the confined space of the fire room.

Charlie and Father cleaned out the byre, the small barn-room attached to the house, and brought in their old draught horse, Bottom, from the pasture. The milk cow and the yearling calf along with several ewes that were due to lamb in the early spring filled another stall. Lizzie soothed Gregor's tears because they couldn't find Meggy-monyfeet, though they'd searched around the clachan and the surrounding hills, all the way up to where the laird's fenced land began, and down to Loch Rannoch and along its shore. Lizzie suspected the ewe was pregnant and sheltering in a corrie. To find her now, with snow on the ground, would be practically impossible.

Ma rested often as her lying in time neared. It could be a January baby and winter babies had a tougher time surviving in the damp cold of the Highlands. Lizzie and Annie swept and scrubbed the flagstone floor. Ma's girth made it impossible for her to do heavy labour, yet Lizzie had to nag her younger sister to do her part. Lizzie delighted the youngest sister, Kate, with a rare bath in front of the roaring peat fire. Afterwards they all took turns washing in the bine, the big galvanized tub kept under the bed. Lizzie had set, near the fire, a bucket of rainwater, her secret ingredient to make her hair shine.

After dark on Hogmanay they straightened out the fire room and put on their best clothes. Ma added a lace collar, which had been her mother's, to the neck of her fine gray wool dress that had survived in careful storage since her days as the laird's servant at Aulich Mansion. Lizzie combed her freshly washed auburn hair, tied it up with a green ribbon and pushed an errant curl back into place on top of her head, then groomed Annie's hair. The girls donned with pride the matching red and green patterned shawls their mother had knitted for a New Year's gift.

Donny and Jamie had dug a path to the outhouse and to the gate which opened onto the clachan, the circle of houses that formed their village, Aulich. Fresh snow fallen on this last day of December; had given the world a brand-new coat to welcome in the New Year. Banked several feet up to eye level, it helped keep the stone croft warm as did the animals in the byre.

Anyone coming down the path after midnight would be sure to make a fresh print on the snow. Lizzie wondered who their first-footer would be. She secretly hoped it would be the Campbells and maybe she'd get a chance to talk, or even dance, with Jock. Leaning over the deep window-shelf in the only bedroom, Lizzie's watched the snow sparkling in the moonlight, her anticipation mounting.

She waited.

CHAPTER THREE

The Campbells Are Comin'

And there's a hand, my trusty fiere,
And gie's a hand o' thine:
And we'll tak' a right guid-willie-waught,
For auld syne

Soon after midnight Lizzie heard John Campbell coming round the stone fence. By the sound of him, he'd been at some other parties before this. He sang an old Covenanters song with some lusty help from his grown sons.

"It's the Campbells, Ma." Lizzie checked herself in the mirror and straightened her ribbon; in the light of the paraffin lamp her green eyes shone and her cheeks were pink from excitement. She caught her breath and said to Annie, "Och, I hope Jock brought his fiddle."

"Why? Are you going to sing again?" Annie curled her lip. Lizzie knew her sister couldn't carry a tune, and couldn't understand why she was never invited to sing but to avoid the topic, Lizzie said, "We'll all sing," or Annie would take a huff and try to spoil the evening.

"Are ye there, MacGregor? We're coming in," yelled John.

"Sweesht, John. Ye'll waken the bairns," said Nellie Campbell in a hoarse whisper.

"Och! Woman, what kind of Scot young or old sleeps on Hogmanay? Open the door, MacGregor. I have a wee dram for ye."

"Comin', John. Comin' right away." Pa never answered the door, that was a job for one of the women, but tonight he forgot himself in his enthusiasm.

Lizzie's family crowded the door of the croft to be sure the appropriate first-footer gained entrance.

Over the noise of the Hogmanay greetings and the wind howling down the glen, she heard the Robertson's piper across Loch Rannoch playing "Auld Lang Syne."

Aleck Campbell, the oldest, tallest brother, led the parade to the threshold. Aleck had the darkest hair of the sandy-haired family. Lizzie had hoped Jock would be the first-footer but he was bringing up the rear.

"Aleck, carry this in." Nellie called to him and shoved her fragrant pot of mutton stew into his grasp.

"What for, Ma?"

"Ye can't walk in empty-handed. Ye'll bring the MacGregors bad luck, ye glaikit big tattiebogle."

His brothers laughed at the tall fellow getting lessons in Highland etiquette from his diminutive mother.

Aleck blushed, caught in the unmanly act of carrying food, and tried to refuse it. Yet to walk in empty-handed would have been an affront to his host.

"Och! For God's sake take the kettle from yer mother and let us all get indoors out of this howlin' wind." His father pushed the inebriated Aleck towards the door; Aleck stumbled, then regained his balance and what little was left of his decorum. "It's an act of honour and good-will. Ye should be proud to be the MacGregors' first-foot," said his father.

"Aye, Pa." He grabbed the pot and resolutely made his unsteady entrance, mustering dignity to demonstrate the importance of his mission.

They filed in and arranged themselves by the fire—women on one side, men on the other.

Jock entered last. Saying, "Evenin', Mrs. MacGregor. Evenin', Annie," he smiled and touched his cap, then took it off and walked past Lizzie towering over her and close enough for her to see his blue eyes, no longer smiling. He gave only a slight nod in her direction, taking care not to brush against her in the tight space. He drew his fingers through the thick mop of wavy red-gold hair that glinted in the lights from the candles Ma had set on the table. He headed for a place on the bench next to his pal, Charlie, and whispered something to him that made her twin brother laugh out loud.

Lizzie's heart dropped. Why did he treat her like that? What had she done?

"Here's a bottle of the best, Flora." Jock's father said.

"Aye, I'll get glasses out right away, John."

Nellie helped Ma bring out the food. Lizzie put some more peat on the fire, while Father, Charlie, John Campbell, and his three boys sipped the whisky.

Her mother retrieved a bottle of her homemade elderberry wine from her kist and poured two glasses. She slid one across the sideboard to Nellie, who favoured her with a wide grin that revealed several gaps in her teeth—about one for each nine-month it took to birth these braw big sons, she always said.

"Not too much, Flora." But she accepted the full glass with a girlish giggle.

"Here's a drink to those we miss—a toast to the old ones—gone but not forgotten," said John, using his best ceremonial lilt. He took a long draught from the cup, exhaled, and wiped his mouth with the back of his hand. "To yer father, Rab." John sighed and raised his glass to his friend. "A finer man ye'd never meet than old Gregor. Clung to the old ways he did. I think he was still waiting for a Stewart to show up and claim the throne."

Lizzie stared into the fire, watching the shimmer of the peat flames and the soothing sound of the boiling, bubbling water and breathed the spicy aroma of the dumpling cooking in it. Her thoughts reconnected her to the old man who had been so much a part of their lives until recently.

"There was a man could tell a yarn," John went on. "Remember the one about the MacGregors?"

"What MacGregors? We're all MacGregors one way or another in this glen."

Her father's voice was sharp, but she knew it wasn't directed at John. It was a sore point with the folks in Glen Orchy and Rannoch Moor, many of whom claimed ancestry to the outlawed Clan MacGregor but carried different names due to a quirk of history.

John's family had been MacGregors of Glen Orchy back in the 1600s. "My forebears were living here before it was Menzies or Campbell land," he'd tell anyone who'd listen, thumping his chest with his fist. "That was before the proud name of MacGregor was proscribed in 1603. Fancy word, that—proscribed. Means the bastards wouldn't even let us call ourselves 'MacGregor.'"

John Campbell's whisky was talking. Lizzie knew they were going to hear the stories of the MacGregors, whether they wanted to or not.

"Back in 1595 the MacGregors caught a Drummond who needed hangin' and did the job. The man took it on himself to cut off the ears of the MacGregors for what he called poaching. Och! I know they carried it too far but, being proud of what they'd done, they presented the Drummond's heid to his wife on a platter, and I mean really on a platter, at her own dinner table. After that yon King James made it legal to murder our clansmen, whip and brand the women, and sell our wee ones into slavery. Back then the only safe place for MacGregors was Rannoch. We fought back as long as we could, and then yon English King banished the name MacGregor on pain of death, and forced us to take the name of any other clan. My folks in Glen Orchy had to take the name of the tacksmen, those bloody land-grabbing Campbells—never held any pride in it. For how many long years did we slave four days in the week to turn <u>their</u> soil so we could have our own wee tract of land to subsist on?"

Lizzie felt her blood rising. No matter how many times she heard the stories that had been passed down, she still seethed.

Pa tried to appease his friend by offering a toast. He raised his glass to the level of the only decoration on the stone wall, a cross-stitched banner his fiancée, Lizzie's mother, had made as a wedding gift to him. It bore the proud MacGregor motto: "'<u>S rioghal mo dhream</u>.'" "<u>Royal is My Race</u>."

"To the MacGregors wherever they are or whatever they're called—in Bonnie Scotland or roaming in foreign lands. It's about time ye changed yer name John. It's been legal since seventeen-seventy-four to call yerself MacGregor."

"Aye, well I need to do that." John said lamely, no doubt hating to give up the cause that made his blood boil.

"To the MacGregors." They solemnly raised their glasses.

Lizzie settled down on a milking stool near the fire for the storytelling, and took Gregor on her lap. The fire lit the faces of the expectant gathering. Lizzie's eyes met Jock's; he quickly turned his head and said something to Annie that made her simper.

Jock taken with Annie? The very notion sent a chill through to her heart. She tried to dismiss the thought, but Annie had placed herself right across from Jock. She giggled at everything Jock said and kept adjusting her new shawl around her shoulders, drawing attention to herself.

Finally Mrs. Campbell said, "Aye, it's a braw shawl ye have there, lassie. Did yer Ma make that for ye?"

Then she whispered, "Now if ye'll jist sit still, Annie, ye'll not knock me off this bench."

Jock's father signalled to his wife to refresh his drink.

"Seems these English bastards . . ."

The twins, Donnie and Jamie, seated on rugs on the floor, giggled and punched each other. Pa cuffed them. "Wheesht, you two."

"You mind yer tongue, John Campbell," Mrs. Campbell warned.

So John told his stories for an hour and when the laughter subsided, Jock's mother said, "Enough of yer tall tales, John Campbell. Let's have some music."

"C'mon, John, lad, give us a tune on the fiddle," John Campbell used the formal name of his namesake, who was usually dubbed "Jock" to avoid confusion.

CHAPTER FOUR

Give Us a Song

Ilka lassie has her laddie,
Ne'er a ane hae I,
But a' the lads they smile on me,
When comin' thru the rye.

Lizzie watched every delicate movement of his work-roughened hands
as Jock took out of its case the ancient instrument he had inherited
from his grandfather, and looked around for a spot to place the case
and the bow. Lizzie started to lean over to assist him, then drew back feeling self-conscious . . . Would he accept her help? . . . Would the others see
her as too eager? Instead she turned away and helped Mrs. Campbell and
her mother get out the sweetmeats and spread them on the sideboard and
prepared to make a pot of tea while Jock tuned the violin.

They loaded their plates with black bun and shortbread while he played
"Flora MacDonald's Lament." Lizzie cherished that he had learned it to
honour her mother, Flora MacDonald MacGregor.

Ma gave a little curtsy. "My, yer getting awful good on that instrument.
Ye'll be playing next year at the feeing market in Dalmally."

"Play one Lizzie knows. I'd like fine to hear her sweet voice. She never
sings loud enough in church. It's hard to hear her over yon Mary Buchanan's
skreiching," said Jock's father. "Did ye hear yon woman at the Christmas Eve
service? Och! I'd sooner listen to ten bagpipes in a coop full of chickens."

15

Lizzie cocked her eye towards her father as though to dare him to deny her singing ability now, for he always made her sing quietly in church, "out of respect" he said, but Lizzie knew Pa's philosophy about knowing your place in society and Lizzie shouldn't be showing up the laird's daughter. Pa smiled sheepishly and said, "Now, John, there's nothing worse than a woman with a swollen head."

"Och! The lassie's head's not swollen. If she's got talent, let her enjoy it. Let's all enjoy it."

With that introduction, Lizzie stood up beside Jock, who moved away from her as far as he could in the cramped room. Lizzie stared at him bewildered, then noticed the reaction of Nellie and Ma, who nudged each other and hid smiles. Hmmm!

"I'd like to sing 'Comin' Thru the Rye,'" she announced, with more confidence than she felt.

She threw her shoulders back, took a deep breath, and tried to envision herself out in the field walking alone and singing like she did every chance she got. She tried to ignore these cramped quarters with everyone staring at her, and Jock Campbell with that silly look on his face and it almost the same colour as the fire. What is the matter with him? she thought. Maybe he can't play it. Och! Everybody knows that one, surely.

Lizzie gave Charlie the raised eyebrows, 'help me here,' and he gave Jock an encouraging nudge, Jock gave her a few bars of introduction, her voice rang out clear, supported by his perfect accompaniment. He must have been practicing, she thought, and gave him a nod of appreciation when the assembled gathering, except for Annie, broke into applause.

Now it was time for the clootie dumpling, which Ma fished out from the simmering pot and removed its cloth cover. The rich, fragrant pudding smelled of cinnamon and nutmeg and bursting with raisins was presented with ceremony, steaming hot, on Ma's precious blue-and-white Prestonpans platter she kept in her kist for safety.

That bottomless kist of Ma's, Lizzie thought. The ancient wooden box, an heirloom from her mother's family bore heavy iron handles on each end and stayed padlocked till Ma needed something. Though only big enough for two children to sit upon, her mother continued to produce surprises out of it, never offering an explanation. Lizzie saw Nellie Campbell cast an envious eye on the platter. The rest of the party was only focused on seeing its contents divided and shared.

"Time for a wee bit more of the uisge beatha, the aqua vita, as the laird might call it." John poured whisky into the traditional quaich, a silver, two-handled cup that Ma set out beside the dumpling.

"Slainte mhath!" He raised the cup and proposed the Gaelic toast, then passed it to Lizzie's father.

"Aye, John, to your good health, too."

Lizzie's mother sliced the dumpling and served generous portions, first to the men and boys, next to Nellie and the girls, then served herself a piece. Gregor cried out in delight when he found a paper-wrapped ha'penny in the slice of pudding Ma had selected for him.

"A toast," said Pa. "To the Auld Laird. May he have a long life."

"Aye, he'd better. Wouldn't want yon Miss Mary makin' decisions about our glen." The whisky was making Jock's father somewhat maudlin.

It seemed as though a shadow passed over the adults and Lizzie felt a strange fleeting apprehension.

"Slainte! To the Auld Laird." Everyone raised a glass to toast the land-lord. The older ones had whisky; the younger ones got a wee taste of elder-berry wine for a treat.

"Heard tell he's not that well. Getting worse by the day. Terrible gout in his foot, they say." Nellie delivered this inside information with an air of importance.

"Living with those women he has to live with, he likely has pains in other places too," John tossed back at her. "Flora knows what it was like living up at that big house with those spoiled bitches, don't ye Florry?"

"Time to go to bed now." Lizzie's mother told the children, to protect them from gossip or to change the topic, Lizzie wondered which. Lizzie carried Gregor and Nellie took baby Kate, who had fallen asleep during the storytelling. Ma shooed the twins into the sleeping room amidst sleepy complaints.

"You too, Annie," Ma said.

"Pa," she appealed, "Lizzie got to stay up last year when she was my age and the year before."

"Och! Don't start her greetin', Florry. The tears'll be trippin' her and she'll spoil the evening." Pa was having a good time. He got up and placed two more peats on the fire even though the room was toasty warm.

"All right then, just for a couple of hours," said Ma.

Charlie overheard Lizzie groaning and gave her a sympathetic grin.

"About the laird, John." Pa showed as much interested in the laird as the next crofter.

"Aye! Like I was saying." Jock's father leaned heavily on the table. "He's getting older, like the rest of us. Charlie Buchanan's been a wild man in his day, don't ye think, Rab? Those braw good looks. He was all over the world before he married Menzies' oldest daughter here in Rannoch. She was starting to get a bit long in the tooth. Her father made Buchanan's father honour some kind of obligation by having him marry her."

"Nice way of saying he was forced into it," said Nellie.

"Is that a fact?" Aleck stuffed his mouth with dumpling and almost swallowed a ha'penny.

"Mind yer manners," his mother cautioned.

"He didn't come from hereabouts, then?" Jock seemed to be just as curious about the gentry as Lizzie. The cup was passed again.

"He's a Buchanan from Loch Lomond way, is he not?" Lizzie appreciated that Jock's mother, Nellie, tried to move the story along. Mr. Campbell could digress for hours.

"Aye . . . younger son . . . I think. Though some say he had a twin that died after the war. Anyway, it seems our laird got all the Buchanan money one way or another."

* * *

Close to morning the singing and storytelling ended, and the Campbells bundled themselves against the blowing snow and took their lanterns to light the way to their croft a few hundred yards round the hill. Chickens fluttered down and the cock crowed from the roost in the entryway.

Lizzie crawled onto her straw-filled mattresses for an hour's rest. The New Year had been properly welcomed.

"Here's a wee kiss for ma dearie." She heard her father say in the next room. "Ye did us proud. Yon black bun was better than even my mother made." The highest compliment he could pay.

"It was a grand evening, Rob. The best in the seventeen years we've spent together."

Hogmanay. A New Year. A time to re-affirm commitments.

Lizzie remembered Jock's red face. Och! If only things could be the same as when we were children together, she thought. Was it partly her fault? She felt different about him, too.

Very different.

CHAPTER FIVE

The Kirk

Spring 1860

Here some are thinkin' on their sins,
An' some upo' their claes;
Ane curses feet that fyl'd his shins
Another sighs and prays:
On this hand sits a chosen swatch,
Wi' screwed up grace-proud faces;
On that a set o' chaps, at watch,
Thrang winkin' on the lasses.

Sundays you gave to the Lord, Lizzie knew, but Och! On a braw day it wearied her to be indoors, even in the beautiful new church. The Reverend Mackenzie routinely timed his advance to the pulpit to precede the entrance of the gentry, while the rest of the congregation twisted around to gaze at the elegant folk strutting down the aisle. Her twin, Charlie, crossed his eyes and curled his lip when she looked at him. She had to smile.

The Lord of the manor, Colonel Charles Buchanan, and his entourage paraded into the Kirk like they owned it, which, since they owned the land, they did. Today, as usual (when Miss Mary Buchanan and her mother weren't gallivanting off to London, that is), the Buchanans arrived late, led by the patriarch, who always dressed in full highland regalia. The colonel's regimental bonnet, a stately headpiece with plaid ribbon, impressive insignia, and black-and-white plumes sprouting from the top, made him look much taller, for he was a short, stocky man who never removed his hat till he took his seat. The brass buttons on his stark black jacket appeared ready to pop and expose his mammoth midriff. His kilt, a dazzling red-and-green plaid, woven from the finest yarn swung like a fan from his rear. His sporran, decorated with a fox head, hung from his waist. White wool socks barely covered his fleshy calves. His silver-buckled shoes landed heavily on the board floor.

Lizzie watched the familiar procession till it arrived at the velvet-covered pew opposite the bare plank pew that overflowed with the ten members of her own family. Which now included the new baby, wee Archie, innocently awaiting his christening this morning.

Mary Buchanan and her mother, Lady Isobel, heads held high in new, fashionable chapeaux, bestowed haughty looks on their inferiors. Those two had more bonnie hats than a Glasgow milliner. Lizzie wondered what it would be like to have all that finery to select from. Was Miss Mary pretty? Lizzie couldn't make up her mind. She certainly spoiled the effect with the sour look she always wore.

Lizzie pictured herself in that royal-blue velvet dress; she could almost feel the comfort of the heavy material hugging her curves and holding off the bone-chilling cold of the airless building. The colour would be as perfect for Lizzie as the laird's daughter, who had the same peach complexion. Lizzie glanced down at her own coarse hodden skirt and her best blouse, pressed to a shiny finish and almost perfectly white except for the stain just below her left breast, a gift from wee Gregor when he was feverish and puking.

She inspected her shoulder, covered by the hand-knit green wool shawl, where a ringlet lay, loosened from her cap. She surreptitiously pulled it into view to reassure herself that it had the sparkle of burnished copper. Wisps of Mary's reddish-brown hair that escaped the elaborate bonnet reminded Lizzie of a squirrel.

The laird stepped aside, and with a grand gesture invited the ladies to sit. He sat himself down at the end of the row, took a deep breath, exhaled, removed his hat, and put it down between him and his wife. The service could begin.

"Stop gowping at me," Lizzie mouthed at Duncan Cooper and Sandy Robertson. Strange, those two always sat directly in front of her and stared at her when they turned to get their hymnals. They should be seated in their own family pews. She curled her lip at their silly grins and turned away with a toss of her head that sent a curl over the top of her starched, white bonnet. She renewed her inspection of the laird's daughter. Mary reached out a kid-gloved hand to retrieve her hymnal. Lizzie glanced down at her own Sunday-scrubbed hand, bearing fine etchings of dirt in the soda-dried rough skin around her knuckles. She feebly attempted to cover them with the fringes of her shawl.

Pa nudged and frowned. "Stop fidgeting, lass," he ordered.

Jock's family sat two pews down. She turned her attention to Jock Campbell. Just looking the back of his head gave her a warm feeling. She imagined standing close to him and running her fingers through his hair.

She, Charlie and Jock had played together all their lives. As wee ones, they romped safely in the confines of the walled clachan, chasing chickens and each other. She winced at the memory of the day they climbed together on the dyke and Lizzie playfully pushed Jock off, breaking his arm.

When they were old enough to go school, they walked back and forth together to the dominie's house where they got their lessons with the other young children. Only a few summers ago the three explored the glen beyond the clachan together almost every night till twilight, their mothers calling them, repeatedly, to come indoors. Not any more! Och! He hardly even talked to her.

Seated, he was much taller than the other two farm lads pestering her, and almost as broad in the shoulders as his older brothers. Red-gold waves of hair covered his high collar as he turned his head slightly. Jock's hair needed a trim, but at least he was gentleman enough not to stare at her. But why not?

Perhaps too busy signalling something to her brother to notice her sitting nearby. Jock and Charlie were so close that they seemed to connect wordlessly, almost the same way that Lizzie and Charlie could tell what the other was thinking sometimes. Her mother said it was often that way with twins. He kept turning his head. Was it accidental that her eyes met Jock's briefly? The strange jolt she felt caused her to gasp. She felt heat rising to her face and covered her distress by fumbling with the book in her lap.

Father tapped her hand to remind her to open her hymnal. She did, and let her vibrant voice ring out above the heavier voices around her. Music, the one gratifying element of the service, diverted her attention until she heard Mary singing out strong, her blue ostrich feathers bobbing in 4/4 time. Lizzie felt her voice swell to prove she could sing better than Mary Buchanan, but Pa whispered in her ear, as he always did, "Ye know, she's a trained singer, Lizzie." She knew her father didn't want her showing off; he believed modesty in a young woman to be an admirable trait. Subdued, she sang quietly.

His restraint dampened her spirit, and made her bashful and self-conscious. She longed to be out on the heath with no one nearby, heeding the silent sermon of the moor, surrounded by hills that spoke of eternity with an eloquence no pastor could command. The strong smell of furniture wax from the pews, the musty odour from the ancient songbooks, and the proximity of stale, well-worn clothing assailed her nostrils. She'd rather be savouring a clean, rain-washed breeze to clear her head of the fearful pungency of fire and brimstone that the minister threatened to the doubter.

The back of Jock Campbell's head merited just so much attention; she'd while away the forced obeisance by reading a psalm. She opened to Psalm 23:

> "The Lord is my shepherd
> I shall not want
> He maketh me to lie down in green pastures . . ."

CHAPTER SIX

In the Service
of the Lord?

All hail, Religion, maid divine!
Pardon a muse sae mean as mine

The thought of green pastures transported Lizzie to the shores of Loch Rannoch. Out there the lapping of the wind-driven water and the murmur of the breeze through the tall grass soothed her spirit in ways the fierce words of the reverend never could. Out there her voice opened up in song. "Comin' Thru the Rye" was her favourite. The familiar melody rang out clear, echoing off the hills. Out there she "made a joyful noise" to whatever benevolence had created the beauty of Rannoch—her wild moor—the most beautiful place in the world, her own corner of Scotland's Central Highlands.

"...'Toil in the fields of the Lord.'" The minister's exhortation startled her into the present. But how much harder could a person work?

"'Give unto God what is God's.'" Did he mean support the church? Her family scrounged a few ha'pennies to put in the plate. Surely God understood. Please let this boring sermon be over soon, she pleaded silently. I don't care how Christian it is to work your fingers to the bone.

Then the mouse flew out of the pew two rows down. It sat stunned in the aisle before it scampered straight to the Buchanan pew. Lady Isobel screamed, stood up and shook out her skirt. The wee beastie made its second appearance in the aisle escaping from the fluttering skirt and the fearsome screaming and Charlie grabbed Lizzie's shawl and threw it over the terrified creature and carried it quickly to the door. The reverend halted his sermon. Lizzie glanced around at the laird's surprised grin, at her discomfited ladyship and those two dolts sitting beside Jock, looking her way as if to say, "Are you amused by our trick?"

This was not the first time vermin had interrupted the service, intentionally or otherwise, so the congregation settled down quickly. After an apologetic smile in the direction of Lady Isobel, who was trying to regain her composure, the reverend droned on where he'd left off.

"Serve your rightful master." Was that in the Bible? He must mean God, but why did Lizzie always suspect he supported the cause of earthly masters? She saw his furtive glance towards the velvet pews and witnessed the laird's nodding approval at the obsequious orator. "Obsequious orator." She liked that; she must remember to share it with Charlie and thank him for his fast response to the "accident." Her twin shared her love of language, Gaelic and English and Latin. They would spend hours together discussing books they had read.

She began to wonder if all the lessons this plodding parson preached were indeed from Holy Scripture. Her personal Bible study, under her mother's guidance, led her to understand that we are all one in the sight of God. Did the reverend illuminate God's plan, or did he corrupt the message? Did each being answer to God directly? Was God the only "rightful master," or did He designate authority to earthly beings to govern over others, making them "rightful masters?" If He did, there was no mistaking who they were.

Another philosophical point to discuss with Charlie. Lizzie doubted she'd learn much here. She sighed and shook her head in an involuntary gesture, dismissing the stupefying boredom of the sermon. Father's warning frown reminded her she questioned authority in ways he would never approve if he knew her thoughts.

When the reverend began to pray, Lizzie tuned out the cheerless monotone and let her mind drift to the afternoon. Maybe she would take a walk by the riverbank and gather spring wildflowers for a wee bouquet for the Sunday dinner table. Apart from dinner preparation and other vital tasks, her father allowed nothing but church attendance and Bible reading to fill their Sundays. Think of an excuse, she told herself. Walking out to check on the spring lambs was an important—even "vital"—task. She'd use this ploy to get out of doors after dinner.

"...may the Lord remove this affliction so that our beloved laird can shepherd his fold for many years to come. Amen."

"What's the matter wi' the laird, Flora?" her father whispered over her head to her mother, who had gone pale.

Her mother shook her head. "Wheesht." She hushed him.

The sudden restlessness of her kinfolk, talking shamelessly in the midst of the reverend's overlong prayer, drew her attention.

Lizzie reached for her hymnal for the closing hymn and stood with the others, but focused on the patriarch across the aisle. She barely knew the heavy, red-faced Lord of the manor, but she secretly considered him arrogant. She studied him now, mulling over what she had heard about him. Others, including her parents, considered him to be a fair man, which she preferred to believe, since the well-being of her family, indeed of all the tenant farmers, rested entirely in his hands. Colonel Buchanan's fiefdom, part of the Menzies clan's great estate, stretched from Loch Rannoch all the way north to the boundaries of the private land of the overlord, Sir Robert Menzies. Lizzie remembered that as a child she rode in a cart with Charlie and Pa to make a delivery to the imposing Menzies Castle, even bigger than Aulich House, where the colonel lived.

Like all the crofters, her family farmed Colonel Buchanan's acreage and inhabited his cottages at the laird's sole discretion, a fact of life like the sun rising in the morning over Schiehallion's white crest. On the rare occasions that this came up for discussion at their hearth, her parents would recall stories of clearances of tenants from other parishes. But the laird, they said, would never do such a thing.

"My loyal folk will never be thrown off the land," Colonel Buchanan always promised on his rare tours of the crofts. "There'll be none o' those damned clearances at Rannoch. No Knoydart here," he boomed, referring to that region northwest of Rannoch whose population had been evicted and shipped to Nova Scotia in 1853.

Lizzie once asked her father about the infamous "Highland Clearances." His answers were reassuring—in a way.

"Nothing to worry yer bonny head about. The last time crofters were thrown out of Rannoch I was a boy about eight years old. It's all over, lass, back in the days before Charlie Buchanan became the laird. Och! A crofter might give up and leave because he can't pay the rent or think he can make his fortune in Canada or America, but that's their choice. Do ye see what I mean?"

Lizzie thought she saw, but wondered privately how a whole family could work the rock-strewn plots from dawn till dusk every day and not be able to come up with enough to stay on the land they rightfully called home.

Charlie Buchanan, as his tenants affectionately referred to him out of earshot, had become Lord of the manor and the legal owner of the land Lizzie's family tilled when he married the heiress of the Archibald Menzies estate. In true Highland tradition the MacGregors had given him their loyalty after Archibald's death. The colonel went on to gain their respect and fealty to the point of their naming a son after him, or making "Buchanan" the middle name of a daughter. Lizzie's brother they'd named Charles Buchanan MacGregor, and she was Elizabeth Buchanan MacGregor.

The strains of the hymn died away and the congregation sat back down, ending Lizzie's musings.

The wee babe in Ma's arms, now two months old, would be christened today and given the name Archibald MacDonald MacGregor. Wee Archie mercifully slept through the short baptism service and Lizzie thanked God that the reverend gave a blissfully short benediction.

The parishioners dutifully waited till the gentry exited the church before beginning, pew by pew, to file out. Jock Campbell's family was almost to the vestibule before the MacGregors exited in their accustomed order. Lizzie smiled and shook her head as Annie, almost fourteen years old and trying to act the fine lady, ostentatiously led the parade, followed by Donald and James, wearing twin scowls on their identical faces as they trudged behind their show-off sister. Charlie stepped into the aisle and offered Ma a hand to get up off her seat, weighted down, as she was, with the baby. He took wee Gregor's hand and preceded her and Pa, who carried the squirming Kate, to the back of the church.

CHAPTER SEVEN

The Invitation

Lord, man! Our gentry care sae little
For delvers, ditchers and sic cattle;
They gang as saucy by poor folk
As I wad by a stinking brock.

Walking down the church steps into the cluster of gossiping parishioners, Lizzie fine-tuned her escape plan, paying scant notice to the conversations around her until she overheard talk of an auction at the Angus MacGregor cottage on the Blair estate that joined the Buchanan holdings.

Despite what Father said about the clearances being over, or "Thank God it can't happen here," stories like this one about Angus MacGregor were more common than she liked to think. Another hard-working cottar and his family turned out of their place, and a roup, a humiliating public auction, of their possessions which happened if this harsh land couldn't produce enough for a growing family, or their cottage deteriorated faster than they could do repairs; sometimes they often left voluntarily or ended up penniless and were evicted for back rent. She imagined what the exiled cot-folk might be feeling as they headed down the road to Glasgow or Edinburgh or God knows where, to search for work.

And now the laird was ill. What would that mean for the cottars on this land?

"Did ye hear that minister prayin' fervent for the laird?" Jock's father said to Pa. "I wonder how bad off Buchanan is?"

"Och! Just the Reverend currying favour, John. The laird looks hail and hearty to me," said her father.

Everyone shushed when the Buchanan family finished talking to the Reverend Mackenzie—no doubt telling him what a fine sermon he'd preached. Lizzie yawned. She was impatient to leave, but it was customary to wait till the laird left the Kirk yard before the crowd dispersed.

When the throng parted to allow the minister to lead the gentry towards their coach, her spirits soared—free for the day, if she could be convincing to Pa. Och! It would be fine. She suspected her father understood her love of the moors and the forest.

She took off the restricting bonnet, shook her hair loose, and hurried to catch up with the rest of her family. That curl fell again onto her forehead; she blew it out of her way, where it stayed for a second before it tumbled back. She had to pass a group of the parish's "finest," laddies who had nothing better to do than stare and call after a girl.

"Hey, Lizzie with the curls, Jock wants to know if you'll be walking by the burn later in the day."

"We heard you on the moor singing 'Gin a body, meet a body, comin' thru the rye.' Aye, we were wondering if you'd like to meet Jock out in the rye field?"

Lizzie's heart sank. Those yokels had been listening to her when she thought she was all alone, not performing to an audience. She felt naked.

"Jock says he's going to catch ye down by the bridge and see if you'll give him a kiss."

Jock Campbell, all red-faced and shuffling, nudged his tormentors. "Och, Lizzie, that's not true. I never said the like." He raised his lids, changing a shy expression into a direct gaze.

She "tut-tutted" to express irritation, and cover other feelings she couldn't fathom.

As if it weren't bad enough putting up with these fools, the Buchanans saw and heard it all. The Auld Laird chased them off with his deep rolling voice. "Don't you rascals have to get back to the fields or the stable or some such thing?"

Their bravado dissipated. They doffed their caps and pulled on their forelocks, blushed and stuttered, then scattered, leaving her alone with the Buchanans and the reverend who was, at first, indignant, but decided to act jolly when he saw the gentry was entertained.

Lizzie wished the ground would open and swallow her. She hated to have anyone think she encouraged these fools. Thank God her family had moved out of earshot. She stood rooted to the spot, wondering what to do next, when Mary Buchanan, of the elegant chapeaux, intervened.

Casually tying the yellow satin ribbon under her chin, she said, "Papa, who is that girl? Girl, come over here. What's your name?"

"Lizzie's my name, Miss Mary." She remembered to curtsey.

"Well, Lizzie, come up to Aulich House this afternoon. I have something you could use."

"Yes, m-m-miss."

"You can go now. Just be there around two." Lizzie could barely understand her affected English accent. Lizzie turned to go.

"Wait a minute." It was the laird. "Aren't you the little MacGregor girl? My! Yer all grown up. How old are ye, lass?"

"I'm sixteen, sir."

"Aye, and quite pretty, too, don't you think?" He asked no one in particular. "Why, she's a fair Scottish beauty," he said, answering himself and unabashedly eyeing Lizzie from top to toe. "No doubt about it."

She stood transfixed, embarrassed by the colonel's penetrating appraisal.

"Are you Flora MacDonald's lass? Och, ye must be. Ye have the look of yer island mother, and that's the truth."

She watched the heavyset man rock back and forth on his heels; his kilt swung out in a bright coloured fan with every motion of his ample backside. His red face bore a grin. "Look at the fine lassies that are born and raised on Buchanan property."

Does the pompous ass think I'm prime livestock? Lizzie wondered, and then remembered her manners. "I'm sorry you're ill, sir."

His voice softened and he patted her on the top of her wind-blown hair. She wished she hadn't removed her bonnet earlier. "Don't you be worryin' now, lass. You'll be just fine. Everything is seen to. Do ye hear me?"

"Thank you, sir." Lizzie had no idea what he meant.

Lady Isobel gave her husband a scowl to which he responded with a shrug of his shoulders.

"Oh and give this to your mother for the bairn." He handed Lizzie a silver coin. She curtsied, said "Thank you, sir," and walked off, wondering what his remark and his wife's reaction meant. It was customary to give a christening gift, but why not hand it to Ma? And what of Miss Mary's command? What did Miss Mary have in store for her? A lecture about her unladylike behaviour, talking to boys so near the church, perhaps? Or had Lizzie's singing provoked her ladyship?

What would she tell Pa, or even Ma? Lizzie had never been to the big house before. A mysterious invitation.

One thing she knew, she had to get out of the house this afternoon and respond to the summons and do it without alerting her parents and having to tell them about the embarrassing episode in the churchyard. She felt sure they would assume she was in some kind of trouble. She reckoned she'd still use her original excuse to get out of the cottage, then go to the big house instead of walking on the moor.

She strode down past the cemetery, not quite fast enough to catch up with her family, imagining her face still flushed.

* * *

Sunday dinner seemed to take forever reaching the table. Father, all fired up about the sermon, picked up where the reverend left off.

"In His plan, God assigned 'some to lead and others to follow.'" Father knew that for a fact, for it was in the Bible. "In His wisdom, the Lord has placed the likes of us in our station, the minister to spell out His eternal plan, and Colonel Charles Buchanan as the final authority in all other matters in this glen. May he go from strength to strength." Lizzie squirmed in her seat, but when Pa started to give a Bible lesson, it was not wise to get up and leave.

"God has said, 'Thou shalt serve thy rightful master and do unto him as you would unto God Himself.'" Father believed if you used words like "thou" and "unto" in a certain tone of voice, you were quoting scripture.

Lizzie groaned inwardly, she and her mother were much more conversant with the Bible, Ma never took exception or qualified anything her husband said, and Lizzie didn't dare. Pa had a free rein to interpret what the good Lord expected of his faithful followers. And so she took a deep breath, folded and unfolded her hands in her lap, and kept her thoughts to herself. The old clock on the mantel chimed on the half-hour after one. Now or never.

"Father, I think yon wee sheep with the crooked foot is about ready to lamb. I know where she was yestere'en. Maybe I can find her."

"Aye, Lassie. The Lord would not mind his servant tending the flocks, even though it is the Sabbath. Go on now and be about yer business."

"And, Ma, here's a gift from Colonel Buchanan for wee Archie." She pressed the coin into Ma's hand, grabbed her cap and shawl, and bolted. As she unlatched the door she glanced back and connected with her mother's questioning stare. She'd tell Ma later. Maybe.

CHAPTER EIGHT

The Big House— First Visit

I see how folk live that hae riches;
But surely poor folk maun be wretches.

Lizzie flew up the hill to the big house, arriving sweating and out of breath at the high stone wall that surrounded the mansion. Still a fair walk to the gate, she slowed so that she would appear composed when she reached the big house.

What did they want with her? What was the inside of the mansion like? What did Mary wear while she relaxed at home? Some fine velvet robe, maybe. What style did she wear her hair under that bonnie hat? She had inspected Mary in every detail these many Sundays while the parson sermonized. Mary's reddish locks, though lack-lustre, were groomed to perfection. Lizzie pushed her own unruly mane back off her forehead and wiped her sweaty brow with the sleeve of her old gingham dress, faded by years of wear and stretched out to capacity by her burgeoning figure. She hadn't dared to wear her best Sunday clothes when she left the house on her fictitious mission.

* * *

Lizzie pulled a chain hanging adjacent to the huge oak double doors and heard a chiming sound off in the distance. Startled, she retreated to the foot of the stairs and watched the door, wondering what to expect. She shifted her weight from one leg to the other several times before the door opened to reveal the sharp face of Kate MacKay, Buchanan's housekeeper, peering short-sightedly at her.

Lizzie, painfully aware of her dishevelled appearance and unsure whether she should speak first, backed down the path a few more feet.

Miss MacKay let loose at her with her famed ferocity. "Who are you, girl? If ye came for a job ye'll not be gettin' it. Ye should know servants use the back entrance. Have ye never been in service afore?

"One o' those lowland wally-draggles tryin' to get into service with a genteel family in order to raise yer station in life? Well, not if I can help it! I've seen enough of ye come and go." She continued to rant as though Lizzie wasn't even there. "Useless! Scampering back to their mothers and their cottages before the week is out."

"But Miss MacKay . . ."

The woman barged on in Gaelic now. "A good Highland girl I might hire, or better still a crofter's daughter from the islands. You could get a full day's work out of them and they'll listen to correction without running home cryin'."

Lizzie resolved not to do that, though she felt close to tears. Instead, she took a deep breath and approached the stairs. "Miss MacKay . . ."

Her emboldened step seemed to further exasperate the laird's caretaker.

"Well, Missy, what is it you're wanting here? We have no need of beggars or extra hands, and we get all our supplies from the farm or the village, so make it quick. I have no' got all day to stand around blethering with you." Miss MacKay stepped out of the door onto the landing.

Unsure if the housekeeper wanted to physically remove her or get a better look, Lizzie stood her ground.

"Oh no, Miss MacKay, Miss Mary ordered me here. I'm Elizabeth MacGregor, miss. They call me Lizzie. You kent my mother well when she worked here as a parlour maid."

"Come up," she ordered, taking spectacles out of her apron.

Lizzie climbed the stairs.

"Heavens above! You're that MacGregor." Kate MacKay covered her mouth with her hand. When she removed it her face had a lopsided smile.

"Och well, if that's who ye are, come right away in then. Why'd ye not say somethin', lassie? I haven't seen you since Ne'erday before last. Didn't recognize ye. Oh my! Growin' up very bonnie, ye are. Well, ye would be, of course. Flora was always the pretty one."

The older woman tucked errant strands of thin hair back under her cap and sighed. Lizzie followed her, through double doors into a sumptuous room. Miss MacKay showed her to a dark green velvet wing-backed chair overlooking a cheerful window.

"Flora's lass . . . all grown up. I cannae believe it. Och! I remember yer mother when she was your age. Flora's all right, is she?" There was an edge to her voice. "Having bairns is fine as long as yer strong and healthy. She's stronger than her mother Elizabeth . . ." She seemed to stop herself.

Lizzie didn't reply. She always found it sad to think of Ma growing up without a mother.

As though reading her mind, Miss MacKay said, "Och! Not to worry, lass, Flora had a wheen o' mothers, myself included, though I was only twelve when Cousin Elizabeth passed on and left the bairn. Aye. Everybody in the family loved our bonnie Flora."

Lizzie smiled to think of Ma surrounded by doting relatives. Och! This woman was kin, just a wee bit prickly on the outside.

"Wait a wee minute. I'll find out what her ladyship wants with ye. Not been in any trouble, have ye?" Lizzie submitted to further, more kindly, inspection.

"I'd fair hate to see any lassie of Flora MacDonald's straying from the straight and narrow. Yer mother and I both hailed from Stornoway. Came here as lassies we did. Did she tell ye that?"

Lizzie knew something about it and would have loved to learn more, but as Miss MacKay didn't pause for her answer, it seemed that none was expected.

"Och! I can't believe you're a young woman already . . . and your brother Charlie? Flora and her twins! Poor lass. Doesn't come from her mother's side of the family. Charlie's still in school, I hope."

"Oh, yes, Miss MacKay, and I am too."

"Fancy that. You're a scholar, just like your gifted mother."

Lizzie smiled at the compliment.

"Lot of good it did her, mind ye."

"Miss?" Lizzie gave her a quizzical look at the turn the conversation had taken.

"Och, never mind me, lass. 'The best laid schemes o' mice and men gang aft aglee.' Rabbie Burns said it best." She pointed to a leather-bound book of Burns' poetry lying open on a nearby table.

"I have to take the family their afternoon tea now. Mary'll want that before she receives anyone. You'll be all right here for a wee while, eh?"

The grandfather clock behind her rang out the Westminster chimes surprising Lizzie before she could answer. By the time she recovered, Kate MacKay had breezed out the door, a vision in gray gingham and white cotton starchiness, wafting the odour of carbolic soap in her wake. Lizzie suspected that neither a louse nor a flake of dirt that came near Miss Kate MacKay could ever survive.

Lizzie's gaze took in the immense room, bigger than the croft her whole family lived in. It didn't look as though anybody slept in it, nor was there a table for eating. What did they use this fancy room for anyway? A log fire crackled in the open hearth and not even that cold outside. She hung her shawl on a ladder-back chair.

A portrait of a handsome young man resembling the Auld Laird hung over the stone fireplace. Dressed in fox-hunting gear, he carried a hunting rifle over his right shoulder and sat proudly astride a fine dapple-gray horse. It took Lizzie a few moments to realize it <u>was</u> Charles Buchanan, in his prime. The artist had captured a serious expression on his face, and a determined set to his jaw that contrasted with the jaunty, blue polka-dot cravat he wore. His gaze captured her eyes for a moment—something about it haunted her. The eyes. Yes, the eyes. They were sky blue, about the same colour as the fancy neckerchief.

She never remembered meeting the colonel's gaze before. She'd been taught humility in the presence of her betters; yet she felt sure she'd encountered these eyes and had locked on to them many a time. They seemed to follow her around the grand room with an indulgence that invited her to explore, enjoy, and make herself at home. A smile curled her lips at her own whimsy—Elizabeth MacGregor, lady of leisure.

Her gaze fell on a peculiar piece of furniture in the alcove by the bay window. She sidled over for closer inspection. This must be a pianoforte. A huge instrument—bigger even than the organ in the parish church. She had never seen one before. She was tempted to touch its shiny ivory keys but didn't dare.

She continued her scrutiny of the room. Over in the darker corner bookshelves rose all the way to the ceiling. Must be the library, she decided. A ladder, like she'd seen in a farmhouse for people to climb into the loft, was positioned to get to the dozens upon dozens of books on high shelves. She wondered how long since anyone had opened one of the musty-smelling volumes. Oh, how she and Mother would love to spend a few weeks in this room exploring its treasures, as would Charlie.

Her heels sank into the carpeting. She yearned to remove her boots to feel with her bare feet the rich deep texture of the rug with its intricate pattern of gold, green, and red. The power of the beautiful piano lured her across the room again. She couldn't resist plunking one of the keys. A rich tone rang out, startling and delighting her. This must be the instrument that accompanied Miss Mary when she got the voice training Father always reminded her about. Lizzie wondered what her own singing would sound like with someone accompanying her on such a grand instrument.

She returned to the chair to wait. From the enormous window she beheld the manicured lawn and the formal gardens beyond. She envisioned what a magnificent display of colour there would be in a few weeks when the countless tiny buds on dozens of rosebushes opened themselves to the sun. A perennial bed ran close to the high stone wall, protected from the wind. Yew hedges, which were clipped in the shapes of birds and other animals, not only delighted her eye, but impressed her with their effectiveness as they circled the formal gardens, far enough back to allow optimum sunlight yet shielding the more delicate plants from fierce weather.

Miss MacKay seemed to be gone forever. Lizzie had inspected every detail of the sumptuous room and was now at a loss to keep her mind occupied by anything other than the ominous fact that she had been ordered here. What if they thought she had encouraged those lads outside the kirk? Did they mean to chastise her or punish her family in some way for raising such a wayward daughter? She couldn't wait to get to the bottom of it. Where did Miss MacKay go? How long could it take to make a cup of tea?

She cautiously opened the door and stepped into the long hall. Seeing no one, she walked, mesmerized, farther down the corridor.

CHAPTER NINE

The Other Half

Reader, attend! Whether thy soul
Soars fancy's flights beyond the pole,
Or darkling grubs this earthly hole
In low pursuit;
Know prudent cautious self-control
Is wisdom's root.

Lizzie started at the sudden clatter of dishes in the distance. It must be the kitchen. She heard Kate MacKay's voice instructing someone to "Give me that tray right now, girl. They can't wait all afternoon for their tea." Then she heard the click of heels on the distant scullery floor and into the hall.

Lizzie pressed her body against the nearest door on the right wall of the corridor, trying to disappear. She felt behind her for the heavy doorknob, turned it, and almost fell backward into a room pervaded by a heavy, flowery perfume. Her eye fell on a lavender-skirted dressing table strewn with powder puffs, combs, brushes, bottles and jars, and a silver hand mirror. It must be Miss Mary's bed chamber. The clothes Mary had worn to church were thrown on the satin-quilted bed. Her shoes lay at the foot of it, amid a puddle of white cotton hose. She spied an open wardrobe crammed with gowns and Mary's famous hats filling the top shelf.

Her heart beat wildly. If anyone caught her here, she would really be in trouble. She must get out of danger and back to the library. She leaned out

41

of the door to see if the coast was clear. Seeing no one, she stepped into the hallway. The heavy oak door banged behind her.

"Quick, Agnes," it was Miss MacKay's voice. "The mistress is coming to see what's taking so long."

Lizzie expected Lady Isobel to appear any moment. She tried the door of Mary's boudoir, but it wouldn't open this time. She must have tripped the lock.

Trapped in the passage, too far down the hallway to return quickly to the rooms she'd left, she spied a door only slightly ajar across the way and took refuge just inside. She stood, back pressed against the wall and listened. All was quiet, so she gently opened the door, eager to make her retreat to the library, then froze when she heard voices. Afraid to alert anyone in the vicinity to her presence, for they seemed that close, she stood very still, barely breathing. Their voices continued in the same resonance, apparently unaware of her closeness. The sound came from the other side of the long room beyond the open French doors. Curious and emboldened, she crept towards the light. Maybe there was another exit.

The room she had stumbled into opened onto an atrium where the laird, his wife, and daughter were relaxing informally. With his noble head supported by two lace-covered pillows, Colonel Buchanan lay prostrate on a chaise longue facing his wife and daughter, both busy with embroidery, enjoying the afternoon sun in this sheltered corner. Mary, minus her dress, petticoats, and hoop, wore a powder-blue satin wrap over her chemise. Lady Isobel had removed her corset; her full-blown figure bulged under a gaudy flowered robe.

From her vantage point behind the brocade curtains, she could peek out on the domestic scene. Ashamed of her audacity, her heart pounding in her chest, she could barely hear the quiet conversation among the three until Miss Mary's petulant voice rang out, demanding to know where Kate MacKay had disappeared to with the afternoon tea.

As though on cue, the housekeeper appeared in the courtyard. Well, Lizzie thought, at least Miss MacKay doesn't have to come back down the corridor to get to where the family is. It would be safe for Lizzie to make her escape the same way she had come.

The housekeeper carried a tray loaded with sandwiches, scones, and shortbread. To Lizzie it seemed like a feast for Ne'erday or a christening or some other special occasion.

"And where is the Dundee cake you promised, Miss MacKay?" Mary demanded.

"Sorry, Miss. Ye know we're shorthanded in the kitchen. I didnae have the time tae bake."

Lizzie sensed Miss MacKay's irritation from the overly noisy clatter of the china cups and plates she laid out within reach of each of the three Buchanans.

"I'll be back in a wee minute with the tea things." She exited with her characteristic bustle.

Mary barely waited till the door closed. "Papa, that woman is not respectful enough of me—or Mama. Can't we hire an Englishwoman of a higher social class?"

Mary's mother answered. "Don't bother petitioning him again about that housekeeper. He is unyielding in his support of these Island people. You know what I think, Mary. Barbarians—all of them."

Her ferocity astonished Lizzie, and her accent, like Mary's, revealed her London schooling.

Before the laird could reply, if indeed he meant to dignify the discussion with a rejoinder, Miss MacKay reappeared at the scene with a large silver tray and matching tea service.

Mary said, "You didn't bring Dromedary sugar, Miss Kate. Do you always forget it intentionally, just to annoy me?"

"No, no, Miss Mary, I'll fetch it right away. Oh and, miss, Lizzie MacGregor is here waiting to see ye." Kate MacKay smiled thinly at her. Lizzie's heart leapt at the mention of her name.

"Lizzie who? Oh, that wild-haired young woman at the church. Now why did I want her to come?" She raised herself from the settee to take a finger sandwich from the piled plate.

"Oh yes, give her a comb off my dressing table. I can't abide to see such a bedraggled bunch of parishioners each Sunday. Maybe if the girl tames that awful hair, it will be one less ugly sight to behold on the Sabbath."

Lizzie felt herself blush.

Mary took a big bite of her sandwich, and with her mouth full, sputtered in her father's direction. "Papa, couldn't you have built them their own church? They smell worse than the barn. And I hate the way they stare at us."

"If you and yer mother didnae wear new hats every Sunday you'd not be givin' them such a show." At least he spoke with a normal Scots tongue. Lizzie, hurt and angry but intrigued by the conversation, temporarily forgot the precariousness of her position.

The colonel continued, "And how can you talk like that, Mary? You, who have had everything all of your life, should be grateful and have a wee bit of compassion for these poor people. They are our tenants. They've lived on this land for generations and likely love it."

"They can love it all they want, Papa. I can't wait to return to London."

"Ye've no interest in this place, have ye?" No mistaking the sadness in his voice.

"Please, Papa, don't start." Lizzie couldn't believe a daughter would challenge a father this way.

"I just need to know. That's all." The laird pleaded.

"All right, Papa. Is not giving a gift of something I treasure an act of compassion?"

He seemed not to notice she'd switched the subject.

"It surely is, my Mary. The Lord will bless you for that act of kindness. And He will enrich you according to your generosity."

"Oh, and Katie MacKay, those are all ivory combs on my chiffonier . . . see you don't give her the one with the silver inlay I got from that nice English officer, Cedric Something-or-other. What was his name, Papa?"

Lady Isobel provided the name. "Cecil Winterbottom. His name is Winterbottom, girl . . . Captain Cecil Winterbottom. English name." She curled her lip.

"You're going to need a husband, Mary, and soon." The laird sounded aggravated. "But could ye not find a real Scotsman wi' the balls to produce a grandson for me? Yon Englishman looked like the only thing he could get up would be his wee finger while he held a teacup."

Lady Isobel waved her hand towards Kate MacKay and frowned, indicating that her husband needed to mind his tongue in front of the servants. "Perhaps your father can arrange for him to have some sort of title so you don't have to go around with such a silly name should you decide to accept his suit."

"Can you arrange that, Papa?"

"We'll see. We'll see. Meantime, I've invited Colin MacPherson and his family over next week for a shooting weekend. Now there's a real man for ye."

Mary groaned.

"Do ye want to see the girl, Miss?" Miss MacKay turned to leave.

"Yes," said Mary. "She needs some instruction on..." Lady Isobel's eyes glared caution at her daughter.

"No, no. Of course not . . ." Mary quickly changed her mind. "See to it for me, Miss MacKay."

Lady Isobel's tone was terse and dismissive. "Leave us."

The laird waited till the door closed behind Kate MacKay. "Can ye not show some of yer aristocratic family's genteel manners around the servants, Isobel?" His voice dripped with sarcasm.

"Kate MacKay should know better than to bring any spawn of Flora MacDonald's into my presence. She knows how I feel."

"Isa, don't start that again. Ye've no reason tae resent her."

"Oh bother, Papa! I didn't realize it was that MacGregor when I invited her." Mary pouted.

"Lady Flora of the Hovel."

"Stop it now, Isa."

"You brought that uppity servant Kate and yon Flora MacDonald from Stornoway. It's a disgrace, Charlie. When my father gave you my hand in marriage, he thought you were an honourable man."

"Enough, Isa! Yer father knew I was a wealthy man. That's all he needed to know. He needed my family's money to bail him out of his damned gambling debts. This land would have gone to some Sassenach deer-hunter. Lost forever to the Scots. 'Keep the land in perpetuity.' That's what he wanted, and I agreed. I've fulfilled and exceeded old Menzies' expectations. The servants I brought from Lewis are no concern of yours."

"Servant, you call her . . ."

"Isa! The hours I spent with that lassie reading and listening to the sophisticated ideas she gleaned from the books she read were a pleasure to me. No-one ever touches that library now. The books are left to get mildewed."

Lizzie realized he was talking about her mother. She lost the thread of the conversation for a moment. When she trained her ears on them again they were still squabbling.

"You think you can fill Archibald Menzies' shoes?" said Lady Isobel ignored his explanation.

"Aye. I know I can. I can more than fill them. He wasnae exactly a shining star in the clan Menzies. He jist happened to have a nice wee bit of land I fancied. You're well provided for, and the crofters are more loyal and content than when your besotted father ruled the roost with a heavy, unsteady hand."

"Please, Mama, Papa. Stop before Kate comes back. Where has she disappeared to anyway? All I asked for was some sugar. Is that so difficult?"

"And you, girl, will have the responsibility of this place some day. I have made my wishes very clear to you."

"Father, I will not stay forever in this godforsaken, primitive glen . . ."

"Then you'll pay the consequences. I have made provisions for your noncompliance. I won't see you starve, but you'll do my bidding or . . ."

"Charlie, Mary's right to the land is clear. It is her inheritance. You may have taken advantage of my father's misfortune to make yourself a landowner, but my daughter will be the mistress of Rannoch some day."

"Stay out of this Isobel. You know it isn't that simple. I need a male heir. It's never so cut and dried when a title or property are left to a woman. Maybe your daughter will do a better job than you did of providing an heir."

"You're a cruel man, Charlie Buchanan. I grieved my sons too." His wife was sobbing now.

"Papa, do we have to have this argument every Sunday? It's supposed to be a day of rest—not battle."

Lizzie felt a chill down her spine, her cheeks flushed in embarrassment, privy to a conversation never meant to be heard outside of this warring family.

"Then get the girl married off . . . and soon."

Lizzie saw Miss MacKay approach before they did.

"Charlie! Wheesht!" Lady Isobel cautioned when they saw her.

Lizzie wondered how long she dared stay in this risky situation. Her curiosity piqued, she risked staying a few minutes longer, Miss MacKay would be busy for a while attending the family.

"Your sugar, Miss." Kate MacKay placed the bowl in front of the sulking girl.

Mary reached for the sugar and popped a lump into her mouth before she dropped three into her teacup. "What took you so long?"

But Miss MacKay was already out of the door, returning a tray to the kitchen. After that, Lizzie presumed, she would come down the hallway to the mistress's dressing room. Lizzie made good her escape to the library.

CHAPTER TEN

Aulich Hill

It's hardly in a body's pow'r,
To keep, at times frae being sour,
To see how things are shar'd

She sat in a high-backed chair in the farthest corner from the door, trying to regain her composure. Shamed at her bold eavesdropping, and embarrassed at the insults heaped on her and her family, she felt stinging humiliation spreading through her. She breathed deeply and twisted the folds of her skirt. She had wanted to find out more about the gentry. But this overwhelmed her. And she could never tell anyone what she'd heard. How could she explain her audacity? Plus, she couldn't understand their animosity towards her family, especially her mother. No, she wouldn't tell. Not even Ma. Especially not Ma.

She shot out of the chair as if it were on fire when Miss MacKay suddenly appeared at her side. Lizzie trained her eager eyes on the woman for any hint in her demeanour to indicate if she had somehow discovered that Lizzie had sneaked through the house.

Miss MacKay put her at ease with one of her rare smiles. "Och! Sorry ye had tae wait so long. Here, I brought ye a wee cuppa tea and some of my famous Dundee cake."

"Dundee cake? Ye do have some? I mean, thank ye, Miss MacKay."

The housekeeper handed her the china cup. "Sit ye down and enjoy. Not to worry, lass. The mistress saw that bonnie hair of yours and wanted you to have this comb for a wee gift."

She pulled the comb from her apron pocket.

Lizzie's eyes widened and her jaw dropped at the sight of the silver comb inlaid with ivory. It must be one of the combs Miss Mary had forbidden Miss MacKay to donate, one of the combs Lizzie had seen in the elegant, untidy bedchamber.

"Miss MacKay, I can't take that. My father would send me right back here with it. I mean it's not even Ne'erday or my birthday or anything like that."

"Just tell Robert MacGregor some folks up here think there's nothing too good for a dochter of Flora MacDonald. Her, a descendant of the girl that saved the Bonnie Prince Charlie, and carries that same proud name herself. Brought up a good Catholic, she was, too. Not like them that lives in this big hoose."

Lizzie bit into the orange-and-almond-flavoured cake, savouring its buttery moistness and the sweetness of the currants. She sipped her tea as delicately as she could, but Miss MacKay seemed oblivious to her and carried on a prolonged, intense conversation with herself.

"It would have been different if Prince Charlie had sat on his rightful throne, and we had the fine royal line of the Stewarts supporting Scotland. But what do we have? Germans . . . Protestants . . . turncoats, all of them. Och, I would never speak ill of yer mother. A lass has to go to the same kirk as her man, I suppose, even if it is Presbyterian. I'm sure it was what God intended. Aye, you tell him that . . . that rascal! Took my best worker and friend and made a farmer's wife out of her. She could have married any gentleman on Lewis or Harris . . . that smart lassie. Himself was teaching reading and writing to her. Charlie Buchanan kent how clever she was. Then she off and marries a ploughman . . . just a poor cottar . . . doesn't even have the proper Gaelic. She would have made a fine governess one day . . . but No! She has to fall in love with . . ."

"Miss MacKay." Lizzie's shocked interruption silenced the housekeeper's tirade.

Och, this news bewildered her already reeling mind, and Miss Mackay began talking rapid fire again.

"Aye, Flora was always the quiet one; kept herself to herself she did. Flora never flaunted her former station in life in front of you children, then?"

Lizzie shook her head.

"Never bragged to her daughter about her talents or the opportunities she gave up to marry Rob MacGregor?"

"No, Miss MacKay. Please, Miss MacKay . . ." Lizzie indicated she was out of her depth in this conversation.

"Well, that's the way it should be. Women should be modest, and children should be taught respect for their fathers." She straightened Lizzie's cap in a surprisingly maternal gesture.

"Your father is a fine, hard-working man. The laird has often said so hisself," she finished lamely.

Lizzie handed the crockery back to Miss MacKay, curtsied and thanked her. She walked to the front door trying to watch where she was going without taking her eyes off the comb for more than a second at a time.

"Oh, and Lizzie—"

"Yes'm." She retrieved her shawl on the way out.

"Wait, girl." The housekeeper reached into her apron pocket. "Miss Mary insisted you have this bar of French soap and this bottle of pomade to use for yer bonnie hair. But she doesn't even want you to thank her. She knows her generosity will be amply rewarded by the Lord."

* * *

Out on the lane Lizzie walked in the shade of the stone wall, several feet taller than she, eyes pointed down towards the cobblestone pavement without seeing it, her mind buzzing with the happenings of the last hour.

She had stepped into another world, one where people gave priceless objects away at a whim. Shelves of precious books full of fascinating tales and interesting information were taken for granted, ignored, and left to rot. Sumptuous rooms full of superfluous furnishings gathered dust till white-aproned servants bustled through to sweep and shine. Beautiful gardens were filled with exotic flowers; trees were laboriously trimmed and shaped just to please the eye that should happen to glance there.

From that library window the Buchanans could survey land that they owned, stretching as far as the eye could see. She was mystified, awed, full of curiosity, and something else that crept in like a cold draft under a door . . . envy.

Only in her imagination had it been <u>her</u> glen.

CHAPTER ELEVEN

Below Aulich Mansion

The eagle, from the cliffy brow,
Marking you his prey below,
In his breast no pity dwells,
Strong necessity compels.

Lizzie tramped beyond the length of the wall to the steep footpath that led down Aulich Hill. At the halfway point, she heard the barking cry of a sea eagle, then the noisy flapping of his huge wingspan as he plummeted to the earth, talons at the ready. He snatched some unfortunate creature, a mole perhaps. Lizzie's eyes followed him as he flew back to his aerie to enjoy his catch. From a craggy ledge, she looked back and up, making a final inspection of the panoramic vista of the splendid grounds and of the house where she had gained illicit access to some of its secrets. Looking down, she saw the view of the valley that Aulich House commanded: the hillside, dotted with sheep; Loch Rannoch glistening in the late afternoon sun; and the tenant houses of Aulich and Craiganour, where most of the laird's tenants lived.

Winding down the hill, she could see, through a haze of her own, the black smoke curling from each chimney and disappearing into the twilight. It poured forth continually from the peat fires lit all year round for cooking and boiling water and to warm the cottages.

Lizzie stumbled on a rocky protrusion and almost fell. Who knows how far she might have plummeted if she hadn't been able to right herself.

The fright cleared her head and forced her to return to her own world, a world now somewhat diminished by her recent other-worldly experience.

Lizzie inspected the clachan below. The group of two-room cottages, similar to the MacGregors', was surrounded by a wall, built by generations of her kinfolk from the stones they dug out of the unproductive land they cleared to plant their oats and potatoes. She could not see her own cottage, one of six that formed the clachan, nestled, as it was, under the rugged slope that gave it some protection from the north wind. She could see figures dimmed by the gray dusk; animated dolls moving around the communal yard. A figure emerged from the Campbell croft, maybe Jock going out to bring in peat for the fire. Could she ever move fast enough to 'accidentally' run into him?

The sun set early this time of year. She had dawdled as long as she dared. A sharp blast of wind funnelling through the glen caused her to wrap the shawl more tightly around her head and shoulders and pick up her pace. If she hurried maybe she'd get to share a few words with Jock.

The sun had dropped to the top of the mountains at the west end of the loch by the time she opened the latched gate and stepped carefully through the muddy yard. Through the tiny window of the Campbell croft she saw Jock and his brothers around the supper table. She watched him telling the others some story and heard their laughter.

Lizzie sighed, turned away and viewed the facade of her own home as if for the first time or as though she'd been gone for weeks or months. It would feel good to be inside the thick dry-stone walls, which shone silver in spots from the lichen that dotted them. A beam of light from a lamp, no doubt placed there by Ma to brighten her return, shone from the only window halfway up the ancient walls that rose the height of her father to the thatched roof. She noticed that despite the lattice of thick strands of woven heather, tied at each end around a boulder to hold the rope in place, some straw had blown away in the fierce winds that had whipped down from the mountains all winter. Time for spring repairs.

When she opened the door onto the entrance room, about two paces across and six paces to the rear wall, Lizzie smelled the customary odour of domestic animals housed in the attached byre to her left, the largest of the croft's three rooms, which extended about fifteen paces to the west wall. She felt their heat; the cows and sheep helped keep the place warm all winter, and the poor brutes couldn't survive in the gales out on the moor. The smell of the French soap in her apron pocket masked the odours somewhat, but now the thought of being shut up with the stench of animals for even a few more weeks dismayed her after the luxury she'd seen.

The hens danced angrily around her in the entryway. Charlie had constructed an ingenious heather net strung across the half door that opened onto the byre that kept them confined. An incongruous image of Mary Buchanan's white cotton hose lying in the middle of these droppings and feathers occurred to her.

Lizzie opened the door to her right into the living area where the family had congregated, as was customary at dusk. The soft murmur of Charlie's and Pa's voices, engaged in congenial discussion about taking the animals back out to pasture for the warmer months, soothed her jarring memories of the Buchanans' bickering and her disappointment over missing Jock. In the cramped quarters she felt warmth creeping back into her bones.

Annie gave her a snide look and tossed her head, daring her into an argument about the ribbons she had in her hair; Lizzie's ribbons that she'd left out to dry in the windowsill. She'd see to her sister later.

Wee Gregor chirped from his stool on the rag rug near the fire, "Yer home, Lizzie," and held up his arms.

She picked him up to be petted. She could never refuse the frail wee lad. She sat with Gregor on the box bed against the west wall across from the fireplace. Gregor chattered about his day, but Lizzie's attention wandered around the overcrowded shadowy room, lit by one oil lamp and the firelight.

A dresser stood next to the fireplace on the flagstone floor. The engraved wooden piece, quite splendid by local standards, seemed out of place next to an assortment of hand-hewn wooden chairs and stools. She could, more clearly now, imagine the elegant setting where it must have originated. The piece of furniture might have been decorative in a place like the big house, but utilitarian here. All the food was chopped and mixed on its well-worn surface, and only crude dishes filled its shelves. Ma's few pieces of china were put away for Ne'erday celebrations.

Ma rocked baby Archie's cradle with her foot and stirred the delicious-smelling concoction she had in the iron pot suspended over the fire.

Lizzie handed wee Gregor into Annie's reluctant arms. Her younger sister didn't dare refuse, caught, as she was, using Lizzie's stuff.

Lizzie approached Ma and tapped her on the shoulder. "I have an essay to finish for tomorrow, Ma," she whispered, risking the white lie to escape to a private corner.

"Better not let your father catch you doing school work on the Sabbath. Go on, lass. I know ye've been kept busy around here. Your Pa and Charlie will be going out to feed the livestock presently. I'll keep our Annie busy."

Lizzie escaped into the dark sleeping room to be alone with her thoughts. She lit a lamp, set it on the windowsill, and quietly pulled her own personal kist from under the bed. She inspected the silver comb again before placing it under a tangle of homespun yarn and the half-knitted socks she meant to finish before Ne'erday, gifts for her brothers. She fished out her school jotter, laid it on the chair, locked the box, and slid it back under the bed. Lizzie breathed a sigh of relief, glad for the solitude, and absently opened the writing pad to the essay she had already completed.

What had it been like for Mother, living in that mansion? Until today, Lizzie had considered it inconsequential that her mother had worked at the big house. She'd never bothered to discuss it with her. After all, many in the village had taken jobs at the manor. In fact, employment there was coveted, for it paid real money, paid in silver florins, which came in very useful to buy items they couldn't produce themselves, like the china Ma kept safely in her kist, all paid for in Scottish pounds and dragged from Pitlochry by horse and sleigh. But if Ma had been considered for a governess—well, that indicated a special status. Could that be why the Buchanan ladies were so vicious? Were they jealous of her island mother's intelligence—or perhaps her grace? Of course, her mother still had fine looks and an almost regal carriage, despite the years of effort to keep the growing family comfortable in the stone cottage.

Close to Ma as anyone, she knew her heart and found it pure. Hard to believe anyone could judge her mother harshly. Mother was different in so many ways from other farm wives; Lizzie supposed her stately air might have been mistaken for an attitude of superiority. Her mother could discuss literature and politics; educated "beyond her station," some said. Lizzie now had an inkling about how Ma's uniqueness had been acquired.

But what right did Mary Buchanan have to malign a decent woman like Flora MacDonald MacGregor? And what did her ladyship mean by "spawn?" Lizzie's heart swelled in pride and anger. She wanted to run out into the fire room and tell her mother and father what she had heard and wait for their soothing explanations. But that simple solution wouldn't work in this instance. Suddenly she felt older, wiser. Lizzie would have to go carefully into the many questions she had for her mother. Any kind of probing—even from Lizzie—easily triggered Ma's natural reticence. Flora MacGregor had the reserved ways of her Hebridean Island forebears.

Her mother rarely talked about her early years, but Lizzie knew that Ma had been raised by her mother Elizabeth's clan, the clan MacDonald, and had always been referred to as Flora MacDonald. Ma said little about her father. He had been wounded in combat in France and travelled by boat out to the Isle of Lewis, as far as he could from the fray and still be in Scotland. There he met Lizzie's grandmother, Elizabeth, and married her. It was a short love affair, for Elizabeth died within a year, when she gave birth to Lizzie's mother. Something about Ma's father's death irked Ma still today; probably his being wounded for a cause so alien to his Highland roots. Ma believed it futile for Scots to give their lives in English wars. When Flora used the expression "cannon fodder" like an embittered soldier, she always startled Lizzie, for Ma rarely made waves; she was serene, dependable, and the rudder that kept the family on course.

The school jotter, crammed with reports, slipped from her hand. As she picked it up, she thought about reading from it in Kilichonan School tomorrow. Och! It would be fine. She'd worked hard on it. She was a good student and the teachers always valued her efforts, especially her appreciation for prose and poetry. Her mother had insisted that Lizzie stay full days at the one-room schoolhouse till she was fourteen and had persuaded Father to allow her to attend for half-days for the last two years despite his constant complaints.

Mother was unusually adamant. "Lizzie, ye're staying at the school. Ye've always loved to read and learn. I, too, acquired a taste for literature when I was in service at Aulich House."

That was all Mother had said about her connection to the Buchanans at the time. Now Lizzie wanted to know more.

She'd not yet invented a scheme to get Ma by herself when she heard Pa and Charlie's noisy return from the stockyard.

Time for supper.

She hoped Pa continued his pontificating over supper. It would cover her confusion and the turmoil inside her that she feared might be obvious.

"Where's Lizzie?" She heard Pa in the other room, impatient to start the meal.

"Here, Pa," she called out.

"In there workin' on books again? If I've said it once, I've said it ower many times; ye've had enough school. It's bad enough Charlie fillin' his head wi' multiplication and long division when I need him tae help cut the peat."

"Here, Rob." Ma tried to distract him with a bowl of steaming potage.

"Aye, Florry, it's all your doin'. Ye've been readin' those books to her since she was at the breast. Her head is full of ideas way beyond what any lassie needs to be a good wife and mother."

Lizzie scooped a generous portion out of the big iron pot and took her place at the table.

Pa wasn't finished. "Ye'll get too uppity to settle down with a plough-man or a shepherd. Then what will ye do? Be wantin' to run off to Glasgow or Edinburgh."

Lizzie knew if she began to argue, it would go on throughout the meal. Ridiculous! Glasgow? Edinburgh? They seemed as far away as Canada or America.

CHAPTER TWELVE

Flora's Secret Life

The morn that warns th' approaching day
Awakes me up to toil and woe;
I see the hours in long array,
That I must suffer lingering slow.

ext day Lizzie awoke sobbing, beset with her old nighmare.

Her mother shook her head, sighed, and gave her eldest daughter a tired smile.

"I'll get you some water, child. I think you've caught a chill."

"I'm fine, Ma. But wee Gregor feels feverish."

Her mother disappeared into the living area where she and father slept. Lizzie could hear her, through the open door, pouring water.

Lizzie's father asked, "Is wee Gregor wet?"

"No. Go back to sleep. Lizzie had another of her nightmares."

"Och! She's too old for that nonsense," he grumbled.

Lizzie felt her already flushed face heating up. Normally, she shut out or ignored sounds and conversations from the adjoining room, but she felt anxious and vulnerable now. Though it vexed her to incur her father's criticism, she would never tell him the frightening vision that had returned in the night, and which had haunted her since Gregor's first episode of croup at five months old. That wracking cough kept coming back for three years and left him weak and vulnerable to chest infections. Ma had confided in her that she thought the boy had developed consumption, and Lizzie saw the wee lad spit a red stain in the snow.

* * *

A shaft of sunlight woke Lizzie. The light that shone through the window barely lit the room most of the time. It must be late, noon most likely. The sleeping room had been tidied and swept. The hand-sewn quilt and the straw mattress were smoothed on the adjacent bed. On Ma's kist, her private box of treasures she'd had since before her marriage, a posy of wildflowers had appeared and replaced the dried herbs that decorated the windowsill all winter. Lizzie had missed school. She sat up and felt her head throbbing. Gregor, still asleep in the bed beside her, coughed when she moved the weight of his body off her legs. Ma appeared at the door.

"Why did ye not wake me for school?" Lizzie asked.

"Ye've got the Influenza, I think. Ye stayed out too long in the dampness yesterday. Where were ye, anyway?"

"I'm fine, Ma. What's the matter with wee Gregor?"

"He's having one of his bad turns. Keep him in bed with you today. I've made some thin porridge for the two of ye."

Lizzie tried to eat the porridge. Ma had even sprinkled sugar on it and topped it with cream, but it turned her stomach. She wakened Gregor, who was even less interested in the food. She lay back down, threw her arm around her brother, and felt her mind floating off. She had no idea how long she slept and thought she must be dreaming when she heard Kate MacKay's voice in the next room.

In the close confines of the cottage, it was considered bad manners to listen in on private conversations that occurred not more than a few feet away. Living in such proximity, she had cultivated an ability to go inside herself, even in the midst of chaos. How else could you read and think and memorize or even sleep? But the previous day's experience made her keen to find out what Kate MacKay might know. There was a lot to learn by eavesdropping. And so Lizzie's curiosity overcame her ingrained reticence, and she pricked up her ears.

"... making your lassie come all the way up ... must be two miles ... and the wind fit to blow her off Aulich Hill ... and not to remember why she summoned her. Och, Florry, it's just pitiful. Did the lass show ye the comb I picked out?" She gave a hearty chuckle.

"Well, no ..." Her mother's voice trailed off.

"Did she no' say?" But Miss MacKay didn't wait for a reply. "The high and mighty Mary decided to tame Lizzie's bonnie hair with the gift of one of her fine ivory combs. No skin off her nose, mind ye. She must have had five o' them cluttered about her bureau; one from yon English captain who's tryin' to win her hand. He better come with a fist full of siller if he wants to court Miss Mary. There's not tuppence worth of charity in that wee madam's soul. It's chust pitiful. She thinks she's superior, Florry, but she knows you're better educated and more refined, and don't you forget it, lass. That's what sticks in Isobel's craw! Do ye ever worry what will become of us when Auld Buchanan goes? I do. Och! I hope I'm deed and buried by then."

"Wheesht, Kate. Lizzie is home sick from school. She's sleeping in the other room."

"She's a bonnie one, right enough, Florry. Aye. Maybe ye made the right choice after all. I'm still takin' care of Charlie's spoiled brat and too late to have my own bairns. That last bairn took its toll on ye."

Her mother mumbled a reply.

"It's time Rob MacGregor found some other hobby. Ye're wearin' yerself out."

"I'm fine, Kate," her mother whispered.

Lizzie gently disentangled herself from Gregor and crept closer to the door separating the rooms.

"I know ye worry about me, Kate. I'll never repay ye the gratitude I owe for taking care of me when my mother died. You weren't much more than a child yourself, taking care of me, a baby."

"Nothing to thank me for. I swore I'd protect you if anything happened to her. It was a sacred trust. And how was your father going to tend ye, with him so sickly? Damn the English and their wars."

"Kate, about my father ... remember he entrusted Colonel Buchanan with my birth certificate back in Stornoway?"

"Aye. Ye never got that baptismal record. Did ye?" Kate's voice had taken on an exaggerated whisper Lizzie had no problem hearing. "He means for ye to have it. It's probably slipped his mind. Why won't ye talk to him?"

"Och, Kate. Better if I stay away from them. Isobel Menzies suspects the worst about me."

"That's as it may be, but mark my words, the laird may not get the male heir he yearns for from Mary and he won't tolerate her abandoning the land. He always pledged to take care of ye. He has that fierce clan loyalty, too. There must be a will somewhere. Maybe he made some provisions. Stranger things have happened . . ." Kate seemed to be rambling or talking to herself, as usual.

"Kate!" The warning in her mother's voice could not be mistaken now. "Just see if you can get it without creating any fuss. It would be nice to pass it along to my bairns."

Lizzie heard the chink of teacups.

"There's some shortbread there in the basket I brought." Kate said.

"Kate, we manage fine. Ye don't need to bring me stuff."

✳ ✳ ✳

All went quiet in the adjoining room. Lizzie assumed they were drinking tea and eating. She wished she could have some too and realized that, if she were hungry, she must be feeling better. Wee Gregor stretched and whimpered. She crooned quietly to him and dried his sweaty brow with a towel. She hoped he'd go back to sleep so she could hear more. Lizzie listened carefully but heard only the sound of Ma's knitting needles clicking rapidly. She picked up Gregor and took him into the fire room to get a drink for both of them. Kate had vanished. Lizzie disturbed her mother stuffing items into the dresser.

"Come here, my wee lamb, are ye feeling better? How's that bad old cough?" Her mother gathered Gregor into her arms. "Miss MacKay was here." She raised her eyebrows and gave Lizzie a questioning look.

Lizzie didn't know whether her mother was fishing to find out how much, if anything, Lizzie had overheard, or if she wanted Lizzie's version of the visit to Aulich House. Lizzie chose to believe the latter. She needed time to grasp the significance of the conversations she had inadvertently heard over the last two days before she discussed any of it with her mother.

"She told you about the comb then?"

"Aye, she did, lass."

"I was going to tell you, Ma. It's just that Pa might have been cross with me if I'd said where I'd been, because I told him I went to tend the sheep."

"So what happened?" Her mother fed thin gruel to the boy on her lap. Lizzie returned to the bedroom and dug the comb out of her kist. "This is it."

Ma's eyes grew big. "She gave ye that? Not like Mary Buchanan to do a kindness to us. She's never been known for her generosity." Ma tapered off, bit her lip, and then smiled at her daughter.

"Miss MacKay chose it, I think."

Her mother chuckled in obvious delight as she turned the ornate piece over in her work-roughened hands. "It's the brawest comb I've ever seen. Here, let me dress yer hair. Gregor's asleep . . . Och! Never mind. I hear the others coming home from school. Ye still look like yer ready to drop. Go lie down, take wee Gregor, too. I'll get Annie to help with the supper."

Lizzie made a hasty retreat just as Charlie, Annie, and the twins burst into the room all talking at the same time.

* * *

Annie peered around the box bed. "Are you sleeping?" She said in a loud voice that would have wakened Lizzie from a deep sleep.

"No. Why are you so late?"

"Och, we were havin' such a great time with Jock." She tossed her head in a manner Lizzie recognized as her own habit.

"Doing what?"

"Och, just talkin' and laughin'. He said I was the prettiest girl in the whole school."

"He said no such thing." Lizzie was emphatic.

"He did so. Ask our Charlie. He heard him."

Lizzie didn't believe Jock, or any other boy she knew, would say such a thing in the company of other lads. Annie had Pa's wavy brown hair and dark eyes; she'd filled out this last year. And, yes, she had grown pretty. She flirted with any young lad who gave her the time of day. Surely Jock wouldn't be taken in by that. He'd known her since childhood to be the surly, selfish tattle-tale Lizzie and Charlie left out of their adventures. A strange chill rippled through her body, which may or may not have been related to her slight fever.

CHAPTER THIRTEEN

Treading with Caution

The best laid schemes o' mice and men gang aft aglee.

Lizzie's return to school felt like a holiday after three days of being shut up in the farmhouse with Gregor and baby Kate demanding her attention every minute. It was Thursday, and Mr. Kennedy, the travelling librarian, would be coming to school to tutor the older children after the others went home. In this year's class, the older children consisted of Charlie, her, and Jock. The spirited discussion on the books they studied in class continued on the way home. Lizzie treasured this rare opportunity for the three of them to be together.

Until today.

Mr. Kennedy asked Lizzie to read her report to the class, and Lizzie suddenly regretted her choice of subject. Charlie and Jock raised their eyes to the ceiling when she announced her topic, Shakespeare's "Romeo and Juliet."

Mr. Kennedy seemed pleased, though. "Class, this play is often dismissed by scholars, or at least not compared favourably with some of his other works. But I believe it has depth and structural complexity and . . . Och! Let's hear what Lizzie made of it. Go ahead, Lizzie."

Encouraged, Lizzie stood up and read for about half an hour. She talked about Romeo's pining for Rosaline as being quite immature, and in her analysis he deserved the teasing he got from his friends and relatives. "He finally realized he was infatuated with the wrong girl." She looked straight at Jock, just as Charlie kicked Jock under the desk and Jock's face turned red. Mr. Kennedy, however, seemed too intent on Lizzie's presentation to notice.

"Lizzie, that was an excellent piece of writing. Boys, this is the kind of book report I want to hear from you two lads when we reconvene in September. You'll have plenty of time to study over the summer. Leave your notebook with me, Lizzie; I want to show it to Mrs. Kennedy. Class dismissed."

They would be out of school for months but that did not mean they would have free time. The big lads would be helping in the clachan and in the fields and Lizzie would be busy with cleaning and gardening all summer.

On the walk home, Charlie and Jock talked constantly, as though she weren't there at all. Lizzie felt a tightening around her heart. The strain in her relationship with Jock now spoiled this precious time too. She loved Jock the way a woman loves a man, and that changed everything, and now it seemed he couldn't even be her pal. He and Charlie shut her out.

"I want to go to America or Canada, or even New Zealand or Australia; make my own way," said Charlie.

"Aye," Jock said. "This land is all used up . . . too many people, too many sheep; can't grow a decent crop."

Charlie continued, warming to his subject. "Those maps in school of North America . . . Australia, too . . . got me to thinking about leaving this place for someplace where there's open land, good farming."

"Is that what you want to do, Charlie . . . be a farmer?" said Jock.

"Maybe . . . or maybe I'd get a boat and go fish the Great Barrier Reef or cut timber in the British Columbian forests over there. I don't know, Jock. It's just what I think about when I'm walking in the fields or fishing in the burn."

Charlie had told Lizzie often enough that he would leave the glen when he got older. She knew he meant it. But, growing up, she'd always thought she would go with him. She sympathized with his views that there were no opportunities for someone like him. So why did they not include her in their conversation?

The three had been pals all their lives. What had gone wrong? Why was she left out? Could it be true that Jock liked her sister? How could he?

Nobody liked Annie. After being ignored for about twenty minutes, Lizzie thought she might burst into tears of frustration.

"I'm running on ahead," she told them. "I have to pick some kale for the soup."

Both boys turned as if they had just noticed her.

* * *

The next day the house was quiet. The twins and Gregor had gone to the pasture with Charlie. The baby and wee Kate slept in the other room. Annie had gone to a neighbour's croft, most likely to avoid work.

In a reflective mood, Lizzie stirred the iron pot suspended over the fire with a big wooden spurtle. Uncertain about tackling the delicate topic of her mother's past, she had waited many weeks for the opportunity to have a long, undisturbed talk with Ma. She still hesitated, afraid of seeming too inquisitive and sending her mother back to her customary silence.

Ma opened her private kist and retrieved a volume of poetry, which gave Lizzie an opening.

"Ma, where did ye get all the books ye have in the kist?"

"From the big house; from Colonel Buchanan."

"Why, Ma?"

"Ye mean what made him give them to me?"

"Aye. Ye lived there for a long time then left." Lizzie thought if she threw in this oblique reference to her mother's tenure at the mansion without asking a direct question, Ma might elaborate on her explanation.

After an awkward silence, her mother began talking in a dreamy, quiet voice, as though hearing aloud, for the first time, the words of a story she had often told herself. "Ye know...the laird caught me reading over his shoulder one winter night. Och! He thought it was grand that a girl from the Islands was wanting to learn from books. So fascinated was he that he allowed me access to his extensive library. As the years went by, he began to ask me, 'What book are you reading now?', and we'd get into a bit of a discussion about this novel or that bit of scripture, usually while I was polishing the woodwork in his study.

"Sometimes it was a wee bit difficult for me to share my thoughts in English with the colonel, which he encouraged me to use. It was easier for me to think things through in the Gaelic back then. He has a bit of the Gaelic himself. He was gie patient for a nobleman. I'll say that, all right."

She stopped, got up, set down her book, and poked at the peat fire. Before she sat down again, she gave her daughter an intense look.

"Lizzie, we are sharing a story here for your ears only."

Lizzie nodded and waited for her to continue, but the baby started to cry, commanding her mother's attention, and the boys could be heard roaring down the hill behind the house. Oh, no, Lizzie thought, yet another missed opportunity.

It was almost twilight and her father would be home soon, wanting his supper. She hastily threw another peat on the fire under the big cauldron and added salt, from the box at the side of the hearth, to the boiling water. She barely noticed the turmoil the boys created, caught up, as she was, in her speculations. She stirred the iron kettle absentmindedly and wiped her sweaty brow. Her eyes were smarting, for the chimney was not drawing, and smoke had backed up into the room probably from the north wind blowing down Aulich Hill.

The laird and her mother . . . hmmm! . . . talking to each other casually . . . just not done! She knew her father would think it strange. Aristocrats did not treat servants as intellectual equals. And yet the auld laird must have thought peasant girls could have intelligence and refinement if he devoted so much time to Ma's education. Was her mother the one who taught him that?

She felt suddenly protective of Pa. Had he ever suspected the laird's motives? Och! The ancient tradition of <u>droit du seigneur</u>, a maiden being taken first by the ruling lord, only happened in ancient tales. She let her imagination run away with her. If Pa had any reason to be jealous or angry, she surely would have sensed it.

Lizzie absentmindedly sprinkled too many oats in the pot. She quickly added boiling water from the kettle before the porridge could stick or get lumpy.

Lizzie had always rested securely in the bond of affection that existed between her parents. It was difficult to imagine what Ma's life would have been like if she hadn't met Lizzie's father. Even though he was years older than Ma, he must have been handsome when he won her mother's heart. Did Ma ever regret her choice that had led her to a life in a cottar's shack when she could have lived on at the big house, in comfort?

Now she found herself wondering what old Buchanan made of her mother's decision. Probably hard for him to understand a woman's desire to have her own roots, no matter how humble. Whatever attitude of affection or special favour he had bestowed on her mother in the past was no longer evident; she'd never seen him do anything but nod in Ma's direction just as he did with all his other tenants. Sure, Kate MacKay sent down packages from the big house addressed to her mother from time to time, but that had nothing to do with the laird, did it? She probably distributed "kindnesses" to all the tenants—noblesse oblige.

But her mother had not yet told her about the books. Compared to the contents of their neighbours' bookshelves, a family Bible and perhaps a volume of Sir Walter Scott, her mother had a veritable library. Where did the books come from?

Lizzie served her father and the children a bowl of porridge with fresh milk to wash it down. The fire blazed cheerily now that the chimney was drawing like a charm, the wind must have changed. She retrieved the horn spoon Kate was banging on her wooden platter and fed her little sister. She'd have to get Ma talking again; after all these years, her quiet, reserved mother could still surprise her.

* * *

Pa and the children fell asleep soon after supper. She could hear his snores from the box bed on the other side of the room.

"Get yer comb, and I'll take some of the tangles out of yer hair, Lizzie."

Though she knew her mother must be tired, Lizzie grasped the opportunity to find answers to the questions that haunted her.

"If ye were in service at the big house, how did ye meet Pa? Was he working up there?"

"It was when the new church was built. We all went . . . the Buchanans and the staff. I was not sure if I should sit with the family or on the other side with the farm folk. Yon wee Mary Buchanan, only a bairn she was, started to cry. 'Papa,' she says, 'Miss Flora has to sit with the plain folk. You said this was our own side.'

"He tried to dissuade her. And with that she started in to screaming like she always did to get her own way, and Charlie, ah . . . Mr. Buchanan says to me, 'Sit over there, Miss MacDonald.'

"So I did, and the only place left was in the MacGregor pew. Och! Yer father was a fine figure of a man. He was nigh on thirty-eight years and never picked a wife. I had begun to accept that I would spend the rest of my years in service, for I was already twenty-six. But, och, it was love at first sight for the both of us, I think. Aye, it is safe to say."

She smiled and drew the comb through Lizzie's hair. "He started calling on me at the big house the next week. I don't think the auld laird was too happy about losing me . . . I mean about losing a servant. He had a long talk with your father, but in the end he gave us permission to marry. He knew the MacGregors were a good family. That's how it happened."

Her mother appeared to have finished her storytelling for the time being. Not too many details, Lizzie thought, but good enough for a beginning.

The grooming completed, her mother turned Lizzie's face towards her to see her handiwork in the firelight's glow.

The fire flared up and cast a gentle radiance onto her mother's countenance making her look younger than her years. Lizzie could imagine her mother as a lass. She must have been bonnie, with her red hair and blue eyes and her calm, soothing ways. Tonight, she was convinced; she was being introduced to a secret part of her mother no one else knew.

Darkness crept in on them, and they lit paraffin lamps that shed enough light in the cottage for Lizzie's mother to do some mending on socks the boys would need for school tomorrow. Lizzie still had an essay on the Beatitudes to do before Friday. It would have to wait till tomorrow. Lizzie picked up a sock with the heel worn out and began to lace wool across the hole.

Her mother seemed deep in thought and could remain this way, silent and stitching until bedtime, unless Lizzie initiated something.

"So what happened, Ma?"

"Well, lass, like I was saying . . ." She picked up her story as though she had never left off. "The laird thought it would be fine to have a Scottish woman to teach his bairns. He's not like all those that have to hire English governesses to teach their children to talk like they're not even Scots. He said he could never find anyone who had a better grasp of literature than his Miss Florry. That was me, you know."

Lizzie whispered to her mother. "You still didn't tell me how ye got the books, Ma."

"It was a wedding gift, Lizzie. The laird allowed me to choose half a dozen books from his library. I have never told anyone about it, not even your father . . . especially not him. He could never have understood a servant girl talking to a master the way I did. He might not understand."

Lizzie felt sure he wouldn't. She began to wonder herself.

Ma's intense gaze made Lizzie blush, feel transparent.

"I, of course, chose some works by Robert Burns." Her mother returned to safer ground.

Lizzie nodded. She would keep her mother's secret. Relaxed by the hair-brushing and hypnotized by the peat fire, she almost dozed off.

"I think Buchanan did not respect Rabbie Burns." Her mother's voice startled her. It took her a moment to remember what they had been discussing.

"He admitted there was no question about his literary genius, but I overheard him with the Duke of Argyll—telling him the plain folk were welcome to Burns. He says, 'Och! The man's morals are definitely question-able . . . harrrdly a gentleman.' He referred to what he called 'that upstarrrt ploughman's chicanery and debauchery.'"

Ma chuckled, perhaps at the memories or about her own imitation of the colonel whom she mimicked to perfection. "'There's even a fol-lowing erupting among the gentry,' he says. 'It makes for lively discussions over brandy and cigars, of course, but not a suitable subject matter for the ladies.'"

Not exactly a suitable topic of discussion between a master and a young female servant either, Lizzie thought.

Ma read her mind again. "Burns' colourful personal life was not a sub-ject he raised with me, of course. He did, however, share his opinion that some of Burns' topics were a bit mundane and crude. I did not refute him on that, but he suspected I was fond of Rabbie.

"He was not a devotee of Sir Walter Scott either. He met him in Edinburgh at a lecture and subsequently bought all of his books. But the laird thought that Scott, being a Lowlander, had not captured the true nature of the Highlands. His novels were more fanciful than authentic. But that's what I liked about them, so he indulged my fondness for fiction and gave the books to me. I know your favourite."

"Yes, Ma. 'Rob Roy.' I've read it five times. Charlie's read it six."

Ma laughed. "You two! It exhausted me having two sets of twins, but watching my children play and grow together, I almost envied the closeness you twins enjoyed."

Her mother reached onto her kist again. "I was, as you know child, particularly fond of the works of Charles Lamb, and, though the only copy he had in his library was a valuable first edition, he gave this to me on my wedding day. I cried with joy, I must admit, and broke all the rules of proper conduct by giving him a hug in front of Katie MacKay. Och, well, I suppose it was all right—Katie was like a sister to me. We were all a wee bit embarrassed till the colonel guffawed and said, 'It's your wedding day. Save all those hugs for MacGregor. He's a very lucky man. I wish you both a long happy life and a house full of bonnie bairns.'"

Wistfully she added, "I left service then and never had occasion to visit him again, except in church or in the village and when he attended the christening of my firstborn—you, lass, and Charlie. It was the first sacrament in the new church. He gave me a package that looked suspiciously like a book. When I opened it, I discovered a note from the colonel."

Her mother reached into her kist and pulled out a yellowing scrap of paper.

"'April 11, 1843

'Dear Flora,

'May your children inherit your love of literature.

'I have not been able to get my Mary to sit still long enough to enjoy even a nursery rhyme. She definitely seems opposed to any kind of learning unless it is about pretty frocks or ribbons or sweetmeats.

'This will be little Elizabeth's and Bonnie Charlie's introduction to the classics.

'Never too soon to start.

'Regards,

'Charles Buchanan.'

"The package contained Charles and Mary Lamb's <u>Tales from Shake-speare</u>. I put the book in the folds of your baby dress, and on return to the cottage placed it in the kist to await the day when you could enjoy being read to."

"Och, it's one of my favourites, Ma. You've read that book a hundred times to us. I like 'A Midsummer Night's Dream' best."

"That ye do. I remember well the year you first heard the tale, for I had to read it to ye every day. You were Titania, the queen of the fairies, and all the lambs born that spring got fairy names."

"Aye, we still have Pease-blossom, Cobweb, and Moth . . . Mustard-seed got sold at the market." Lizzie shrugged in acceptance.

"The laird often quoted the bard. And even though the little book is intended for children, it has been my only access to the works of the English dramatist and poet since I left Aulich House." She sighed. "I am not likely ever to have a copy of the original plays and even less chance of seeing them acted out on the stage. It has satisfied me to read the tales. And my joy has been to share them with you, daughter."

Her mother folded the note and picked up the leather-bound book. When she opened the book to tuck it back in place, a folded letter of several yellowed pages dropped out. She retrieved it from the flagstone floor and quickly buried it in the back of the book, offering no explanation.

"When I am gone, you take that kist and all that is in it, Lizzie. That chest shipped all of my belongings from Stornoway when I was just a lass of twelve. Och! I didn't even have the English. It travelled from Lewis with me across The Minch in a wild storm and over rough roads in a carriage, and now it is by my own fireside with all those dear books at the bottom of it."

Her mother stared into the fire and picked up her mending.

"And a lock of my mother's hair," she added.

"Did you have any memento of your father?"

"We'll talk again, girl. It is late and we've burned enough oil."

Lizzie wished she could bite back the words; she'd pushed Ma too far.

They put out the lamps and Lizzie found a spot to curl up in the narrow bed already full of tired bodies, arms and legs so tangled it was hard to move Annie without disturbing Gregor. Charlie and the twins were fast asleep in the other bed.

In the other room, Archie, roused from sleep, began crying. Ma must be changing the rags on the baby's bottom. Then she heard him slurping vigorously.

Lizzie lay at the edge of the bed listening to the crackle of the flames from the peat fire. The action of the fire matched her thoughts. Her mind had been ablaze with imaginings about her mother and the big house and the Buchanans. Was there more? Her mother was a silent pool that ran very deep.

Did old Buchanan have a roving eye? She recalled the portrait of the young man in the big house. Something had disturbed her about his very bright blue eyes. They weren't unkind or unfeeling at all. In fact, they were soft and warm like the embers of the fire, which had quieted down now and would smoulder through the night.

He certainly could have turned a young girl's head. But he must have been quite old already when Flora worked there. Young women in service were helpless to thwart the pressures of a rapacious master. Lizzie had heard some stories that eclipsed the novels she read. Surely her mother would not have succumbed voluntarily to the sexual advances of an older, married man. Yet it didn't sound like Mother had been forced into some situation. Her thoughts were running in circles.

Did Father have any inkling about Mother's past? If he did, he never showed any resentment. On the contrary; he always spoke well of Colonel Buchanan.

Lulled to somnolence by the warmth of wee Gregor snuggled up against her back, she put her arm back to pet him and pulled his nightshirt down over his bare, cold rump. He mumbled in his sleep. She couldn't tell if he said 'Mammy' or 'Meggy.' She tucked the quilt around them, noting she or Ma needed to sew some more pieces on to it, for it barely covered everyone.

Lizzie wondered how much more she dared ask her mother or reveal about what she had overheard at the mansion.

CHAPTER FOURTEEN

Lizzie's Secret Place

Among the heathy hills and ragged woods

"Is it time to bring the kie home?" Her mother's smile barely hid her fatigue.

Not that Lizzie had much free time. But on fine summer days like this, when the hearth was swept out and the window and door opened to let the place air out, her mother would say, "Take a basket down to the lane and see if the raspberries are ripe." Which, of course they weren't yet. Or maybe, "Go on out and find me some dandelion greens." Or, "Are the kie headed for the barn yet?"

This last excuse about the cows coming home became a code between them; her mother was offering her a respite from the constant round of work; a welcome chance for Lizzie to slip off on her own without any of the little ones in tow, a signal to go off with a book from Ma's precious collection and satisfy her passion for reading. But the opportunity to indulge herself came with a certain amount of guilt. Her mother could barely keep up with the mounting chores this new bairn had created.

Now close to forty-three and worn out with childbearing, Flora almost died when Archie was born breech in January. Lizzie shuddered at the memory of Ma's screams, which lasted way into the night and scared all of them. At dawn Mrs. Campbell, who was attending Ma, called Lizzie into the sleeping room. By then Ma's cries were moans punctuated by deep sighs.

"Lizzie, push on her belly. We have to get that baby out, or your Ma isn't going to last another hour."

Lizzie approached the blood-soaked bed. Fear crept up her spine. "Ma, Ma, are you all right?"

"Just push, lass. NOW!" Nellie commanded Lizzie.

She obeyed, pulling her eyes away from her mother's gray face to watch Mrs. Campbell flexing her muscular, bloodied arms. Her hands weren't visible, and Lizzie realized with horror that the woman had reached inside her mother's body.

"Push, Lizzie, push. She cannae do it for herself anymore."

Against her instincts, Lizzie pressed her entire weight through her trembling hands against her mother's abdomen. She felt a slight movement under her fingers.

Nellie Campbell's hands emerged with a tiny blue-red leg in her grasp. "Again, Lizzie."

The body emerged in a gush of fresh blood. Mrs. Campbell worked frantically at the birth canal to free the baby's head.

"Please, God. Please, God. Please, God." Lizzie's repetitive entreaty continued for what seemed like an eternity, then she felt the mound under her hands collapse and Nellie pulled the baby from Ma's body.

The exhausted midwife let out a guttural, "Thank you, God."

Lizzie and Nellie raced between the baby and the mother, with Nellie shouting instructions till they heard the child's pitiful first cry.

"Get yer sister."

"Annie?"

"Yes. Have her take the babe out to the fire room and bundle him up near the warmth."

Lizzie handed off the child to the terrified Annie.

"Just keep him warm," she instructed her sister but Pa appeared and gently took his new son and Lizzie returned to Nellie's side to tend to her mother. The next hour was a blur to Lizzie till she saw her mother's eyelids flicker and she hoarsely asked, "Is it a boy or a girl? Not twins again, I hope."

"Not twins, Ma."

"Ye've got another fine wee boy, Flora," said Nellie.

Now, three months later, the memory of that night was still fresh in Lizzie's mind as she watched her mother, still pale and slow-moving, reach down into the chest where she kept her prized books. Ma seemed to come more alive as she pulled out one of the precious volumes for Lizzie.

Before Lizzie escaped with the well-worn book, she checked around both rooms of the but and ben to make sure the babes didn't need changing or the slops emptying, eager to be off, yet loath to leave her mother with the full burden.

Finally satisfied that Mother could cope without her for a while, she tucked the book into her apron pocket and carefully tiptoed on the flat stones spaced a few feet apart leading to the gate in order to avoid the mud from the recent spring thaw. Chickens came clucking expectantly around her skirts, the noisy rooster in the lead. She stepped quickly beyond his pecking bill. That aggression would put him sooner into the soup pot.

Beyond the cottages, she could see the big house, high on Aulich Hill, set in its grove of oak and conifers, surrounded by the imposing stone wall, taller than she. A rider left the stable of the big house. Must be Andy MacFarlane running errands for his aunt, Kate MacKay. Maybe there would be a package for her mother in his saddlebags. Lizzie hoped it would be something good to eat.

* * *

Lizzie held her face up to the sun's rays, absorbing the warmth; exhilaration coursed through her veins as she revelled in the kind of spring day that is rare in the region. The skies over Rannoch never bored her. They changed like a kaleidoscope; never clear blue as Lizzie had read some skies could be; never just one shade of gray either. Sometimes she could see Ben Nevis, grandfather of all Scottish mountains, off in the distance with its permanent, peaked cap of white.

Sometimes she had difficulty distinguishing the far-off mountaintop from the clouds; they each used the same palette of blue, silver, white, and gray. Sunbeams danced on the budding heather and the green pastureland and lit the tops of the evergreens; gold and orange shafts of sunlight glanced off lochs and burns. The dikes gave off an opalescent glitter where lichen had grown and died, leaving a silver crust. The air smelled fresh and new; another hard winter was almost behind them. She would climb north into the upland pastures and see if there were any newborn lambs on the slopes neighbouring the loch. Maybe she'd even walk all the way to Craiganour Forest, five miles away.

As she stepped out onto the uneven terrain and crossed the rye field to the burn meandering through the Buchanan holdings, she felt the muscles of her strong young limbs tighten and relax in rhythm with her confident stride.

She was growing into a woman. Changes in her body she had expected, but the turmoil of emotions confused her. A torrent of tears would arrive for no apparent reason or in reaction to a slight reproach; excitement would surge in response to her fanciful imaginings about walking up to the summer fields with Jock or singing a solo in the church or having a bonnet as elegant as Miss Mary's.

Apart from the hours she and Charlie and Jock had larked about in the yard, she didn't remember ever having been a child—if that meant having no responsibilities or having someone to take care of all your needs. Ma's bairns had come every year; Lizzie had lent a hand when she wasn't much more than a toddler herself.

Halfway up Slios Minh, her keen eyesight picked out ruins of old settlements along the banks of Loch Rannoch. They were now only rocky mounds, regular in shape, covered with grass, deserted by their inhabitants in the wake of the land clearances of 1824 or abandoned by families starved out in the potato famine of '46. She'd heard the tales, but never having gone without herself, such tragedies were hard to imagine—and it was too beautiful a day to bother.

She broke out in song, like a lark soaring over its domain.

"Will ye gang to the Hielands, Leezie Lindsey? . . ."

Far enough from the clachan, she loosened her bonnet and let her long hair flow free. All her worries slipped off her shoulders like an old shawl shed on the first sunny day.

She followed the burn that fed the river, a fast-flowing tributary tumbling over polished stones and into clean, clear pools, a likely place to see brook trout or salmon.

"By yon bonnie banks and by yon bonnie braes . . .," she sang. Like her mother she had many Rabbie Burns favourites.

She climbed the slopes up into the shieling, the group of dwellings where the women and the children used to take the stock up to hill grasses for summer grazing. A carpet of wildflowers grew in profusion around the shieling, where generations of animals had fertilized the soil. Granny Mac-Gregor had told many tales about her childhood in the "summer town." It must have been a carefree time back then to be up here all summer herding cattle, practically living out of doors.

Now the dwellings were neglected; all but one had collapsed, and most of the wood had been hauled away for firewood or fence repairs. The stones used in their construction were added to the ubiquitous fences that criss-crossed the countryside.

Lizzie strode past the surviving hut, which she used as a sanctuary on rainy days. The wind and snow had caused the roof to collapse; she would have to find some broken tree limbs for props.

Something white caught her eye in a crevice between the stones. She pulled it out, bruising and cutting her fingers, and adding yet another blotch to a badly stained and damaged book of poetry by William Wordsworth and a school jotter, both ruined by rain.

Who could have left these in her retreat? She opened the jotter and saw evidence of the fine hand of a writer who had been composing poetry. Had it been Charlie? He was the only other one she could think of who took an interest in books. Mother never came up here; she didn't have time.

Lizzie read silently from the notebook.

"Her lilting voice the songbirds shame
Her milk white skin . . ."

Farther down the page she read,

"I've dreamed a dream of velvet mouth
Of honeyed breath and burnished curls
Of strong young limbs . . ."

The rest was obliterated on the page damaged by rain.

Her brother must have an eye for some lass. Now who could it be? Very flowery poetry. But it had to be Charlie. She couldn't imagine any other boys from the clachan writing such stuff—she could hardly imagine Charlie writing it.

Several times, in the last year, she had wakened to the sound of Charlie sneaking out of the house late at night, his old habit of seeking solitude. If Ma and Pa knew, they never questioned it. He had been capable of taking care of himself in the outdoors for years. He'd usually tell Lizzie he'd spent the night in the barn or up here in the summer shieling, if she asked. But writing poetry? He must be smitten. He hadn't told her about any romance. Sly fox. She'd get it out of him.

* * *

On a dry day like today, she sought her other favoured spot, a great oak tree that had been split by lightning a hundred years before and grown off in two directions, creating a cradle-like resting place. She'd discovered it six years ago—her own aerie, up off the ground. With no one to see her, she could haul up her skirts and scramble unabashedly into its welcoming arms. Many peaceful hours were spent here in the company of an absorbing book.

Today she casually read part of Elizabeth Barrett Browning's "The Cry of the Children," before she hit these poignant lines:

"For oh,' say the children, 'we are weary,
And we cannot run or leap—
If we cared for any meadows, it were merely
To drop down in them and sleep.
Our knees tremble sorely in the stooping—
We fall upon our faces, trying to go;
and, underneath our heavy eyelids drooping,
the reddest flower would look as pale as snow.
For, all day, we drag our burden tiring,
Through the coal-dark, underground—
Or, all day, we drive the wheels of iron
In the factories, round and round."

She knew she shouldn't personalize the poetry. But a lad like wee Gregor working in a pit; the thought of it made her shudder.

Gazing around her arbour for distraction, her eyes met those of an owl squinting at her from a smaller oak. She must have disturbed his sleep. They locked eyes till Lizzie felt mesmerized. The climb up the hill had left her pleasantly tired. She dozed off.

✶ ✶ ✶

Walking through endless corridors of polished wood floors that smelled of carbolic Lizzie heard her Mother's voice. "This way daughter. I want you to see this room." Why was her mother speaking with an English accent? She bid her sit in a red, crushed-velvet chaise and began to comb her hair. Lizzie sighed in pleasure then observed a picture of Mary Buchanan, getting ready to topple off the mantel. Her mother watched too but seemed unconcerned as it fell on the floor—glass shattering. From the shards she heard a voice. "She didn't do that— Lizzie would not do that." It didn't sound like Mary or mother. In fact, it was a male voice.

She opened her eyes wider to see where the voice came from, sat up suddenly, and smacked her nose on a low branch just above her head.

"She's too young, Duncan. She wouldn't do that."

"All lassies do it sooner or later. Would ye no like to be the first?"

"All lassies don't do it, some have better sense and wait." Her heart leapt. It was definitely Jock's voice.

"Och, while we're having this daft conversation she's likely up there in yon oak tree, where she thinks she hides, dreaming about it. She's grown some nice titties this last year—or haven't ye noticed?"

"Shut up, Duncan. I notice everything about Lizzie MacGregor, but I would rather not discuss it with the likes of you."

Lizzie wished she could slap yon Duncan Cooper silly. Pimply-faced fool always smelled like the byre—even on Sundays. What did he know about girls?

Through the branches she could see the boys returning to their fishing; Duncan caught a trout. In the ensuing excitement, while keeping an eye on them, Lizzie quietly descended from her perch and tried to sneak past them using the drove road that followed the river about twenty feet above where the boys were struggling to land the fish.

She glanced down at the front of her dress and noticed the buttons were stretched to nearly popping and one had come off—probably when she climbed that tree.

One minute, worried about buttons, and the next she fell facedown in the bracken. She knew the loud crash would alert the boys to her presence, but with her ankle caught between two logs that had tripped her; she couldn't get up and run as she desperately wanted to.

Lying there helpless, more angry than hurt, she watched Jock Campbell wordlessly approach her. His stealth was for fear of the game warden. She saw him take in the situation. His blush told her he knew she must have overheard his conversation with that fool Duncan, who had taken off down the bank with a fat trout wriggling under his jacket.

"Are ye hurt, lass?"

She waved him away, signalling his help was neither needed nor welcomed.

"I'm sorry, Lizzie. Here, let me help—please." He moved the log, then pulled awkwardly on her arm, which stretched her blouse and caused another button to pop. Jock jumped back, staring at her gaping bodice. She fell hard on the ground when he released her and, though in pain, her first thought was try to cover the exposed skin his eyes were drinking in.

"Just leave me alone, you big lummox."

He handed her a rag and pointed to her nose. The blood dripped down to where the top of her breasts swelled. It began to stain her exposed white corset. She wiped her face. The filthy rag smelled of fish guts.

With his eyes now studiously fixed on the ground, he removed his wool jacket and offered it to her.

She snatched the jacket and buttoned it all the way up to her neck and finally accepted his extended hand. The pain in her ankle caused her to wince.

"I'll carry ye."

The idea of being so close to Jock comforted and scared her simultaneously. A swirling tide of joy expanded from her belly but by the time it reached her heart, she blurted, "Ye will not!" with such fervour and conviction that Jock withdrew his supporting hand. She dropped to the mossy damp ground again, wincing with renewed pain. Jock's expression showed hurt, surprise, dismay. Why did she say that—something totally contrary to what she felt?

"I'm sorry, my love. I would never hurt you, never."

Had he just said what she thought he said? His love? The increasing pain as well as all the doubts and regrets she had harboured for the last year fled from her mind. She reached her hand out to him to help her to her feet, one more time, never losing eye contact with him. The joyful feeling arose in her again reaching her heart, and she knew from the way his eyes bored into hers that he felt it also. She leaned against his shoulder for support, and by the time she had limped back to the croft she'd grown used to the feel of his arm around her waist.

CHAPTER FIFTEEN

Uncle Archie

Alas! life's path may be unsmooth!
Her way may lie thro' rough distress

"Looks like ye have company." Jock alerted her to an unfamiliar old horse clomping around loose in the stack yard amid the diminished pile of peat.

The noise of the chickens clucking and the horse neighing at their arrival alerted whoever was at home.

Lizzie's jaw dropped to see Archie MacDonald, Ma's uncle, come to the door of the croft. His scowl warned Jock he'd better have a good explanation for bringing a lass to her father's door in this condition and his arm around her waist besides. Her mother followed right behind him, drying her hands on a rag.

"What happened?" Her mother ran to her.

"I'm all right, Ma. I just took a bit tumble." She braced herself on the stone wall of the croft and removed Jock's jacket, revealing the bloodied bodice.

Uncle Archie drew his own conclusions.

"And did you take a bit tumble too, lad?" he said with an icy edge to his deep voice.

"She fell. I tried to help . . ."

"Best be on yer way. Ye've done all the helpin' ye're going to do this day."

Jock ambled off shamefaced. By the gate, he shrugged into his jacket and smiled in her direction with an apologetic tilt to his right shoulder.

"But Uncle Archie—" Lizzie began.

"Get you inside, gurrl."

Lizzie obeyed. There would be time for explanations later—maybe.

Uncle Archie stayed outdoors—seething, she supposed, while her mother cleaned Lizzie's bloodied face and sewed buttons back onto her dress. Lizzie told her the right way of it, and her mother assured her she would talk to Archie before he vented his spleen on Father.

"What's Uncle Archie doing here, anyhow? I thought he went to Glasgow to work."

"Och. He's had a bit of bother down in the Lowlands, and he's not feeling too well. He's getting to be an old man, ye know. He was my mother's older brother. He must be over sixty. I think he's going back to Stornoway for good this time."

Lizzie rested in the box bed that overlooked the fire room, her leg elevated on a straw pillow. The dose of Godfrey's Cordial Ma had given her to relieve the pain made her light-headed and dreamy. She heard the men coming in from the fields and the sound of supper being prepared and eaten.

Annie brought her a bowl of broth. "For you, your ladyship," she snipped, but Lizzie didn't care.

Father pulled aside the curtain to her box bed.

"Feeling better, Lizzie?"

Sleepy-eyed, she tried to smile at him and felt it slide into a lopsided grin, "I'm just grand, Pa," she said and meant it, snuggling into the quilt. The opium in the medicine was doing its work.

"She's not feeling any pain now, Flora. How much of that dope did ye give her?"

"Och, not too much, Rob. Let the poor lass get a good night's sleep."

"She'll be dreaming about her knight in shining armour before long." The three adults laughed, and Lizzie smiled in contentment. Ma had straightened out the story for the two men.

"That lass puts me in mind o' my sister Elizabeth," Archie said. "She looks jist like our Beth."

"Does she, Uncle Archie? Ye always said I did."

"Ye both have my sister's fine looks: bonnie hair and eyes, quiet gentle ways. Didnae rub off on me though." He chuckled till it triggered a coughing fit.

"Here, drink this," said her father.

"She got older," Archie continued. "Ye'll need tae watch the lads. Is that boy to be trusted?"

"Och! Archie, They've grown up together . . . like brother and sister," said her father.

"Not the way he was lookin' at her, not brotherly at all, at all." said Archie.

"Hmmm," her mother said.

After Pa went to bed, she heard her mother and Uncle Archie talking quietly. "What will ye do back in Lewis, Archie?" Ma's voice showed concern.

"No matter what I turn my hand to, it can be no worse than working like a mole burrowing under the earth, digging down to hell in that filthy town of Coatbridge."

"It was that bad, eh?"

"Better to scratch a living from the land or drown fishing in the Minch than work in the bowels of hell or beg on the filthy streets of Lanarkshire," he said in his carefully and slowly enunciated English, which he'd had to learn since he'd strayed from his roots in the Isle of Lewis. His lament was punctuated by the hacking cough.

"Human beings were never meant to live like that. I saw wee boys like your own twins sitting in a wet cart, sorting out lumps of coal till their fingers bled and they were blinded with coal dust. Bonny lassies like yer own, bent double from carrying bags of coal heavier than themselves." Lizzie heard him pour himself another glass of Pa's whisky as she dozed off again.

* * *

The pain in her ankle awakened her. Wee Gregor had rolled to the bottom of the bed. His head lay on her foot. She gently repositioned him and settled back down.

The voices murmured softly now in Gaelic. Father must be asleep. She could hear only Mother and Uncle Archie's intense discussion.

" . . . he should never have taken ye. Ye were too young to leave with only Kate to look out for ye." Archie's voice expressed a surprising amount of passion which led to a coughing spell. She heard her mother fill him a glass to drink. "Here Archie, a wee dram for that chest of yours."

"Charlie had to for . . ." Lizzie couldn't hear the rest of her mother's soft conciliatory reply.

"Ye were our flesh and blood, too."

"I know. The MacDonalds treated me well. They thought . . . we all thought I'd be better off coming to the mainland."

Archie further entreated her mother in Gaelic spoken in a very low tone.

She replied. "He did what he could, Archie. It may not be much, but this is the best house in the clachan and I have everything I need."

"Aye. That's as may be." Archie's voice was gruff.

"Och! It's better than the old blackhouse we grew up in." Her mother seemed to be cajoling him.

Archie laughed. "Can't deny that."

Her mother said quietly, "If he'd offered any other special treatment—Isobel Menzies would have . . ."

Lizzie couldn't make out the rest of it. Sleep overcame her again.

She awoke at sunrise and went outdoors to relieve herself. Archie's horse whinnied. She limped over to pat the old brute.

The events of the night before hazily returned—snatches of conversation she had heard—or had she dreamed them?

The household started to rouse when she went back indoors. Ma nursed the baby cradled in one arm while she stirred the porridge with her free hand.

Archie drank a mug of tea and asked Father general questions about the farm, then talked to Charlie about what a young lad could do here in Rannoch to better himself.

"Not much, Uncle Archie. Maybe I'll come up to the Isle of Lewis and see you in Stornoway."

"Save yerself the trouble, lad. Nothing there but sheep and rocks. Go to Nova Scotia. Young man can do well there, they say. It's chust sublime.

Good fishing, good hunting, good land, and ye can own a piece of it for your own self. Chust grand.

"And what is this wee lad's name?" he asked, as Lizzie took the baby from Ma to give him a change.

"I thought ye knew. This wee fella is called Archie. Isn't that right, my wee lamb?" Lizzie smiled and shook her curls at the tiny baby, who chortled in delight. She saw Uncle Archie pull himself up to his full height and swallow hard, pleased his niece had named her son after him.

Under the bluster Lizzie could see Uncle Archie was a broken man, stooped and bent from too many years of howking out a narrow coal seam, hacking and coughing from breathing the foul air, and spitting black into the spittoon Ma had thoughtfully provided near the hearth. He had a look of wet clay about him. A man who should never have been transplanted from his native island soil. He would go back to the family croft and live the simple life he understood—but for how long?

The image of his haunted face etched in Lizzie's memory as he took his leave of his niece.

"I'll see ye next time I come through, Florry."

"Aye, Uncle Archie, we always look forward to yer visits. Here's a wee bit something to see ye on yer way."

He took the bottle of elderberry wine and placed it in his saddlebag. Ma handed him a bundle wrapped in a new kitchen towel. Must be some of Ma's scones. They stood silently; each with a hand on the bundle for a few moments till Ma released it, turned away quickly, and hurried into the cottage with the hem of her apron held over her mouth.

Lizzie knew Ma would never see her mother's brother again—the last link to her island family.

CHAPTER SIXTEEN

Wee Gregor

We twa hae run about the braes,
And pu'd the gowans fine;
But we've wandered mony a weary foot
Sin' auld lang syne.

Lizzie stood with her brothers and sister watching Uncle Archie mount his horse and ride off silently. He nudged the reluctant beast through the shieling yard, out of the gate, and down the drove road toward the loch.

"Let's go inside. It's getting chilly." Charlie said.

Lizzie followed the others into the cottage with a final backward glance down the hill.

"He's goin' on a big journey, Ma," Gregor called through the house to his mother.

"Aye, Gregor," Ma's strained voice floated from the sleeping room.

* * *

Lizzie banked the fire and half-filled the cast iron cooking pot with water. Better feed this lot before they start pestering Ma, she thought. "Charlie, put this over the fire while I peel the potatoes."

Jamie, already headed into the other room to investigate his mother's withdrawal got distracted at the window, and called out in an excited voice, "There's a horse coming up the hill."

"Is it Uncle Archie?" His twin asked.

Lizzie and the others headed for the door to find out. Ma appeared from the other room with a dazed expression.

"He came back?"

The horse and rider arrived at the gate just as the MacGregors reached it.

Andy MacFarlane had a wild-eyed look. The horse snorted and stomped; his coat was lathered from being hard-ridden.

"It's the laird, Charlie. He took bad and died this morning. I've to tell all the tenants, but my Aunt Kate said to come here first."

Out of the corner of her eye, Lizzie saw her mother retreat into the croft. They all trudged after her.

"Charlie, better find Pa."

"He'll be here directly, Lizzie."

"Ye need to hurry him along. Ma is in there sobbing. I don't know if it's about Uncle Archie or about the laird."

"She's sad about her uncle, Lizzie."

"Aye. Get Pa anyway."

* * *

Lizzie and her family all attended the service and the burial along with the villagers and the local gentry. Mary Buchanan was more conspicuous by her absence. She could not return from London in time.

Three days later, Lizzie, her family, and the Campbells were standing around in the kale yard still talking about the laird's passing and wondering what changes might be in store for them, when Charlie brought the news that Mary Buchanan had returned from London with her new husband, Captain Cecil Winterbottom, recently returned from India and much decorated. Charlie told Lizzie he didn't care what kind of medals this foreigner wore on his puffed-out chest.

"Damned Sassenach," he whispered to Lizzie.

Pa said, "That's the thanks the Auld Laird got for sending Mary to that fancy finishing school in London. Couldn't even show up when her father was near death's door."

John Campbell added, "Rich folks get to keep more of their bairns, Robert, but some still die young. Three Buchanan sons buried on Aulich Hill—and Mary goes and finds herself an <u>Englishman</u>."

Pa said, "No good will come of it. 'Ne'er trust muckle to an auld enemy or a new freen.'"

No question in Lizzie's mind that the English were "old enemies." Whether or not this particular Englishman would be a "new friend" concerned her.

And nothing seemed to help Ma. She dragged herself around the cottage for a week or more. As though Uncle Archie had already passed. Or was she mourning the laird? She didn't say. Lizzie did what she could to help. Ma didn't even ask how Lizzie's ankle was but it felt better each day.

* * *

Lizzie was still wearing the black armband in the laird's memory a month after his death. Mary Buchanan and the Englishman had returned to London and the MacGregors breathed a sigh of relief. Ma had resumed her usual share of the daily chores and Lizzie felt freed to tend the sheep and take wee Gregor with her that day. Ma thought the fresh air would help the poor wee soul. It hadn't rained for a week, and the sky shone blue. A few airy clouds scudded across Loch Rannoch. Early summer in Scotland.

They had almost lost five-year-old Gregor three times that winter. He had the fever twice, followed by the whooping cough. All through the very cold spring and early summer the lad was too weak to go outdoors. He still had a bit of a cough but begged to go out. Bored with the toy sheep Pa had whittled for him and weary of listening to the baby crying, Gregor got into mischief, throwing his wooden toy up in the air, nearly crowning Archie in his basket.

"Hap him up well if ye're taking him out. There's a chill in the air today, I feel a storm coming in." Her mother had warned, nodding towards the old worn wool jacket hanging on the nail. Lizzie scrubbed his grimy face and put the jacket on him. Far too big, it covered his knees and went almost to his ankles. He looked comical but stood proud.

Charlie came in from the byre and appraised the wee lad. "Gregor Mac-Gregor, yer jacket's ower long."

"This is <u>my</u> new coat. It used to be yours but it fits me now."

The women hid their merriment. It would keep him warm out on the moor where the wind blew cold even this time of year. Lizzie jammed a woollen cap on his shock of blond curls, noting she would need to give him a haircut before he went to school, or the bigger boys would tease him.

Lizzie sang for the boy while they meandered down the path that led to the burn.

"Scots, wha hae wi' Wallace bled,

Scots wham Bruce has aften led;

Welcome to your gory bed,

Or to victory!"

He knew all the words even though he might not understand them. His little voice piped up in good tune as he followed in her trail, marching along like a soldier.

"Wha will be a traitor's knave?

Wha can fill a coward's grave . . ."

He hadn't seen his favourite ewe, Meggie-monyfeet, all winter and spring. She had lambed this season after Big Tam finally caught up with her. Her lamb would be months old.

"I hope the lamb is in the pasture yonder."

Lizzie hoped so too. She slowed her usual brisk pace to accommodate Gregor, who lagged behind now.

"Or maybe up the first slope of the Ben, Lizzie."

But just in case the lad might be disappointed, she had brought along a book to read to him. He loved stories from books or, his special treat, Lizzie spinning him a yarn about valiant Scots like Robert the Bruce or William Wallace or Rob Roy MacGregor. All the heroic tales she had heard in school or read from the books in Ma's kist. Gregor would start school this year; he could hardly wait to learn the reading for himself.

The singing and brisk walk caused wee Gregor to cough till his face reddened and he gasped for breath. Lizzie got scared. "We'd better get home—"

"No, No," he whined. "You said I could see the wee lamb."

"We'll sit here for a while, Gregor. I'll get you a drink from the burn."

She carried the tin cup, tucked in her apron pocket, to the sparkling, ice-cold water. The burn flowed much faster than it had a week ago; the warmer weather had created run-off. Rivulets poured down the mountain. The shrinking diamonds sitting atop the pewter slopes of Ben A'Chuallaich were half the size they'd been last week. She must remember to tell Pa. If this mild weather continued and the snow kept thawing at this rate, or if they got some heavy rain, this stream and others like it could be in spate with little warning.

Lizzie shielded her eyes to scan the glen. The lower pastures had greened up. The sun shone on the steep rise of the distant mountain, giving the thick heather's young buds an amethyst shimmer. The nearby field of bluebells added a sapphire glow to nature's majestic gems.

Wee Gregor had stopped coughing when she returned with the water, but the effort had worn him out. He took a few sips. "Can you carry me, Lizzie?" He could barely hold up his scrawny arms towards her. "Just for a wee while, Lizzie?"

She bent down to allow him to climb onto her back. "I'll be the sodger and you can be the cuddy, right Lizzie?"

She often played horse and soldier with him. This poor horse would have to carry its burden a lot farther than planned. There would be no cantering today. She plodded on back the way they had come, disappointed not to have seen Meggie-monyfeet. Gregor needed some cheering.

The rugged countryside had twists and turns that followed old deer tracks, up steep inclines and down into soggy, marshy valleys. Buttercups and daisies were in full bloom and the trees were leafed out.

At the crest of one of the hills, her eyes wandered over a heathery knoll and off to the meadow beyond. In a cluster of the animals she spotted the black-faced sheep. The white lamb scampered around its mother.

"Look Gregor, there she is."

The boy gripped Lizzie around the neck. "We found her, Lizzie. We found her."

Meggie bleated in greeting. Lizzie let the delighted child down onto the ground by the lamb, and he threw his arms around it. "You'll be my own wee lamb. Won't he, Lizzie? What can we call him?"

"How about Cronie?"

"Aye, that'll be a fine name. He can be my friend. When he's big, I'll be big too. Won't I, Lizzie? He'll be like Big Tam the ram and I'll be big like my Pa."

"Aye, lad. Now we have to go. See that cloud coming in from the loch? That means rain. Can ye walk for a wee bit?"

So heartened by the success of their venture he thought he could.

The mists seem to come out of nowhere. She could find her way back, that was not a problem—but could Gregor walk the distance?

Then they saw Pa and the nightmare of the eviction began.

CHAPTER SEVENTEEN

The Clearance

Rannoch Moor Summer 1860

Man's inhumanity to man
Makes countless thousands mourn!

A sudden chill wind blew across Loch Rannoch heralding rain. They were almost home when it started, gently at first, soon lightning lit up the snow-peaked hills, as it will in summer in the Scottish Highlands, followed quickly by a roar of thunder that reverberated through the glen and set the sheep to bleating. Lizzie grabbed her wee brother's hand and speeded up the pace. It would be risky to let him get chilled. He'd barely survived last winter.

Wee Gregor saw him first. "Look, Lizzie, it's Pa."

She was surprised to see their father appearing through the mist from the direction of their croft. The old mare he rode was lathered up by his attempts to push her to greater effort.

"Pa, where are ye goin'? There's a storm comin' in."

He waved his arm toward Aulich Hill and the mansion house. "Up to the big house. Git home, lass, yer mother needs ye—and hurry."

Lizzie hoisted her fragile young brother on her back and ran, toward the keening cries she could now hear from the direction of her cottage. She hadn't heard that eerie, yowling sound since her mother had grieved her last dead babe, and it was her mother Flora's voice now.

Had someone died?

Rounding the hillock she stopped in shock, and surveyed the scene. In the muddy barnyard her mother sat on her prized possession, her kist. She was surrounded by stools, the big iron kettle off the fireplace, a chest of drawers. Other household items from their cottage were strewn in the middle of the stone-walled enclosure. The sampler Ma had made for Pa before they married that bore the proud MacGregor motto, my blood is royal, stitched in the Gaelic words, 'S rioghal mo dhream, was trampled into the mud. Sunday clothes were thrown in a soggy heap on the ground on top of quilts and blankets. Even the china chamber pot with the flowers she'd painted on it—her whimsical artistic creation—lay out in full view. Since the piece had never been fired, the painting of sunset over Ben Lomond looked more like an egg had been smashed on the side of the vessel.

Lizzie counted the children. Six with Ma in the yard and she had Gregor with her. All accounted for. No one had died; but what had happened? Lizzie ran the last few yards.

The children crowded around their mother. Two-year-old Kate slid around in the mud and animal droppings, happily covering herself in filth. Baby Archie suckled at his mother's breast so hungrily the mayhem did not distract him.

Charlie hauled a heavy dresser towards the barn, stopping every few steps to wipe away tears pouring down his cheeks. He motioned with his head towards Ma indicating she needed Lizzie's help. They didn't need words between them.

"Ma, Ma, what happened. Oh God, what's happened? Ma, stop crying, tell me, please, tell me."

Her mother's wails got louder. She made a choking, gasping sound and seemed to stare right through Lizzie.

"Wheesht, Mother." She put Gregor down and placed her arm around her hysterical mother's shoulders.

Charlie came over to Lizzie. "We're out," was all he could say as he bent to rescue Kate from the filth.

"Charlie, what..." But he'd left carrying the screaming Kate to the barn out of the now-heavy rain.

"A big man on a horse came and threw us all out," Her sister Annie said in a self-important manner. She knew something her big sister did not. Despite the gravity of the news, she seemed to savour her moment of glory. "He said he was in charge now. A MacNab man, Duncan by name, he's the new factor and he'll be managing Rannoch till Mary Buchanan's new husband gets here, and Pa has no job with the Buchanans anymore, so we can't live rent-free on this property."

Lizzie looked at her unconvinced.

"It's all true. That's exactly what he said." Annie took a moment to bite her lip, then arms akimbo she eyed Lizzie, a disdainful expression on her face. "Ask oor Charlie when he stops blubberin'." She nodded her head in the direction of the barn and her big brother.

Lizzie didn't know whether to smack her sister, shake her, or start crying herself. Something had to be done right away. The rain had started to pelt. They were all going to catch their death of cold out here.

"We'll go back in the house for the night," she said.

"No, no, we can't." Annie's bluster left her; her lower lip trembled. "The man said if we're in the house when he comes back, he'll smoke us out."

"Pa's gone up to the big hoose to see if we can stay in the laird's hay barn the night," Charlie told her. "Pa told me tae take charge. Ma isn't makin' any sense. She told Pa to go up and talk to Colonel Buchanan like she's forgotten he died last month. See tae her, Lizzie."

"Ma, take the baby into the barn," Lizzie yelled over the now pounding rain.

Her mother stared at her from deep, dark orbs. She seemed to have retreated to an unfathomable place inside herself. She quieted long enough to follow Lizzie's commands. The other children, Jamie and Donnie, trotted along behind their mother, dripping wet and shivering.

Lizzie had just piled straw on her brothers and sister, the only thing dry she could find to keep them warm, and was climbing down from the hay loft when her father returned. Pa's cap was gone; his sandy hair fell in wet curls around his ashen face. He had a wild air about him. His shirt, wet with sweat and rain, clung to his broad shoulders. His boots were covered in mud.

Lizzie followed him back up the ladder into the hay loft. Father's voice was agitated. "We have to git out, lass," he tried to tell Ma.

"No, Robert, we can't leave here. We have no place to go. You go back up and tell the laird."

"It's useless," he told her. "With the Auld Laird gone, Mary Buchanan and her new English husband are making decisions about our lives. Yon weasel MacNab is in charge, he's the new laird's factor now. He showed me legal notices. Eviction, Flora, I can't believe it myself."

Ma answered with only a blank stare.

Lizzie's heart went out to her. The shock is too new, she realized. Ma's forgotten the colonel is dead and his daughter Mary is in charge. Ma will understand better in the morning. I'll have to think for both of us. Thank God the rain is letting up.

Pa supervised moving the remaining possessions into the barn.

"Charlie, get some wood for a fire so we can get the claithes dry. Lizzie, see if there is any bread or oatmeal or anything else we can get out of the kitchen for to eat and to feed these bairns. Annie, help yer mither with the wean."

"Why do I always have to change wee Kate? She's filthy, Lizzie can do it."

"You're not too big to get the back of my hand. No more cheek...DO IT."

Annie scampered off.

During the long night they huddled together in the loft. Lizzie slept fitfully and awoke at regular intervals when her mother started wailing and calling "Robert, Robert." Pa was up half the night comforting her.

"We can't leave, Rob—the babes." Each time she roused, she lamented about her lost infants, the two little boys who never made it through their first winter, buried in the family cemetery on the hill. "How can I leave them up there all alone?"

Lizzie heard Annie whimper and complain about the cold, then the baby awoke crying, and getting no comfort from his agitated mother, Pa crooned him back to sleep. The twelve-year-old twins, Jamie and Donald, were entwined in each other's arms and startled awake at each unfamiliar sound. Charlie quieted them and threw more straw on their tangled heap.

Gregor slept close to Lizzie; his feverish, dry little body roused listlessly each time the turmoil set in motion. She feared he might be ill again and getting worse. She hoped and prayed he'd be well enough to travel to wherever they were going tomorrow. Where <u>would</u> they go, for God's sake?

After another round of settling the younger ones back down, Pa talked hastily to Lizzie and Charlie about what needed to be done on the morrow. Though appalled to hear they would head out for Glasgow, she said nothing, just looked at Charlie who shared her consternation. It was almost dawn before Lizzie collapsed in the straw and muffled her sobs into wee Gregor's sleeping back. Exhausted, her mind wandered, seeking escape.

This very year, only eight months ago, they'd had the best New Year party ever and her biggest worry had been about Jock Campbell, wondering if he would he ever feel the same way about her that she felt about him.

Now, she might never see Jock again. Her stalwart twin couldn't hold back his tears. Her favourite wee brother was dangerously ill and her mother seemed to have lost her senses. They were all in mortal danger; thrown out into the wilds of the Scottish Highlands without shelter or food.

Then Lizzie must have fallen asleep.

CHAPTER EIGHTEEN

The Morning after the Eviction

Perhaps a mother's anguish adds its woe

fter a hellish night and little sleep, the rhythmic thud of horse's hooves approaching the barn wakened them. Lizzie shot out of her bed of straw, followed by Charlie, both fearful it was Duncan MacNab, the new factor, keeping his threat to smoke them out. The horror hit her; we're going to Glasgow, a terrible place.

Instead, Charlie's friend Andrew McFarlane, the stable boy, had "borrowed" the Auld Laird's fine gelding. He called her father out and confirmed that they were determined at Aulich house to have the evicted families out and on the road today.

"Who else is pushed out?" her father asked.

"Everybody in this clachan. Some Stewarts from up the glen."

"The Campbells too?" Charlie asked.

"Aye, them too. I'm goin' there next. Mrs. Mary Winterbottom is bossing everyone around since the Auld Laird passed." He sneered. "Her new husband, "Freezy-arse," is coming to inspect the glen—maybe today. My Aunty Kate says Miss Mary's turnin' Rannoch into a huge sheep farm. Auntie Kate is fit tae be tied. The telegram came yesterday. A shipment of Cheviots arrives tomorrow by train. It's 'cottars out' and 'sheep in place,' and it all has to be done before the Sassenach arrives or there'll be 'hell to pay.' Those are the turncoat factor's exact words."

Andy's horse stomped restlessly.

"I have tae go."

He reached into the saddlebags.

"Aye, and this is for Mrs. MacGregor from my auntie, Katie MacKay."

He showed the envelope engraved with the initial "B" to Pa.

"I'm covered in mud. Take it, Charlie."

"What is it, Andy?" Lizzie said, reaching for it. Could it be a reprieve?

"It's awfy important. My Aunt Kate said the laird entrusted her with it before he passed."

Lizzie's heart sank. Was it an old letter or just something her mother had left behind at the big house? Not something to help them in their immediate predicament, she thought. But if it was Ma's baptismal certificate, Lizzie wanted it in <u>her</u> hand, this link with her mother's heritage.

Andy drew his hand back. "Auntie said I should give it into the hands of Flora MacDonald. That's your mother, Mrs. MacGregor, is it not?"

"Aye, Andy. She's the one all right." Charlie said. "But she's no in her right mind now. I'll see she gets it."

The lad hesitated, but Charlie's authoritative tone must have convinced him. He handed the envelope over and got back on the horse, calling back over his shoulder to his pal. "This clearance is all over the glen, dozens of folks routed out. Ye'll meet yer neighbours on the road to Kilichonan. Better get goin'; MacNab's bringin' in the law tae enforce it. Good luck, Charlie. Goodbye, Lizzie."

She managed a feeble smile and a wave of her hand. Out of the corner of her eye she saw Charlie tucking the envelope absentmindedly into his shirt with his free hand.

"Charlie, maybe we should open it. Maybe Miss Mary changed her mind."

"Yon bitch never in her life thought about anybody else. I'll take care of it," Charlie said, an edge to his voice.

"But it might be important . . . Kate MacKay said..." Lizzie held out her hand.

"Kate MacKay can't help us now." Charlie's dismissive tone shocked her.

"Just let me see it, Charlie," This was no time for a contest of wills. "I'll give it back."

Charlie handed the envelope to Lizzie. "Hurry up."

She pried it open and saw a yellowed official-looking document. She had no sooner read the name "Flora" than Charlie grabbed it. "Satisfied?"

"See Ma gets it," she said. Lizzie had never seen Charlie in such a foul mood.

No time to think of that now. She needed to get busy. No time to reconcile with her newly forceful twin either. She'd remind him about the envelope and they'd give it to Ma after they got on the road and her mother calmed down. Though Lizzie suspected Ma wouldn't calm down any time soon.

Charlie gritted his teeth, pulled himself up to his full height, towering over Lizzie, and blinked back the tears that moistened his eyes. His worn old shirt stretched over the muscles that flexed across his chest and upper arms where the field work had speeded his growth from a raw lad to a strong and virile young man—too old to cry.

"Charlie . . .," Lizzie tugged his arm in a gesture of support and comfort. He jerked his arm away and strode towards the barn. Her brother, her twin, her confidant, her friend, growing up to a man, yes, but growing away from her? An intolerable thought. She heard him muttering under his breath; "If that fucking Englishman shows up, I'll cut his ballocks off and feed them to the pigs."

* * *

The twins straggled out of the barn half-awake. "Wee Gregor won't get up," Jamie said, rubbing his eyes, immediately diverted by the fine horse trotting off down the bridle path.

Lizzie ran from the door of the cottage, dropping a bag of flour that exploded onto the barnyard. "Oh, Father, wee Gregor."

She flew up the ladder into the hayloft, her father on her heels. Too late—the child was gone. His frail body had given up its struggle for life sometime in the night. Still well covered in hay the way Lizzie had left him, his tiny hand had gripped a clump of straw. Lizzie dropped to her knees sobbing. "No, no, Gregor. Could ye not have held on for a wee while?"

She picked him up and peered into his dirty face. The tears that dripped from her eyes made streaks down his waxy cheeks. His pale lifeless body had turned cold already. Pa took the boy from her wordlessly and carried him from the loft.

"Flora, come here." His voice was barely audible, as though wishing she'd never have to hear what he needed to tell her. The children stood around with their mouths open, gawking from their brother's body in their Pa's arms to Ma, to Lizzie, and back to their father.

Ma's screams echoed throughout the glen. All except Charlie and Pa started to wail.

"There's no time for grief, Flora. We have to bury another bairn in the MacGregor cemetery. There's no time to have a proper ceremony. Other things—for the living—have to be done this mornin'."

Lizzie felt like she was trudging through a dark tunnel trying to find the light. She heard, in the distance, Pa issuing orders.

"Lizzie, Lizzie. Do ye hear me? Take care of yer mother and the baby. Charlie, before ye start packing that cart for the journey, ye'll have to go to the cemetery and dig a hole for Gregor. Take the twins to help ye. Get going now."

Lizzie stared at her father in disbelief for what seemed an eternity, then snapped out of it and moved across the barnyard to her mother, who sat wide-eyed in the mud.

Charlie's jaw dropped.

"Did ye hear me, Charlie? Git the shovel. Now, I said. There's no time to waste," Pa yelled at him.

When Charlie regained his senses, he pushed past his shocked father to go into the barn. He was outraged. "Aye. I'll git a shovel, and it'll be to kill that English bastard and his fucking factor."

"Charlie, may God forgive ye. I'm not going to take the belt to ye the noo, but never let me hear you talk like that in front of yer mother again."

Lizzie knew Pa's heart wasn't in the customary reprimand.

From where she knelt by her mother, Lizzie saw Charlie, tears blinding him now, stumbling into the darkened barn.

They had to obey Father. Whatever forces had combined to wreak havoc in their lives, Lizzie knew it wasn't Pa's fault; he was doing what had to be done.

Charlie continued to mutter. "Someday—somehow—someone will pay for this."

Lizzie shivered.

The twins stopped crying to watch the drama unfolding, as though they couldn't believe Charlie would get away with this affront to their father.

Lizzie was relieved that those two had the wisdom to move fast and forestall Pa's expected reaction. They quickly found shovels and set off across the field, calling to Charlie to follow them to the little plot with the rough-hewn stones that honoured the memory of their forebears and the two wee ones taken with the fever.

Pa wrapped Gregor in a plaidie and set him in a tinker's cart the men used around the yard. "That's anither of oor wee lambs God has called back to be with him. Flora, ye need to come down to the cemetery so we can bury this bairn."

Ma stared off into space. "We buried our bairns already." She was clutching the infant, Archie, who badly needed a change, which she hadn't done for him since Annie cleaned him up yesterday.

"Come on, Ma. I'll carry the baby for a while." Lizzie practically pried her mother's fingers from the baby. He smelled foul. She took him to the pump and cleaned the urine and feces off the screaming babe's raw and reddened bottom. She dried him and found some fresh rags to cover him, put a dry dress on him she'd found in the house, wrapped him in a blanket, and set him down in the barn on a heap of straw. Exhausted, he went off to sleep.

She couldn't keep her eyes off the old cart and the plaidie that covered her beloved wee brother.

"C'mon, Ma." She linked her mother's arm through her and headed down the path.

Ma obediently followed her to the cemetery. When she saw them put the child's body into the newly dug hole, she started wailing again. She made that keening sound they did on the Hebrides. Crying the coronach, they called it. It cut deep into Lizzie's heart and got all the other children crying again. They piled dirt on the bright tartan blanket that covered the little corpse and pulled a big boulder over from the stone wall to mark the spot. Someday, she thought, I'll come back and put up a proper stone.

They all said the Lord's Prayer and sang from the Scottish Psalter, Psalm 23. It was hardly recognizable, for they were choking on their tears.

"'The Lord's my shepherd, I'll not want . . .

. . . And in God's house for evermore my dwelling place shall be.'"

"Your brither was a pure wee bairn. He's gone to be with Jesus now. He'll have a fine robe and live in a mansion in heaven. He'll be fine. Ye don't need to worry about him."

The twins stared at their father. "Makes ye feel a lot better to think wee Gregor's singing with the angels rather than lying down in that dark hole. Does it not, Jamie?" Donald said as he pushed the cart out of the way.

"Aye, Father must be right, he knows all about the Lord," his twin agreed.

Lizzie wretchedly studied the mound of dirt; her arms ached to hold her little brother one more time. The words of Mary Lamb came to her.

"'Thou, straggler into loving arms,

Young climber up of knees, . . .'"

She had not realized she had spoken out loud till she heard her mother's voice finishing the verse.

"'When I forget thy thousand ways,

Then life and all shall cease.'"

Ma had quieted again and seemed resigned to follow behind Father and be guided by his directions. And now he had orders for everyone.

"Charlie, pack what you can in that cart. Lizzie, help him sort out what needs to go. We can only take what we can lug on oor backs and in that cart. The big pieces we burn. We're not leaving anything for thon factor to sell. Annie, help yer mother with the baby and pack some bundles for the twins to carry. Everybody has to do their bit—no slackin'."

Her father didn't need to worry. They scurried around more than glad to be busy—to keep their minds occupied. Even her stalwart father couldn't shield them from the elements or from the whims and edicts of indifferent strangers. There's not much protection against them with no conscience, Lizzie released a deep sigh. Overnight this haven of peace and security that had sheltered and sustained them all their lives had turned dangerous.

* * *

The drizzling rain lowered their spirits even further, if that was possible, but her father pointed to patches of blue.

"See, the sky off towards the west is clear, and that's the direction we're headed."

The sorting and packing operation was moved into the barn. They couldn't afford to get everything wet again with no time to dry it out.

She shook her head, trying to bring herself back to the reality of the situation, and blindly gathered up what she could for their journey. "Father, I should never have taken Gregor to the pasture yesterday. That soaking chilled him through and brought on his death."

"Naw, lass, don't blame yerself. Would it have been better if he'd been thrown from the cottage out into the rain with the others? Naw. He was sick all winter. Ye know that. He probably would never have survived this journey. Better he is buried here with his kin."

* * *

The weather was fine that day and by midmorning the family was ready to go, and, true to his word, Pa made a pile of everything that wouldn't go on the cart or onto their backs and set fire to it. It was a small gesture of rebellion and all that he dared. She saw, for a second, a smug look brighten his grave countenance as he surveyed the roaring blaze. Lizzie knew someone would be sent down from the big house as soon as they saw the flames to be sure the departing tenants hadn't destroyed buildings or equipment.

"Let them worry and scurry, Lizzie. Nothing they can do. You still can't hang a man for burning his own possessions."

Lizzie was comforted to see a resolute squaring of her father's shoulders as he set out in his long, determined stride with the others following. The baby snuggled against his mother's breast, quieted by her familiar smell. The rocking motion soon soothed him into a peaceful slumber.

Her mother seemed to be studiously ignoring the precious possessions of a lifetime going up in flames. Lizzie knew what mattered to her mother. Ma had her family with her—well, most of it—and her kist containing her books and a few items she valued. Father had not challenged taking the kist for all it meant to Ma, even though it took up most of the space on the wheelbarrow Charlie pushed. Lizzie's fine silver comb was in there and a lock of hair from each of the dead bairns. Lizzie had remembered to cut off one of wee Gregor's curls.

* * *

"Father, oor Annie's got yon wee, wild cat from the barn hidden in her apron," said Jamie.

"Annie, ye can't take that wild kitten on the train," Pa said, kindly enough. Annie started to whine.

"The train?" Jamie and Donald squealed in unison. "Are we going on a train, Pa? Can we sit at the window? Will they blow the whistle? How far are we going?"

"Wheesht, you two, and don't start that girning, Annie MacGregor. Ye ken fine I told ye no animals were going with us. If I wasn't pushing this cart, ye'd get the back of ma hand for yer disobedience."

Annie started to bawl even louder.

"Och, I wish I hadn't told him about the wee cat. She's going to girn all the way there," Jamie told Lizzie and Donald.

Annie snivelled till they reached the main post road, and other families, dragging all their earthly belongings, approached from other parts of the glen, diverting her attention.

Part Two

The Journey

CHAPTER NINETEEN

Trek from Rannoch

To lie in kilns and barns at e'en,
When banes are craze'd, and bluid is thin,
Is doubtless great distress!

news of her brother's death rippled through the swarm of evicted crofters congregating on the post road that skirted Loch Rannoch. Lizzie heard muffled snatches of conversation from these victims of the clearance; stunned villagers who sat on their bundles or adjusted their backpacks or called out anxiously for their younger children to make sure everyone was accounted for. All the parents truly commiserated with the MacGregors; most of them knew the unbearable pain of losing a child and were relieved not to have to deal with <u>that</u> tragedy on top of the eviction.

Jock's father caught up with Pa to talk to him about the scandalous actions of the new factor.

"Do ye not mind him, Rab? He had a drink with us down in Kilichonan. He's that Duncan MacNab from Tyndrum. Been snooping around here for weeks asking nosy questions. I told oor Sandy not to tell him a thing, but he talked civil to the wee bastard anyway . . . went to some school in Glasgow and learned all about economics and modern farming or some such thing—how to make his own Highland folk suffer, is mair like it. Like to get ma hands around his scrawny neck."

Mrs. Campbell walked in respectful silence beside Lizzie's mother; no mere words could fit the occasion of a child's premature death.

* * *

Lizzie set a stiff pace despite the heavy bundle she toted, and strode out to the front of the group. Her heart missed a beat and she felt herself flushing when, out of the corner of her eye, she saw Jock, who had caught up to her. She noticed his awkward sideways glance. It took her a moment to realize he might still be embarrassed about the incident with Uncle Archie. She gave him a wistful smile and nod that was supposed to tell him that she welcomed his presence but had nothing to say. He took one of the heavy bags from her and walked alongside her in the silent sharing of their tragedy.

"Yer wee brother . . ." The rest of what he tried to say got lost in her violent sobbing. She wrapped her arms around him and hid her face in his jacket.

"Oh, Lizzie," he crooned into her hair, his arms enfolding her wracked body. He held her till her weeping quieted.

Over his shoulder she could see two or three dozen dejected souls pouring out of the glen—a rag-tag procession of emigrants forming—families that had held on through the major clearances thirty-odd years ago. Since the best land had already been taken for hunting estates and large-scale sheep farming, they must, like her, wonder why anyone would want their few worn-out acres of land.

Lizzie didn't know she had voiced her thoughts till Jock said, "Aye, it doesn't make any sense."

Crofters from Craiganour, who were already dragging their belongings along the military road that followed the north bank of Loch Rannoch, joined up with the folks from Aulich.

Lizzie and Jock walked towards Learan, followed by the families of cottars grimly hauling what they had salvaged from their crofts. Families, purposeful and proud, struggled with their cumbersome bundles and barrows, trying to hold their heads high above the shame of what was happening.

Women wept softly not to disturb the suckling infants at their breast overmuch, but many of the older women were crying the coronach, keening and wailing, as they did for funerals, giving the bedraggled procession its own eerie music.

Some of the ponies loaded with bundles had a child perched on top, king of the parade, happy in their innocence.

Anything with wheels had been called into service. Men hitched themselves up to farm carts, piled high with the possessions of a lifetime—tools, iron pots, griddles, Sunday clothes. Kists, not as elegant as Lizzie's mother's, surely contained irreplaceable treasures—a bit of fabric, woven by a skilled grandmother, being saved for a wedding coat; a jar of herbs guaranteed to cure the rheumatism; a few shillings that had been put aside towards a disaster; and, of course, the family Bible.

Elderly grannies, carrying the smallest babies, led the dejected parade behind Lizzie and Jock. Grown men stooped to pick up tired toddlers, giving them a cuddy ride on their backs. Every able-bodied man, woman, and child carried a load balled up in a sheet or a plaidie.

Lizzie had never seen so many people in one place at the same time, except on special occasions at the kirk, and then they wore their Sunday best. Now the men wore jerseys and dark jackets, caps, hand-knitted socks, and home-made leather shoes. The women's long skirts, of a uniform dark, heavy cloth, were bunched up in the back to help support their bundles; colourful tartan plaidies were tied round their shoulders. Boys were in knickers and otherwise dressed like the men, if they were lucky, or barefoot in most cases. Girls wore white cotton aprons that they usually tried to keep clean. Lizzie observed that today some of the peenies were whiter than others and no one cared.

Kilichonan buzzed with the news. Seemed that everyone was out on the street staring in disbelief. The tradesmen and shopkeepers, heads hanging, watched their long-time customers leaving Rannoch.

The sounds of "goodbye" and "fare thee well" rippled along the road in the wake of the procession. The traditional "Haste ye back" had a hollow ring.

Some of the girls in Lizzie's class ran up to her and tearfully told her how much they would miss her. She couldn't talk to them and pushed past, blinded by her tears.

* * *

Lizzie and Jock climbed high above the Falls of Gaur, which gave them an unobstructed view of the valley and the loch, and watched their families plodding their weary way down the meandering road towards them. In happier times they had come here for Halloween, from Kilichonan School. They'd lit a fire that could be seen all over Rannoch to scare away evil witches and warlocks.

She gazed with haunting sadness on Schiehallion, that spectacular mountain, the Fairy Hill of the Caledonians off to the east, and to the south, Loch Rannoch and the ancient Black Forest, what was left of the rainforest that covered much of this land in antiquity. She knew this land like her own image in the stream and was as acquainted with its history as she was with the stories of the MacGregors.

Jock offered his hand to assist her onto the rocky perch where they rested. "Where are you goin'?" she asked him, turning her head sideways to meet his honest, straightforward gaze, breaking the silence they had maintained on their climb up the crag.

"To Canada," he said dreamily.

"To Canada?" Her head shot up and almost hit him on the chin—he was very close.

"Och, I don't mean right away." He explained. "Charlie and I want to go to Hudson's Bay and make our fortune someday."

"Aye, Charlie always talked about that."

Once he started talking about his dreams of travel, he couldn't seem to stop, though at times when she fixed his gaze his face reddened and he stammered.

"But first we are going to Lanarkshire. Father has heard there is work there. I have to make some money first for the fare. My Auntie Jean is over there in Ontario. She told Father he should come over there, too. The work is good, and a man can buy his own place instead of workin' for landlords or factors or such." His voice dropped to a whisper. "Did ye ever think of going there, Lizzie?"

He stood so close to her as he spoke of his hopes for the future that she heard the sound of his heart thumping. Every embarrassing emotion was lighting up his face. He looked so vulnerable. Her interest in what he was saying seemed to encourage him to go on. Each time she blew that stubborn curl off her forehead she felt his eyes following.

He touched her arm to turn her around and draw her attention to the familiar hills, the valleys, and the moors. "God's view, Lizzie, our beautiful glen." He raised his voice with passion and force. "Is it not the most wondrous place? And do you think those foreign rogues will love it like we do? Who else can appreciate this? Generations of our families, back even before the Covenanters, have cried out their sorrows into these echoing mountains, raised their families, died to protect them."

He quieted, reached out, and put his arm lightly around her shoulders. "And you, Lizzie, are the essence of this place. You're part MacGregor."

"The best part . . ." She smiled wistfully, remembering her grandparents.

"My own grandmother was Helen MacGregor, and she was just as feisty as her grandmother, the chieftainess, the wife and right hand of Rob Roy. I used to think of it when I watched you walking out on the moor—well, some of the time." He melted her heart with his smile. "And I'd think how proud my great-great-grandmother would be to see how her folk survived. How happy to know that MacGregors still walked these trails. Maybe she does know. We'll be back, Lizzie. We'll be back." He stroked her hair.

She knew it comforted him to think so. But how can I believe that? she thought. Down there by the stream is my broken family dragging away their few precious belongings, and over there in my glen the smoke rises . . .

She turned to face him; their lips were so close; when she could no longer bear the sweetness of his gaze she closed her eyes; he kissed her lightly on the mouth.

His tenderness eased the hurt, fear, anger, and despair of the worst day of her life. She put her arms around his neck and crushed her mouth against his then buried her head in his rough jacket while the tears flowed.

CHAPTER TWENTY

Charlie's Revenge

My son! My son! May kinder stars
Upon thy fortune shine

Lizzie and Jock descended Slios Minh, the gentle slope, to greet the advance party at a sheltered resting place near the Bridge of Gaur. Mostly men, they had the foresight to start a fire and get a huge cauldron to boiling. When the women got there, they tipped the potatoes into the iron pot to cook. The group's bundles made backrests and pillows for the short respite they allowed themselves. They sat down on the familiar moor, and shared the hurriedly packed oatcakes and black pudding.

One enterprising fellow even got an enormous salmon out of the stream, which he cooked over the fire and shared with the Campbells and the MacGregors.

"How do ye like yer salmon, Robert?" the lucky fisherman asked Lizzie's father.

"Och, I like it fine poached, Murdoch," said her Pa, to his friend's great glee.

"That's one guid meal for us and one less for yon English bastard's table. May he rot in hell!" The fisherman's heartfelt blessing added relish to the feast.

While they enjoyed their forbidden fruit, a two-horse carriage approaching from the west caught their attention. It could only be someone headed to the big house on this narrow back road. It had to be the factor, or Mary's

English husband. It was unlikely to be Mary herself; she'd probably never set foot on these moors again. "Selfish bitch," Lizzie muttered.

Her brother Charlie was up ahead of the crowd on the other side of the drove road. Lizzie had tried to find him and talk to him but he had stayed off by himself all morning. From where Lizzie stood with Jock, Pa, and John Campbell, she saw Charlie running from the hillock across the field, scooping up rocks into the pouch he'd created with his shirttail until it was full of stones and spilling over as he loped over the uneven ground.

He reached the road just ahead of the chaise and started pelting the carriage. The surprised groomsman let loose a volley of curses and waved his whip frantically in Charlie's direction. The startled horses reared up and took off galloping toward the safety of the stables, giving whoever was inside the ride of their lives and splashing mud on anyone close to the road. Lizzie watched, from behind Pa, as they stampeded past at breakneck speed and saw, inside the vehicle, the terrified face of a pale, bewhiskered man holding onto a strap with one hand and his top hat with the other.

"Seems to be in an awfy hurry," John said, pulling out his pipe and cutting a plug.

"Aye, maybe he's afeart he's going to miss the bonfire," was Pa's thoughtful comment as he took off his cap and used it to wipe the spattered dirt off his face.

Lizzie got a quick glimpse of the fancy carriage, designed for sedate city riding, as it flew by. A few hundred feet down the rough road it struck one of the many rocks that protruded, and dislodged a wheel. Loosened from its axle, it began to wobble precariously. The careening vehicle tossed its elegant passenger into the gully. The horses dragged the disabled carriage a few more yards before giving up and coming to a standstill, whinnying and tossing their manes.

The group around Lizzie stared, transfixed, at the spot where the tall, skinny man had disappeared. They watched in fascination till he crawled out of the ditch and stood up, his green velvet doublet, tan breeks, and silver-buckled shoes covered in mud. The Southron shook his fists impotently at his recently banished tenants, who laughed and applauded this impromptu act of Highland justice—the traditional respect that they had afforded all their lives to landed proprietors had evaporated overnight. Lizzie saw Charlie across the road, a satisfied smile on his face. He smiled and winked at her. She felt a surge of pride at her twin's rebellion.

Why, she didn't know, but a stanza from "Man Was Made To Mourn," Burns' poetry that Charlie often muttered when he was frustrated, rang in her head.

The sun that overhangs yon moors,
Out-spreading far and wide,
Where hundreds labor to support
A haughty lordling's pride—

She knew Charlie was wounded to his core and probably blamed everyone, including Pa, for not standing up to the bullies.

Pa and Mr. Campbell shared their views on the "haughty lordling."

"With a wee lick of dirt on his breeks and sporting some Hieland mud on his fine jacket, he'll look a bit more Scottish-like on his trek ower the glen . . . would ye not think so, John?"

"Aye, if he could lose that silly lookin' hat, it wud help too."

"Git you over here," Pa yelled over the merriment to Charlie, who had started down the road kicking rocks into the ditch.

Charlie yelled back some forceful retort that got lost in the east wind, turned on his heel, and headed west away from the others. Lizzie saw Pa taking off his belt, which meant only one thing.

"Och, Rab. Ye're not going to leather him for that, are ye?" said Mr. Campbell. "It's only what ye would have done yerself when ye were his age."

"That's the second time the day that lad has acted foolhardy. He has to learn some control or he'll get in a load of trouble and I'll not be able to help him at all, at all."

"Och, let him be, man. There's plenty else to worry us," said John.

Her father inspected the ragtag bunch and had to agree. "I'll see to the boy later." He put his belt back on.

"Yon English fop can't stand the sight of real men on the property . . . especially Highland men. Did ye ever see sich a get-up as he was sporting? He'll not last one winter in Rannoch. He'll freeze his arse off on our mountains."

"Aye, Captain Freezy-arse he'll be when he's riding his fancy horse on the moor and gets thrown into an icy bog," offered Pa, eager to mete out imaginary justice to the Sassenach tormentor.

* * *

Jock chuckled. "I can't believe Charlie had the temerity to act so brash." He sounded envious. He and Lizzie ran up a nearby hillock to get a better view of the Sassenach and his flunky, off down the military road, attempting to right what was left of the fancy carriage—still a mile or two away from its destination, the manor house, which Lizzie could see too from this vantage point. She wondered if Katie MacKay might be watching the sad exodus of the crofters from the bay window, or was she too busy making tea for yon new laird? Lizzie bristled to think of it. Had Kate even tried to intervene? She thought of the envelope—and Charlie running off to God knows where.

* * *

Lizzie and Jock rejoined the main group to share the simple meal and listen to stories the crofters told of their individual evictions and discuss the painful alternatives for their future. From what she could hear, many MacGregors, Campbells, and Stewarts were headed along the River Gaur and around Loch Eigheach to the Black Corries, west to Glencoe to join other members of their clans. Their Highland relatives would provide for them until they could re-establish their lives there or make preparations to move on to greener pastures. Others were headed to Oban; some to Fort William, and a few were returning to the Outer Isles where they were born.

This was as far as some of her neighbours had ever travelled in their lives. At Bridge of Gaur the refugees from Rannoch Glen divided their ranks and said their last farewells to aunts and uncles and second cousins and other relatives, for everyone in the glen was related in some degree by blood or marriage.

Lizzie listened to them talk about the weather, as country folk do— anything to postpone the painful goodbyes. Though some of the women and children wept, the men were stoic and simply tugged at the skips of their bonnets and mumbled phrases that had more soul than meaning.

"We'll all get together again in a better time."

"Och, aye! Come and see us in Oban when you get up that way. We're taking up the fishing."

"We're off to Glencoe to join with the wife's kinfolk. She's been greeting to get back to her ma since we left. MacGregors are all the same. Talk about clannish. Furthermore, she says she'll have no more bairns till she's near her mother. Been sleeping in the other bed for months, and I've been getting cold comfort. Now there's a good reason to go visit the mother-in-law."

"Ye'll do weel in Glasgow, Donald. Hielanmen have got some grit in their craw, not like those Lowland Scots. Some of them's not much better than Englishmen, if ye were to ask me. Aye, ye'll do fine."

Lizzie was grateful the rain stayed away despite the threatening clouds that lifted over the snow-capped mountains as she watched her kinsmen, people she'd known all her life, walk on down the road to their uncertain futures.

CHAPTER TWENTY-ONE

Uncharted Territory

These northern scenes with weary feet I trace;
O'er many a winding dale and painful steep,
Th'abodes of covey'd grouse and sheep,
My savage journey, curious, I pursue

Lizzie's family bid goodbye to a few neighbours who had been planning emigration to North America for some years and were now figuring out the quickest route through these mountains to Greenock, where they could board a vessel for the faraway shores they knew only by reputation. Now that the clearance had precipitated their mass departure, they were counting every saved penny to see if all the family could go or if only a few of the able-bodied would be sent to pave the way.

Lizzie's family, some other MacGregors, the Campbells, and two families of Stewarts were headed across Rannoch Moor to connect with the main road near the Bridge of Orchy to find a way south to Clydeside, where there was work at the mines, the ironworks, and the shipyards.

"Pa, do we have to go to Lanarkshire?" Lizzie was walking alongside her father and John Campbell.

Her father directed his answer to John.

"Lizzie's remembering what Uncle Archie said. He had a bad experience there." He turned to Lizzie. "Och! I'm younger and stronger than Archie; the Glasgow area means jobs."

"Fifty-six isn't that young, Robert, but ye are strong. I'll say that," John said.

"What choice do I have, with eight bairns to feed and clothe and Flora, weakened and grieving and not much help."

Lizzie saw Ma talking to Pa's cousin from up the glen. The women stopped and put their arms around each other and began to wail, slowing up the march. She remembered, with a sudden gripping feeling in her chest, that there were only <u>seven</u> bairns to feed and clothe now.

"Rob, ye'll no need that old crookit foot. There'll be good land and modern shovels where ye're goin," said John.

Her father still had a "cas chrom" on top of the pile on the tinker's cart. She'd often seen her father working alongside Mr. Campbell wielding its unpolished wooden shaft, the height of a man by the handgrip, worn smooth by rough hands; thrusting the iron "foot," with his homemade boot, into the peaty soil. Her grandfather had prized that old hand plough. How many times had Auld Gregor delved and scooped the infertile soil with that implement?

Her father wordlessly jettisoned the ancient tool. It would be rough crossing the long stretch of moor south of Loch Rannoch on the seldom-used trail. Jock's father was right—no point in lugging a useless relic. Though she was relieved, she couldn't look her father in the eye for a while.

Pa yelled at the twins to take turns pushing the creaky cart, and shrugged his shoulders to adjust the sleeping Kate's weight. Lizzie's young sister had run up and down the braes for the first half hour with all the enthusiasm of a two-year-old and, finally exhausted, begged to be carried.

Lizzie and Jock set a steady pace for the others, stopping every few minutes to let them catch up, and reached the shelter of Rannoch Forest that night just before dark. The fatigue reached deep into her bones as Lizzie helped her father set up a lean-to with branches the twins had scavenged. Lizzie draped quilts and plaidies over it to create a shelter from the west wind. She gathered bracken to spread under the blankets to cushion their rest. The fire Pa built and the porridge Ma and Annie made soon soothed the children into a deep slumber and allowed Lizzie and her parents a short respite before they collapsed beside them.

Lizzie lay next to her mother and the baby, fighting sleep and listening to the drone of her father's voice.

"And where will ye go, John?" Her father came as close to tears as she had ever heard him. He and his friend had worked side-by-side. All their adult lives they had turned over that infertile Highland soil they thought they owned.

"My lads and me will get work in Motherwell; the wife's relatives bide there."

Lizzie wondered, where in the world is Motherwell?

Mr. Campbell droned on. "Nellie says her cousin'll give us a cot till we get settled. Thank God for MacGregors. This cousin is married to a Maclure from Coatbridge, out on the other side of Glasgow. Isn't that where your wife's uncle nearly killed himself, Robbie?"

Lizzie hoped Uncle Archie would never have to hear of this horror they were going through. In the quiet she heard the men drawing on their pipes.

"Rob, are ye still bound and determined to go by road? The rest of us are taking the boat to Glasgow."

"We'll do fine by road . . . at least to Callander. Heard tell there's a new train station there. The twins are gie keen to go on a train."

Lizzie knew her father would never admit that he was prone to seasickness. She remembered him coming home very green after a stormy afternoon on Loch Rannoch fishing. But, John knew that, too, and didn't press the point.

"Is there any way ye can lighten yer burden? Yon cart is getting awful heavy for yer young boys . . . and no sign of Charlie, yet. Ye could get rid of that old kist," Mr. Campbell said.

"NO! No, Charlie'll be along." Father shrugged as though it was of no concern. "Probably taking goodbye with some lassie back at the Bridge of Gaur. He's following us, John. I saw him this afternoon hanging back on the trail. The lad and me, we had a bit of a squall back there at the croft. He'll catch up when he's ready. Charlie's a mountain man. He'll find his way."

Lizzie was relieved to hear news of Charlie and dozed off into exhausted slumber.

* * *

Lizzie rubbed the sleep from her eyes. Despite the hard ground conditions, she'd slept hard. The morning breeze had a hint of warmth in it and, thank God, the rain had stayed away.

"Do ye think we can make it as far as the Bridge of Orchy today, Rob?" John Campbell was up at daybreak.

"We can but try," Pa said. "If we can find a dry path along the ridge by the Water of Tulla, we can be in Crannoch Wood by afternoon."

Ma had said nothing since yesterday. This was her way, Lizzie knew. She was grieving quietly after the initial tumult. There was nothing Lizzie or her father could think of to take away her pain. Lizzie knew Pa was afraid if he talked to his wife, he might end up spilling some tears himself, and that wouldn't do at all. Pa had to get this lot packed up and ready for the day's march.

They got beyond Crannoch Wood in the afternoon just as the rain started. It slowed them down. The men tried to protect the smaller children by carrying them close to their bodies, while Lizzie and the other women struggled with their long heavy skirts hampering their stride. The biting wind that howled over the crystalline top of the Black Mount and across the angry waters of Loch Tulla added to the misery. Lizzie and Jock, out ahead of the others, announced the welcome sight of the old tower ruin at Achallader. The news brought cheers from the group. The overcast skies had created an early dark when they dragged themselves into the hamlet.

Nellie Campbell's mother hailed from this area. Seems Jock's mother had kin all over Scotland. Nellie expressed the hope that some MacGregors still lived here, for they would never turn away a stranger from their door—and certainly not family. It was an obligation of Highland hospitality.

Sure enough, Nellie learned from the innkeeper that her cousin, Dougald MacGregor, lived close by, which meant shelter for the night for Lizzie's family as well as Jock's. The innkeeper didn't mind giving out that information to Nellie, for the two families of Stewarts in the party were all his inn could accommodate. Nellie's cousin Dougald did not even know, after these many years, that he had family in Rannoch Moor. But, aye, he remembered his Auntie Jessie when she married and left with yon young Campbell lad.

"You're the spitting image of her. She was a local beauty," he told Nellie, stretching the truth a bit, Lizzie thought.

Dougald's wife, Isobel, took the MacGregor and Campbell women and bairns into the croft to dry out their clothes and feed them. Dougald led the men to the hayloft where they would spend a more comfortable night than the previous one.

When she saw Ma had plenty of help, Lizzie offered to go out to the barn with cold meat and sliced bread for the men.

As she climbed the ladder she heard Dougald say, "We'll have a wee dram, bye and bye, but keep quiet about it. Isobel is a Methodist and doesn't approve of the whisky."

Lizzie served the men and helped herself to the fine food.

Dougald sneaked back saying the women were nicely settled. "The coast is clear. They're all in there warm and coy-like, sharing stories or recipes or some such thing." He winked at Lizzie who had found a place near Jock.

Dougald unplugged a jug of whisky and took a long pull on it before he passed it to John.

The men stopped passing the jug around the circle long enough to gobble the food.

Dougald showed no interest in the food. "I'll go get my fiddle and we can have a wee bit of a song." His gait was unsteady as he headed out of the barn.

"Dougald, do ye think that's a good idea?" John cautioned, having more of his wits about him than his host did at that juncture. "It's been quiet over there at the house these many hours."

"Ye're right, John." He was disappointed. Lizzie surmised it would mean trouble if Isobel saw him now. Then he brightened up. "I'll just sing for ye, never fear."

He had a fine repertoire of all the old songs and Lizzie left Jock's side, from time to time, to join him for a duet and returned sitting closer to Jock each time till she had to leave, reluctantly, to join the women.

Dougald was still singing when she woke up near daybreak to go outside to the privy.

The group wolfed down the hot breakfast Isobel served them. She was the soul of hospitality, and only Lizzie's keen observation revealed she was less than pleased with her husband as balladeer.

"Looks like you're getting eggs and ham...I'll likely get a cold shoulder and that's the truth," Dougald told John in a loud whisper. He might have thought he was jesting, but Isobel's "while-the-company's-here" smiles told it all.

* * *

Lizzie strode down a road that skirted around Loch Tulla and wound its way south close to the bank of the River Orchy. It was little more than a deer path here; she startled a doe and her fawn, which bounded into the bracken around the next curve. The twins tore after them, but the anxious mother and offspring loped out of reach of the noisy youngsters.

By noon they had moved out of Menzies and MacGregor country. Crofters left their ploughing to come to the stone dykes and inquire tactfully about the strange band headed down the road. Lizzie had no doubt that these Highlanders must have courted the same conviction that the worst of the clearances had been carried out and finished in their parents' time and that in this Year of Our Lord 1860 it was over. But now the spectre of fellow cottars evicted had to bring home to them the uncertainty of their own situations; no one could predict when a landlord might want to make different use of the land. It was the choice of the landowner, and his alone, to create huge sheep farms that didn't need much labour or to turn over the great estates to hunting and fishing for visitors from England or abroad who were able to pay handsomely for the privilege.

When they got wind of the reason for the dejected parade, women ceased their frightened gawking and withdrew themselves and their children behind closed cottage doors, as though contact with the wretched exiles might be contaminating. One old crone, remembering her Highland hospitality, re-emerged from her cottage with a bulging kitchen towel. She tripped on a rock and spilled a couple of potatoes onto the ground but quickly retrieved them and gave the bundle to Lizzie's mother.

That act of kindness, a good night's sleep and dry clothes worked wonders for her spirits. She pretended it was her usual walk on the moors as she set out on the long hike to the Bridge of Orchy and even felt good enough to sing. Jock caught up with her and startled her. Her song ended in a tight little squeal of surprise.

"Don't stop, Lizzie. I love to hear ye. I've listened to your singing for all these years up on Aulich Hill."

"Ye didn't—I never thought anyone heard me. Those lads teasing me in the churchyard . . . what they said was true then?"

"Of course. And the teasing I got about it was fierce. But I didnae care. Och! The beautiful sound of your voice singing the old songs surely was heard by the angels."

"Ye've quite a way with words, Jock Campbell."

His face flushed now. "Aye, so my brothers say. Our Colin always says to me, 'What kind of Scotsman talks like that?'"

"Ye really like ma singing then, Jock?" Though her eyes were downcast she felt his gaze fixed on her. Looking up she saw them shining with unabashed pleasure.

"I did so," he said quietly, taking hold of her hand.

She felt her body tremble in pleasure.

"We can rest for a bit on this dead stump till the others catch up, Lizzie."

She sat down on the dry perch from where she had an unobstructed view of the river. They were close enough to hear waves lapping on the pebbled shore. A stand of pine shielded them from the freshened breeze; a thrush warbled from one of the higher branches. Jock remained standing. He took a deep breath.

"Your pleasure was like a radiance that surrounded you. I never approached you; I sensed solitude was what you wanted." His voice had a throaty quality. "But I listened—and I saw you when you walked along the bank and into the stream. I could almost feel that bracken under your bare feet and the chilly water swirling around your ankles."

His wistful smile transmitted thoughtfulness and regret. That era had passed, a dream that was forever tied to the home of their birth. One that had disappeared like a young doe into the Highland mists just like all their yesterdays. What future could they have? Not old enough to venture out on their own, and committed to helping their families in the alien land to which they must go in order to survive.

"Sometimes you passed my secret place; for I had a refuge too, Lizzie, where I would try to write a verse that would capture your charm . . . I'm still working on it." He laughed. "William Wordsworth wrote about you, though."

Her head jerked up; her mouth opened wide in astonishment. "It was you then . . . it was you who wrote the . . ."

He forged ahead, deeply absorbed in recollecting the poem.

"Behold her, single in the field,
Yon solitary Highland Lass!
Reaping and singing by herself;
Stop here, or gently pass!
Alone she cuts and binds the grain,
And sings a melancholy strain."

"Jock, ye have Wordsworth memorized. Ye never did that in class."

"Not there, Lizzie, this is for you."

After a deep breath that betrayed the catch in his throat, he continued:

"O listen! for the Vale profound
Is overflowing with the sound.
No nightingale did ever chaunt
More welcome notes to weary bands
Of travellers in some shady haunt,
Among Arabian sands:
A voice so thrilling ne'er was heard
In spring-time from the Cuckoo-bird,
Breaking the silence of the seas
Among the farthest Hebrides."

Jock smiled in her direction. He couldn't have missed the tears streaming down her cheeks. She dried her eyes with the corner of her shawl.

"Then the poet goes on later to say, as if he wrote it just for my Lizzie:

'Whate'er the theme, the Maiden sang
As if her song could have no ending;
I saw her singing at her work,
And o'er the sickle bending;—
I listened, motionless and still;
And, as I mounted up the hill,

The music in my heart I bore,
Long after it was heard no more.'"

He delivered the verse in a clear, ringing tone—no hesitancy in his lilting voice. As soon as he finished the last line of the recitation, he lowered his steady gaze, and the telltale crimson began to creep up his neck and face.

"Jock." She smiled to assure him she was pleased. "I never before allowed myself to suppose that I could be the object of the romantic poetry I love so much."

He pulled himself up straining under his heavy bundle and reached out his hand to help her to her feet. "Lizzie, somewhere in this world a man," suddenly shy again, ". . . and a woman . . . can surely find a place to live a good life, a place where they can realize their dreams. Maybe not in this land—but somewhere."

When they approached the Bridge of Orchy, she knew their short time together was coming to an abrupt end.

* * *

"Och! Afore ye know it ye'll be all settled in a fancy new house in Lanarkshire, Robert. With all your fine family to help ye, ye'll be back on yer feet in no time at all." John Campbell offered encouragement to Lizzie's father.

The two old cronies were not about to dissolve into tears or show any signs of the sorrow or dread they were experiencing at the sudden and total loss of everything familiar—lands they had thought they would always inhabit, friends they thought never to lose. Their farewells consisted of backslapping and bluster that fooled no one—certainly not Lizzie.

Jock approached her with a solemn face. "Lizzie, Charlie crept into camp last night."

Her foreboding increased.

"He's going to try to get a boat to North America. He begged me not to say anything in case his Pa would try to find him and talk him out of it."

"He's cut to the quick; he can't face Pa." Lizzie felt the heartbreaking truth tightening her chest and reached for Jock's hand.

"Aye, he said that." He grasped her hand and raised it to his lips. "Charlie had been anticipating a ploughman's wages this year. To work like a man on the land at your father's side; he wanted that more than anything."

Lizzie's somber thoughts were with her twin and her slim hope. Might he change his mind and follow them at a distance? It didn't sound like it. He was devastated. Everyone knew that, but only Lizzie knew why he wanted a pocketfu' o' siller—so he could get away from what he considered servitude. Get away to where he dreamed he'd be free. Charlie was quiet; his feelings ran deep.

"I can't keep this from Pa." She was dazed. Her brother gone and not even a goodbye.

"It wasn't just that. He says he fears Winterbottom will set the law on him, Lizzie."

"He's too young to go out in the world all alone." She gulped her tears.

"I think he's afraid he'll kill the man if he stays in Scotland. I've never seen Charlie like this. He needs to go, Lizzie."

He kissed the top of her bowed head. "Do what ye think is right, lass. He always meant to go to the colonies. I knew that; so did you. Seems he decided to do it sooner than later."

"I can't tell them right now. Maybe he'll get in touch later . . . but how can he?" If Charlie's staying might endanger him, she had to let him go. But to keep this from her parents!

"I'm so sorry, Lizzie."

"He has the envelope . . ." Her voice tapered off.

"What envelope?"

"Maybe it's not important." Her mind raced.

"I have to go, Lizzie. They're waiting for me. What about you and me? We have to meet again somehow."

"Of course. I don't know how," was all she could say before her voice choked off.

Charlie and Jock torn out of her life in the same day. How could this be? She felt a great empty place in her chest filling with tears she could not yet shed.

Jock's back was poker straight when he abruptly disengaged and left her side to join his mother and brothers.

Lizzie swallowed hard. For the last few years she had misunderstood his shyness and let herself grow apart from the treasure that was Jock Campbell, this mature, gallant, handsome, insightful young man. Too late to concern herself now about the lost years; she would probably never see him again. Jock, his parents, and his brothers were headed for Inverary and the paddle steamer to Glasgow and some place beyond. How far from Glasgow? She had no idea.

And Charlie. Was he still up in the Highlands or on his way to a port?

Her father inclined his head towards the long road headed south. She knew he wanted to get away from these painful goodbyes quickly and be on his way.

"Charlie better show up soon before he loses track of us," Pa said.

"Charlie never lost track in the glen," the twins piped up in chorus.

He'll show up . . . he'll get over it, she told herself, but a bad feeling gnawed at her. Charlie meant what he said and said what he meant. His secret visit to Jock was his way of letting her know his plans, she felt sure.

Jock and his brothers faded into the morning mist, lugging their possessions across the bridge and down the road to Inverlochy, then Dalmally and on to Inverary to wait for the next steamer to Port Glasgow or Greenock. They'll do well, she thought. With so many able-bodied sons to go to work, they'll manage.

She peered once more across the bridge in the direction the Campbell family went. She thought she saw someone turn around and wave, but they were too far away to tell who it was. She decided it must be Jock. Joy and sorrow jolted her body. The dark form receded and disappeared into the haze. Her heart emptied any hope into the rolling shroud of gray mist.

CHAPTER TWENTY-TWO

Where's Charlie?

Adieu, dear amiable youth!
Your heart can ne'er be wanting!
May prudence, fortitude, and truth
Erect your brow undaunting.

Following a paved road that was easier to travel on, they were leaving Lizzie's beloved wild Highlands. She stole a glance up the road. Would she ever come back?

She adjusted the shawl around her head, picked up her bundle, and headed south to the Lowlands, to Glasgow and the Clydeside, and whatever strange country lay beyond that.

Lizzie observed her family and realistically took stock. Pa would find work, of course; she could too, and Charlie . . . no, not Charlie. Her guilt at keeping what she knew from her parents pained her.

"Where's Charlie?" both twins piped up at once, a disconcerting habit they had retained from infancy.

"Never mind," said their father. "He's probably gone off behind the hillock to do his business."

They giggled. "Will we wait for him then, Pa?"

"Naw. He's old enough to fend for hisself. He'll catch up with us in no time at all, oor Charlie." Pa's words rang hollow.

Ma hadn't said a word. She must have believed Pa's assumption that Charlie wasn't far behind. Or did they both know he had gone his own way and were struggling to accept it?

All these changes, and it wasn't over yet. What next? Nary a handy rock for footing to get you across the raging torrent that was ripping through their lives.

Ma had all she could do to hold herself together and mind the baby. Annie would have to take more responsibility for the younger ones so that Lizzie could get a job of some kind. Annie wouldn't like it. But Lizzie knew that without going out to work herself, they would not be able to manage. Uncle Archie's words came back to her about women working at the pits.

She threw her head back and gave that curl a puff of air. I'm not afraid of work, she told herself, and I'll do what I have to do, and maybe some day . . .

Jock's dreams had lit a fire in her. To live someplace and have a piece of land of their own. It was an idea she had never entertained before, but now things were different. Her world and her way of thinking had changed overnight.

She couldn't abandon Pa now, though. He was counting on her, but in a few years—when she was older . . . Why not? Lots of Highland folk went to Nova Scotia or Prince Edward Island or British Columbia.

* * *

"Guid afternoon," Pa hailed the young lad fishing off the bridge.

"Looks like rain." The boy jerked his fishing pole and a trout leapt out of the churning water.

"I hope it holds off. I want to get my family to Tyndrum afore dark."

"Aye, ye should make it fine, mister. To the inn at Tyndrum, is it?"

"Och no! We like it fine staying out of doors," Pa lied.

"Aye, that's the best way," the boy said politely. "About two hours walk down the road." He returned to his fishing without further comment, intent on reeling in his catch.

Ma passed around the cooked potatoes from the old lady at Tulla, and they set out gobbling down the food. The sun rode high in the sky; its welcoming warmth on their left shoulders cheered Lizzie. No rain, yet. Thank God. If it would just stay away till they could get to Tyndrum.

Lizzie could see that her mother was tiring. She offered her relief by taking turns carrying Archie. He got to ride on top of the piled up cart in the centre of the soft blankets and quilts when they could get wee Kate to relinquish her throne and run on ahead for a time.

"We have to wait for Charlie, Robert," Ma said.

"Oor Charlie will jist have to catch up with us or else make his own way. Och! He's all the man he's ever going to be." Pa's attempt at sounding indifferent wasn't too convincing.

"Aye. He could make his own way, Pa." Lizzie emphasized the concept as a good reason not to tell her folks what she knew. She'd decided to wait until they were well on their way.

Pa and Ma had walked ahead of the others. At the crest of the hill that descended to the Tyndrum Inn they stood facing each other in a heated discussion. Finally her father shrugged.

"All right, you lot," he called back to them. "We're staying at the inn tonight."

"We are?" The twins dropped the cart and almost tipped the baby onto the road.

Lizzie was thrilled. She'd never been in an inn before. Annie wanted to borrow Lizzie's silver comb, but it was in the kist and too difficult to access. Lizzie wondered: How did she know about it? But this was not the time to question Annie.

She whined, "Finally we get to live like gentry, and I have to go in looking like a scarecrow."

"Well, that's better than the way ye usually look," said Jamie.

"Aye, like an auld witch," said Donnie.

"Quiet, you two! Don't get her greetin' again," said Lizzie. "Here, ye can wear my Sunday cap." Lizzie reached into the kist and found the white frilly cap on top of the tightly packed chest. Anything to stop Annie from whining. The cap was a bit crushed, but Annie was pacified.

Mother gave Lizzie a handful of shillings and sent her into the inn. "Get two rooms, or at least two beds . . . and find out how much for supper."

Lizzie came back in ten minutes with the cost totalled to tell Ma, sure that would be the end of it.

"We'll take it. Go and tell them."

"Afore ye go," Annie begged, "tell the twins to wipe their snotty noses. They look like pigs."

Lizzie gave them a frown and a nod, for once in support of Annie's request. The twins grumbled but wiped their faces with their sleeves.

Annie sashayed, à la Mary Buchanan, into the hallway with the twins behind her, making faces to each other and silently imitating their sister's antics.

They were just in time for a fine dinner of venison stew. Lizzie was vaguely aware that her family was not as well turned out as the other guests. She knew they were the object of scrutiny and probably disapproval; she was too hungry and tired to care. They had two rooms with fireplaces. While Lizzie helped her mother tend the baby, her mother confided to her. "Wee Archie has to be under cover for the rest of the trip. I think he's getting a fever."

Lizzie fell asleep in the luxury of beds with sheets and blankets as soon as her head touched the feather pillow. They were up in the morning to a plate of porridge and rich cream. Annie sat in the dining room supping her porridge with her pinkie stuck up in the air.

"Get a gander at oor Annie. Thinks she's gentry," Jamie whispered to Donald.

CHAPTER TWENTY-THREE

The Help O' Kinfolk

'An' forward tho' I canna see,
I guess an' fear!

For the next two days the road was fairly even and the cart moved well on it, but they were all tired, and their shoes, designed to walk on moor and fields, were wearing out. The twins had discarded theirs and walked barefoot on the soft grasses by the side of the road.

Tonight they had to camp in Glen Ogle, they'd sleep under the full moon.

"Tomorrow is Sunday, Florry. What say you we go to Balquidder? It's not much out of our way. There's MacGregors there, kin to my mother. Haven't seen them since they left Rannoch before you and I were married. They'd want us to stop and visit, that's a fact." Pa tried to console his wife with the promise of a roof over her head the following night. "And we can go to the kirk there. Heard tell Rob Roy MacGregor is buried in yon kirk-yard. We can leave for Callander on Monday. We're not tinkers yet. We can observe the Sabbath like guid Christian folk should."

* * *

So it was settled. Lizzie and her mother were glad to have the help of women kinfolk who made a fuss over wee Kate and boiled up barley gruel to treat the baby's fever.

Their relatives heard the saga of wee Gregor, wept with Lizzie and her mother, and shared their own sad stories of bairns who succumbed to fevers and accidents beyond their control.

The MacGregors would have been content to stay in the supportive company of caring relatives for a few more days beyond the Sabbath, but Pa had information that the train ran on Mondays for sure—probably in the morning. The cousins weren't too sure about other days.

Pa raised a glass to his cousin Meg. "Thank ye for yer fine hospitality. We'll be up afore dawn and on our way. No need to tend to us in the morning. I ken ye have plenty to do on the farm."

"Hoots mon, are ye daft?" Meg's elderly husband was affronted. "My wife will cook ye a fine Highland breakfast and you'll be riding down the road in yon wagon right after I hitch it up to the old mare. Walk is it? Have ye not walked this wife and these bairns far enough, Robert MacGregor?"

"I'm much obliged to ye, Duncan." Pa's voice echoed the relief Lizzie felt. Now surely they could get to the station in Callander in time for the Stirling train.

* * *

"Robert, what do ye suppose has happened to oor Chairlie?" her mother asked in the morning. Lizzie thought she looked like she'd been crying. "Maybe we should wait till tomorrow." She said in a querulous voice.

Lizzie plunged into guilt.

"We've talked enough about it, here's nothing to be done." Pa said in a grumpy voice. Then more gently, "I don't know, lass. We can't stop now. These other bairns are bone weary. Duncan says we'll be at the station in an hour. If we can git on the train the day, we can maybe git to Lanarkshire by nightfall. Duncan will put the word out in the village and tell the postman who delivers the whole of this area to look out for Charlie and tell him where we're headed."

They reluctantly left without Charlie when the wagon was loaded half an hour later.

"Maybe he went north with his cousins," Pa said, apparently moving away from the conjecture that Charlie was nearby.

"Maybe he went on the paddle steamer with Jock Campbell," young Jamie volunteered.

"Wish we could have gone on the steamer," said his twin. "I've never been on a big boat."

"A train's better'n a boat."

"No it's not. A boat's bigger."

"No it's not. A train's bigger."

"Father, make them stop fighting. Do we have to listen to that all the way to Stirling?" Annie was relishing the adult adventure and no doubt wishing she didn't have to put up with her uncouth younger brothers.

"Charlie'll be all right, Ma," Lizzie ventured.

Her mother looked at her quizzically.

Her mind raced to convince her mother not to tarry. "We need to get the baby someplace where we can tend to him."

"Yer right, Lizzie."

When the wagon reached the main road to head south, Lizzie studied the steep road back north they had traversed for two days before, and strained her eyes for sight of a lone traveller.

* * *

They trailed onto the tiny station where about thirty people were waiting. The group had formed a straggly queue by the time the stationmaster appeared and scurried to open his ticket office.

"No, the Striveling train is not here yet." Using the old name for Stirling, he responded to their eager questions.

Her father relaxed visibly. "When does it usually arrive?"

The little man in the official Caledonian railway cap pushed it to the back of his head and scratched his bald pate.

"Och! She'll be here afore ye know it. Sometimes sooner and whiles she's a bit later . . . and sometimes afore that."

Lizzie had to giggle. Pa seemed to be digesting that bit of useful information. He found a place for his wife to sit so she could change wee Archie, who had been crying for the last mile or more.

"Lizzie, come over here." Ma's voice was weary. "Open the kist. There is a bag of siller down in yonder. See to it yer father gets enough for the tickets."

Her father never concerned himself much with money. Ma was inclined to be secretive about the kist and its contents, including the current state of their reserves, but she invariably came up with 'the necessary' in any emergency.

Lizzie pushed aside the books and the cigar boxes of treasures to find the leather bag her mother had indicated. Of course, it was at the very bottom of the chest. It was heavier than she expected. She took out a handful of coins.

Pa came back from the ticket office crestfallen. "Kin you believe it? They want four shilling each for third class or two and sixpence if yer willing to stand. Who can come up with yon kind of money?"

"We can," said Ma with a determined set to her jaw. It crossed Lizzie's mind that Charlie came by his willpower quite naturally.

"Flora, yer a fine wife for managing the money. I don't know how ye do it." Ma started to smile but a tear slid down her cheek.

Lizzie, like Ma, felt the loss of Charlie and tried to cover it. She counted out the coins in a business-like way. "You and Ma can get seats, and the rest of us will stand," she told her father.

"Och! Do ye think I'm an auld man? I don't need a seat, lass."

"Pa, if ye get two seats we can take turns. Two times six is twelve and four tickets at two and sixpence is ten shillings more. Here's twenty-two shillings. We shouldn't need to pay for Kate or the baby." She counted out eleven silver florins into his hand.

His eyes opened wide. "To have a daughter who can add like that in her head—it's a wonder. Ye must have yer mother's cleverness with the money." Unlike Lizzie, he never seemed to concern himself with how Ma did it.

He came back with six tickets. "He gave me two seats and four stand-ups. Oor stuff can go in the luggage compartment. It'll cost another shilling for the cart." Pa waited for the women to decide.

"Och! Ye might could use it," Ma said, returning his grateful smile.

"The wee man said this track was built recently, and the train just started to provide service to Callander one year ago. The locals keep him busy now they've discovered fast travel. This is the modern world, boys," Pa told the open-mouthed twins, who had never seen such sights in all their twelve years.

The station master opened the door to allow the passengers onto the platform.

Lizzie piled her bundle onto the rest of the gear and took charge of wee Archie.

They could see it now, its black smoke puff-puffing into a billowing cloud, which disappeared into the clear Highland air. The twins jumped up and down and ran to the edge of the platform when they saw it and heard its clickety-clack. When the deafening train whistle blew, they began to jump and squeal and punch each other in the shoulder. They were in danger of falling off the edge onto the tracks in their excitement. Pa had to restrain them. The train thundered closer. When the front of the engine came into view the rest of the train was hidden behind a veil of white and black smoke. It looked like it was on fire.

"Git back here, you two." Their father's yell was lost in the din of the approaching locomotive. He grabbed one with each hand and pulled them back out of danger as the engine squealed and ground to a halt, shrouded in acrid smoke.

* * *

They all clambered on to the incredible vehicle. The compartment was crammed. Pa, with Kate perched on his lap, did sit down for a while beside Ma. Her exhausted mother reached out and patted his rough, work-worn hand resting on his knee. He turned his palm up and gripped her hand. His eyes misted and he swallowed hard. "Well, we've come this far, Florry."

"Look over there, Kate. Wave bye-bye to the wee man in the cap," Lizzie said to distract Pa and reassure her little sister, who seemed unsure whether to laugh or cry about rumbling along at breakneck speed in a noisy, packed train.

The tickets were good all the way to Glasgow, Lizzie told her father when they alighted at Stirling. She made some inquiries and came back to them with the information that a train would leave for Glasgow in about an hour. They would have to change platforms in Buchanan Street station if they meant to go farther. This was beyond her understanding. How many tracks did they have in Glasgow? Farther! Surely they would find work in Glasgow.

The twins found a corner to sit on the floor of the carriage and soon fell asleep, leaning up against each other's backs. Annie was deep in conversation with a Glasgow girl, who was filling her head with city stories. Lizzie noticed Annie had put as much distance between herself and her crude brothers as she could.

"Do you have a house in Glasgow?" the well-dressed girl about fifteen years old, like Annie, asked.

"Och! We're just going to start out in something small. My father is waiting for word about a job in Glasgow, then we'll move." She saw her sister glance over at her family; Lizzie quickly turned her head towards the window and pretended she hadn't heard the boasting lies.

"Sauciehall Street has the very best shops in Scotland. My mother takes me there in our carriage at least once a week, and then we go to tea. It's grand. Perhaps you could join us sometime. My mother wouldn't mind. We have a Highland maid."

Lizzie was furious, but apparently Annie didn't know she'd been slighted and was fussily adjusting the borrowed cap in her reflection in the window. *Hmmm! Have to get that cap back before Annie claims it as her own.*

Two hours later, when they poured out of the carriage onto the Buchanan Street station. They stood on the platform in a huddle not knowing which way to go.

"Ye need to keep moving," said the enormous muscular porter, who had the ruddy complexion of a Highland man and an accent that sounded a lot like Uncle Archie. He had retrieved their luggage and was easily piling it all onto the cart.

Seeing their uncertainty and consternation, he inquired, "Where are ye going?"

Pa seemed less sure of himself in this bustling city than he had been when they started out on the train journey, but he apparently decided to trust the fellow countryman. "We're looking for a place to lodge till I can find work and support my family."

"Is that a fact, now? My sister takes lodgers in a wee village not a far train ride from here. Whifflet, it's called. I think that's part of Coatbridge. Och! Another sixpence in fares'll get ye there . . . I'm Angus Macleod." He reached out his big paw and grasped Pa's hand and nodded acknowledgment to the rest of the family.

"Robert MacGregor and my wife, Flora." Pa shook the red-faced giant's hand. And these are my bairns."

"Do ye have a place to stay?"

"No, we left oor place with little warning."

Lizzie thought that was the understatement to beat all.

"Och! My sister Jessie's got a fine big house, I hear. Never been there myself—got as far as Gleska' and found work. Oor Jessie wid be proud to give a Hielanman and his bairns a place for the night and the best bowl of purritch in Scotland in the morning. I'll give ye her address. Have ye got something to write on? Here, let me see that ticket."

He took Pa's used ticket and pulled a stub of pencil out of his vest pocket. He licked the end of the pencil thoughtfully, his eyes raised to the heavens trying to recall the address of his generous sister.

"Hozier Street. Aye that's it. Right above the blacksmith's shop. Ye can't miss it. Tell her Angus sent ye, and she'll do ye proud."

It sounded like a solution to Lizzie. How would they find their way in this big, noisy city, she'd been thinking.

Ma's nod of approval was all Pa needed. "And where do we get on the train?"

"Follow me."

They all trailed after him. Angus walked at the same leisurely pace he probably took strolling footpaths over the moors of his home. People naturally got out of his way. It was easy to follow him to the platform, especially now that he was transporting most of their luggage.

"Take the train for Coatbridge—it'll let ye off at Whifflet—comes through here in a wee while. Sit down and take the weight off yer feet."

They thanked him profusely and he promised to visit, "When I get out to see our Jessie."

"Oh, and Angus, if ye see a good-lookin' young chap with brown hair wearing a green jacket, ask him if his name is Charlie MacGregor and tell him where ye sent us."

"Aye, I'll do that. Is he some kin of yours?"

"He's ma oldest son," said her father, barely disguising the lump in his throat.

The twins were revived after their nap and ran hither and yon and climbed up the overhead crossings to get a better view of Glasgow. The tall buildings, the smokestacks, the bridges, and all manner of engines and carriages, and the scurrying people in every kind of garb were a wonder to them.

At her mother's bidding, Lizzie got more shillings out of the kist and bought their tickets for Whifflet, not indulging in the luxury of seats for this part of the journey, which would only be an hour or so.

Part Three

Whifflet

CHAPTER TWENTY-FOUR

Arriving in Hell

In this strange land, this uncouth clime

The MacGregors spilled out of the train at Whifflet into a world Uncle Archie could never have described adequately.

The sulphurous fumes filled Lizzie's lungs and made her cough. A hot day in Hades, Lizzie thought. The twins screwed up their noses at each other, and Jamie nudged Donnie.

"Did you do that, ye wee stinker?" They laughed and started to punch each other, till Annie called to Father to intervene.

The buildings were black with sooty grime, and the people's faces smeared with the same dirt.

"Hozier Street? Ou-aye! It's jist a hop, skip, and a jump frae here," said the porter. Welcome tae Coatbridge." He surveyed their meagre belongings with a jaundiced eye.

"Is this not Whifflet?" her father asked.

"Ou-aye! This wee bit is Wheeflet and yon wee bit up there is Roseha' and ower there is Langloan. We call the whole lot Coatbridge. And nane o' it is too fancy."

Yes, he knew Jessie but didn't know if she had room for any more lodgers. That daft brother of hers directed every teuchter to Whifflet that got off the Stirling train at Glasgow.

Lizzie took charge of Archie, who was still burning with fever, as they trudged the last few hundred eager yards up the gentle incline from Whifflet

151

Station to Hozier Street to find Jessie, hoping she would be willing and able to accommodate them.

Black smoky fog hung in the air. Over her shoulder, she could see the source of the pollution. Great chimneys belched sooty clouds into the foul air, burned her eyes, and blotted out buildings in the near distance. She covered the baby's face loosely with his blanket and her own mouth and nose with her apron to prevent breathing in the solid black flecks floating in the haze.

"Surely it is not like this all the time? How do the folk breathe?" her mother said.

But Lizzie remembered Uncle Archie's warnings.

"Och! That means there's a lot of works nearby. We'll get jobs in no time at all." Pa tried to put a good face on it.

"It must be round the corner," chorused the twins.

Above the thunder, grinding, and explosions of the furnaces battering their ears from every direction, they heard the lighter sound of metal striking metal.

They entered a wide, cobblestone close with a sign above it that read "D. B. MILLS & SON." In smaller print it said, "Blacksmith. Horseshoeing and General Jobbing." Huge horses were tied up in the courtyard, and the blacksmith could be seen through the open door as he hammered on a horseshoe; sparks flew off his anvil. Pa tried to get his attention while he held back the boys, who were straining to get closer to the operation.

"Ou-aye! Jessie Macleod lives up they stairs. Do ye have business with her?" said the smithy.

"We need a place to stay." Pa said.

Lizzie studied the man for some sign that this might not be an impossible request. He was noncommittal.

"Ye'll have to ask Jessie. Jessie?" he yelled up the stairs.

"What is it, Davie?" A large-bosomed woman, her head wrapped in a scarf and wearing a flowered apron, came to the landing and took in the situation at a glance. "I suppose ye met Angus Macleod in Gleska. That brither will be the death of me. They are hanging aff the rafters in here already. Come on up. Ye can stay the night. Sixpence each and that includes purritch. Most of ye will be on the floor. Oor Angus must think I've got a castle here."

"Put yer wheel-cart in here for the night. Could use a wee bit fresh grease to the axle, I think," said Davie.

Pa tried to show his gratitude for the kindness. "Maybe I can repay ye with bit of work."

"No bother at all. Jist take me a wee minute. Ye'll find paying work here. They're needin' workers at the Rosehall pit, up at the top o' Whifflet Street. How old are yer lads?"

"We're almost eleven." Jamie said.

"What kind of horses are they?" Donnie wanted to know.

"They're Clydesdales, Lad. Best draught horses around. You boys will get work . . . and both o' you lassies too. Yer wife can stay home an' put her feet up."

Lizzie's glance at the smithy's face revealed he was kidding. Ma couldn't go to the pit. There would be plenty for her to do—of course, both men knew that.

Lizzie gave the baby back to her mother. "He's awful hot, Ma."

"Aye, I know."

Jessie showed Lizzie how to use the water closet at the head of the stairs, then Lizzie instructed the rest of the family on this modern marvel.

It was nightfall when they got settled. The weary travellers almost fell asleep over their porridge. Every inch of available space was taken up in the two-room house. One of the hole-in-the-wall beds was for Jessie. She offered them the other, and the men went into the back room to make the best of it with six other lodgers who rolled in at all different hours, and made pallets on the floor with their extra clothing.

Jessie let wee Kate crawl in behind her to make more room in the bed that Ma, Lizzie, Annie, wee Archie, and another woman and her bairn occupied. The overcrowding was bad enough, but the noise from the town was a shock that Lizzie, used to the peace of Rannoch, could barely tolerate. The blasting woke her and the others at regular intervals. Lizzie was amazed that Jessie slept through it. How could anyone get accustomed to that din?

She crawled out of bed in the night, sweating from the unaccustomed heat and the close quarters and went to the fancy outhouse with the pull chain. She had no trouble finding her way, for the sky was lit up at regular intervals from the nearby chimneys shooting flames high into the night sky. Instead of climbing back into the crowded bunk, she found herself an old over-stuffed chair in the corner, which turned out to be more comfortable than the bed full of thrashing and flailing arms and legs.

Her father was up and gone before dawn. She saw him leave quietly with a purposeful set to his jaw. She pretended to sleep. There was no way for her to assist him or even get him a bite to eat in this unfamiliar house.

He came back as the church bells chimed six, filthy with coal dust. Yes, they were hiring at the Rosehall pit. He was starving. He had worked all day without food . . . and very little water. He needed to carry a billy-can to drink from to get a cup from the water boys down in the pit.

CHAPTER TWENTY-FIVE

Work For All—
And Plenty O't

And, in the narrow house o' death,
Let winter round me rave;
And the next flow'rs that deck the spring
Bloom on my peaceful grave!

The good news Pa brought was that a house had just become available in the miners' rows. He told her mother to go up the hill to the Rosehall Rows. Their new house was in the Back Row.

"It's right next to the pit," he said.

Next morning Jessie let them borrow an old pram to put Archie and Kate in to climb Whifflet Street to Rosehall, the next mining village at the crest of the hill.

"Rosehall," her mother said. "What a beautiful name."

It hardly fit. The whole village, strung out from the top of a steep gradient that descended to Whifflet, seemed to be nothing more than an extension of the pithead. There was neither a rose nor a hall anywhere that Lizzie could see, just four rows of low-roofed, single-story narrow cottages, strung together in ascending steps along the flagstone walkway. The red-bricked fronts were blackened with soot and streaked where the rain poured freely down the walls, which had no roof gutters. Lizzie called to the twins to stay on the paving stone out of the street, which smelled foul and was slippery with slops thrown from the doors of the houses, doors that were only about six paces apart. Women and children stood on the single doorsteps or peered through windows. Their impassive faces scrutinized the new arrivals.

Their new home was "tied" to the job Pa had explained when he left for work before dawn. The mine owner, a Mr. Addie, was their landlord. He'd come by at the end of the week to collect the rent. "I'll have a pay-packet by then, so don't worry," he told Ma. He slipped and said that the "laird" would inspect the house at that time. Lizzie saw a shadow pass across her mother's face. Once again they were vulnerable to the good graces of another type of "lord," a landlord and Pa's boss.

"Hullo! Are you the new tenants? I'm Maggie Maclure. We live on the Front Row. This is my son, Wullie." The woman, with a shopping basket over her arm and a black shawl covering her hair, seemed to be headed down the hill on a mission.

The young man stuttered a "howdyedo," doffed his cap, and stared at Lizzie. She ignored his attention, as she was busy with the effort of keeping the younger ones out of the mud and pushing the pram up the steep incline. He had grime on his skin and clothes, but so had everyone else she had seen so far. His cap and the coal dust obscured his features, but his strong build and white-toothed smile were not lost on Annie, who ogled him unabashedly.

Maclure, Lizzie thought. Now there's a name I've heard before, but where?

"Ur ye goin' tae live in McGivern's auld hoose?" he asked in the coarse accent she heard everywhere.

Both girls shrugged. They didn't know.

"We're the MacGregors," said her mother.

"Hullo, Mrs. MacGregor." The plump woman picked up her skirt to avoid a black puddle and stepped towards her mother. "Jist between you 'n me, and I hate tae be the one tae say it, but I'll bet that place o' the McGiverns is a sorry mess. They laid him off at the works when his cough got sae bad. He only lasted a few weeks after that. That puir old wummin moved down tae . . ." Mrs. Maclure raised her voice over a thunderous explosion that made the Highland folk jump. " . . . THE AULD MONKLAND POORHOOSE."

When it subsided, she continued. "Och! Ye'll get used tae that racket, it's just the foundries blastin'. There's half a dozen within ear-shot, aye, earshot." She laughed at her joke. "All the McGivern sons went tae America. People don't care aboot their auld folks the way we did in Ireland. Oh, by the by, a wee word tae the wise .. . women never use that privy. It's the worrld's worrst!" She held her nose and screwed up her face.

She knew the woman was only trying to be helpful, but Lizzie was becoming more discouraged by the minute. She'd never seen anyplace as barren or foul smelling as this. The east wind carried an additional chemical odour that stung her eyes. Children were floating boats made of old news-paper in the sheugh, the drain that flowed down the middle of the road. Rain in the night had probably made it flow faster, carrying refuse with scraps of discarded food and brown sludge as well as the children's fragile boats to God knows where.

"When the privy gets full, they cart it off for fertilizer—about once a fortnight." Mrs. Maclure was a wealth of information.

No fancy flush toilets here. Not one.

"Then some brave carter goes in and sluices the rest doon the sheugh. They just cleaned it oot. It would be a good time for ye tae show yer lads where tae go.

"Weel, ah'm aff afore there's nothin' left at the shops." Mrs. Maclure started down the steep hill.

Lizzie accompanied her mother to inspect the disreputable outhouse. The stench of the dry toilet stopped her as soon as she turned the corner behind the First Row. It was worse than an ill-tended barn. She thought of the fancy painted chamber pot, which they would now have to use, and made a mental note to remind Ma to buy another one. They would need at least two.

Between the row houses and adjacent to the foul outhouse were mid-dens, stacked with refuse, and washhouses with copper boilers for doing laundry. Well, at least they could get their clothes clean.

Lizzie and her mother returned to the house. On the way, she noted where the pump was. Only one for all these houses and a good fifty yards from their door.

Jamie and Donnie had been invited to sail a paper boat in the drainage ditch.

"Let them be, Lizzie. We need to get to work."

Lizzie gritted her teeth and entered her new home. It was one room recently vacated by some very dirty tenants, as had been reported. She wanted to cry, but controlled herself because her mother already looked close to tears. Ma sent Annie to the store to buy carbolic soap. Lizzie and Ma threw out broken furniture and filth and swept the floor.

"Lizzie, there are still a few chunks of coal under the hole–in-the-wall beds; use them to start a fire in the fireplace and get some water boiling in the cauldron. We'll go over every inch of this place with hot water and soap."

"Aye, Ma." A rat scurried from under the bed and, fortunately made it out of the door before Ma saw it.

By the time she got a fire going, Annie returned with the soap. For once she'd hurried.

They got to work. Lizzie gagged at the malodorous human waste and spoiled food she scraped from the floor. Carbolic fumes made her choke and cough, but the job got done. After hours of sweeping and mopping they discovered that the floor was flagstone.

"Don't say anything to yer Pa about the mess this place was in. He's doing the best he can."

Lizzie's father's jaw dropped, and his eyes opened wide when he stepped inside the door of their new home. Lizzie could tell he was trying to cover his feelings at its bleakness by complimenting them profusely on fixing up the place.

"In a day or two it'll be cosy," Ma said.

Lizzie thought it would take more than a "day or two." Tearing the damned rat trap down and rebuilding it might help.

This seemed as good a time as any to tell them what she knew about Charlie. At least it would distract them. If it would please them or distress them, she wasn't sure.

"Ma, Pa, I need to tell ye something."

Both jerked their heads towards her, probably readying for more bad news. The room was silent. Even the twins stopped tussling.

"It's about oor Charlie," she said, tears coming into her eyes.

"What, girl, what?" her father said.

"He went to the colonies."

"How do ye know?" her mother almost whispered.

Lizzie told them about Charlie getting word to her through Jock. How she had to keep it secret. How Charlie wanted to protect them should the law come after him. She silenced any notions they had about Charlie going north with his cousins.

"He's gone. I just know it." Lizzie told them about the vision Charlie had nurtured since he was twelve about travelling abroad and chasing his dream.

"Where would he have gone?" said her mother.

"That I don't know, Ma."

When no one said anything, Lizzie added, "There's more. He took a package with him that came from Kate MacKay the day of the eviction."

"Why would Charlie do that?"

"It was supposed to be handed to you, Ma, but in all the confusion Charlie took charge of it. He stuck it in his jacket, then probably forgot about it. Maybe it was your birth certificate."

Her mother gave her a quizzical look. Lizzie remembered, too late, that she knew about the certificate from eavesdropping.

Ma didn't pursue it. There were more important concerns, like stretching the family's earnings so that they could eat, pay the rent, and provide some measure of comfort.

CHAPTER TWENTY-SIX

Swallowed Into the
Maw of Progress

Thou Pow'r Supreme, whose mighty scheme
These woes of mine fulfil,
Here, firm, I rest,—they must be best,
Because they are Thy will!

Every one of them who was able worked at the mine, which meant Pa, Lizzie, Annie, and even the twins. But among the five of them they made barely enough siller to put food on the table and pay rent on the house.

Ma did whatever she could to make it comfortable, but despite her best efforts it was damp, cramped, and offered little protection from the elements. One of the first things her mother did after they took up residence was reach into the kist for the siller to buy bedding: two mattresses for the hole-in-the-wall beds to replace the louse-ridden chaff mattresses left by the former inhabitants. That accommodated everyone except the twins. They shared a trundle bed that hidden from view under Ma's bed during the day. Before the cold weather set in with a vengeance, Ma purchased wool blankets to go under the quilts they'd brought from Rannoch. She was not about to allow her family to sleep on the floor on heaped straw like she saw when she peeked in one neighbour's door, she said. It might be all right with them to share the floor with vermin, but she'd come from better.

Lizzie noticed that Ma's titbits of stories about the wee croft where she was born in Lewis got grander as the gruesome new environment drained her spirit.

No question of the twins going back to school after the summer. The children's formal education had ended. What they'd learned in the Highland school would have to do; they could read and write well enough; they could add and subtract. Annie didn't seem to care about school. All she talked about was going to work in Glasgow or, at least, at a clean job where she could wear decent clothes and meet a better class of people. But it saddened Lizzie that there would be no more schooling for Jamie and Donnie. They had keen and inquisitive minds. She'd try to teach them what she knew. But with winter coming, they wouldn't see the light of day for months, for they'd leave for the Rosehall pit before sunrise and come home after sunset, too tired to care about scholarship. And lamp oil was a luxury.

* * *

Through summer and into the autumn, Lizzie and her family fell into the same routine that ordered the lives of the entire village. Wakened by the siren at six, families moved into action with one thought, to get the workers to the pit.

A half-hour before the siren blew, Lizzie awoke, stoked the fire, and threw some oats in the cauldron. She found her way around by the meagre light that the gas streetlamps spilled into the room. She sponged her body with some of the water left warming over the fire all night, then wakened Annie so she could clean up and dress before the men arose. They all supped porridge, trying to rouse themselves for the long day. Now that colder weather had begun, those growing lads needed a good breakfast in them before they headed down into that cold, damp blackness. Annie polished the boots; Lizzie wrapped food for everyone in newspaper. Usually they had bread and butter, bread and jam, or bread and cheese, but today, Ma had made pies with onion, potatoes, and a bit of meat, a special treat to carry to work to fight off the hunger and cold. Pa and the twins put their pies in a jacket pocket; the girls dropped theirs into the pocket of their aprons.

Lizzie wrapped her shawl around her layered jumper and cardigan, and stepped out into a cold drizzle. She joined the ragtag army of undisciplined soldiers, marching heads down, anticipating defeat. Each unit up and down Whifflet Street disgorged from its door its full quota of bundled-up workers.

While Pa and the twins went down the pit for twelve hours a day, Lizzie, alongside her sister Annie, sorted coal brought to the surface by pit ponies. She pitied the poor brutes, blinded by the lack of light, with sores on their haunches where the straps rubbed; they had a short, hard life. They knew her smell and nuzzled her when she led them to the area where they got a short respite and stood placidly beside her while she worked. She picked fist-size pieces of coal from the carts and threw them in a heap. These coals were prized for fireplaces and would end up in bags shipped to the better homes on the other side of town. With winter approaching she hoped the MacGregors would have enough coal to keep their house warm.

Gloves with the fingers cut out gave little or no protection. Her wet fingers froze, and she stopped frequently to swing her arms across her body to encourage the circulation. But she daren't let the gaffer see her slacking, or she'd be docked a sixpence.

The whistle blew at noon for the workers to take a break and eat. She lit a fire and warmed her billycan of water. Sometimes she had a little tea to put in it—not today. But did that pie taste good!

She renewed her efforts after lunch. Her pay fluctuated according to her output by a system she hadn't figured out yet. So far she'd had a full pay-packet only once in six months.

* * *

Lizzie looked forward to the popular Sunday walk after kirk, from Whifflet to the Old Monkland cemetery, a beautiful, peaceful place overlooking gently rolling hills. The road wound through pastoral land before it reached the well-tended grounds. Perhaps anticipating that some of them might not survive for long in this torn-up corner of God's earth, where trees and grass were replaced with packed dirt or slimy mud from the frequent rains, where filthy air and fetid water killed flowers and children, Ma bought a plot in the local burial ground. She picked out the spot, and Pa didn't object, although it was in the most expensive part of the cemetery up on a hill next to an ornate stone bearing the name "Buchanan," where there were even a few sheep grazing. Her mother imagined it was probably some cousin of the Auld Laird, and nobody tried to convince her otherwise. She said it would be grand to be buried near a family member of her respected mentor.

The subject of the Buchanans hadn't come up for a while amidst all the confusion and changes, but that Sunday Lizzie took the opportunity when they arrived back in Whifflet after their walk. The rest of the family had gone into the street to "neighbour," leaving Lizzie alone with her mother and the wee ones and the responsibility of getting dinner ready.

"Ma, ye have such respect for the Auld Laird, I hate to bring this up, but don't ye ever get angry about him not leaving things so that we could have stayed on?"

"Aye. But it wasn't his doing. He would never have hurt me. He was sworn to help me . . ." Her mother took Lizzie's chin in her hand and smiled into her eyes. "Ye've known there's more to it, haven't ye?"

"I wondered, Ma." Lizzie could feel the excitement grow inside her. Would her mother resolve the mystery? "I heard Mrs. Buchanan and Mary talking about you that time I went to the big house. They were vicious."

"Aye, no doubt, but they had it all wrong . . . put salt in those tatties, Lizzie. When Charlie Buchanan brought me frae Lewis he was performing a kindness to a wounded soldier of his clan . . . my father, James Buchanan."

"O-o-o-oh!" Lizzie tipped too much salt in the pot.

"Aye. When you heard them talk, you were old enough to put two and two together and come up with the same suspicions that Isobel Menzies always held . . . that I was Charles Buchanan's bastard."

"Ma!"

"Och! I'm sure it's what they called me behind my back." Her mother took the baby Archie on her lap to soothe him. She rocked the bairn while they waited for the potatoes to cook. "He never did tell his wife the whole story. Or, if he did, she didn't believe him. Isobel suspected I was Charles's love child, and I know it was the gossip around Rannoch."

"Why didn't the laird tell the whole story?"

"Out of loyalty to a fellow Buchanan. Telling the whole story would mean revealing that my father was a deserter."

"No!"

"Listen, Lizzie, my father was an honourable man in a dishonourable fight. He served in the same regiment as Colonel Charles Buchanan. My father took a bullet in his thigh, which they removed in an army hospital over there in France in the Napoleonic War. But he never fully recovered, not for the rest of his life. They ordered him back into active duty anyway. But he'd had time to think in that foreign hospital, while death hovered over him. He was a boy when he enlisted, but he grew into a man."

"Ma, isn't dinner near ready?" Jamie stuck his head into the room.

"Aye, son. Call the others. We'll have to discuss this later, Lizzie."

"Does Pa know?"

"He knows that much, lass."

* * *

Lizzie sat by the fire with her parents after the others had gone to bed.

"Rob, Lizzie and I talked today about my father."

"Ou-aye. Time she learned her ancestry. We're proud of his story, no matter what the English care to call him. I think the Sassenachs have contrived a way to rid Scotland of the troublesome Highlanders . . . for that's what they've always thought of us. Used us for soldiers in their struggles to expand their empire. Your grandfather saw that first-hand. We all know that Scots' blood is shed first in their wars. Some of the glens were emptied of young men in those days."

Lizzie sat on the three-legged stool to be close to her mother and out of the draught from the ill-fitting door. Ma picked up the story. "Murdoch MacKay, Kate's father, served with my father over there and had a minor injury in the same battle. He and my father watched, day by day, their Highland regiment passing through that gory hospital ward . . . dead and dying, maimed and bitter. The fearless Highland warriors were always killed disproportionately to the English. Murdoch told me their regiment was just cannon fodder."

Lizzie nodded in sympathy.

Flora continued, a catch to her voice. "The war lost its glory for those young men. My father refused to lead any more of his country-men into certain death. As soon as Papa could walk, he left the bat-tlefield to the English and escaped with some of his Highlanders. He made the long, painful journey with Murdoch MacKay home to the Isle of Lewis."

"What happened to him then, Ma?"

"He had to hide out there for the rest of his life. The English consid-ered him a deserter. Charlie Buchanan told me all I know about him."

Her father covered her mother's hand with his rough, coal-ingrained one. "Colonel Buchanan was in Lewis on some family business when he ran into Flora's father, a poor crippled soldier from his regiment. As a fellow Buchanan, the colonel promised your grandfather that he would do what he could for your mother and brought her and Kate back to Rannoch. If he hadn't, I would never have met your mother." He picked up her hand and held it against his lips.

Lizzie wondered how she had never heard any of this story before. When did Ma and Pa have their private moments to discuss all this?

"Then your father, my grandfather, met my grandmother there, right, the one I'm named for?"

"Aye. He married Elizabeth MacKay MacDonald, kin of Murdoch. And two years later, in 1816, I was born. I never knew her."

Her mother stayed quiet for a while.

"Then what happened to my . . .uh . . .grandfather?"

"He refused to set eyes on me because he'd lost his Elizabeth. So Mur-doch MacKay's family raised me. They always called me 'the wee MacDon-ald lass' after my mother, their kin. Aye, it prevented any questions arising about my father, I suppose."

"I'm sorry, Ma." Lizzie thought how awful it must have been to grow up without loving parents.

"No, no, lass. They were all kind to me." Flora smiled. "When the colonel brought me to the mainland, he thought I should go on using the name 'MacDonald' . . . no point stirring up any old resentments among those that have different loyalties than we do. Anyway it always felt right."

Pa nodded in agreement. "But for a simple soldier's daughter, yer Ma had opportunities for education and refinement not usual for our class. We have tae thank the colonel for that."

"Aye. That's why her ladyship and Mary resented me, because the laird favoured me. Och! He did what he could. We always had a bit extra to make life easier. I liked the simple life anyway . . . and, of course, there was Robert MacGregor . . ."

Her father leaned over and kissed his wife on the forehead. Lizzie noticed how tired she looked. Had it been the emotional conversations of today, or was her mother's health failing?

Lizzie prayed her mother's purchase of the cemetery plot didn't portend more disaster. Did her mother think she would be the next to go?

Lizzie continued to worry about her mother but could do little to help her. Ma had her hands full taking care of little Kate and baby Archie, especially Archie, who never really got over the chill he got on the road to Tyndrum that weakened his lungs. At night Archie woke often with a harsh cough, and Ma sat up with him by the fire feeding him a syrup she'd made with herbs brought from Rannoch in her kist.

* * *

Her fears for her mother were unfounded; in the end it was Archie they buried on a blustery day in November '60, two months before his first birthday . He had been a hardy wee soul though, holding on for months till the damp from the water that trickled down the inside walls of their single-room house got to him.

Lizzie could hear her mother rocking in the night by the open fire. She'd moan softly, "Archie, Archie" then "Charlie, Charlie," and some nights she'd cry out for Gregor.

Kate was taken with pneumonia and they feared she wouldn't last the winter. Her mother screamed, "Take me back to Rannoch, Rob. This god-forsaken place is a death trap for bairns."

Lizzie thought Ma might lose her mind from grief, but she knew her mother was right about the deadly living conditions. Many were buried from the rows, dead from consumption, cholera, typhus—any manner of fevers. Coffins made their way to the Old Monkland cemetery with persistent and frightening regularity.

If only they could get a better house. Trying to keep this place barely habitable used every last ounce of her mother's energy. Lizzie learned that having so many members of the family employed at the pit might make them eligible for a two-room house in the Middle Row. But dare she push for a better house? She couldn't afford to get fired.

* * *

She'd have to go through Peter Shanks, the pit manager, whose reputation for cruelty and lack of common decency or pity she'd heard discussed by the colliers. The gossip was that Peter Shanks had recently arrived in Coatbridge from Fife, in the east of Scotland, by way of Glasgow University. His engineering degree and his air of confidence impressed the local ironmasters and pit owners who owned this town. This minister's son liked to quote biblical passages to support his harsh decisions. Lizzie became the object of his unwelcome attention when he caught her stroking one of the pit ponies, giving it a nibble of her bread crust. She still had ten minutes left of her break when he accosted her.

"If you've finished eating, get back to work."

"My time isn't up. I was just petting old Floppy," Lizzie said, and then bit her tongue. The men loved to make crude jokes.

She thought she might be safe from any of Shanks' salacious remarks, covered in coal dust as she was. But he raised his eyebrows in a seductive way.

"Come over here, girl. I'll give you something to pet that isn't floppy." He dodged and weaved towards her in a dance that must have been his idea of scaring or taunting her.

Some of the men in the area laughed. Tears of humiliation stung her eyes. She moved away from his penetrating gaze as soon as she dared.

He had carte blanche to deal with the labourers as he saw fit, as long as the owners made a profit and the loss of life didn't become notorious.

The workers called him names behind his back; the kindest of these was "Fifer." To his face they were more respectful—out of fear.

Shanks' appearance was almost handsome; some of the other girls harboured romantic notions about him. His tall, spare frame gave him a youthful appearance. But his narrow face had a pinched look and typically displayed a sardonic grin.

After that incident she was leery of approaching Shanks in case he might consider her openness an approval of his disgusting teasing.

* * *

When Kate died in December, they took the bairn to The Old Monkland Cemetery to Flora's plot. Lizzie's heart-broken mother stayed in the wall bed for a week afterwards through the dismal New Year's Day of 1861. Father tried to comfort her but he seemed to be sinking into melancholy himself.

Lizzie had to do something. She dreaded bringing herself to Shanks' further attention, but finally got up the courage to approach the feared pit manager with her request.

At his office she was told that Shanks had left for two months to settle some disruptions at another pit. When he returned in February, in the bitterest winter she had ever known, Lizzie decided that in spite of the risk of his lechery, she had to try for a better house. That noxious place they lived in had killed her brother and sister. If they could just get a bigger house, two rooms with space to breathe. She decided she would keep after him, be a nuisance, and hound him to find her family a house in the Middle Row.

* * *

Lizzie pondered what she knew of this man who held their lives up for ransom. If, indeed, he helped them, she hoped she could avoid any propositions he might feel were his due. He was the personnel manager for several pits and foundries in the area, so he showed up at Rosehall only for a week at a time, and then he travelled on to toy with the lives of hundreds of other folk just like herself. If he didn't respond now, she might not see him for weeks.

At dusk, when she got off her shift, she went to his office to beg.

"Hullo." Shanks' greeting was loaded with insinuating invitation.

"Mr. Shanks, ye know ye promised my father, Robert MacGregor, last year ye'd put his name on the list for a two-room house."

Peter Shanks' expression altered in a second.

"Please, Mr. Shanks, we can't survive in that cramped space . . . my wee sister and brother . . ." she trailed off.

His screwed-up face was suddenly ugly as he pushed past her—closer than was necessary. He opened the door and gestured for her to leave.

"'Blessed are they that mourn: for they shall be comforted,'" he said and closed his door behind her.

So he knew about her family's tragedy, and didn't give a damn. So why should that surprise her? He was just mouthing platitudes. She stood in the hallway thinking, *the devil can cite scripture for his purpose.* The familiar quote ran through her mind. Was it Shakespeare? Yes, "The Merchant of Venice." She hadn't had a chance to read a book since she got to this place. She longed for a quiet hour to read, or just be alone with her thoughts. An extra room to go to for a bit of privacy would be blissful. One more, somewhat selfish, reason to pursue her objective.

* * *

Pa came home a few nights later and mentioned a house in the Middle Row that was coming empty. "I wonder if we're near the top o' the list yet."

The next day Lizzie arose before the others and scrubbed herself in cold water till the lamplighter extinguished the gas lamp across the street and she had to fumble around in the dark to dry herself. She threw more coal on the fire and had a hearty blaze going by the time Annie awoke. Her sister felt around the floor in the half-light for the men's boots and began to spit-polish them amid muffled curses.

"Why do I have to do the boots?" She asked the same question every morning. "You think you're going to get yourself out of this dump by snaring a rich man. Don't you, Lizzie?"

Lizzie hesitated in the middle of combing out her hair. "What?"

"Peter Shanks—you think you have a chance with him. Don't you? Didn't take you long to forget Jock Campbell."

Lizzie slapped her sister across the face and stormed out the door.

CHAPTER TWENTY-SEVEN

The Job Interview

All hail, Religion, maid divine!
Pardon a muse sae mean as mine

Lizzie was on the verge of tears all day. To be so cruelly reminded of Jock, when each and every day she struggled with the sorrow of his loss. It was a constant effort to try to disregard the painful recurring thoughts of her hopeless love for her Highland troubadour. And now she had to put on a brave front in order to meet head-on this uncaring man who held sway over her family's future. "A chance with him!" How wrong could her stupid sister be? Lizzie despised him.

With his bowler hat perched on his head and an umbrella serving as a walking stick, Shanks walked out of his office and practically collided with her.

"Mr. Shanks, I heard there might be a house coming available in the Middle Row. Wullie Maclure told my Pa. He said you mentioned it to him at the Big Tree Bar."

He stared at her. It was very unusual for anyone male or female to question his decisions.

"He did, did he? Ye find yon Maclure to yer liking? He jabbers about ye nonstop when he's had a few."

Lizzie gaped.

"C'mon, lass. Would ye no like tae spend some time with a man who, at least, has a clean face?" He cocked an eyebrow. "Yer lookin' very nice today, Miss MacGregor."

"Please, Mr. Shanks. My parents are getting old before their time in that place."

"Sorry. Spirited and bonny, though ye may be," he chuckled, "there are people ahead of you on the list."

Shanks was toying with her, dismissing her. She swallowed her pride. He was well aware of the death rate in Rosehall. She bet he'd never actually walked into one of their filthy row houses.

"That awful hovel—" she started.

He nodded gravely in her direction. "'Blessed are the meek for they shall inherit the earth.'"

"We're not asking for the world . . . just enough to eat and a decent place to live," she said.

"'If any would not work, neither should he eat.'"

"There's five MacGregors workin' here in the pit, so we should be eligible for a bigger house."

"Eligible, is it?" he hooted, pushing his bowler hat back off his forehead, creating an air of informality, he tried his hand again at flirtation again. "Do ye know any more big words like that—and can ye spell it, lass?"

"Of course."

She watched his eyes following her unconscious gesture as she blew the curl back off her forehead. "And tell me, can ye write them a' doon?"

"That I can." She gave him her unwavering stare, determined that this circuitous talk would not help him to avoid the issue.

"Mr. Shanks, can ye not tell me one way or the other, . . . sir?" She feigned respect.

"Not often pit lassies are so bonny." He leered at her for what seemed an eternity, then began to rifle through his desk.

She held her breath.

"Here, lass. Fill out this form wi' yer request."

It was needless, really. He had the power to move families in and out of those rows at will. He must have another reason.

Lizzie looked at the blank sheet of paper and the arrogant smile on the manager's face. She supposed that if he got it in writing, it would go to his superior. Maybe. She wrote formally and in a neat hand:

March 20th 1861

Dear

Inasmuch as the MacGregor family has five able-bodied workers employed at Rosehall pit, I, Elizabeth MacGregor, do hereby appeal to management to give immediate consideration to our request for larger accommodation for our family.

I respectfully await your response.

Yours sincerely,

Elizabeth B. MacGregor.

"I left a space at the top of the page. How should I address this?" she asked.

He hunched over, stroked his chin, and nodded, wrinkling his forehead. She'd once seen Mr. Addie using this same expression when talking to Shanks.

"Never mind about that. I'll see it gets to the proper authorities. 'The Lord works in mysterious ways,'" he said, avoiding her resolute gaze. "Come back tomorrow."

Next day she awoke even earlier and left the house, clean and groomed, before Annie arose.

She was on his office doorstep before daybreak.

"Oh, Miss MacGregor. I am verra glad you came back," he hailed her an hour later. He'd never called her that before. All the girls at the pit head were addressed by their first names if not by, "Hey you, lassie."

"I have permission to give your family the next available but and ben, which is a two-room mansion in the Front Row, <u>near</u> the Maclures."

She ignored his insinuation. The Maclures? Annie would be pleased. She'd taken a fancy to Wullie Maclure. Lizzie had seen him all summer walking past her house, staring in. Her family had a nodding acquaintance with the Maclures, but not time for much more than that. The Front Row looked out onto the street. She could hardly believe her luck.

"Miss MacGregor?" Shanks interrupted her reverie.

"Thank you, s-s-sir," she remembered her manners and added a wee bit more for good measure. "I appreciate your kindness, sir."

He nodded slowly and smiled like a pastor offering a blessing. The pompous ass didn't even doubt her sincerity.

"We are always willing to help people with bairns. Jesus said, 'Suffer the little children to come unto me . . .'" He was beginning to sound like the Reverend MacKenzie from Rannoch.

Enough! His slathering sanctimony made her gorge rise. "'But who so shall offend one of these little ones which believe in me?'" Lizzie quoted. "'It were better for him that a millstone were hanged about his neck, and that he were drowned in the depth of the sea.'"

She watched him recoil, and she tucked away the knowledge that this bully was also a coward.

He squared his shoulders and harrumphed, seeming to collect his composure. "Management has decided to offer you different employment." He leered at her, causing her confidence and enthusiasm to evaporate again. There was so much at stake. Had she pushed him too far? Her apprehension mounted. She knew he could and would fire her without hesitation. Instead he walked around her, eyeing her from every angle, smiling that tight little smile that never quite reached his eyes.

"We need more office help in Mr. Addie's foundry where I travel to. Where I spend most of my time. You would have to take up lodgings there. That's not a problem . . . I'll be glad to arrange something for you."

So that was the bargain. He'd have her near him for thinly disguised reasons.

". . . and you're offered the job. It will be more money . . . not much, mind you. It will cover your expenses. What do ye say?"

She recognized right away that this was highly irregular. These jobs were given to <u>men</u> who had completed some college courses.

"I can't leave my mother with the whole burden and move to lodgings, Mr. Shanks." Would he withdraw the house offer now? She felt regret tinged with relief.

He practically spat out his frustration. "You teuchters stick together like glue. Ye all look and sound the same—dirty, whining bunch of savages. I thought you were different; yer spirit and eloquence intrigued me. And to think the trouble I took to persuade Mr. Addie to hire a woman."

The silence in the room became palpable till Shanks spoke, though he seemed to be talking to himself. "Och, maybe he's as tired as I am of the sight of those bespectacled, bald-headed clerks every day . . . and for half the price of that row of dull, sickly-lookin' bores." He sighed as though convincing himself of his own argument. "And I thought they could use a lass to work in the office at Motherwell. Bright, responsible lassies are hard to find. It would dress the place up a . . ."

"Motherwell. Motherwell? How far is that?" Lizzie forgot herself and interrupted him.

The vague recollection of a conversation flashed across her memory. Where had she heard of that town before? Yes! John Campbell had told her father on that long cold night on Rannoch Moor. "My lads and me will get work in Motherwell." That's when she'd heard the name Maclure mentioned. Was this Maclure one of Jock's relations? How common was the name?

"About five miles," he said.

"I could take the train."

She ignored his grunt of disappointment. Jock might be a short train ride away. Yes. I have to go there. She felt hope fill her chest and lost her caution with this monster.

"How much more money?" She couldn't believe she'd just said that.

His eyes opened wide. "Well, how much more will ye need?"

"Ma sister, Annie, will have to work less hours at the pit to take up the slack at home." She did the mental arithmetic. "A shilling a day more would make it work."

He made a pious bow to her. "'Ask, and it shall be given unto you.'"

She stared directly into his eyes, not bothering to hide her disdain. "Goodbye, Mr. Shanks."

How much would she have to see him in this new office? She was savvy enough to recognize when a man wanted her. The thought of his coming near her made her flesh crawl. Motherwell . . . that's where Jock's family went. She was sure of it now. She deliberately shrugged off any qualms. There was a chance she might find the Campbells. She might find Jock. She started to hum "The Campbells are coming Ho-Ro, Ho-Ro!" and giggled at herself.

She was practically skipping down Whifflet street to the but and ben when she almost collided with Wullie Maclure, coming in the opposite direction from the foundry.

"Lizzie." He tipped his cap.

"Wullie." When Lizzie slowed down, he stopped immediately and turned to face her.

"In a hurry as usual?" She heard the defeat in his voice. Was she, rather than Annie, the reason Wullie always stared into their house? Maybe Peter Shanks was serious about Wullie's interest in her. If so, then too bad for him. She'd never intended to encourage suitors here in Whifflet, and certainly not now!

"No. Well, yes I am. Just got a new job in Motherwell and can't wait to tell my folks."

"Oh, Motherwell." He sounded disheartened. "Will ye be movin' there, then?"

"I hope not. I think I can take the train there and back every day."

"Is that right? Ye make it sound like it's just round the corner. There's a train every day to there now?"

"Aye. Have ye ever been on it?"

"No, but my mother has some family from up your way that was supposed to move there." Lizzie drew in a sharp breath. "If they've added passenger service now, maybe they'll come and see us."

"Wullie, was their name Campbell or Stewart?"

"Campbell. Did ye know them?"

Lizzie threw her arms around him and squealed. "They were our next door neighbours in Rannoch."

Wullie blushed and stammered, "Aye, Rannoch, that's where they hailed frae."

"I have tae tell my folks." She ran on past him to her own door, then called back, "Have ye heard from them? Do ye know where they're staying?"

Wullie just shook his head and stood rooted to the spot.

The news about the Campbells and about an impending move to a better house seemed to hearten her mother, and Annie was only too glad to work fewer hours at the pithead, which she hated. She would maybe even get a different job, like Lizzie had, which was what she wanted to do anyway.

* * *

Lizzie had not been beyond the town of Coatbridge since they arrived in Whifflet two years before. Nobody from the rows travelled far or knew much about any place beyond Coatbridge—or even beyond the villages of Whifflet and Rosehall. Money for travel, and the free time to do it, was in short supply to the mine workers.

Now that she worked in an office setting, she dressed in decent clothes that didn't have to get boiled and washed once a week. Her mother found a few shillings for her out of the kist, and Annie accompanied her to Bank Street to Mrs. Purdie's Ladies Emporium.

Annie wanted to make a good impression on the owner, for she saw her future in the fashion trade, she said. Annie did all the trading in her most polite, professional manner. "My sister needs a dress for office work; a Lindsey material, perhaps, in a dark, practical colour."

"How tall are ye?" Mrs. Purdie appraised Lizzie.

"She's about five foot tall, bust thirty–four, waist twenty-two, and hips thirty-six," said Annie. Lizzie had to smile at her sister's efficiency. She was surprised that Annie remembered these details from helping her let out their church dresses this year.

Her sister certainly had a flare for colour and design and helped her pick out a pretty forest-green dress. The collar and cuffs were trimmed with cream Ayrshire lace that could be removed to be washed and starched. Lizzie viewed the effect in the mirror and noted proudly how well it fit and how the deep green matched her auburn tresses. The tangle was combed out of her wild curly hair and it had a sheen to it now —thanks to Miss Mary's silver comb.

Mrs. Purdie was so impressed with Annie's assistance that she asked her to help out on Saturdays.

"Your career in fashion is on its way," Lizzie teased.

Annie missed the sarcasm. "Aye, some MacGregors will come up in the world . . . you wait and see."

Dressed in her new finery, and without the coal dust, Lizzie caught the eye of passing males. They flirted with her on the train and in the office. Lizzie knew how to give them an air that, except to an absolute oaf, let them know how far they could go. She had neither the time nor interest to take up with any of them and after the first week the clerks and businessmen talked in their own huddles and eyed her occasionally.

Motherwell wasn't so far away after all, nor was possibility of finding out what happened to the Campbells. Could Jock have been only five miles away all this time? She scanned the main street each day on her way to work from the station for a glimpse of any of the Campbells. But once at work, she had to devote her energy to the job and learn the receptionist duties.

Today, as usual, she was first to arrive at the office building; she rubbed her sleeve automatically on the brass plaque with the ominous inscription "Head Office" to polish the already gleaming sign and opened the heavy, gray office doors. She set about lighting a fire in the open grate and went outside to the pump to fill a kettle, which she placed on the modern gas ring Shanks had ordered installed recently. The tea would be ready when the others arrived at eight o'clock. She filled the inkwells and made sure all the pens had fresh nibs. She changed the blotting paper, estimated the paper each clerk would need for the day, and placed it on his desk.

Mr. Addie's operations were the major employment in Motherwell, so her best chance to track down the Campbells was right here. Surely one member of that large family was in his employ, but a week had passed without seeing one of them.

Finished with the morning's preparations, she used the remaining time alone to search the employee records. They revealed many Campbells, but none with "Jock" or "John" or "Sandy" or "Aleck" as first names.

She, very casually, asked the clerks, if any of them had heard of anyone by that name in the town, to no avail. Discouraged, she gave up. They must have gone someplace else or moved on from here soon after their arrival.

CHAPTER TWENTY-EIGHT

Unwelcome Suitor

I'm o'er young, I'm o'er young,
I'm o'er young to marry yet!
I'm o'er young 'twad be a sin
To tak me frae my mammie yet.

Lizzie took the train every day, six days a week, to Motherwell. Shanks maddeningly dangled the reward just out of their reach for over a year, until the MacGregors finally did get their two-room house in the summer of 1862.

Lizzie was satisfied—for a time.

But, Peter—he insisted she call him Peter—began asking her to take notes. She sat as far from him as she could and scampered to her own desk as soon as he finished, before he could say, one more time, "So when are ye goin' tae step out wi' me?"

Lizzie had so far pretended to believe he was joking and laughed it off. How much longer could she spurn him without provoking his ire?

Sometimes he followed her to her desk and would "assist and advise" her with his arm casually draped around her shoulder. Though it offended her, she felt relatively safe, since she shared the back office with the prim, silent clerks. Nevertheless, Shanks' unwelcome attention only deepened her loneliness and reminded her that she might never see Jock again. Instead, she might have to spend her life tolerating louts like Shanks.

Soon, Shanks began asking her to compose letters by herself, letters to lawyers or contractors—work he should have been doing. She often heard him taking personal credit for her work and her ideas.

Within six months she began to help with the accounting, and informally took over the supervision of the office before the end of the year. Emboldened by her job success, Lizzie resolved to ask Shanks for more money. With winter approaching, her father could no longer do overtime in the bone-chilling pit. He was doing more than a man his age should be doing and was wearing himself out fast. She wanted to make up the difference in the family's income and add to what her brothers brought home.

* * *

Lizzie felt the gravity of her mission that cold November day. The 7:05 train steamed into the Whifflet station and swallowed the dark, bundled up passengers; the whistle blew and the engine chugged into action. She sat across the carriage from a pair of clerks identically dressed in dark suits, high stiffly starched collars, and bowler hats. The three often shared the same carriage, and the routine was always the same. The men generally talked to each other in a low murmur. She'd see them casting glances in her direction and looking away quickly should they catch her eye. In the past she had wondered: Are they scheming and hatching ways to better themselves in the respective organizations they serve? Do they resent me, a country girl, going to an office job? Are they attracted to a young woman travelling alone but trying to pretend disinterest? But she had long ago given up speculation as to their motives and simply nodded and wished them a good morning. Today, Lizzie didn't care about anything except the firmly rooted idea that she would get Shanks to pay her more money.

* * *

Perched on her stool, she went over the accounting she had finished yesterday and checked for errors. She was amazed to see the profits that derived from coal mining. At first she had wondered, where did it all go? It did not take her long to figure out that most of it went into the pockets of the owners. Peter Shanks was invaluable in keeping wages down and the colliers' housing expenses to a minimum. Workers came in to the office from time to time to see him and make requests about changing shifts, getting a day off for a christening or a funeral or, heaven forbid, requesting more money. He had a stock answer to any request: "No."

She was deeply involved in her ledgers when the rest of the staff came in, stomping their feet from the cold outside.

"Is the tea ready, Miss MacGregor?" Shanks poked his head into the back office.

He must be in a good mood, she thought. This early he usually called her name in his grumpy morning voice. Today would be the day to present her request.

"Here's your tea, Mr. Shanks . . . uh . . . Peter. May I talk with you later today?"

"I'm free now." The arched brows, the slanted smile, the flourish when he held the door for her, were as familiar as the arm around the shoulder that she, as usual when she was alone with him, shrugged off.

"What would you like to talk about? Do you have problems you haven't told me about, Lizzie?" His silky voice, in contrast to the yelling and cursing she often heard when he talked to the workmen, warned her that he was inviting intimacy and would attempt again his clumsy efforts to inveigle her into a tryst.

She steered him away from that with her matter–of-fact reply. "Oh no, sir, no problems to report."

Apparently recognizing he'd been rebuffed again, he assumed his gruff demeanour. "Then speak up, girl."

"You're pleased with my work, sir?"

"Ou-aye! It's all right." His voice lacked enthusiasm.

"I'm always on time."

"Aye." He gave her a questioning look.

"I stay late and finish up projects when necessary."

"Aye . . . Aye. Get to the point, Lizzie."

"I need more money."

"You what?"

"I need a raise, Mr. Shanks. I think I've earned it."

The heightened colour of his face discouraged her. She thought he was winding up to say no.

Instead, he said, "When ye get more used to yer duties and prove my good judgment to Mr. Addie in hiring ye, maybe it'll be time to ask for a raise—maybe ye'll not even need to work, Lizzie. It's time I settled down and raised a family." He spoke in a quiet, conspiratorial voice, not to be overheard by the nosy clerks.

She chose to confront the implication, even if he were simply using it as a clumsy ploy to entice her. The audacity of him presuming any kind of future with her! "Ye'll need to find a different lass, then. If my bid for an increase is predicated on anything but my good work, I'll do without."

"Predicated . . .," he sputtered. "We'll talk later."

* * *

"Miss MacGregor. Would you come in here, please."

The others had left; Lizzie had stayed to finish addressing some letters she had written. Her heart leapt to her throat. She couldn't afford to lose this job. Had she gone too far? Her timing had been all wrong.

"Here are some letters for your signature." She tried to be nonchalant.

"Aye. I'll attend to that later." He sat down behind his desk and left her standing. His hands formed a steeple, supporting his frowning face. "Ye see, Lizzie. They'd never pay a woman more than you're gettin' already."

She plopped down in the chair, crestfallen.

Then, in a silky voice: "I've been thinking, Lizzie. The postmaster says your sister is trying to get on there at the Whifflet post office. Those jobs are hard to come by."

She jerked her head up and searched his face, which had reverted to its usual cynical cast.

"Aye?" She narrowed her eyes, trying to figure him out.

"I have some influence around here; what if I put in a good word for her?"

"You'd do that?"

"Aye, any way I can help a struggling family. Is your sister more appreciative than you are?"

He'd never shown any interest in Annie in the past, when he met both of them at the pit. This was a veiled threat. Give me what I want or I'll pursue your younger sister. Annie would be fair game, too, for she was overeager for a beau and would see Peter Shanks as a superior catch. Lizzie hoped her bland smile camouflaged the trapped sensation his words provoked.

* * *

He got her sister the post office job. Annie, now seventeen, was ecstatic. It was more money than she dreamed of making, and she could still work at Mrs. Purdie's on Saturdays. When she learned that Peter Shanks had facilitated her new employment, she lorded it over her until Lizzie was sorely tempted to tell her it had less to do with Annie's charms than his malice towards her. How far would Shanks go to exact retribution from Lizzie or her family?

Lizzie assumed that the whole question of his taking advantage of Annie became moot in the early spring of 1863, when Peter was obliged to marry Sophie Dixon, the rather plain niece of the Whifflet pit owner. Miss Dixon was in the family way and quite far along. They were wed in Glasgow, away from the prying eyes of the local folk. The talk in the office gave great credit to the persuasive efforts of the enraged Mr. Dixon, who, when he learned belatedly about his niece's dilemma, had forced Peter Shanks to do the right thing or find other employment.

Lizzie congratulated Peter on his marriage and received in reply a "Harrumph."

Mrs. Shanks gave birth to a boy on an unusually hot August night. She almost died in the process and never left her bed again.

CHAPTER TWENTY-NINE

Heartfelt Reunion

But urchin Cupid shot a shaft

arlier on that particularly hot Saturday at the end of August, Lizzie was perched on the high stool by her desk, trying to ignore the bickering among the clerks, who were no doubt feeling stifled in their starched collars. She thought how glad she was that it was her half-day, when she heard a voice that made her jump and create a big inkblot all over her morning's work. She wanted to go out into the main office to identify the speaker but couldn't move from her seat. She was paralyzed with fear, joy, and anticipation.

That sweet remembered voice. Could it be? Could it be Jock? He was here in Motherwell? Had he been here all along? Why had she not been able to find him?

"Wheesht!" she practically hissed at the office staff, who obeyed, surprised by her tone. What was he saying out there beyond the thin wall?

"Who the hell do ye think ye are?" she heard Shanks say. "Ye're jist a teuchter upstart. This company has been good to you and yer lazy brothers—heathen savages that they are. Do ye think we're made o' money?

"But Shanks, you were right there when Addie suggested you put me in charge of the gang."

"You'll call me Mister Shanks and show some respect, MacGregor."

185

'MacGregor', did she hear right? It had to be Jock. Though it had been two long years since she heard it, she could never mistake his voice—but why did Shanks call him "MacGregor"?

"He might have talked about ye gettin' a different job, but Mr. Addie didn't say ye were tae get more money. There's twenty or more who'll take the job for the same money or less. Take it or leave it." Shanks was doing what he did best.

"But, Shanks, let me talk to Mr. Addie. There's been some sort of mis-understanding."

"That's enough out o' you. Misunderstanding, my arse! You're the eejit that misunderstood. Yer fired. Now get yer dirty face out o' ma sight."

The door slammed and Shanks cursed. He conveniently forgot she was there when he lost his temper.

At first Lizzie sat glued to her stool from shock. Despite an overwhelming desire to see Jock, she stayed put till she knew he had left because she did not want him to know she had overheard his humiliation.

She had trouble concentrating for the rest of the morning. No other young man had ever caused her to feel the way he had. And she suspected no other man ever would. She was light-headed at the sound of his voice. She had carried the memory of Campbell in a special place in her heart for so long, over two years, that there was a sense of unreality and consternation in his being so close. He _was_ here in Motherwell. His voice took her back to the most momentous day of her life.

Come Monday, she'd search the employee records for an address and track down the Campbells, or the MacGregors, since that was apparently the name Jock was going by, then she'd scour the town.

Her thoughts tumbled over Rannoch memories of wee Gregor and the croft and the eviction—and Jock. He was here in Motherwell! And she might lose track of him again. She was still shaking when the bell rang at quitting time.

She had to get rid of the mess she had made on the ledger and redo her work, which meant she'd have to stay late and miss the earlier train. The later train usually filled with workers; she'd have to get there as quickly as possible to avoid the crush. She had been anticipating taking her mother for an outing to the park or the shops. Ma was in poor health now. She'd just have to take her out after church tomorrow instead.

Lizzie barely had time to complete the ledger before she had to leave for the train.

Motherwell station was a familiar place to her now. Sitting on a bench reading a book, she heard that voice again.

"Lizzie, Lizzie is it really you, lass?"

Jock's intense gaze made her catch her breath. He seemed more self-assured, older, more filled out and so handsome, his blush less evident. His hair curled around the edges of his cap. He was scrubbed clean and wearing what must be his best clothes; she wondered at that. Where was he headed?

"I'm going to Whifflet. I have to find work. Ma cousin Wullie Maclure lives there somewhere. What are you doing here?"

"You won't believe this, Jock. I live there in Rosehall, the village next to Whifflet. The Maclures live a few doors down in the Front Row. I ken them well. I just found out they are your kin."

"How long have ye been there?" He was older, more self-confident and his red-gold-coloured hair sprouted out under his cap. His blue eyes were even more direct and intense than she remembered. She felt chaotic inside with disbelief, excitement, confusion and a familiar passion only Jock Mac-Gregor ignited. She tried to make small-talk.

"We came straight here the day we left the glen. I feel like such a fool. Here we have been practically neighbours for two years, nigh on."

"Why do ye live in Whifflet and work in Motherwell?"

She stammered something about her job at the mining office, omitting to tell him about the spiteful conversation she had overheard that morning.

"Jock, I've been looking for you for months. Your name wasn't in the employee files."

Jock laughed and said. "No, it wouldn't be. Pa thought it would be a good time to call ourselves MacGregor again. Ye know how he felt about bein' a Campbell, even though it was in name only."

They sat quietly together for a delicious moment. Today the hard wooden seat felt supportive and comfortable below her; the smell of cling-ing smoke that permeated the station seemed exciting, suggestive of the beginning of a journey.

When the train arrived, they got into the third class carriage "stand-ups." There was so much to talk about even though they were crushed by other standing travellers and assailled by the odour of unwashed bodies and jolted by each chug of the train building speed.

Jock was close to tears to hear about wee Kate and Archie, the bairns that couldn't thrive in Whifflet, and told her his sad news that his brother had lost a leg in a pit accident. Jimmy had a wooden leg now and a job at the pit head tending ponies.

Jock said he would stay with the Maclures till he could get a job in Coatbridge.

Lizzie was locked on to that gaze that had haunted her for two long empty years. She was totally unaware of the other passengers, till the train lurched at the Whifflet Junction and a heavy-set woman with a suckling baby practically knocked the two of them over. Lizzie was saved only by Jock's quick response to reach out and break her fall.

"Are you all right, missus?" he asked, over his shoulder, as he continued to hold Lizzie.

"Och I'm fine, son. Yer heid goes out the windy at times. I mind when I looked at oor Sandy like that an' see what it got me." She indicated the baby in her arms that burped on cue. Her remark brought peals of laughter from the other travellers. Now Jock did blush, and Lizzie felt her cheeks get hot with the realization their newfound rapture was so apparent to others.

They walked up Whifflet Street from the station, still amazed at this turn of events. "This is where the Maclures live, Jock."

"Can I see ye tomorrow?"

"Aye, come to the house after church. I'm taking Mother to the park. Ye'll have dinner with us, will ye not?"

"Who's that at the door talkin' tae the bonniest lass in Lanarksheer?" Wullie Maclure shouted out the door.

"It's me, Wullie. Yer cousin Jock from Rannoch. Lately of Motherwell," he added as an aside to Lizzie.

"Well, why'd ye no' say so. Come away ben the hoose. Where have ye been? We thought we'd never see ye."

"I have to go, Lizzie. See ye tomorrow."

She fairly floated into the house.

"Would ye look at oor Lizzie. She's got a silly grin on her face. Who was that you were coming up the hill with?" Jamie nudged Donnie.

"Jock Campbell."

"No, not Jock Campbell from Rannoch?" Her father was almost as surprised as she had been.

"The verry same." She told them about meeting him on the train and how he was now staying at his aunt's.

"Did ye ask him about oor Charlie? Did he ever see him?"

She was ashamed to admit she hadn't asked but Jock would surely have mentioned if he had any new information. Her parents still thought maybe Charlie had caught up with the Campbells or some other family from the glen on that fateful day.

"Ye can ask him yerself," she responded to her father's puzzled expression, ". . . When he comes over for dinner tomorrow."

"Oh, it's like that, is it?"

"Och, Father. I was just trying to be polite to an old neighbour."

"Right, lass. Ye get top marks for politeness."

"Oor Lizzie's that polite, isn't she, Jamie?" The twins nudged each other.

"Och! She's the most politest lady on the Rows," agreed his twin.

They would keep it up till she put herself back in charge of the situation. "Go and get cleaned up for your dinner, you two, and brush yer boots for church tomorrow."

"That's women's work. Oor Annie's supposed to scrub the boots when she gets home from work," Jamie said.

"Annie is working late at the post office. And ye know she works on Saturday for Mrs. Purdie. Ye'll just have to learn to scrub your own boots."

"Och! She's just a show-off. She acts like a toff with her new clothes and putting on that accent," said Jamie.

Lizzie had to agree that Annie vaunted her newfound status. She did act much happier now that she knew for certain she was out of the job at the pithead. But instead of showing appreciation for her new position, she swore she'd only stay at the post office for one year. She was awaiting a permanent opening at the "Fashion Emporium," as she preferred to call the dress shop.

* * *

Everyone, even Annie, helped with the preparation for the dinner to honour Jock Campbell. Ma sent her running to the butchers for beef. Jock's mother, Nellie, often cooked that in a stew for her boys. "Ye're just in time for dinner. Pull up a chair, Jock Campbell. You're the first visitor we've had from Rannoch."

"What do ye hear about the old clan?" her father asked.

Jock told them what he knew about who went up to Glencoe and who sailed abroad. They reminisced for a while. Lizzie and her father described their trek; Ma listened quietly, apparently bathed in her own thoughts.

Finally her father asked the question Lizzie knew he was bound to ask. "Did ye see anything o' oor Chairlie, Jock?"

"Och, it's a funny thing happened. We got off the paddle steamer in Greenock and our Colin says, 'See you, Pa, there is a lowland sailor over yonder; spittin' image of Charlie MacGregor from Rannoch.' And we all looked over and there was this lad slipping onto a boat. It was a great big one, ye know, the kind that crosses the ocean ..." He stopped at her mother's gasp.

"Jock, it _was_ oor Chairlie. Lizzie told us how he swore you to secrecy after he disappeared at the eviction. We've never seen our boy since."

"Aye, Mrs. MacGregor. I think it could have been Chairlie. Where would he get money for passage?"

Pa collected his wits enough to say, "Ye said 'slipping', did ye not, Jock?"

"Aye, he seemed to be sneaking onto it. I noticed that at the time."

"Charlie had no money," said Lizzie quietly. "He must have been a stowaway."

"Charlie would never do that." The twins defended their big brother's integrity. Then, "Would he?" With gathering excitement, they gaped at each other.

"Oh, yes. He would," said Lizzie in a tight, small voice that settled the argument. And they all sat quietly for a few minutes, each alone with his or her thoughts about Charlie's voyage.

Her father broke the silence. "Oor Chairlie can take care of hisself. Probably went to the Caribou and built hisself a log cabin."

"Naw. Oor Chairlie wis headed for America."

"Son, did you know that for a fact?"

"Well," said young Donald, "he said often enough he would go there when he saved enough siller for the fare. I heard him tell oor Lizzie."

"Aye, he said that often, Father," Jamie supported his brother's claim.

"He must be in America, right enough." Her mother seemed relieved to have the matter settled.

Ma had lived too long with the agony of uncertainty. Her fading glimmer of hope was reignited into a luminous beam of conviction. "Charlie'll do well. I can just imagine him in a little croft in a village on the water—someplace that resembles the shore of the Isle of Lewis. Or in a great city in America, with a fine job." Ma said, conjuring up images of her oldest son prospering in the New World, the land of opportunity.

They all began with great enthusiasm to reminisce about Charlie while Lizzie quietly revisited her grief about the loss of her twin.

"Charlie could put his hand to anything," her father said. "He might be a quiet lad, but nobody would put anything over on him. Remember yon time when he tipped that English landlord out of his fancy carriage. I thought I shoulda skelped him for that. But he was right. No point in preserving good manners with them that's out to deprive ye. Charlie wid have hated the confinement of the pit and the lack of green fields in the Wheeflet."

"He showed us how to catch rabbits," said Donnie.

"Aye, and how to skin them too and how to fleece a sheep without hurting it," his brother added.

"Charlie loved the land," her mother said. "It was a deep hurt that sent him off like that. He didn't abandon us. He did what he had to do to save himself. He's found a place to settle down and build a new life."

Lizzie's eyes locked with Jock's. She remembered his sharing the same aspiration, which had stirred her that day on Rannoch Moor—that day when she thought she'd never see him again but here he was, larger than life . . . and some day, she thought, some day I'll see Charlie, too.

"He might be a great sea captain by now, Jamie."

"Naw, he's got a wheen of cattle and sheep and a braw house." The twins were off arguing about their heroic big brother, who by now had conquered the world. Before the evening was over, Charlie MacGregor was a legend.

* * *

"I've been thinking. What if we sent letters to the post offices in all the big cities in America?" Jock said.

"That's impossible." Lizzie remembered that geography had not been Jock's best subject. "It's a good idea, but we'd need to narrow down the scale of it."

Finally managing to snatch a few precious hours to themselves, they walked south on the dirt road that led to Kirkshaws and the open fields. They had walked in silence for almost a mile before Jock suddenly stopped, placed his hands on Lizzie's shoulders, and turned her to face him.

She saw his eyes mist up. "Oh, Darlin'!" His voice was harsh, it was not a cry, nor yet a sob, it was an animal sound. She felt herself tremble. He gripped her so tightly she could hardly breathe. Then he relaxed and brought his hands to frame her face, kissing her deeply. She responded to his embrace with all the suppressed passion she had contained for so long.

He kissed her neck slowly. She didn't, couldn't resist as his mouth moved down towards her breast. His hands brushed against her bodice. Her button popped open, allowing him to slip his hand under the fabric and reach her swollen nipple. She drew in a sharp breath.

They forgot they were close by the road until they heard the jingling of a harness and drew apart. An old carter hailed them from his perch. "Ah hope ye know what yer doin', laddie. Keep yer heid or ye could get in a load o' trouble." He chuckled and snapped the reins on the horse, moving off into the evening sun before Lizzie could regain her composure.

"Whew, that was close. I forgot myself. See what ye do to me, lass."

Lizzie shook her head to clear it. "We'd better start home, Jock."

They turned back towards Rosehall, walking slowly, hand in hand, eager to prolong the magical closeness.

Jock broke the stillness. "Now where was I? Oh—about Charlie."

"Aye, maybe it was him at the wharf. We could find out where the boats sail to from there. Send letters to those places, for a start." Lizzie's felt her hope igniting again. At least she could do something.

CHAPTER THIRTY

Lovers

So fair art thou, my bonnie lass,
So deep in love am I;
And I will love thee still, my dear,
Till a' the seas gang dry.

The few trees left standing in Whifflet made a pathetic display of their autumn colours. Lizzie usually dreaded winter, but nothing could dampen her spirit that Sunday morning when she marched with her whole family down Whifflet Street, behind the Maclures. She sang right out in church—no "trained" voices here to put her to shame. She could see Jock in the pew across from her, seated with Wullie Maclure. Every time she glanced sideways, either Jock or Wullie was staring back at her with the same love-struck expression. The cousins resembled each other: same build, same lopsided smile, same alert eyes, except Wullie's were hazel and he had dark brown hair and a moustache—and Lizzie was not in love with him.

They all walked up Whifflet Street to the Rows after the service.

"Can ye come to dinner?" she asked. Both men nodded. Lizzie got flustered. This was not what she had intended. Wullie saw how they looked at each other and withdrew.

"Och! I jist remembered Sandy MacLaren said he'd be over later." He said, stepping away. "I better bide at hame."

193

Jock gave his cousin a puzzled look. Lizzie wondered if he had only just realized how Wullie envied him.

Jock smiled at her. "I'll just tell ma auntie where I'm going and come over."

They parted, and Lizzie caught up with her parents to confirm the dinner guest.

"C'mon, Ma. I promised ye a walk to Whifflet Park today. Come with Jock and me. It's a fine day."

"Och, lass, why don't ye go on ahead with Jock. I have enough to do to get a nice dinner going for later." Lizzie knew her mother was being tactful. She would bow out. All Lizzie's days had been fine since Jock showed up. Ma shared her happiness. Lizzie changed into her old shoes and waited at the door for Jock.

She saw him come out of the Maclures and heard Mr. Maclure's admonition, "Back afore dark, lad."

"Och, Uncle, I'm having ma dinner over there."

"Tatties and mince no' good enough for ye?" piped up Mrs. Maclure good-naturedly.

"Mind you, Jock Campbell, she's a well brought-up lassie. Keep yer hands tae yersel' and stay out o' the bushes." This from Wullie in a different tone.

Lizzie nipped back into the house, not wanting Jock to know what she had overheard. The twins were emptying the ashes out of the fire.

"I thought ye were going courting with Jock."

"Och, he's no daft. He got smart and changed his mind."

"Och, Jock wouldn't say he was coming and not do it."

"He doesn't have sisters like we do, or he'd stay away from them allthegether."

The twins were getting impossible to manage. At fourteen, they were too big now to have their ears cuffed.

She was rescued from more of their teasing by the knock on the door.

"I'll be back to help with the dinner, Ma." Lizzie attempted to regain her authority over her young brothers. "You two take out those ashes then get the stove going."

"Try bossing Jock around like that, and see how long he takes ye out."

"Aye, she probably smiles at him and gives him wee kisses and hugs."

Mercifully, she made her escape but tripped over the threshold in her haste. Jock's outstretched arms prevented her from falling down the two steps onto the cobbles or farther into the dirt of the street.

She squealed, then whispered, "Thank you, Darlin', for being there to catch me." She wrapped her arms around his neck and hid her face in the angle of his shoulder.

"I'll always be there to catch you, my love," he whispered into the soft abundance of her hair.

They walked without speaking for a while up the hill and over to the east towards an open field that skirted the ironworks. She still jumped in alarm at the explosions down the hill and saw Jock doing the same.

They held hands. Jock gave words to a thought that was always on her mind. "It's not like Rannoch Moor. Is it, Lizzie?"

She raised her eyes to his face; all her recent sorrows overcame her, tears spilled over, and trickled down her cheeks. Jock pulled her gently into the shelter of the lone, surviving oak tree in the open field, out of sight of the village. They were quiet, time was suspended for Lizzie. When she finally looked up and saw his adoring gaze, a sob escaped her lips. It contained all the sorrow but now, too, the joy of recovering her lost love. She responded to his rough embrace with a strangled cry and threw her arms around him. He kissed away her salt tears. They both ignored the cap that tumbled off his head.

She felt the roughness of his wool jacket, the pressure of his arms around her waist, the warmth of his body, and the way he drew her up so her feet barely touched the ground. She felt for a moment the pressure of his chest against her breasts, then all she was aware of was his kiss, which at first had a calming effect on her, like coming home. It took her back to that gentle kiss they shared on Rannoch. He tightened his embrace and kissed her deeply. She felt herself go limp; her instinctual response startled her. She was totally yielding to what might happen next, as if she were in a dream state.

Jock released her, drew in a deep choking breath, and disengaged himself resolutely from the hypnotic tangle. "Lass, I've thought about ye every day. Holding ye like this." He pushed her hair back with his trembling hand

and kissed her forehead. "I don't want to get ye in trouble. If ye'll have me, I want to marry ye as soon as I can find work here."

"Yes, Jock, yes." She closed the distance between them and raised her face to be kissed again. She had barely heard what he said. Her body had never before experienced such irresistible urgency, and she was afraid he might stop.

Her passion roused Jock to fever pitch. They hastily, clumsily, unfastened each other's clothing. Lying on the soft bed of fallen leaves she accepted his slow penetration. She was surprised by the pain that his entering her created but felt drugged by the closeness of him. He was spent in a few wild moments and collapsed beside her.

"Bonnie, bonnie lass. How I have missed ye. Oh Lizzie, ye're my own true love. Are ye all right? Did I hurt ye?"

She could not find words to express what she felt, but kept repeating his name: "Jock, Jock, Jock." She wiped her eyes with the back of her hand. "I'm fine. It did hurt some, but there had to be a first time—and it had to be with you."

"And with me for the rest of your life. I want to marry ye as soon as we can. I've always known we'd marry. You and me together . . . we can handle anything."

"Let's keep our plans secret for a wee while," said Lizzie, "It's all so new and exciting. I'm not ready to have other folk know what we share." She suddenly felt bashful about others having any hint about their intimacy.

"If that's what you want, Darlin', though I don't think we're fooling anyone." He kissed her eyelids and her still-moist cheeks, her neck, softly at first till his excitement began to grow again.

She guided him inside her, a bit tense, afraid it would again be painful, but he slipped inside her easily this time. She pushed against him, matching his passion, lost in a frenzy of mounting pleasure that carried her out of her body until the spasms jolted her. A loud moaning sound accompanied her paroxysms of bliss. It took her a moment to realize that the sound was coming from her. She wondered if the wetness on her face was fresh tears shed in their moment of profound bonding. She had been unaware of crying. Jock caressed her face, murmuring endearments.

It was well into the gloaming when their passion subsided and they reluctantly rose up from their love nest.

* * *

They struggled to regain their composure before returning to the Rows. They brushed the leaves from their clothing, making themselves respectable looking again. He untangled fragments of dried leaves and moss from her hair. "There will be enough teasing. No need to give anyone ammunition." Jock said as they approached the village hand-in-hand.

Jamie saw them first coming down the hill. "Och, look at Jock Campbell, Donnie. Oor Lizzie's making a sissy out o' him."

"Och, she'll be having him doing dishes next," said his twin.

Lizzie cast her gaze down and sauntered past them with feigned nonchalance, followed by Jock, whose crimson colouring would have betrayed them to others more observant than the twins.

"I think there was some kind of game going on up at the park when we were there," Jock said. He caught Lizzie's eye and winked. "They were having fun."

"Do ye tell me?" they chorused.

"C'mon, Jamie. Maybe we can get a game of fitba' before dinner." The twins took off running—football was their favourite.

Lizzie covered her mouth to prevent the burst of laughter.

Jock and Lizzie were still laughing when they entered the kitchen. Her mother was mashing potatoes at the stove. "Have a nice walk, did ye?"

"Aye, braw day for a walk and such, Mrs. MacGregor." Lizzie grinned at him. You couldn't fool Ma. He shrugged his shoulders behind Lizzie's mother's back.

The twins came in disappointed that there was no football game at the park.

"Och. That's too bad, lads," Jock said. "The fun must have ended when we left."

"Aye, right," they chorused, silly grins on their faces revealing they understood they'd been hoodwinked.

Lizzie grimaced. Jock shrugged his shoulders at her when no one was watching. *What was I supposed to say?*

CHAPTER THIRTY-ONE

Rejected Suitor

An' forward tho' I canna see,
I guess an' fear!

Wullie Maclure talked to Mr. Rankin, the foreman, about getting Jock a job at Calder Ironworks. By September they took him on as a labourer.

Lizzie's young Highlandman stayed on at his aunt's house and started to save every penny he could—as did Lizzie. She got herself a wedding kist from the joiner in the village and had him fashion the wooden box so that it would fit under the bed. She began to collect linens and dishes in it to be ready to start housekeeping for her and Jock one day and carefully salted the money away in its depths every payday—hers and Jock's.

He spent as much time at the MacGregors' but and ben as he did at the Maclures'.

* * *

Every day Lizzie ran home from the Whifflet junction and changed from her office dress into her old skirt and woollen jumper, threw her shawl around her shoulders, and waited on the step. She and Jock escaped with cursory goodbyes to her family, eager for a short respite from the close quarters.

A long stroll put them far enough away from the clamour of the endless foundry activity and from the dirt and stench. The green, rolling hills to the south felt more like the foothills of their home; without, of course, the majestic mountain backdrop.

Lizzie and Jock walked farther afield each day and found friendly, sheltering trees and stone dykes that provided quiet places out of view of the seldom-travelled road. The shawl she wore on these outings offered her a measure of anonymity as they left the village, as well as a quickly assembled nest for their lovemaking.

* * *

Her parents feigned surprise, and everyone was pleased about their intention to wed—except Wullie, who became sullen and withdrawn and started to spend more time and money at the Big Tree Bar. Donnie and Jamie said he was getting into skirmishes when he was the worse for liquor, especially with Catholics.

Lizzie asked Jock about Wullie's attitude.

"Och! He holds a rankling aversion towards Catholics. His grandfather was an Orangemen from Ulster. He started Lanarkshire's first Orange Lodge. Wullie's father headed up the lodge here, and Wullie's following in his footsteps. He's a big man around here with the Orangemen. Wullie loves a fight."

"Aye, well there's plenty of that goes on. Sometimes it's hard to get any sleep for the noisy brawls out in the street, especially on paydays."

Lizzie found Wullie's self-righteous superiority strange. She and Jock agreed that they were all in the same boat here, Catholics, Protestants, Lowlanders, Highlanders. All scratching for a living in Uncle Archie's hell.

* * *

Lizzie assumed Shanks had moved on from his obsession with her; he seemed preoccupied, which she construed as contentment, now that he had a new home with his wife, ill though she was, and his baby boy. His sister from Fife had moved in to help run the household. He boasted often about the child and showed a tender side that Lizzie had never expected him to have. As a result, she dropped her vigilance around him and even offered to stay late and finish some note-taking for him one evening after the clerks had left for the day.

"How's the wee boy?" Lizzie asked, trying to set a friendly tone.

"He's fine."

"And Mrs. Shanks?" Was that a tear in Shanks' eye? Lizzie began to have some trepidation about the direction of this exchange.

"I'm sorry, Lizzie."

"Is she worse?"

"She'll never be any better. I had to marry her, ye know. It was always you I wanted."

Lizzie was so caught off-guard that she bolted upright and dropped her writing pad on the floor. "But I have a lad, Jock MacGregor." The words were out before she anticipated the impact they might have on Peter Shanks.

"Which MacGregor?"

"Oh, just someone I knew from Rannoch."

"Which MacGregor?" His reddened face was screwed into an ugly grimace. He reached across the desk and gripped her wrist.

"Are ye courtin' that bloody thief? Ye'd rather have a filthy labourer than me. Is that what yer sayin'?"

She assumed he knew, but he hadn't been to Whifflet for a while; her brothers hadn't seen him at the Big Tree Bar.

"That teuchter hasn't heard the last of me. Ye don't steal women and property from Peter Shanks and walk away a free man."

"Let me go, Mr. Shanks. Are you forgetting you're a married man?"

"Hijacked me. That rich bloody bitch tricked me." He let go of her wrist and slumped down on his desk.

Lizzie thought this might be a good time to make her exit. "You'll feel better in the morning, s-s-sir."

She edged towards the door.

He yelled after her. "Do you teuchters marry yer cousins because nobody else will have ye?"

Was Peter Shanks crazed? She had no idea what he might do next; probably fire her for a start. Whatever it was, she and Jock were in danger from him.

Shanks did not come to work for the next few days. His wife had taken a turn for the worse. Sophie Shanks succumbed to a fever a month later in October '62 and was buried at the Old Monkland Cemetery.

* * *

When Shanks began coming in later and later to work, Lizzie assumed more of the burden in the head office. Her brothers told her he was often at the Big Tree Bar now. Not the kind of place a man of substance would frequent.

At the office there seemed to be some kind of unspoken truce between them. Lizzie trod quietly around him. She couldn't understand why he hadn't fired her except, of course, he needed her. He seemed to be losing his grip on his responsibilities, and Lizzie quietly and efficiently filled the void.

She needed the job, especially now that she could see how going down the pit every day affected her father. Lizzie felt almost guilty about the relative physical comfort of her office job. Pa's back was stooped with the crawling he did underground in tight spots. He had developed the cough that so many of the miners suffered from. When he came home each night, wearing soggy clothes, he stripped and soaked himself in the bine to get clean and warm. But even though his clothes and his boots were spread out in front of the fire to dry all night, they were sometimes still damp in the morning.

Her mother fared little better. The twins tried to haul all the water she needed before they left for work, but she still had to keep the fire stoked, drag the dirty clothes to do laundry in the boilers provided in the wash house, and cook and clean. Lizzie wondered how she put meat on the table so often and how she found the money to buy new, warm clothing for the men, which they needed for the quickly approaching winter down in the pit. But she did.

* * *

On Saturdays, her half-day off, Lizzie helped Ma make black bun and shortbread. Plans for Ne'erday could never be as exciting as they had been in Rannoch, but Jock's folks were finally coming to Whifflet to visit the Maclures. And for Hogmanay!

He and Lizzie were eager to share their news with his parents.

The Maclure house was bursting at the seams with the arrival of Nellie and John Campbell—"MacGregor," John proudly corrected anyone. He spent as much time visiting with her father as good manners towards his Maclure relatives allowed.

"Robert, this town has taken its toll on ye, I hate tae say. Can ye no take it a bit easy and let your lads take up a bit o' the slack?"

"It takes all of us workin' just to afford this place. If I could grow a wee bit of barley or oats or have a few chickens, we'd eat better. But ye cannae do it here. Lizzie, make a cup of tea for Nellie and John."

Lizzie's mother said, "I have a bit of dumpling left from the twins' birthdays; it would go well with that." It warmed Lizzie's heart to see her mother cheered by the company of her old friend, Nellie.

"Florry, yer still the great housewife ye always were," Nellie said. "I can't tell ye how pleased John and I are to have our son marryin' into yer family. Ye've taught her well and Lizzie'll make a fine wife. And such a bonnie lass." Nellie put her arm around Lizzie's shoulder as she leaned across her to take a piece of the dumpling.

"There'll be some braw grandweans, Florry," said Nellie.

Lizzie excused herself to go and change. But not before she heard her mother confiding in Nellie her worries about Annie.

"She won't mind us, Nellie. We've never been ones tae leather our lassies, so she never felt the strap, but nothing we do or say seems to make a difference. Won't say where she goes or who she's with. She has me worried."

"Never had lassies. Sometimes they can be worse than lads."

"She never gives me anything to help run the house."

"That's not right." Nellie was shocked.

"And the way she spends money . . ."

* * *

Hogmanay fell on a Friday night, which was the usual bath night in the Rows. With Pa sitting by the fire reminiscing and Ma cleaning up the supper dishes, it was almost like the old days. Annie, under protest, helped Lizzie draw water at the pump between the Middle Row and the Front Row; the twins pulled the bine out from under the bed; Pa got the fire roaring to heat the water. The girls insisted they use the water first, since they didn't add coal dust to the tub. All the others, except Ma, were sent outdoors or into the back room.

"Hurry up, Lizzie," Annie said. "I'm going out later. Can I wear your bonnet tonight?"

"I suppose so." Seems Annie had lots of occasions to get dressed up and go out.

Like her mother, Lizzie wondered where Annie spent all her time, but she wouldn't risk taking the sharp edge of her sister's tongue by asking her questions. Lizzie hoped Annie's secrecy was to avoid the inevitable teasing from her young brothers.

Lizzie and Annie dried and changed in the back room. Lizzie still wore the dress she got when she went to work at Motherwell, while Annie's fancy new clothes appeared regularly from Mrs. Purdie's. The wool dress she sported now, in a rich royal blue with tartan-covered buttons, she'd got especially for Hogmanay. It must have cost a pretty penny. Lizzie resented Annie's show of prosperity and chided her, one more time, about not contributing to the household. Her excuse was, "Och, I'm hardly ever here."

Lizzie could hear her father in the next room; his rattling, productive cough and the sizzle from the fire when he spat into it.

"Are ye up for going out, Rob?" Her mother's concern mirrored her own.

"I'll be fine, lass. We promised tae go tae the Maclures. Ye know I wouldn't miss spendin' Hogmanay with John Campbell for anything."

"Aye. It's grand seeing Nellie again. I wish they were here for longer than two days."

"Pa!" Lizzie called out as her father and mother went out the door. "Remember to call him 'MacGregor.' Ma, send Jock over when ye get there."

When they left, Jamie produced a pint of whisky and offered a drink to his brother.

"Och! I've got my own. Give some to the lassies."

"Just a wee nip," Lizzie said.

"Keep yer cheap whisky to yourselves. I'll get better where I'm going." Annie waved an arm dismissively and slammed the door behind her.

"I wonder where she's going," Lizzie said.

"Ye mean ye don't know . . ." Donnie grinned as he poured a dram for his sister.

She lifted the cup to her lips and took a sip.

". . . our Annie's keeping company with Peter Shanks," he finished.

Lizzie coughed and choked on the bitter liquid.

"We're goin' out. Don't expect us back before morning," Jamie said.

"I know it's Hogmanay. But you two be careful out there. Watch what ye say, and stay away from any fights."

* * *

Jock came over to get Lizzie after the twins had left. She felt a bit light-headed from the unaccustomed effect of the whisky.

"Oh Jock, I love you so much my heart can barely contain it." Tears came to her eyes.

"Are you all right, Lizzie?" He cradled her on his lap on Pa's big chair.

She answered by wrapping her arms around him and pulling him to his feet.

"Wha—!"

"Ssshhh." She put a conspiratorial finger to her lips and led him to the bedroom.

She unbuttoned her dress on the way, and stepping out of it, almost tripped. She giggled and pulled the string on her drawers, stood unsteadily on one foot to rip them off, then her stockings, and fell into the middle of her bed.

"Hurry up, Jock."

"I'll be right there, lass."

By the time he reached her, she was in a high state of anticipation. She kissed him hungrily and dug her nails into his back until he cried out.

"Easy, Lizzie." He sounded surprised but not displeased.

She easily pushed him over on to his back; raised herself up and straddled his body. She wriggled down onto him; her hands pushed against his shoulders, her mind totally focused on the eager, compelling motion of her body till she drained every last drop from him.

Lizzie collapsed at Jock's side, sighing.

* * *

She awoke from a suspended, dreamless, ecstatic state to a loud, persistent knocking on the door in the other room. Jock was no longer by her side, and his clothes were gone. Her clothes had been draped over the end of the bed.

"Oh, come in, Wullie."

She heard him in the other room.

"It's past midnight. Yer supposed tae be at oor hoose. What's the matter wi' ye?"

"Lizzie was just finishing up dressing."

"Aye, right." Wullie must have been drinking for a while. He sounded angry. "A wee bit common decency is called for here, cousin."

"Take it easy, Wullie. It's Ne'erday. Don't spoil it."

"Spoil, is it?" The sarcasm dripped off his tongue. "You just walk in here and take whatever ye've a mind tae."

It wasn't clear whether he meant "walk in here" to the house or the village or his life.

"I'm ready," Lizzie called out.

She joined the two men in the kitchen. When Wullie saw her, his lip curled in a gesture of disapproval. What she had been doing must have been written all over her face.

The surprise exchange didn't really affect their Hogmanay, especially since Wullie went off to the Big Tree and avoided the party at his parent's house.

At dawn Lizzie stumbled home with her ma, pa, and the twins, who'd joined them sometime in the night.

"Where's our Annie?" Her mother asked of no one in particular, so no one answered.

Annie crept in to bed next to Lizzie midmorning.

"Jamie said you might be with Peter Shanks," Lizzie said. "I hope it isn't true."

"What if it is? His sister went to Fife to be with her mother for Hogmanay. I just went over to help with the wee one."

Lizzie found this hard to believe but let it go for the moment.

CHAPTER THIRTY-TWO

Lizzie's Secret

March 1863

But deep this truth impress'd my mind—
Thro' all his works abroad,
The heart benevolent and kind
The most resembles God.

Lizzie opened the window and door to let the place air out in the early spring afternoon. She had waited nervously for days for an opportunity to get her mother alone. She needed to talk to her—privately. Ma sat on the rocker, darning socks.

Lizzie sat at her feet. "Mother, it's been two months since I had my courses." She buried her head in her mother's lap. She didn't expect rejection, not from Ma, but what <u>would</u> her reaction be? ". . . And I've been queasy in the morning just like you were with Archie. Ma, there's a bairn on the way."

She felt her mother's arm around her and the kiss to the top of her head. Lizzie lifted her head to search her mother's sweet face. A sob of relief escaped her lips. "I'm glad you're not upset, Ma."

Her mother smiled. "A bairn, lass, that's grand. It's not that uncommon for young folk who are promised to each other to get the cart before the horse—so to speak. But ye'll need to get the wedding banns called right away. We can talk to the minister and do it next Saturday afternoon. I noticed your bonnie work-dress was stretched a bit across the bosom." Ma smiled. "What does Jock say?"

Lizzie wasn't smiling. "Mother, I haven't told him yet. He's wanted to hurry it along . . . the marriage, I mean, by getting a better paying job at the works. They've promised him a job as a moulder. It would mean more money."

Ma looked concerned. "Don't wait too long. Ye need to be wed now."

"Ma, I think it is too dangerous. I've asked him not to do it. If he learns about the baby, I know he'll try to get the new job as soon as he can. He would want me to stop work too, and I'm starting to get a nice wee pile of siller in the kist. Och, I'll wait a while longer . . . at least till I'm sure."

But even a few weeks later, when she was sure, she didn't tell Jock, and she kept going to Motherwell every day.

Peter Shanks' new smiling demeanour put Lizzie on edge. Lizzie guessed it had to do with Annie, but the subject was never discussed. He must know it tortured her to have him seduce her young sister, but Lizzie had no influence over Annie. Shanks must know that by now.

He had begun to complain about her work, which she knew was just as efficient and effective as always. He must know he would have to work twice as hard if she quit, which seemed to be what he was driving her to do.

"Miss MacGregor, the rubbish basket is overflowing." He barked at her as he swept through the outer office. One of the clerks sniggered.

Lizzie no longer did janitorial type work. He had said it was foolish to waste her time and talents.

"And when you've finished with that, come and empty my basket, too."

Lizzie entered his office, red-faced, eyes cast down. She crossed behind and reached past him for the almost-empty basket. The stretch proved too much for her tight bodice, which popped several buttons. Despite her quick reaction he must have seen her breasts protruding over the top of her shift. He quickly reached towards her and laid his right hand on her bosom while he pulled her towards him with his left hand encircling her waist.

He poured out words of endearment. "You are so, so bonnie. Ye know I love ye. Just give me a chance. Please, Lizzie."

Lizzie was winded from the force of his embrace. She caught her breath and jammed her hands against his chest and pushed him away from her.

"If Jock MacGregor hears about this, he'll give you the thrashing of your life." She slapped his face.

His grin told her he didn't know she was serious. "Och, c'mon, Lizzie. Yer not still interested in that dirty wastrel, are ye? Give me a chance." He reached for her again.

She brought her knee up and caught him in the groin.

"Aaargh." He bent double and she sprang back. His face had turned beet red and tears spilled from his eyes. He groaned and mumbled curses at her.

Someone knocked on the door. "Are you all right, Mr. Shanks?"

He obviously could not answer. Lizzie pulled the edges of her bodice together and called out as casually as she could. "Mr. Shanks tripped. He's all right."

She escaped into the adjacent cloakroom and found her winter shawl and secured it with a brooch from her dress. She had to walk through his office again looking straight ahead, ignoring Shanks to reach the outer office.

* * *

Lizzie knew this would be her last day to work here. She would not give the clerks the satisfaction of walking out in the middle of the day. Mr. Addie made his weekly visit that afternoon. How would Shanks handle the incident?

Everyone could hear him in the outer office. His voice, louder than usual, suggested that this time he meant to be overheard. "I've been meaning to talk to you about replacing Miss MacGregor," she heard him saying to the owner.

Lizzie thought, so he's going to use this moment to humiliate me in front of the clerks. She feigned riveting interest in her ledger. The room was very quiet.

"I thought you liked Miss MacGregor," the owner said.

"She's not bad, sir. But you know . . . once a teuchter always a teuchter."

"Some of those Highland folk are our best workers, Shanks. What happened to that bright lad, MacGregor? What was his name? Jock, was it? Related to Miss MacGregor? I wanted to promote him. He had more than the ordinary savvy these folks have. See to it he gets every encouragement."

"Sir, I thought you heard about MacGregor. We caught him taking some tools out of the repair shed. Ye know, Mr. Addie, they were cattle thieves in the old days, those MacGregors. Some o' them haven't changed much. I fired him on the spot."

So the bastard was going to get to her through Jock, as well as her sister.

"Knew you liked the boy, so I didn't call in the constable." Lizzie's stomach turned at the pure malice Shanks was capable of.

"Well, bless my soul, I used to be a good judge of character. That boy certainly fooled me. A thief . . . a common thief. I think it's time we followed up on some of those petty thefts; they're costing me a fortune. We really should consult a solicitor and decide if we need to take action. See to it, Peter."

"I don't think he'll be any more trouble, sir. But if you want me to . . ." Sanctimonious, sneaky rat. Making dumb Mr. Addie think it was his idea.

"All right, Shanks, do what you think best . . . a thief . . . my, my!"

The little worm—lying to cover his own tracks. He had fired Jock only out of spite. Now he had taken the opportunity to justify it to Addie. This was payback to her for rejecting him. How far did he plan to take this—this atrocious lie? She didn't know whether to be more upset at her own humiliation at his hands or the maligning of her man. She had meant to leave with the last clerk but now she had to see him, even though it was risky. She was bustling about the office, dusting and wiping after the other workers left. She had just grabbed a mop to work off her frustration when he came into the newly shined room, mumbling to himself.

He came right up to her and spat the words. "If that teuchter crosses my path again, I'll . . . Well, Miss MacGregor . . ." He nodded towards the mop she was pushing around the clean floor. "Finally found the right job for yersel. That's what ye'll spend' yer life doin' if ye marry that Highland man o' yours."

"You maligned his character. I heard you. You . . . you . . . liar, you cheat. What tools? There weren't any tools missing. That's how you justified getting rid of someone Mr. Addie valued. Were you jealous of him even then, before you found out about him and me? He's more of a man than you'll ever be, Peter Shanks, and you can't stand it. You're not fit to polish his boots." The words tumbled out on top of each other.

He looked stunned, "What did you say?"

"And while I'm at it—keep your filthy hands off my young sister."

"And who is jealous now?"

"I would never willingly submit to you, Peter Shanks. I have always found you despicable. Surely you know that."

"Empty your desk, Missy. You're finished . . . and don't try for a job anywhere around here. You're blacklisted. Git out. Git out," he sputtered.

Lizzie ran to the station as though he were pursuing her. Sweaty and dishevelled, she boarded the familiar six o'clock train to Whifflet. Shanks might never deliver on any threat to her man. But then again, he might. She had just witnessed an example of his patience to wait for the most propitious moment to get his revenge.

All the way home to Whifflet, her mind sifted through what she knew about his influence: Shanks' sphere of authority grew in proportion to his reputation as the man to keep the workers in line. Ironmasters and pit owners in Coatbridge were coming to him for advice on issues all the way from how to increase production to the thorny political problem of keeping Coatbridge, a district of scattered villages, unincorporated. Without a municipal policy, the owners pretty much ran the town their way, the profitable way, which meant substandard housing, contaminated drinking water, and filthy air. Without burgh status, public health laws were unenforceable. She had observed enough of Shanks' devious mind to fear what it might conjure up. Oh, yes, she'd learned a lot taking notes from the indispensable Mr. Shanks.

She wouldn't tell Jock about what she had overheard. What could he do? He might make matters worse coming to his own defence. He had a job and a chance of promotion. No point in jeopardizing that She prayed he'd get that promotion soon; work that would take him farther away from the pot room, farther away from the molten lead. Shanks was not aware Jock had found employment at the Calder Ironworks; she hoped he never did. In any case, or as far as she knew, the powerful Mr. Dixon, who owned Calder Ironworks and several coal mines, had never consulted with Shanks. For now she only needed to tell Jock about her being out of work. She sadly surmised he wouldn't be dissuaded from taking that foundry job in the pot room now. She needed to tell him soon about the baby.

213

That evening they took their usual walk. In his company her tension eased. It would be all right. Together, they could handle whatever life presented. She wanted to float tonight on the cloud of their passion—despite the fact that other clouds were threatening overhead, and the biting wind was blowing at their backs.

They fairly flew up the hill to one of their special places and made love in a desperate, needy kind of way under the darkening sky. They had not been together for a week and couldn't keep their hands off each other. He always excited her, and tonight was no exception; the rain, when it came, did not dampen their ardour. The oak tree protected them for a while, till the bigger drops dripping from the leaves began to get their attention. They laughed together. What difference did a little rain make?

After the lovemaking, she pored over his handsome, honest face, the ingrained dirt in his hands from heavy labour, the worn coat. It was all so unfair. He hadn't been given the chance he deserved, and she didn't want to tell him what she knew about Shanks' actions. She feared that any response from Jock would make matters worse.

She told him a few days later that she wasn't working at the Motherwell office any more. She made it sound as though her mother needed her and she was looking for a job closer to home. He listened and nodded, but she suspected he knew there was more to the story. She loved that about this man—it was a Highland trait—he simply allowed things to unfold in their own time and had faith in her judgment and wisdom. She knew he would love to help in any way he could.

As though he were reading her thoughts, Jock said, "I've been thinking about how to reach Charlie. I talked to Mr. Rankin. His son works at the docks at the Broomielaw in Glasgow. Ye know—where I last saw Charlie. I'm sure it was Charlie. He asked me what the boat we saw looked like and what day I saw it. I couldn't remember the day, but I'll never forget that giant steamship with the red, white, and black funnels. Mr. Rankin says that was a boat of the Allan line, and they leave once a week for the St. Lawrence River ports. I've sent two letters already addressed to Charlie in care of the main post offices in Montreal and Quebec. Even if he gets one of them, it'll take two months or more for a reply."

"Aye, but it's worth it, Jock." She squeezed his hand. To find Charlie, after the joy of finding Jock, would make her world complete.

"Jock, I have to tell you something." Lizzie said quietly. It was about time she told him she was in the family way.

"I have some news, too."

They went to the back room to get away from the twins and sat on Ma's kist.

"What's your news, Jock, love?" She poked her finger at a tear in his jacket—burn holes.

"I can tell ye now. Next week I'm to be gaffer at the moulding room. Mr. Rankin recommended me. It just has to have Mr. Dixon's approval."

She grimaced. "Ye've been working in the furnace room, haven't ye?"

"Aye, lass, just for one more week; then I'll be at a safer distance. Paddy Riley needs a wee bit more experience to take over from me." He stroked her head in a conciliatory gesture.

"I don't want ye doing it, Jock."

"I know, Lizzie. It's been hard keepin' it from ye. One more week. I'll make almost twice as much money. We'll get our own place . . . start a family."

She blushed and smiled into his adoring face, tempted to share her news but wanting to allow him his special moment.

He wrapped her in his arms, sighing with joy. "Our son'll have a better chance than we did."

Was he reading her mind? She ought to tell him now.

"He'll have a guid hoose and the verra best of food and we'll read to him, send him to school and college . . . and we'll do the same for all his wee brothers and sisters."

"Jock, I . . ."

He started to tickle her until she squealed for him to stop. The twins came through to see what all the ruckus was about.

"Lizzie and I are getting married soon."

"Och, is that all? Everybody kens that. C'mon, Donnie. I'm going doon to the Big Tree for a pint. Can ye not see what happens to a man when a woman starts running his life? They start acting soft and daft."

"You're too young," Lizzie said. "I don't want ye going into that place."

Lizzie only knew the workmen's bar from the outside. The smell of stale smoke and spilled beer that emanated from it was only a little less offensive to her than the cursing and fighting that often spilled into the street. When she couldn't avoid walking past it, she came to the unwelcome attention of the patrons who stood leaning against the wall or the lamppost outside, making loud comments about the pit girls hurrying by. It wasn't a place for her wee brothers.

"We are not too young. Or haven't ye noticed Donnie and I were fourteen last month. We're shavin' now, fer Chrissake."

Jock kept quiet. Lizzie recognized a losing battle. It was common to see lads their age passed out on the pavement.

"Are ye coming for a dram, Jock?"

"I'll see ye later," Jock said.

"Och, we'll no see hide nor hair of him. C'mon, Jamie."

"Ye're right. That's what happens when ye relinquish yer manhood. It's a sad thing tae see." Donald released an exaggerated sigh.

CHAPTER THIRTY-THREE

A Village Mourns

Had we never lov'd sae kindly—
Had we never lov'd sae blindly
Never met—or never parted,
We had ne'er been broken-hearted

"It won't be long now," Jock told Lizzie, after a few weeks of waiting. Despite his confidence that his promotion would happen soon, Jock admitted to Lizzie that Mr. Rankin hadn't confirmed it, and the man would retire soon. Would a new manager give him the same consideration? She knew he worried about that. He was embarrassed and apologetic when he handed over his paltry wages for the kist.

Jock tried to make sense of it. "'They'll put ye on a higher pay rate in no time.' Rankin told me that last summer, and I know him to be a fair man. Something's goin' on beyond this gaffer's control. I mean tae find out. 'Just learn the ropes, see if ye can handle the men,' they said. Well, I've got Paddy Riley trained to take over the cauldron from me. I know ye'll be glad about that. It's a better paying job for Paddy. They didn't want to give it to him at first, him being Irish and a Catholic. Ye know how they are. I put in a good word for him. He's been a friend to me in the pot room, and Paddy's a fine worker."

"What is it you've been doing exactly?" Now that his stint at tending the cauldron was almost over, she wondered if her wild imaginings about the dangers had been exaggerated.

Jock hesitated. "Och! It's not as bad as it sounds. After the cauldron, suspended by a heavy chain from above, is maneuvered alongside the blast furnace, it gets lined up under the chute that guides the molten metal into it. The tricky part that I've been teaching Paddy, and he's almost ready to take over, is when he has to climb the steps at the side of the furnace to the lever that opens the door below."

Lizzie was getting an all too clear picture of the hazards he faced in this job. Her hope was to talk him out of it. But if she told him about her condition, he would be more determined than ever.

Jock's voice showed his enthusiasm and pride in the skills he'd learned.

"Tapping it, they call it. It takes a steady hand tae hold that bar till just the right moment when the cauldron is filled; then drop it closed. The heat is fierce. Wait too long, and ye've got surplus materials pouring into the pot room and out of control."

It was more hazardous than she had visualized in her worst nightmare. Thank God he'd hand the job over soon. Her dress was snug at the waist. She figured she must be two months along. She couldn't wait much longer to tell him. Ma nagged her every day about it. She didn't worry too much about gossip. It was fairly common for lads and lassies to marry after a baby was on the way. Och, in the old days they waited till they were sure.

But a week later Jock said, "Lizzie, we may have to wait to wed."

"No, Jock, I can't."

"Oh, Darlin', ye know I feel the same way. But I don't want us trying to live on a labourer's wages, and I found out the problem wi' my promotion."

"According to Mr. Rankin, the owners have hired Peter Shanks to advise them on hiring. Mr. Rankin said something else. It seemed a bit strange. 'Have ye heard anything from Lizzie's brother? Why don't ye join yer countryman in Canada and take that bonny lass away from here?' It's as though he's trying to let me down gently. Damn!"

Lizzie drew a deep breath; she felt a band tightening around her heart as she digested his news. Should she tell him now about Peter Shanks' accusation or his actions towards her? She hesitated. If Jock knew, he might do something brash. She feared what Shanks might do if Jock met him head-on. Jock didn't know him like she did. She'd come to the conclusion that Peter Shanks had moments of total irrationality. He was vindictive and had the ability to hold a grudge deeper and longer than anyone she'd ever known.

They walked in silence for a while, trying to put some distance between themselves and the unfriendly village they had been forced to call home.

"I thought my problems with him were over after I left the pit in Motherwell. I won't let him throw me out again." He drew Lizzie into his arms. "I'm going to have to confront him."

Lizzie shuddered. "Ye can't, Darlin'. He's insanely jealous of you, Jock. He tried to compromise me with that job in Motherwell. He thought he had a chance with me, thought I'd marry him, even." No need to go into more details. "Then he blacklisted me. That's why I haven't been able to get work. He's furious that I rejected him. I think his attention to Annie is just part of his revenge."

"Bastard! But he can't give the owners that as a reason for not promoting me."

"He won't. He'll accuse you of stealing from the company." She bit her lip, but it was too late; she'd put his pride and integrity on the line.

"He's a liar. Ye know I'd never do any such thing."

"I know that, but I heard him convincing Mr. Addie otherwise. Stay away from him, Jock, love. He's treacherous."

She'd never seen Jock so incensed.

"Jock, please, we'll manage. I'll get a job. Maybe Annie can get me on at the post office or something . . ."

Her days to work were numbered. Soon she would show, and nobody hired a woman in the family way.

* * *

A few days later, Lizzie was drawing water at the well when she heard repeated, long siren blasts that brought everyone rushing out onto the streets. It was coming from Calder Ironworks. She dropped her bucket and joined the crowd racing off in the direction of the dreaded sound that pierced her ears and her heart and ran into her mother, who was coming home loaded with baskets of groceries.

"Ma, Ma . . ."

"Don't go down there, Lizzie." She felt her mother's restraining arm.

"Come home. Jamie and Donnie are headed to the foundry. They'll bring back any news. We'll pray nobody got hurt."

"It is the foundry then?"

"Aye, come home."

Pacing back and forth in front of the door of number twelve, she saw Jamie and Donnie racing up the street a half hour later, part of a crowd of young people, spreading the news as they went. The distress of screaming and wailing relatives spread out a stream of turbulence in their wake.

Lizzie ran to meet them but they deftly linked arms with her on each side and propelled her to the door of number twelve.

"Tell me." She felt the terror rise in her breast.

Jamie and Donnie seemed to be dumbstruck. They stared at each other.

"Bad accident . . ." Jamie started out.

"Five men killed, they say." Donnie was obviously stalling but their haunted eyes and deathly pale faces said it all. Donnie tried to finish the news. "Aye, he was in there, lass."

"Maybe he didn't go in . . . Maybe he stepped out . . . Maybe . . ." Lizzie couldn't take it in. Unwilling to believe the truth, Lizzie looked to Jamie for confirmation.

"It was Jock's crew, Lizzie. . . a giant explosion . . . then a spill of molten metal that destroyed the pot room took out the whole crew on furnace number three." Jamie gulped back the tears. "Shanks made the announcement."

"Shut up, Jamie." But it did take this kind of detail for Lizzie to believe the horror.

She collapsed onto the floor before her brothers could catch her.

* * *

Still in the clothes she wore two days ago, she stirred from a troubled sleep to the sound of his voice coming through the thin walls of the bedroom.

"Ma." She called frantically. "Who is that?"

"It's Wullie Maclure come to the door to say it's time for the service. The minister is over at their house."

It sounded like Jock but it wasn't him; just Wullie Maclure, his cousin. They all said he was dead, but how could he be? She'd held his living, breathing, beloved body in her arms yesterday—was it only yesterday or two days ago? The anguished groan escaping her throat threw her into paroxysms of coughing.

"Lizzie, we need you out here." The sound of her father's hoarse voice barely reached through her fog. "Do something, Wullie. We can't get Lizzie out of the other room."

From her perch on her kist, she uncrossed her cramped legs to turn towards the door to confirm it really was his cousin.

Wullie Maclure approached her where she sat unmoving on the precious box, the last place she and Jock had held each other. She turned her head away from him.

"It's time, Lizzie." He repeated it several times, shook her, gently at first, then more vigorously.

Lizzie felt hands firmly gripping her shoulders and her head being jerked around. She squinted at him, her face crumpled and she turned her head in bitter disappointment. She heard piteous wailing. It took her a few seconds to recognize that these sounds came from her own throat.

Wullie picked her up and set her feet on the floor. "C'mon, Lizzie. The service is about tae begin. We're all waitin' for ye."

She followed him blindly, grabbing a piece of old rag from the chest in the front room to wipe her face. Wullie linked her arm through his and guided her into Whifflet Street, which was crowded with mourners.

At the service, Lizzie saw, through a haze, Mr. and Mrs. MacGregor and all Jock's big brothers standing around, listening to the kind words of Jock's new associates and friends. Their eyes shared with her what their words could not.

Peter Shanks, who stood next to Annie, represented the foundry owners. Lizzie could hardly believe the short speech he made insinuating Jock's "youth and inexperience" should be forgiven. Her mind was trying to grope with what he had just said, so she didn't catch the Bible verse he quoted next. The other mourners said nothing till he left.

The men who had worked the second shift that day, who had survived by a twist of fate, told Lizzie and Jock's family they'd never seen a better worker. The Mighty Teuchter they called him.

Jock's counterpart on the second shift told them, "I dinnae trust that Bible-thumpin' hypocrite. And anyway, how could Shanks accuse Jock of sending Paddy Riley up on the furnace platform when they haven't even found his body in the disaster area? Och! Paddy might have got homesick and left for Ireland like he was always threatening to do. Paddy and Jock worked well together. Problem was, Jock was probably working like a navvy alongside him when the furnace exploded, instead of staying at a safe distance and sending in an Irish labourer like most of us do."

The workmen stood around with their caps in their white-knuckled fists, nodding in agreement with their gaffer, Ronnie MacAllister. He went on talking rapidly—it could just as easily have been him and his crew, Lizzie thought in one of her moments of clarity.

"Ou-aye. We're up on that platform leaning ower that soup till we near pass oot. The owner doesnae care as long as we turn out the purest iron in Scotland. It's no' the first lad that's given his life in that damnable place, and I'm feart it'll no be the last. I cannae understand it. I checked that equipment myself when I finished my shift."

"No one will ever know what happened in that pot room, Ronald," Jock's father said in a weak voice. "I just know my braw son is gone, and his mother will never be the same. And this bonnie wee lass is near dead with grief. If some man is responsible, God will surely take vengeance on such evil."

Lizzie's attention settled lightly on Jock's parents. Mr. MacGregor, older than she remembered, had lost his feistiness, and his graying hair had thinned. Mrs. MacGregor's thin arm clung to her man, her eyes averted from the blackened form they said was her baby, her Jock.

A space was cleared for Lizzie to stand at the head of the casket. Wullie guided her to the appointed place of honour to the pine box laid out on the table in the Maclures' front room. She almost collapsed when she saw her lovely man. His hair was burned off from the blast, and his handsome features weren't distinguishable.

"Sit down, lass." It was Wullie's voice. "He must have been standin' closest to the blast; he's was burned the worst."

"This is not my man," she screamed.

"He never knew what killed him, Lizzie. It must have been over in an instant." She heard Wullie's voice and its comforting tone; but she couldn't make sense of his words.

She tried to kiss the distorted reddened mask but pulled back, revolted. She could smell the burnt flesh. She tried to discern any recognizable features through her blurred vision. Tears trickled from her eyes, her nose dripped. Her mother put her arm around her and dried her face with a handkerchief. When Lizzie felt her mother's presence, she clung to her and started to scream, "Mother, Mother, make them stop. This isn't Jock. Find him. Where is he?"

His skin had shrunk, his body dehydrated from the blast; his best suit hung limply on his body, and despite the undertaker's best efforts, the open casket exuded a scorched odour.

Her mother stroked Lizzie and held her close. "Aye, lass, it's Jock, right enough. I'd take this pain away from ye if there was any way on God's earth I could do it." She reached beyond Lizzie and smoothed out Jock's tie.

Lizzie followed her mother's lead. She touched his lapel. No holes in his Sunday suit. Was it Sunday? That was the one he had planned to get married in. She couldn't think straight. The minister was talking about Jock. What a fine young man he was . . . hard worker . . . taken from us too soon . . . attended church regularly . . . credit to his family. She heard her name mentioned . . . young couple had a future planned together.

The baby! Don't tell anyone, she thought, *it's our secret, Jock's and mine. No, I haven't told him yet. Let's keep my secret a wee while longer. If Jock knows he'll take that awful job at the foundry, just for the money. It's too dangerous. Why isn't Jock here? Everyone else is. The horror hit her again. Why did they insist that the seared corpse was Jock, her life, her hope, her future, and the father of the new life that was fast growing inside her? How could he leave her now?*

Through her confusion she heard the minister paying respects to the other dead workers. "Every family has been touched in some way by this sudden tragedy—this loss of five lives. The whole village of Whifflet is in mourning for its sons, young men cut down in their prime. Three young widows and their children will have to find some way to survive, by the grace of God, without homes or income, and eventually someone in County Derry will hear the sad news about their fellow countryman, Paddy Riley. We pray for all the souls burdened by this tragedy."

It did not comfort Lizzie to know that there were others who had lost their hope for the future.

Lizzie rode with her mother and father in the cart that was hired for older family members. Following behind were coal carts, milk carts; anything a horse could pull had been cleaned up for the biggest funeral procession the town of Coatbridge had ever seen. Like she was in a nightmare, she saw crowds lining the road from Rosehall down the brae to the cross at Whifflet and out the Monkland road, past the Old Monkland Poorhouse and the Coathill Hospital, on to the cemetery. The walk to the cemetery, which was sometimes a Sunday outing, was a desolate march today. Anyone in "The Whifflet" who could walk the two miles did.

It took almost an hour. The icy rain started spitting as they approached the Old Monkland and got heavier during the actual burial. The undertaker had some new-fangled umbrellas that he offered to the family members.

Lizzie refused the strange contraption. She stood in the rain, soaked and shivering, her tears adding to the wet stain on the front of her navy Lindsey dress that was getting tight. She barely noticed the corset that cut into her waist. She barely noticed anything.

She went to throw a handful of dirt on top of the coffin as she had been instructed but slipped in the mud and almost fell into the gaping hole. Hands reached out to save her. As she righted herself, one arm kept its hold around her waist. For a moment she stared in disbelief into the face of Peter Shanks.

"Where is he?" she looked right into his face. She felt her stomach lurch and vomited down his shiny black suit. He recoiled, suddenly releasing her so she once again slipped into the mire.

Wullie pulled her up, held her in one arm, and with the other hand offered his clean handkerchief to wipe the front of Peter Shanks' Sunday suit.

"Take yer hands off me, Maclure." But he grabbed the handkerchief and tried to wipe off the mess and retrieve his bowler hat.

"Git outta my way." He pushed his way through the crowd, followed by Annie.

Lizzie watched as though in a fog as the crowd quickly cleared a path for him. One of the colliers from Rosehall, eager to settle an old grudge with his former boss, snarled, "Yer in an awful mess, Peter. Can ye not show more respect?"

Shanks drove off in his carriage through the gates of the cemetery; as the carriage picked up speed something white flew out of the window.

* * *

Lizzie stood outside the door, looking down Whifflet Street, waiting for Jock as she always did this time of day.

"Come inside, lass." It was Jock's mother. "He's gone . . ." Nellie dissolved into loud sobs.

People spilled over from the wake between the Maclures' house, the MacGregors', and the Big Tree Bar. Neighbours brought over kettles of mutton broth to help feed the crowd and extra bowls and spoons. Her mother and the Maclure women kept busy making sure everyone got fed. Men left the house to console themselves at the Big Tree Bar, and the women and children finished up every drop of the soup. They were hungry from the long walk and all the extra work. Lizzie, still nauseated, did not offer to help with the cleaning up, but retired to the kist without eating. She wanted to be alone, but even this room would be crammed soon. They had to find space for some of Jock's family to stay overnight.

* * *

Lizzie was dimly aware of the noisy men when they tumbled in from the pub, most of them the worse for drink and telling heroic stories about her Jock. She rallied herself a few times later that night and staggered among the snoring bodies, peering into their faces when the burst of light from the furnaces lit up the room—searching for Jock.

"He's gone, Lizzie pet. Come back to bed. Ye need yer rest." Her mother held her in her arms, stroked Lizzie's wild, uncombed hair, and crooned quietly to her till they both fell into fitful slumber.

Part Four

Survival

CHAPTER THIRTY-FOUR

Life Goes On

The creature here before Thee stands,
All wretched and distressed;
Yet sure those ills that wring my soul
Obey Thy high behest.

The next week when the twins came home from the Big Tree Bar, Lizzie overheard them discussing Peter Shanks, who'd been talking to a reporter from Glasgow.

"Can ye believe what he was tellin' the papers?" Jamie hissed in the other room. "'We were RE-considering any plans to promote this man, MacGregor.'"

Donnie added, in his best Fifer imitation. "He worked for me at another location. He wisnae to be trusted. I hate to be the one to point it out at sich a time, but the Good Book does say that the wages of sin is death. Jock MacGregor did not serve his rightful masters well. He never should've let anyone as inexperienced as Mr. Riley so close to expensive machinery."

"Bastard!" Jamie muttered.

"Shanks is using Paddy's disappearance to point the finger at Jock. Maybe the man was blown to bits, but ye know Donnie, maybe he wasn't even there."

"For God's sake, ye're right. What are ye thinking?"

"I don't want to think. Nobody's reported him missing. He had no family here. I heard Shanks say he 'wis only a navvy'. Och! They'll soon enough drop the investigation. Don't say anything to our Lizzie. Better she starts to get over it."

"Ou-aye!"

* * *

She also read about it in the *Glasgow Herald* that Donnie brought home a few days later.

"On March 16 in the year of our Lord 1863, five men died following an explosion at Calder Ironworks in Whifflet, Lanarkshire. A search for the body of the Irish foundry worker, Patrick Riley, at the scene of the explosion, has never turned up anything. Although management is being scrutinized following several unexplained episodes at the facility, a spokesman stated that a Highland apprentice, one of the men dead at the scene, John MacGregor, was responsible for the mishandling of the dangerous, volatile materials. The case is being closed."

"'A spokesman,'" she said to her mother. "Lying sneak is what he is." Lizzie felt a spark of her old feisty spirit.

"Child, ye have tae put it out of yer mind for the sake of the wee one."

"Aye, Ma."

"Your pa is not going to be able to work too many more years, Lizzie."

"Oh, Ma." She put her arm around the stoic woman she loved so much. But Lizzie had known it for months. Pa's coughing was keeping them awake at night.

"Lizzie, that bairn has to have a father."

"He has a father, Ma."

"Stop it, Lizzie.

"Ma, I can't love another man."

"This is no time to live in fantasy, Lizzie. You are here months on the way. There are some practical considerations. Ye can't survive long trying to raise children without someone bringing in a pay-packet. And a woman with a baby and no father is not likely to be treated kindly in this community. I know ye can't replace Jock. I know, lass. My heart goes out to ye and we'll do all we can to help, but your father and I won't be around forever. Ye need a husband—soon."

* * *

Instead of getting bigger, with the child growing inside her Lizzie seemed to shrink. Her mother tried enticing her to eat by cooking savoury soups, but after a few mouthfuls Lizzie felt nauseated and retired to sit on the kist. Nothing interested her, and the April rains that kept the house dark and dreary and turned their filthy street into a quagmire didn't help.

She was fast losing hope that Jock was still alive. Surely he would have tried to get in touch with her.

When Wullie Maclure asked her to take a walk to "get out of the house," Lizzie suspected it was at Ma's request, but the first few times he stepped in the door she let out a loud wail that caused his immediate retreat.

Finally, at the end of the month on a dry day, Wullie did persuade her to take a Sunday afternoon walk to the cemetery and "put some flowers on Jock's grave."

Careless about her own appearance and well-being, she tolerated her mother bundling her in a scarf and woollen tam. She responded, "Aye" and "No" to Wullie's small talk on the long walk to the Old Monkland. She stared at the dark rectangle of earth cut out of the grass and noticed the withered flowers Jock's parents had placed weeks before and shook her head trying to waken from the nightmare. She indicated to Wullie with a nod of her head that she was ready to leave and on the way back from the cemetery, Lizzie started to cry with an abandon that surprised her.

She knew it embarrassed, even frightened, Wullie. He put his arm around her shoulder, then quickly withdrew. When she stumbled, blinded by the tears, he grasped her hand; they walked this way for a while in a cold drizzle. Her immediate grief spent, she met his concerned gaze. This was the first time she had looked him in the face for weeks.

"What am I to do, Wullie? He must be gone, or I would have heard from him."

"Ou-Aye, ye're right lass. He's gone, right enough." He squeezed her hand. "Life goes on, Lizzie. Jock would not want ye grievin' forever. Some day ye'll maybe find another tae love. I had always hoped . . . one day . . . but not like this—not to have to lose ma cousin."

He looked at her with a pleading gaze, which she tried to dismiss as concern. It was an open secret that he loved her, but she just needed a friend right now.

* * *

The weather got warmer in April, and they took to walking to the Old Monkland every Sunday. She told Wullie about the baby. He seemed to take in the information without judgment which vaguely surprised her.

"He'll need a father, Lizzie. He is of my blood, and I have always loved ye. I know it's too soon to expect ye tae love me in return, but I've waited this long . . . a wee bit longer wid be fine. Do ye think ye could ever care for me?"

She hardly knew how to answer him. She was deeply touched by his proposal and the unselfish sentiments behind it. She wanted a father for this baby, of course, but could she ever love this man?

Lizzie talked to her parents that night. They both said they thought highly of the Maclures and that maybe Lizzie could find some happiness after all—in time. Her father said, "This bairn should have a father, and Wullie Maclure's a good provider. Lizzie, I can't help ye. They're laying me off."

Lizzie was simply stumbling through every day. She couldn't imagine the future, never mind plan for it. The reality of the baby could not be ignored. She could feel him moving. She was sure it was a boy. She began to eat better, conscious of the new dependent life inside her and started to fill out in the middle. She could no longer hide her condition. She never remembered actually agreeing to the marriage; she didn't remember disagreeing either. It seemed to follow as a matter of course. The banns were called on two consecutive Sundays at the Free Kirk, and the following Sunday she married Wullie after the regular service.

From Annie's expansive wardrobe, purchased from Mrs. Purdie's Emporium, she let Lizzie borrow an apple green dress with an empire line front.

"It might camouflage your condition. Try not to stretch it out of shape."

"Thank you, Annie. Will you stand with me at the service?"

"Sorry, Lizzie. I can't. You've never liked Peter, and you seem to have ignored the fact that he's courting me. It wouldn't feel right going if he's not welcome. I'll stay away and save everyone embarrassment."

* * *

Wullie, dressed in his Sunday suit with his hair freshly cut and slicked down, looked proud and pleased as he stood beside her in the kirk, repeating the vows in a voice that betrayed his emotions.

Their parents and Jock's parents, who surprised and pleased everyone by coming from Motherwell for the occasion, cleared a path for the newly married couple to exit the church after the simple ceremony.

Lizzie choked up with tears at the sight of Nellie MacGregor, formerly Campbell. But Nellie and John seemed to be in good spirits on that sunny May day. Had they really made such a miraculous adjustment to the death of their youngest son after only two months, or were they putting on a front for Lizzie and Wullie's sake?

Nellie gave Lizzie a kiss on the cheek. "It's all for the best, lass."

Lizzie looked straight into Nellie's dry-eyed stare, but Mrs. MacGregor's usually open demeanour seemed guarded. Lizzie had a fleeting notion that she was shielding something: some kind of emotion or something she couldn't or wouldn't say. Ah well, it must be very difficult for her, too, Lizzie thought.

They made quite a parade of the climb up Whifflet Street to the Maclures, where they'd spend their first night.

When Wullie made love to her, he treated her gently and with obvious passion, but she was reticent and held herself back.

"It's all right, lass, a new bride's expected to be shy. You'll get used tae me in time," he assured her.

She thought, he's put it right out of his mind that there was ever anyone else. But she would never forget.

When they moved in with her family, she had no illusions about what their life would be. She and Wullie could have the front room, with the hole-in-the-wall bed, and the rest of the family would be in the back room.

Ma and Pa would have one bed and the twins the other. They'd have to get a cot for Annie. She wouldn't be happy about it. But maybe it wouldn't be for long. Maybe. Annie hinted, she'd be getting married soon and moving up in the world, which was where she felt she rightly belonged. It seemed that Peter Shanks hadn't got around to proposing, so Annie would have to make the best of it in Rosehall for a while yet.

"Where can I get dressed?" she demanded.

"In our room—after Wullie leaves for work," Lizzie suggested. So they worked it out, though not entirely to Annie's satisfaction. She became more determined to get away from this 'ghastly barracks'--Peter's words.

* * *

Lizzie walked down to Dundyvan Road wearing the roomy smock Ma had bought her, enticed outdoors by the July sun; her first outing since her marriage, to buy herself some new boots at Brady's. Wullie gave her the money as a present. "Buy yerself something braw."

But Lizzie was too practical. She needed sturdy boots that didn't leak. The recent dry spell wouldn't last long. Mr. Brady wrapped the leather boots in brown paper and tied the bundle with string. "Ye'll have these for many years, lass. Yer feet'll be dry a' year. They're the best I have in the shop."

She returned his smile and turned to leave. There, framed in the doorway, was Peter Shanks. She attempted to move past him without acknowledging his presence, but he turned in the doorway and followed her out.

"Why did ye do it?" His voice was a soft murmur.

"Do what?" She stared into his hated face.

"Marry that Maclure. Don't ye know I would have married ye even if ye are pregnant?" He ogled her swelling contour with an expression of ☐ what? She couldn't put her finger on it. Fascination, disgust, pity?

"Peter Shanks, I'd sooner see you in jail than across the breakfast table. I will never forgive you for what you put Jock MacGregor through."

His eyes opened wide and he took a step back from her.

"What are you talking about, woman?"

"If it hadn't been for you, he would be alive today."

"I had nothing to do with that accident. I have no blame in it at all." He had switched to his managerial tone.

"I mean if you hadn't fired him from Motherwell."

"Oh . . . that." He breathed a heavy sigh that sounded like relief.

She eyed him appraisingly. Could he possibly have had anything to do with the accident at Calder Ironworks? He was certainly capable of petty viciousness and indifference to the suffering of others, but the murder of five men? That was too much, even for Peter Shanks.

"So which one of those Maclures did ye marry?"

"Wullie and I were married last week."

"Ou-aye, well. Congratulations. I think I owe that young fella a new handkerchief."

"You owe us much more than that, Shanks. And maybe someday you'll pay."

"Don't you threaten me, missy. That husband of yours still has to answer to me."

CHAPTER THIRTY-FIVE

Love Bairn

He'll hae misfortunes great and sma',
But aye a heart aboon them a';
He'll be a credit till us a'.

Lizzie was too big to get into anything decent, so she cut a hole in the front of her oldest dress and covered it with her pinafore tied around her swollen middle. She figured she would need the midwife sometime after September, because she was convinced Jock's child had been growing in her since Hogmanay.

But it was the middle of August when she awoke before dawn in a pool of sticky wetness. Her back ached relentlessly. She lay there as long as she could, her skin crawling with fear, before she staggered into the other room to waken her mother.

"Annie, get Granny Wilson," Ma said.

"Get Granny," Lizzie repeated feebly. "Get the midwife."

Annie threw on her dress and ran out the door.

"Is it time tae get up, Lizzie?" Wullie rolled over and opened one eye to see his doubled-over wife brought back to their bed by her mother. He leapt out of bed demanding, "Is she all right? Is ma wife all right?"

"Aye, she'll be fine, Wullie. Just go on to work, and we'll send word when the bairn arrives."

And sixteen hours later she gave birth.

"Mother, is the baby all right?" Lizzie could barely hold up her head.

Granny Wilson was bathing the squalling infant. "Ye've got a wee boy, Lizzie. He's got great lungs and bonnie blue eyes. When I wash his heid we'll see what colour hair he has. Ou-aye. Here's a wee tuft o' red hair."

"Ye're fine now, lass. Thank God, it is over. He's a fine wee chap. He has the look of a MacGregor."

"Then that's what we'll call him—Rob Roy." Lizzie smiled, pleased with her choice.

She watched Ma holding the baby. The joy that radiated from the new grandmother lit the room. "Lizzie, there's nothing like a new bairn to give ye hope. Ye're a verry special wee boy, Robbie."

* * *

Wullie came back from the Big Tree after midnight, loudly boasting that he was the man of the hour.

"Even yon Mike Rafferty bought me a pint; though that Catholic ploughboy shouldn't even be at a Protestant celebration." He tumbled into the bed, startling Lizzie and the bairn, who began to squall.

"What's wrong wi' him, Lizzie?" he grumbled.

"Nothing is wrong with him," she said wearily over the child's cries. "Ye just woke him up."

"Well, shut him up." His speech was slurred.

"Be quiet, Wullie. He's just a baby." She hissed at him.

As if making an apology he whispered. "If a man can't have peace in his own house, what kind of world is it comin' to?"

She watched her husband scrutinize their first-born. The baby's face was crimson from his noisy distress. It matched the few wisps of bright red hair that sprouted out of his head.

"No' much Maclure in that yin—must be part MacGregor and part bagpipes, if ye ask me."

Lizzie put the baby to her breast to quiet him. In a few moments, Wullie and the baby were fast asleep. Lizzie cried quietly into her pillow. This wee lad would never know his own father. She prayed Wullie could open his heart and show him some love, but this was not an auspicious start to the relationship.

But if Wullie didn't have much interest in Rob Roy, his other relatives couldn't seem to get enough of him. As autumn slipped into winter, her brothers and her parents petted and played with him every waking moment. The twins bought Lizzie a pram for him. His distinctive shock of red-gold hair grew thicker each month, and when she parked his pram outside the stores, he was admired by every passer-by.

* * *

She was standing barefoot baking scones with her back to Shanks . . . aware of his presence yet carrying on as if he weren't there . . . the fluffy white beauties floated out of the oven; they were so light. Out the window of the croft in Rannoch Moor they flew and up . . . up . . . up where they expanded into puffy cloud formations. A man sat on one wearing an Oriental turban . . . she got closer . . . it was Jock . . . not changed a bit—braw as ever and smiling to his Lizzie.

Now he was floating on carpet, red, green, and gold. Where had she seen that kind of carpet before? She tried to reach out to him, but the celestial traveller was carried out of her sphere. "Come here to me, come here to me," he said. Her body was alive with desire.

She grasped the fringe of the rug, trying to pull herself up on to it. She had almost made it aboard the magic carpet when she felt something pulling her back down again. She heard her own voice cry out like a lost child as he slipped away from her. She thought it was Shanks pulling her back, tugging on her gown . . . a growl of rage escaped her throat.

"Did ye waken me, lass?" Too late, she realized she'd pulled on Wullie's nightshirt and aroused his ardour. There was no escaping his passion; Lizzie felt trapped, and it was so close to morning when the bairn would be awake soon.

"There, there, lass." He stroked her tense back; his hand moved quickly around to her breasts; he turned her over to face him and gave her the full benefit of his fetid breath.

"Och, go back to sleep, Wullie," she whispered. "It's too early to get up."

"Ye're goin' tae have tae tell that tae wee Wullie. He's up an' ready for business." He pulled her hand down to feel his swollen organ and held her wrist firmly there.

* * *

"Mother, how long does it take a man to get used to a new bairn?" She hoped her mother had a good explanation.

Lizzie's heart sank when she saw the sadness in her mother's eyes. "Och! Some take longer than others. Times they don't pay much attention to them till they can talk and play."

"Wee Rob is almost ten months old, and Wullie said last night, 'Is it no time we had a bairn?' like we didn't even have one."

"Lizzie, it is none of my business, but get yer strength back more afore ye get in the family way again."

"Aye, Mother." She cast her eyes down and sighed.

"Och no, lass! Don't tell me."

"I think so. The thought of bringing another wee one into this awful place is more than I can stand."

Her mother's silence filled the room, intensifying her sense of hopelessness. But she couldn't give up; an idea had been gnawing at her for weeks.

"Ma, Wullie and I never took a wedding trip. I'd like to show him where I was born and maybe visit folks we haven't seen for years."

"Aye. If he could get the time off, it would do both of you a world of good." Her mother's penetrating gaze demanded answers—answers about Lizzie's satisfaction with her rushed marriage, answers Lizzie wouldn't admit, even to her mother. The truth was that she regretted her hasty decision, and that despair was her constant companion.

* * *

Before she would tell Wullie about her condition, she planned to talk him, somehow, into travelling north with her before the weather turned cold. If he knew about the baby, he wouldn't want her to take any risks, and the chances of her introducing her husband to her birthplace would be lost. The trip would cost precious siller, but it might be worth it. Lizzie had a plan—and a yearning—that Wullie would love Rannoch the way she did. Her prospects of finding a place to live there were slim, but she had to try.

"Wullie, I want us to go to Rannoch. The money Ma gave us for a wedding gift is set aside for it. We never had a wedding trip. Ma would be happy to take care of wee Robby."

CHAPTER THIRTY-SIX

Rannoch Revisited

Thou'lt break my heart, thou warbling bird,
That wantons thro' the flowering thorn:
Thou minds me o' departed joys,
Departed never to return.

They took the train to Callander and travelled by coach up through Crianlarach to Tyndrum, retracing the journey the MacGregors had been forced to take four years earlier.

She searched his face for reaction to the splendid scenery. Could Wullie love the Highlands the way she did? He'd never travelled out of Coatbridge. The train trip into the pastoral lands that were the gateway to the Highlands, and the coach ride over country roads, were his first experience outside the gray, fiery world where he had always lived. Lizzie tried to point out places of interest and raved about the beauty of the surroundings, but he seemed dazed.

"Is that the Tyndrum Inn just ahead?"

"Aye, that's it."

"Finally we'll have a honeymoon night all tae ourselves." He put his arm around her and hugged her as the coach pulled into the private road leading to the inn.

* * *

"We need accommodation for two . . . uh . . . married people for the night." He blushed.

Lizzie thought he needn't have bothered being bashful, for the innkeeper ignored him and was staring at her. She found it hard to believe he remembered her. Her distressed family must have made quite an impression when they lodged here. "Aren't you the MacGregor girl from Rannoch . . . all grown up and married. What brings you back to these parts?"

"It's our wedding trip," she told him.

"And you want to show your new husband the land where ye were brought up? Thinking about coming back, are ye?"

Wullie gave her a questioning glance.

"No, just a visit," Lizzie said, offering nothing more.

"Were you no' one of that MacGregor clan?" he repeated. A safe guess as he fished for information.

"Some o' yer countrymen from Rannoch tried comin' back, but the constable came around asking about them. They're no welcome by the gentry."

A fleeting vision of Jock crossed her mind. She considered asking him more, then thought better of it. The sooner she gave up hope about Jock being alive, the better. Ma insisted that fretting was bad for the baby, but not a day went by that her mind wandered off into thoughts about how things might have been different, and she'd see Jock walking back into her life; see his smile; hear his voice; feel his touch . . . Then she'd come to, with a start, to the reality of her life.

"Nothing here for ye anyway. Hardly anybody in the glens any more except toffs and Englishmen taking out the deer. Yon Duncan MacNab from hereabouts runs things for Captain Winterbottom, Mary Buchanan's Sassenach husband, up on Rannoch. The Captain's ower fond o' a dram, and Mary spends all her time and money in London."

The innkeeper was kind of nosy for a Highlander. Maybe that's how you grew to be in that business. Lizzie didn't trust him; she'd find out in Rannoch who returned and if they found work.

He pulled a pint of draught for Wullie. "Would ye like a wee bit o' venison for your dinner?" he offered with a sly wink. Wullie's smile answered his question.

* * *

Early the next morning, they took the post gig, driven by one Andra Robertson, who accepted the fare, counted it carefully, and gave them a piece of paper torn out of a notebook as a receipt. He also jotted down the time that he would again make the trip to Achallader, assuming they would need the return ride. But not a word did he say.

By afternoon, they walked into Kilichonan. Lizzie, dismayed to find the one and only guesthouse closed down, began to wonder how her husband would react to sleeping on the moor. But her old classmate, Beth Robertson, now married and eager to offer Highland hospitality in her own wee cottage recognized her walking on the main road.

"Come on up to the house. I can hardly wait to hear all your adventures, and Angus was just talking the other day about you and Jock and Charlie and how good ye were in school."

"This is Jock's cousin, Wullie Maclure, my husband."

A fleeting expression of surprise registered on Beth's face. She quickly smiled it away and said, "My, that's grand," looking Wullie over. "Ye'll stay with us, of course."

"Of course, if ye'll have us." Lizzie said.

"Och, nae bother. It'll be grand and Angus will be glad to have another man to talk to."

* * *

Next morning Lizzie and Wullie walked on the moors of her childhood, where the blaze of heather was past its peak. She proudly showed him the mountains and her favourite streams. Wullie picked his way carefully, not accustomed to uneven terrain.

"Wullie, it's such a braw place; is it not?"

"Aye, if ye like sheep and mountains." He grinned.

Was he joking? She pressed on. "If we could get work here, would ye consider moving?"

"Into these hills?" He looked confused.

"Believe me, Wullie, a wee croft here, simple though it may be, is a far better place for raising bairns."

"It all looks pretty barren. The hills and streams are lovely, but how can a man make a livin'? What is there to do to? Where can ye find work?"

"Ye can tend sheep. Maybe learn how to make farm implements. Ye're a foundry worker, after all, used to working with metals."

"Och! It's not the same at all."

But he didn't bother to explain. He rarely gave her credit for understanding "men's work." She dropped the subject for the time being. She'd have to think of another approach.

The leaves had changed colour on the trees that bordered the dry stone dikes. Blazes of russet red and orange lined the stonework off into the distance. The brilliant foliage ended halfway up the mountains, where trees refused to grow and moss and fern took over. Memories of the old happier days flooded her, roaming in the twilight, singing her songs, the purple of the heather in bloom and the trickling of streams that meandered more slowly as the year drew into autumn.

Facing south across Loch Rannoch, Lizzie feasted her eyes on the stretch of the ancient Caledonian forest that still remained. The Black Hill belied its name today. It was a blaze of colour under a blue sky. Elsewhere, the ancient forest had long disappeared in the service of man and never got a chance to recover itself because of the grazing patterns of the sheep and cattle. The soil eroded year after year, creating the stark, craggy beauty that now characterized the Highlands.

It was a time of year she had loved and yet dreaded, for it heralded winter, a tough time for the cottars. The work would speed up in order to lay in a supply of root vegetables. They salted down meat; children gathered wild fruit. The berries that made it home and not directly into the children's mouths were made into jam that sweetened the scones Ma would make for a special treat.

* * *

So much had happened since 1860; that fateful year. She was lost in recollections as they travelled to the old home, which showed signs of four years of neglect. The thatch had deteriorated and the stone walls needed chinking. Several sheep had discovered the kale yard, overgrown with weeds, and were mowing it down. She called "Meggie, Meggie" and to Wullie's surprise, the black-faced ewe scampered over to Lizzie.

"Och, I never saw such a thing. They a' have names. I thought they were ignorant brutes."

"This one was wee Gregor's favourite," she explained. Then she had to tell him all about her brother and the dreadful day of their eviction.

They sat in silence after her story. Finally, Lizzie stood up and began to pick gowans and bright orange poppies, which she bound with some coarse grass to make a bouquet.

Silently, Wullie followed her up the hill to the cemetery now waist-high in weeds. The stone wall her forebears had erected around it served to keep out the sheep. Mature fir, pine, and larch trees grew randomly in the tiny sanctuary. An ancient tree that had outgrown its shallow root system no longer bore leaves, but made an ideal aerie for the ospreys that had taken residence there many years before. They flew from their intricately engineered nesting place, chirruping their high-pitched tweet that belied their size and strength.

The protective walls around the ancient burial place had allowed nature to renew herself in ways that revealed to Lizzie what had been intended for Scotland's verdant valleys. The sweet smell of the clean, rain-washed air filled her lungs.

"Can ye hear the bird song? It sounds like a mavis."

"A what?" said Wullie, stepping carefully over the stile.

"Oh, you would call it a thrush."

"Ou-aye! Right."

The bird took off as they came closer.

Lizzie approached the rough stone her father had erected and solemnly laid the bouquet as close to her brother's resting spot as she could remember, images of the tiny lad flooding her memory. The stones that did have dates and names on them told the sad story of the many infants buried in this spot.

Lizzie spent a quiet moment at Granny MacGregor's grave. Thank God, the old lady had not lived to see the day when the last of her line was forced from the glen.

When Wullie's arm went around her shoulder, her head jolted upright, for she had forgotten his presence.

"I wish I could have protected ye from this awfu' eviction. Yet, if ye'd never left this place, I wouldnae have met ye."

"Ah, Wullie. Life goes on." She absentmindedly stroked her swelling contour.

"That it does, lass. We better get back. Yon lassie, Beth, we're stayin' wi' will be making some o' that Highland food yer aye braggin' on. Her man might have a wee nip o' their homemade whisky."

They started back across the moor. Lizzie pointed out the big house when it came into view. They gave it a wide berth, just in case they might be accused of trespassing.

Lizzie drew Wullie's attention to the large flock of wild geese arriving from the arctic to winter in Rannoch.

"Oh, no!" she cried as gunshots rang out in the late afternoon quiet and two of the geese fell out of the sky.

She jumped when she saw Wullie drop to the ground in self-protection, and remembered miners always expect explosions. A pair of grouse flew up in front of them, and a red deer buck loped across the footpath and disappeared into the underbrush.

Wullie's glance darted anxiously about. "What's goin' tae happen next?"

"The hunters are still far off, but let's hasten to leave this glen before they get closer."

In his hurry, Wullie tripped over an object in his path, which tightened on his foot. Lizzie knew he was tangled in a rabbit snare.

He let out a yowl and began to tug to free himself. "The damn thing's cuttin' ma foot off."

She held his arm to discourage his exertions. "Stay still. Don't move. That just tightens the noose."

She searched around for a strong, pointed stick and pried it between his boot and the wire, expertly releasing him. The wire had cut into his boot, and badly bruised his foot.

"Och! It's more dangerous than being down the pit," he complained, only half joking.

She tried to imagine what it would be like to start a life someplace like this with Wullie. She silently measured his potential as a farmer, his awkward gait through the moors, and his lack of interest in the farm buildings or the animals. Even the swift-flowing streams with their rich bounty of trout or salmon were just more obstacles for him to cross on their trek.

"Wullie, would ye just give some thought to starting a new life in the country?"

"Ye mean here, Lizzie, here in Rannoch?" He sounded surprised. Her timing was bad again. She'd try broadening his options. "Well, some place like this . . . even in America or the colonies?"

"And leave ma folks? Would ye ask me to do that?" His tone said it all. She knew he'd never agree. She also realized he would never fit into this life.

For three generations now, his family had been town folk. Whatever hopes she had of enticing Wullie into trying something new, of finding a rural life somewhere, here or abroad, she sadly discarded.

"Is that what you'd want, lass, tae live away frae everything?" He sounded offended, even outraged at her suggestion. "What aboot ma pals? Where's the friendly pub to share stories and raise a dram?"

"I was just thinking aloud," she finished lamely, unable to share with her new husband her great disappointment.

"Och, well that's fine then." Wullie said.

* * *

Beth MacGregor's husband, Angus, only too glad of company, produced a bottle of uisge beatha, the water of life, and he and Wullie drank it down after a dinner of haggis and tatties. Under the influence of his favourite drink, Wullie forgot his injured foot.

* * *

Lizzie woke early. Beth sat by the fire nursing her youngest bairn.
"Tell Wullie I've gone up to the cemetery."

"Aye. Have some porridge afore ye go. Ye have plenty of time. Your man will not be walking on that foot today."

"I want to go before they start their shooting, Beth."

But Lizzie hoped she could get to her destination before the hunters were even awake. She was going to the big house, not the cemetery. She had to see Kate MacKay. She had to find out if the climate at the big house had changed enough to allow her, or anyone related to her, to come back to the land. Also, the innkeeper's chance remarks had fanned a dying ember. What if Jock had survived? Where would he go? Was he one of her countrymen who'd tried to return to Rannoch? Her one remaining thread of hope was fraying. Her hosts had made no mention of any MacGregors returning after the clearance. Was the nosy innkeeper just blethering?

She climbed Aulich Hill in the half-light and found her way to the tradesman's entrance at the back of the great house. Fearfully she tapped on the door. What if by chance Mary answered, or MacNab? Unlikely but she had to take the risk.

Andy MacFarlane answered the door, all grown up and wearing the jacket and boots of a groomsman. "Lizzie, Lizzie MacGregor. I cannae believe it." He surprised her with a hug. "Is Jock with ye?"

Lizzie was cut to the quick. "Jock is dead, Andy."

"Did he die on the ship?"

"What?" Andy wasn't making any sense. "No, no. In the foundry . . ."

"I don't understand."

Neither did she. She hated to remind herself of the accident that killed Jock, or tell one more person about it, or even hear the words out of her mouth.

"Is Miss MacKay around, Andy? I don't have much time." Lizzie surveyed the grimy kitchen and wondered if Kate MacKay's mind was slipping.

"Och! Too bad about Jock. I wonder if Charlie got word?"

Lizzie's distress mounted. "Where is your aunt?"

"She went back to Stornoway last year. Her mother had gone blind, and Auntie went home to care for her."

Lizzie felt tears coming to her eyes.

"Lizzie. Is your mother all right? Are ye doin' well in the Lowlands? Och! Yer brother Charlie took those papers. Auntie Kate was furious. She said it was your mother's birth certificate. I hope it didn't end up in Canada. Well, it's my stupid fault. Is your mother here with ye?"

"No. I'm here with my husband. We're staying at Beth and Angus Robertson's place in Kilichonan."

"Jock's here? He didn't go to Canada?"

"Andy, stop it! Jock died in a foundry accident over a year ago. I married a cousin of his, William Maclure."

"That can't be. Jock was hiding out in Rannoch last spring for three months. Then he left. He told me he was going to Canada to meet up wi' your Charlie. He was coming to get you first, but something must have changed his plans. I think MacNab knew he was here; he would have hunted him down like the— Lizzie are you not well, lassie?"

Lizzie gripped the table to stop herself from falling. Great waves of nausea roiled up into her throat from her empty stomach. She tasted bile in her mouth. All she could say was, "Are you sure?"

"Aye, I'm sure. Jock hid out in your empty croft. I took him food from the kitchen. He was a desperate man; some gaffer in Coatbridge had set the law on him, he said. He wanted to go to Canada and meet up with Charlie. But first he said he was going back to Whifflet for you. All I know is a letter came for him from Motherwell. I picked it up at Kilichonan post office. I think it was from his mother. He read it and left. Next day I took him some bannocks and beer but the house was empty."

Lizzie lurched to the door. Out in the kale yard she retched until her head hurt. She stumbled across the enclosure. She couldn't take it all in.

She unlatched the gate, pulled her shawl around her shivering body, and started down the path to Aulich Hill.

Lizzie staggered down the hill and walked to Kilichonan. He must be right, of course. If Jock were alive, it made sense he would go to Canada. Had he heard from Charlie? But when? Why had she not trusted her instincts and waited? But she couldn't. How would they have survived without Wullie's help?

Wullie! Oh, my God, I'm married to another man and Jock is still alive. She reached Beth's house still in a state of disbelief.

One thing she had decided. Not to tell Wullie.

But her body couldn't lie. When he threw his arm around her that night, she turned her back and curled into a tight ball, closing in on herself, repulsed by his touch. When he entreated her, she told him that she was having her courses.

CHAPTER THIRTY-SEVEN

Another Bairn

Thou Pow'r Supreme, whose mighty scheme
These woes of mine fulfil,
Here, firm, I rest, —they must be best,
Because they are Thy will

Back in Whifflet, she struggled with her solitary dilemma. Why hadn't he let her know? There had to be a life-or-death reason for Jock to have abandoned her. She wept secretly and softly, sadness mixed with relief.

Who could she talk to? The need to talk to someone, preferably her parents or brothers, had to be balanced against the dangers of divulging Jock's survival in case Shanks or Addie were still hounding him. Had he made it out of Scotland, or had MacNab caught up with him? He might have been killed when hiding out in Rannoch. Plenty of MacGregor men left their bones to rot on Rannoch Moor, and no one ever knew the why of it.

Did Jock's parents know whether he was alive or dead? At the funeral their grief seemed real enough. Had he contacted them afterwards? Was Andy right? The letter he took to Jock, had it come from Nellie? Of course, Jock <u>would</u> let his mother know he was all right. But why not her? Why not her? He could have saved her some of the pain. And why did Nellie not say that Jock had survived when she came to the wedding? That damned farcical wedding!

She remembered Mrs. MacGregor's cryptic message: "It's all for the best." What right did <u>she</u> have to make such a decision, if Nellie knew back then that Jock had survived? Dear God! It didn't bear thinking about, just how different her life might have been.

She held wee Rob on her lap and parried her mother's questions. Aye, the old place still stood. Yes, she placed a stone for wee Gregor.

"Ma, Kate went back to Lewis. Her mother needed her."

"She did? Lord, her mother must be a very old woman by now. Ye know, Lizzie, she took care of me when I was a bairn. I remember only kindness from Jennie MacKay. When I was only three . . ."

But Lizzie's mind was racing down a different track. What would a letter from Jock's mother contain? What could she have told him that triggered his departure for Canada instead of coming for her? Och! Nellie would have told him about Lizzie and Wullie marrying. That must be it. He must have been devastated. It was too late then for him to come for her. Did he think she got over him so fast? No, he couldn't have thought that. It must not have made sense to him. Would it have made more sense to him if his mother had told him about the baby? He could never have left if he knew his bairn was on the way. Damn! Why didn't she tell him when she had the chance?

She cuddled her son. "Hello, wee boy. Did ye miss yer mama?"

Rob gurgled his pleasure.

Pa excused himself to go to the outhouse. Lizzie worried about his frequent visits to the nasty privy. "Is Pa worse, Ma?"

"Aye. Yer father's not long for this world, Lizzie." Her matter-of-fact voice showed her mother had been preparing herself. "Lizzie, what else did they say?"

"The package Andy delivered, ye know, the one Charlie took with him, <u>was</u> your birth certificate. Andy said his aunt was hopping mad when he told her he didn't give it directly to you."

"Aye. It had to be. She'd promised to get it to me. Och! With everything else we lost, it's a small matter." Her mother touched her on the hand. "There's more; isn't there, Lizzie?"

Couldn't fool Ma! She told her mother what else she had learned on the Rannoch visit—what Andy had told her about Jock.

Her mother's eyes opened wide. "He's alive? Dear God! What about the body we buried?"

"It must have been Paddy Riley, Ma."

Her mother was silent, thoughtful, then: "How would Jock know where Charlie lives? We've never heard from your brother."

"Before Jock died, I mean before the accident, we sent letters to Canada trying to trace Charlie. I wonder if Jock heard from Charlie about the same time he crossed Peter Shanks and had to get away. It's the only thing that makes sense. Andy said that some gaffer in Coatbridge had set the law on him."

"But why did he not let you know?"

"That I don't understand, Ma. Andy took him a letter—"

She stopped herself when she heard her father shuffling in from the privy. He looked pale and barely made it to his chair, where he sat down heavily.

"Pa. What's the matter?"

"Nothing lass, I just . . ." A paroxysm of coughing wracked his body. His mouth filled and his cheeks bulged. His frightened eyes searched for her mother's face.

"Here, Rob." She rushed to his side with a basin.

He opened his mouth over it, and allowed the bright blood to spill out.

Watching the scene, Lizzie realized this was not the first time this had happened. Lizzie rose from her seat by the fading fire and put the baby in the box bed, while Ma led Pa to his bed in the same room.

Lizzie checked the iron pot suspended over the fire, breathed deeply the aroma of leeks simmering gently with the potatoes, and released a sigh that escaped her as a choking sound. She spluttered and covered her mouth, unaware these tears had been stuck in her throat. She gave the leftover soup one more stir.

With any luck, Wullie would eat some soup and fall asleep when he finally wound his way home.

She picked up Rob Roy and plopped down in the old rocker to rest her aching back for a few moments. The din of the ironworks droned on mercilessly in her ears. For once, she hoped Wullie would come home drunk, for how could she hide her turmoil from him? Her heart felt leaden in her chest.

Rob Roy, asleep in her arms, reminded her of Jock. The red-gold hair, the blue eyes like summer skies. He had Jock's nature, too.

No, no. Don't go there. Don't go near that pain. It was bad enough it visited her every night in her dreams. Where was he now? Was he alive and happy somewhere? Maybe her boy would meet his own father one day. But how?

She sank deeply into her grief for a while; the heavy weight expanded in her chest; the pain of it pushed against her throat; she gasped for breath.

The child slept on in her arms while Lizzie stared, mesmerized, at the fire.

The campfire created a rosy glow on the faces of the men. She went from one to the other filling their billy-cans with strong, black tea . . . Lizzie stared into each face, searching for Jock. "He's comin'," one old codger told her with a wink and a smile. She hung her head, embarrassed to have them know she waited for him. They talked about hunting and fishing, ignoring her. The fire burned low. She felt a chill and hunted around for twigs to revive the flames. She heard music in the distance. "That's him," said the old man. "He's come back to get his Lizzie." An animal cried out in the wilderness . . . the sound became more persistent.

Lizzie awoke, and cast her eyes down on Rob Roy's puckered face, the source of the cry. The fire had almost died. She heard singing out in the street. It must be Wullie. The house was ice cold. Lizzie scurried to restart the fire under the soup. Then she changed Rob and went to the door, opening it and scanning the hill in the direction of the noise.

Wullie weaved his way up Whifflet Street, singing one of those Protestant Orange songs he had learned so well from his father. The rhythmic roars of steam hammers accompanied the familiar melody, and the fighting words seemed to blend seamlessly with the endless foundry noise that arose from the bottom of the hill. Lizzie put Rob in bed with her mother and added water to the soup pot.

Wullie rolled in soused and reeking with liquor. He ignored the food she offered and fell into bed with his clothes on, and soon filled the house with his rasping snores.

She crawled in behind him—softly now—don't disturb him. Drunk, he would sometimes mount her and want to thrust until she was exhausted and sore. She reckoned he was so numb it was simply a reflex action that never led to the blessed release he wanted, but kept her from the sleep she craved.

He rolled over towards her and mumbled something unintelligible. Lizzie feigned sleep and prayed he wouldn't touch her. She needn't have worried. In minutes the sound of his deep, even snoring again rattled the room. She soon fell into a restless sleep beside him.

* * *

The next night the men had gone to bed, and Annie wasn't home yet. Lizzie usually treasured these quiet evening hours with her mother by the fire, but tonight was not a night for pleasant relaxation. She meant to find out how much her mother knew.

"Ma, do ye think Nellie Campbell . . . ye know, Mrs. MacGregor . . . Jock's mother, knew a baby was on the way when she came for the funeral?" She could barely disguise her agitation.

"Aye, she knew, for I told her." Her mother raised her eyebrows.

"Did she tell you Jock was alive?"

"No, no, Lizzie. I was taken aback when you told me."

"Would she have told Jock?" Lizzie spoke through clenched teeth.

Her mother turned her knitting over several times on her lap and spoke without looking at Lizzie, using quiet measured tones.

"My presumption is she would keep it to herself, and we never told anyone. She'd want whatever was best for her son . . . and there wasn't much Jock could do at the time."

"Ma, she had no right to make that decision for me . . . and you should never have kept this from me." Lizzie's frustration exploded. "I plan to go and see her in Motherwell and find out the reason for it. She'd better have a good answer."

"Lizzie, I'm so sorry, lass. I know we pushed that marriage on ye. We thought Wullie would take good care of ye and ye'd be safe."

Lizzie sat hypnotized by the fire, grappling with this turn of events, embroiled in her hopeless quandary till she fell asleep by the fire, exhausted.

Next morning when the chores were done, her mother said, "Lizzie, what are ye going to do . . . you know . . . about what we talked about?" Apparently she could barely tolerate opening the topic again.

"I've decided to write to her first. If she knows I'm coming it will pave the way."

"Aye, that's good." Her mother sounded relieved.

Lizzie's letter was polite and to the point, no blame or anger, just that she knew the truth and would call on Nellie to hear the reasons she had decided to withhold the information.

* * *

That evening, feeling calmer now that action had been taken, she slowly emerged from her thoughts to the sound of her mother's voice on a different topic.

"It must finally be getting serious between Annie and Peter Shanks, Lizzie."

"I don't understand him . . . or her, Ma, and you know I don't trust him. But Annie's determined to have him and swears he treats her well," said Lizzie. "I hope he does." She'd not told her mother what had transpired between Peter and herself. Ma had enough to deal with.

"I'm afraid there'll be a wedding before long. Peter Shanks has not been an easy one to snare, despite Annie's persistence," said her mother. "She never stays around the house much. Do you think it's because we might try to talk her out of it?"

"Ma, I've tried. She won't listen to reason." Lizzie sighed. "And I can't very well tell her I suspect the man of . . . what I suspect him of."

"Maybe you should."

"The twins still have to work in this village," Lizzie said. "If Annie knew the half of it, I think she'd tell him and make him more dangerous to our family."

They sat staring into the fire, fretting, and caught in a trap not of their own making.

After a half hour, Lizzie said, "She's been complaining daily and nightly about the wee one crying. She'll be happier in her own place."

"Hard telling what makes that lass happy."

"What are ye knitting, Ma?"

"Socks for wee Rob."

"Maybe ye better get some more of that baby wool out."

Her mother's eyes dropped to Lizzie's midriff. "So ye're sure. Have ye told Wullie yet?"

"I thought I'd wait till nearer the time . . . no point in getting his hopes up."

"Maybe it would put him in a better mood," said Ma.

"Another noisy bairn won't do much for Annie's mood, though." They were both giggling like schoolgirls when Annie came in—right on cue.

"What's so funny? Did ye finally find a place for you and yer sour-faced husband and that red-headed midget to live?"

"Not yet, Annie. In fact, with all the extra space, Ma and I were just talking about taking in a lodger."

More peals of laughter from Lizzie and her mother.

"Ye're both daft." Annie swept through the room to her little corner of the back room, where she changed into a new outfit from Mrs. Purdie's.

Lizzie feared her sister was a pawn in Shanks' game, but Annie would not tolerate interference. She would do as she pleased, and made no secret out of her ambition to elevate herself out of these humble conditions no matter what it took.

* * *

Ma gave up her seat to Lizzie and attended to the pot suspended over the open fire. Lizzie took over with Rob and spun him around the room. He had been aptly named, for his bright red hair suggested he was indeed the descendant of the legendary Rob Roy MacGregor, cattle thief or defender of the poor, depending on your point of view.

"'There was a wee mouse
And he had a wee house
And he lived in there.'"

Lizzie tickled Rob Roy's tummy to squeals of delight.

"'And he gaed creepy-crappy,
Creep-crappy,
And made a wee hole in there.'"

He tightened up his arms around his chest, but she found her way up under his arm, as she always did, and elicited further giggles.

"There was a wee mouse . . . Oh, there's yer Dada."

The door opened, escalating the usual din from down the hill with its accompanying stench and like a thundercloud Wullie entered leaving tracks on the scrubbed floor with his muddy boots and cursing the weather. "Is yer mother cookin' again?"

"Aye, Wullie, she's made yer favourite, cock-a-leekie soup."

"Ye'd think a man's wife could cook for him occasionally . . . Yer spoilin' that wean, the lot o' ye. Goin' tae be a Mamma's boy, he is."

After he hung his jacket on a nail, he turned his backside to the fireplace to dry his saturated shirt and pants and warm himself.

The door flew open once more, revealing the twins, soaked to the skin. Both headed directly to the simmering kettle.

"What smells so good, Ma?" in chorus.

They ignored her admonition to get cleaned up and turned their attention to the child. Robbie squealed with delight to see his uncles.

"Come to yer Uncle Jamie, ye wee rascal."

Rob Roy reached his pudgy little arms out to Donnie.

"See, he'd rather come to his <u>kind</u> uncle," said Donnie.

"Och! He doesnae know the difference," said Wullie. "Is there goin' tae be any food on the table soon?"

Lizzie got up and began to set the table.

"What's wrong wi' you, woman?" said Wullie. "Yer face is trippin' ye."

"Nothing, Wullie."

* * *

On Wednesday night, the twins went to the Big Tree and her parents went to the Maclures, a thinly disguised ploy to leave the house to Lizzie and her husband for the evening. She wished they wouldn't. Oh how she wished they wouldn't! But tonight she had decided to use the opportunity to tell Wullie about her condition.

Soaking in the bine always relaxed Wullie, especially when Lizzie scrubbed his back.

"I'll be glad when ye can be a proper wife in oor ane place. Do we have enough siller tae move yet?" She knew he had the mistaken idea that having their own home would put their relationship to rights. Lizzie wanted to avoid that forced intimacy as long as possible.

"We'll not be getting our own place for a while, Wullie."

When he swerved around in the tub, ready to confront her on the subject, he sent a wake that soaked her dress, causing it to cling to her.

"And why not?"

"Will ye just look at me?"

"Ou-aye! Ye're a' wet."

"Look closer, Wullie."

He scrutinized her from head to toe. "Aye, yer puttin' on a bit o' the beef. Och! Wait a wee minute . . . what are ye tellin' me?"

"Aye, a bairn in the spring."

"A son . . . We'll have a son." She heard the catch in his voice.

"Maybe it'll be a lass." No point in reminding him that they already had a son.

"When, Lizzie?"

"About two months after Ne'erday."

"Now that's a braw way tae bring in the New Year."

* * *

Lizzie had never seen Wullie so cheered. He spent less time at the Big Tree and even went to the kirk with her on Sundays.

What to tell Annie, though? Lizzie knew it would drive her mad to have another bairn in the house.

One night, Lizzie waited up for her.

"What are you doing up this late?"

"I want to talk to you."

"Well?"

"I'm going to have a baby."

"You're what?" She curled her lip and gave a disgusted snort.

"A baby, Annie, can ye not be happy for me?"

"Happy is it? Ye've just got that other brat trained so he doesn't keep us up all night, and now this. I'm leaving before that happens."

"Where will ye go? Places are hard to find."

"Peter and I will get married."

"Oh!"

"Ye don't believe me, do ye? Well, we'll see. I've got a bit of siller laid by, and it's about time I got myself into a better class of society."

"Does Peter agree?"

"He will."

* * *

A couple of weeks later, all business, Annie announced to her parents and Lizzie that she planned to gather up her belongings and move out immediately.

"Where will you go?" Lizzie asked again.

"Since you are content to live in this squalor, it's really none of your business, but Ma and Pa, you should know I will be safe. Peter has offered me a job as housekeeper . . . er, governess for wee Hugh."

"Is he going to marry ye?" Pa asked.

"Very soon." But she didn't sound at all sure.

"Will ye give up your job at the post off—" Ma sounded concerned.

Her rapid reply, "No. No. Not right away," raised Lizzie's curiosity.

* * *

They heard she got married the next month in Glasgow with Peter's sister as a witness, though none of them were invited.

If Ma felt cheated about not attending her daughter's wedding, she never showed it. To Lizzie she said, "I hope she's happy."

Annie was obliged to leave the Whifflet post office. She had signed a required agreement that she would resign if she married.

They heard Shanks had bought a fancy new house in Blairhill, on the other side of Coatbridge, and moved his new wife, his son, and his sister into it.

CHAPTER THIRTY-EIGHT

Sectarian Brawl

November 1864

Twill make a man forget his woe;
Twill heighten all his joy;
Twill make the widow's heart to sing.
Tho' the tear were in her eye

On a raw day in November, Lizzie banked the fire and put a kettle on to make her father a cup of tea. Her mother wrapped his legs in a plaidie. The two women, bundled against the cold, set off down the hill to the shops with wee Rob in his pram. The cupboard was empty and Wullie, Jamie, and Donald had handed over their pay-packets the night before—minus what they held out for their tab at the Big Tree Bar.

She clung to the idea she'd hear someday from Charlie or Jock. At Hozier Street she stopped at the post office to inquire if letters had come for her but the smiling Miss Ferguson dashed her hopes about once a week.

"No, Mrs. Maclure, nothing today," said the postmistress. "We miss your sister around here. But it is a blessing that Mr. Shanks has a mother for his bairn, and Annie is happy in her braw new house. We see her regularly when she comes for the post."

But why did Annie come to Whifflet for mail? Was there no post office nearer to her? Maybe Shanks still received business letters. Then Lizzie learned from the twins that he no longer had any business. Jamie heard he had been fired from all his lucrative positions, though he tried to give the other men the impression he still had power. But he was spending too much time at the bar to be holding down any kind of job. Maybe Annie just liked to come and visit with her former employer. The selfish bisom never bothered to climb the hill to see her mother or her sick father.

Dispirited, Lizzie turned to go.

"Oh, Mrs. Maclure, there was one letter returned to you . . . I'm sorry."

What in the world was she talking about? Lizzie snatched the familiar envelope. It was the one she'd mailed to Nellie. It now bore the stamp "Recipient deceased."

Lizzie stepped out into the cold drizzle that matched her mood exactly and trekked back to Whifflet Street to find her mother. She spotted the baby's shiny pram, now glistening with raindrops, parked across the road outside the butcher's, at the corner of Whifflet and Calder Streets.

Lizzie's basket with potatoes and leeks and a copy of today's *Glasgow Herald* on top weighted her down. She'd be glad to deposit her heavy burden at the foot of the pram. Her mother emerged from the butcher's, and Lizzie, distracted and morose, tread heavily across the slippery cobbles. The basket, perched on her side resting on her distended belly, was throwing her off balance. She had almost reached the other side when she slipped on the glaur in the street. Too late, she grabbed for her mother's arm to break her fall. The thud of her swollen abdomen hitting the ground sent waves of pain and fear through her.

She heard her mother's voice calling out "Quick. Help! Somebody!"

Two colliers leaning against the wall of the Big Tree Bar seemed to take forever to respond. Then one went back into the bar and returned with Jamie and Donald in tow.

She heard her mother say, "Help your sister. What were you two doing in there?"

Jamie responded for both of them. "Och! Ma, we just came off the night shift. We had a thirst on us."

"Never mind that now. Help with Lizzie."

Donnie leaned over his sister. "Jamie, take her other arm."

"Let's get her across the street," said Jamie.

"Get me home," Lizzie pleaded, vainly trying to wipe some of the smelly filth from the horse manure and other road dirt off her best dress.

The twins were strong men now and sensing their sister's distress moved quickly to get her to safety or just out of public curiosity.

"Over there, Donnie, Davie Mills' horse and cart. He must be in the news agents."

"I'll get him."

Lizzie, perched uncomfortably on Davie's cart, pulled her shawl over her face to hide from the prying eyes of the women and children in the street and the men who had poured out of the Big Tree Bar.

"Get Granny Wilson," Lizzie whispered feebly into Jamie's shoulder.

"Get Granny Wilson," Jamie called to their mother, who was already halfway home pushing the pram up the steep hill.

She felt the powerful arms of her two young brothers carrying her to the back room. Her mother and Granny Wilson appeared quickly and took charge.

* * *

She didn't have the strength to cry or ask to see him or respond in any way when Granny told her the little boy was born dead. She simply closed her dull eyes and slept.

When she awoke hours later, the tiny body was washed up and set on the bureau wrapped in a blanket. She heard her mother rustling around in her kist and then read a sad poem. Even in her semi-conscious state she recognized the words by Charles Lamb from the snatches of it she could hear.

"'Ye did but ope an eye, and put
A clear beam forth then strait up shut'
Lizzie struggled to sit up.
". . . 'who can show
What thy short visit meant, or know
What thy errand here below?'
Her head fell back onto the pillow.
"Or did the stern-eyed Fate descry,
That babe, or mother, one must die;

So in mercy left the stock,
And cut the branch; to save the stock . . .'"

Lizzie's eyes misted with tears. Dazed, she saw her mother as though through a frosted pane of glass. Ma cut tiny wisps of hair from the baby's head, wrapped the precious memento in paper, and placed it in Lizzie's kist.

The minister arrived, ending the private mourning of mother and daughter, and the family gathered round Lizzie's bed to baptize the child. Tomorrow they would take him to the Old Monkland Cemetery.

Lizzie tried to rise the next day, but her efforts caused a bright stain to spread across the clean sheets.

"Ye'll stay home, lass. The Lord understands. Ye barely survived this wean's birth yourself."

Lizzie collapsed back onto the pillow. Granny Wilson would stay with her till her mother returned.

* * *

Wullie returned from the Old Monkland Cemetery by way of the Big Tree Bar. Lizzie heard him staggering into the but and ben in the wee hours. He fell onto the bed on top of Rob Roy, who squealed "Mama, Mama."

"Git him oot o' here."

"But, Wullie," Lizzie, only half-awake and still light-headed from the potion Granny Wilson had given her, could not have picked up Rob Roy if she'd tried.

Wullie lifted the squalling boy into his arms and stumbled into the next room.

Lizzie heard her mother and father mumbling soothing words, then Wullie's loud, slurred speech. "My bairn is deid, and this yin is more yours than mine. Keep him out frae under ma feet."

Lizzie wept silently and did not sleep till well after Wullie's snoring was deep and even.

* * *

Lizzie stumbled through the New Year. Wullie drank as though every night was Hogmanay. It took two months to get back on her feet; then she threw herself into a frenzy of mindless work. Spring-cleaning she called it, but she continued through the early summer. She whitewashed the walls of the but and ben, cleaned every corner, and mended every ripped garment.

Wullie, on the other hand, barely hid the anger his grief generated. She thought he felt diminished as a man.

More than once he said. "That flamin' cousin of mine can give ye a bastard, and I cannae even git a legitimate son."

Lizzie had resisted having relations with him for as long as she could, using the excuse about the damage the miscarriage had done to her, but she knew Wullie could see the energy she put into taking care of her boy and her ailing father and well-tended house. Since he usually staggered home the worse for drink, she tiptoed around him till he fell asleep. Thus she avoided what passed for intimacy in their relationship.

Sometimes, especially if he had had "only a coupla beers," he attempted to cajole her.

"The lads at the pit were makin' fun of me and yer brothers." Wullie sat by the fire one evening and watched her polishing the boots till they shone.

"What about, Wullie?" She wondered where this was leading.

"About oor shiny shoes. 'Are ye goin' dancin', Wullie?' they says. 'Och, it's ma wife,' I says. 'She's that house proud everything has tae shine.' 'She needs a few bairns, Wullie,' Tam Whiteside says."

"Is that right, Wullie?" Without looking at him, she spat on the brush and vigorously buffed her brothers' pit boots.

Wullie exhaled an exaggerated sigh. "I'm goin' oot."

Staunch Orangeman as he was, he got into fights almost every Saturday night and usually finished up in the centre of some sectarian brawl. It seemed to Lizzie that Lowlanders fought just to entertain themselves. Constable Graham, another faithful Orangeman tried to keep his friend safe and brought him staggering home several nights. Anyone else he'd have thrown in jail. She had no patience for Wullie's deeply ingrained, bitter attitudes about Catholics and feared he'd start a fight he couldn't finish and end up seriously injured.

July 1865

Lizzie couldn't sleep. She'd had a bad feeling about Wullie's state of mind when he left the house. July started the season of the worst brawls—Protestants against Catholics. The rancour reached fever pitch as the Orangemen got ready for the annual parade on the twelfth of July to celebrate the "Glorious Twelfth."

According to Wullie, Orangemen had been marching in these parades annually since 1796 to celebrate the anniversary of William of Orange's victory at the Battle of the Boyne in 1690 over the Catholic King James. He could hardly be called a scholar, but Wullie knew all about that.

1690, for heaven's sake! And still they fought. The battle here in Lanarkshire gave no indication of letting up, just an excuse for them to get into a brawl, but she kept her thoughts to herself.

She sat on Pa's chair with wee Rob on her lap. She treasured these moments when she could read to him. His eyes wandered round the room, to the fire, to the street noises, to the bed where his Papaw and Granny lay listening. The blue, alert gaze always returned to Lizzie.

After the boy's eyes closed, she read on silently, until the rhythmic snoring of both her parents and the crackling fire lulled her to sleep.

* * *

Over the usual Saturday night noise, a loud drunken rendition of an Orange battle cry intruded into her sleep.

"Ho, we are the Billy boys . . ."

She tucked Rob Roy in with his grandparents and opened the door to check the street. When the sky lit up behind them at regular intervals by the spewing furnaces, she clearly saw the silhouette of three men climbing the steep hill.

When the trio, Jamie, Donnie, and her husband, stormed into the room, the draft caused the fire to flare. Lizzie saw more clearly that Wullie had been in a fight.

"He's hurt bad," Jamie said guiltily.

"Put him in here," she said. Her mother and father rose from the box bed. Ma picked up the bairn and cleared a place to deposit Wullie, who seemed ready to collapse.

"Robert, take wee Robbie into the other room."

Mercifully, the child still slept.

Wullie had gone quiet. The twins dragged him to the bed. Ma lit an oil lamp, and Lizzie poured water from the kettle into a basin to tend to his cuts. Lizzie loosened Wullie's clothes and checked his body for injuries. A small, crescent-shaped gash under his rib cage seeped blood.

"What in God's name is this?"

"He was stabbed, Lizzie."

"Get Granny Wilson." Lizzie feared this injury was beyond her nursing abilities and Granny Wilson, the midwife, was the closest to a medical person available.

Minutes later, Granny arrived with her bag of dressings and rudimentary instruments. She took one look at Wullie and gasped.

"How long was the knife?"

Jamie's slurred speech could have been from drink or tears. "It was Mike Rafferty's, not really a knife, more like a hook. It's the tool he uses to clean the horses' hooves, a hoof pick. Yon Mike's a ferrier. It's not very deep. He's had worse. Is he going to be all right, Mrs. Wilson?

Granny went pale. "Did it bleed much?"

"No. Not much at all," Donnie said. "That's good, isn't it?"

But this information seemed to make Granny even more worried. "We have to clean this wound with carbolic. Lizzie, put a few drops in this water. Not too much now, or it'll do more harm than good."

While Lizzie helped the woman clean Wullie's wound and search for other injuries, Jamie and Donald talked, tumbling over each other's words, eager to exonerate themselves.

"Wullie tried to get Mike thrown out of the bar. You know how he feels about Catholics coming in to the Big Tree," said Jamie.

"Aye, and when that didnae work he started in to let Rafferty know that about all he was fit for was cleaning out the horse stalls."

"Aye, Mike takes care of yon white horse Wullie rides in the big Orange Day parade, and Wullie never lets him forget it."

"One thing led to another."

"They'd both been drinking halfs an' pints for hours."

"Go to bed, you two," Lizzie hissed. They were obviously incapable of understanding the seriousness of the situation.

"Aye. Sorry, Lizzie, it wisnae our fault."

"Get Dr. Murray first thing in the morning," Granny said, with an intensity that scared Lizzie.

"But it's Sunday, Granny."

"Get him."

* * *

Wullie improved for a few days, but the doctor said they'd have to watch him for a couple of weeks and keep the room as quiet as possible.

She heard from the twins that Mike Rafferty, who'd dropped out of sight for a few days, returned to his house on the Back Row when he learned Wullie was doing better.

But by Tuesday Wullie's jaw and neck started to get stiff, and his voice didn't even sound like him. Dr. Murray just shook his head and told Lizzie to prepare for the worst. Soon, convulsions wracked Wullie's body night and day. His form rigidly arched in the bed; the muscles of his face tightened, and he alternated between bitter laughter and crying. Lizzie sponged him to reduce his fever. He couldn't eat or drink. Finally, the paroxysms constricted his throat and he choked.

* * *

Because it took Wullie three weeks to die of the lockjaw, the sheriff's court could not easily make a connection between the skirmish and Wullie's demise. Lizzie suspected that Dr. Murray's reason for signing the death certificate with the cause "pneumonia" was to prevent another man's needless death. As a result, the charges against Mike Rafferty were reduced to assault, but the magistrate, a rabid Orangeman, threw the book at him anyway and gave him eight years in Barlinnie Prison in Glasgow.

Lizzie wondered, in the midst of her own distress, how Mrs. Rafferty and her brood would survive Mike's long imprisonment. Revenge was on the minds of the Orangemen; Lizzie could sense the undercurrent at the funeral. Since Wullie had been a Master in the Orange Lodge, the turnout was like for gentry or even royalty. It was the twelfth of July without the merriment. The weeks of violence that followed offered a sad commentary on Wullie Maclure's contribution to society.

She confided to her mother that she was relieved he was gone. Her mother tactfully agreed saying that he'd suffered enough. Lizzie felt she, too, had suffered enough, but she couldn't admit that even to her mother. On behalf of her son she did feel saddened; Wullie was the only father Rob Roy had known, and his violent passing scared the boy.

Jamie voiced his sentiment. "That wee lad has lost a second father."

It was then she told the twins about Jock surviving. They were amazed and wanted to tell everyone. Lizzie thought it better if they didn't let it get about, even though Jock was out of harm's way.

Aleck MacGregor, Jock's brother, and Wullie's cousin, came from Motherwell to represent the family. The Maclures wanted to know the manner of Aleck's parents' passing. John had died last summer within weeks of Nellie in the cholera epidemic that had ravaged the miners' rows of Motherwell.

Lizzie wanted to discreetly question Aleck about Jock's whereabouts. But at the wake Jamie asked him, saving her the embarrassment.

"Did Aleck have Jock's address?" she asked her brother later.

"I asked Aleck, Lizzie. But the daft big tattiebogle never looked in his mother's things before they were burned after the cholera."

"So he had no information?"

"Ou-aye, he said Jock went to Ottawa."

"He did? Anything else?"

"Ah didnae ask him." Lizzie gave her young brother a contemptuous look.

CHAPTER THIRTY-NINE

Staying Alive

Happy, ye sons of busy life,
Who, equal to the bustling strife,
No other view regard!

Wullie had been dead for six months that bleak Hogmanay of '65. Not much to celebrate going into 1866, except perhaps that they still had their house, thanks to the fact that the twins lived with them and worked at the pit. Her mother had stopped producing siller from her magical kist, so the contributions the twins made needed to be stretched pretty thin.

"Do ye think oor Annie would help us?"

Lizzie thought her father must be desperate or getting senile to come up with such an idea.

"No," she said tersely— then more kindly, "I don't think they've got the wherewithal to help, Pa."

"Lizzie's right, Pa," said Jamie. "Yon Shanks fell out of favour with Mr. Dixon and the other bosses. I think Mr. Dixon put up with him because he got his niece, Sophie, in the family way, but with her gone, God rest her soul, he doesn't need to keep up the pretence."

Donnie picked up the story. "Dixon fired him, and the other owners followed suit. There was some talk about negligence after Jock's team got blown up. He even tried to blame Paddy Riley, insinuating he took off after the accident. Little does he know he attended Paddy's funeral. Just too many accidents happened on Shanks' watch. Talk at the Big Tree was that the investigators found some damaged chain at the site."

"Shut up, Donald. Have ye nae sense!" He nudged his brother and tilted his head towards Lizzie.

"What are ye talking about?" Lizzie asked.

After some hesitation, Jamie told her, "They hushed it up, Lizzie, but some of the foundry workers think the chain they suspended the cauldron on had a weakened link."

"What?"

"Lizzie, don't go upsetting yourself about it. Lots of times the equipment gets old and worn and they don't replace it till something goes wrong. Right, Jamie?" said Donnie.

"Aye, that's about all they could pin on Shanks. I think the man is demented. They probably were afraid of him and his methods." He added, "I wonder how oor Annie puts up wi' him."

His twin said, "Annie would put up with the devil himself if . . ."

"Never mind, you two. She is your sister, after all," said Ma.

But Lizzie didn't care how her sister and brother-in-law lived. "I heard the grandparents are raising Sophie's son. Just as well. It's hard to imagine oor Annie having much patience for a bairn," she said.

"I hope she's happy. Maybe some day she'll have a wee one of her own." Her mother seemed to be talking to herself. "I wonder how they can afford to live in their fancy house."

Nobody else seemed to want to speculate on Annie's fortune or the lack of it. They turned their attention to Rob Roy, now nearly two-and-a-half, who lit up everyone's life.

Lizzie's father had miraculously survived this past year. Ma said he lived on because of Rob Roy. His joy was to spend countless hours with his wife and wee Rob, sharing stories about Rannoch. He didn't miss the coal mine a bit. Lizzie enjoyed the yarns as she bustled around the but and ben.

"Story, Papaw." He climbed on his grandfather's lap.

Lizzie settled into a chair by the fire to read the paper. She'd picked up *The Scotsman* since the last *Glasgow Herald* had been sold out.

"Get up here, lad."

"Ranowk Moo." He snuggled into the crook of his grandfather's arm.

"Och! Rannoch Moor. There you could open the windows and let the fresh air blow through. You could go outdoors and take full deep breaths of it without choking and coughing. You could scout the green fields and the rugged hills without your eyes smarting from the fumes and smoke belching out of mines and factories. You could rest your eyes on green pastures dotted with sheep."

"Tell 'bout the sheep, Papaw."

"Och! You even knew the sheep by name." He remembered some of them. "There was Big Tam the Ram, practically killed the old ewe giving birth to him. Yer mother brought the wet squirmy lamb into the cold spring world of melting snow. He grew up to be a great breeder, always sired great hulking lambs."

"Och! Robert, the wean is too young to understand all that."

"Right, Flora . . ." Her father coughed and spat into the spittoon kept nearby. When he got his breath back he continued. "Then there was 'Meggie-monyfeet'; the weans dubbed her that. That sheep could climb the craggy hills behind the cottage faster than a mountain goat. Yer Uncle Donnie and Uncle Jamie would chase her up the slopes and around the rocks but never catch her. Sheep are more sure-footed than children. Anyway, the fun was in the chase."

Finally, Rob Roy would fall asleep, but the old man would ramble on with his stories, for his wife never tired of them.

"It never bothered us back then that we only got to tend these animals, not own them, did it? Lamb or even mutton was a very rare thing indeed at oor table, or on any tenant's table."

"Hunger makes good kitchen," said Ma. "The Auld Laird did right by us, though. Always a shilling for a new bairn, a bottle of whisky at New Year's, a spring lamb every Easter, a hind of beef before winter set in."

"Aye, and you could keep half the oats and the barley that grew on your acre. Most years there were plenty of potatoes to go around, too. With that and a wee bit of poaching me and John Campbell got away with when the rabbits got kind of numerous and the laird turned a blind eye, a man could live decently and feed his family."

Ma enjoyed the reminiscences. "At butchering time the laird always shared with the cottars," she said. "Remember the sheep's-head soup? That was yer favourite. With a few onions out of the backyard garden plot, some kale and chopped potato, add a bit of turnip, and I had pottage to please a hungry ploughman and half a dozen bairns."

"Flora, ye made the best pot of soup this side of the Minch, simmered all day in the big iron pot over the open fire. Nobody ever turned their nose up at Flora MacDonald MacGregor's good Highland cooking."

"It's not the same here getting food from a shop and not from your own plot," said her mother.

"Aye. Too many things are different. Here the young men die. Jock, then Wullie . . ." Lizzie had told her father that Jock was alive and he was in Canada, but he sometimes forgot.

When Lizzie was reminded of Wullie, she felt guilty because he rarely came to her mind. She worried about how they could scrape by, but that hardly amounted to mourning.

Ma tried to cheer Pa. "Och! Some day we'll see Charlie MacGregor walk through that door."

"Flora, maybe _you_ will. Unless oor Charlie comes soon, I'll not be seeing him."

With Rob Roy safe and happy with his grandparents, and the house shiny and clean, she needed something new to fill her mind . . . something new to stop the intruding thoughts about her lost bairn . . . something to eclipse the recurring dreams about Jock.

She needed to get out of the house; she needed diversion; she needed something to keep the pervading thoughts at a safer distance. Money was tight. It was unfair to expect the twins to give up so much of their pay-packet to run the household. She'd talk to Miss Ferguson tomorrow about a possible opening at the post office.

* * *

The postmistress was happy to offer Lizzie part-time employment Tuesday through Thursday in the mailroom. It felt good to have her mind challenged again. She sorted the mail, attended the counter, and began to learn Morse code in order to send telegrams.

Lizzie worked at the post office only two weeks before her father passed away peacefully in his sleep. Lizzie and her mother tried to contain their grief the best they could in order to attend to the inconsolable Rob Roy.

* * *

Lizzie sent letters to the post office in Ottawa, Canada: two each to Charlie and Jock. With the death of Jock's mother, and his brother's dim-witted carelessness, Lizzie had lost the chance of having a proper address for Jock and Charlie. Sometimes she'd feel her anger growing until it included Jock. Surely he could have contacted her, even if she were married to Wullie. Damn these men and their pride and stupidity! She waited impa-tiently. Even if they got the letters promptly, it would take six weeks for the letters to get there and six weeks for a reply. She could be waiting forever for something that was never going to happen. Damn! Damn! Damn!

* * *

On a cold blustery evening in April, Lizzie came home from the post office to a house filled with warmth from a crackling fire and the welcome aroma from Ma's soup pot, as well as a yeasty fragrance coming from her new oven. Bread. Mmmm! Mother's home-baked bread. Her mother relaxed on the old rocker with Rob Roy wrapped in a plaidie.

"Look, Ma." She waved a letter in front of her mother. "It's from the Isle of Lewis. It has a Stornoway postmark."

After Lizzie fortified herself with mutton broth and several slices of the buttered warm bread, she settled in the chair with Rob Roy to hear her mother read the news from her home.

"It's from Kate MacKay. Her mother passed away. Och! That's sad. My Aunt Jennie was so good to me. More like a mother, she was. A fine lady. But she must have been on in years."

Her mother read on a little farther. "Listen to this, Lizzie. She says she has something for me from my father, his . . . my family Bible. Her mother saved it all these years. Kate writes that it's too precious to send through the post and wants us to come and get it. She is returning to Rannoch . . . 'see enclosed.' Here, read this, Lizzie, the print is gie small."

Lizzie took the newspaper article from *The Scotsman* and unfolded it with some dread. Unlikely though it was, she feared it could be bad news about Jock or Charlie or someone else they knew.

"Listen to this, Ma. 'Lady Isobel Menzies Buchanan and her daughter, Mrs. Cecil Winterbottom of Rannoch, were suddenly taken ill on a trip to Edinburgh. The ladies both succumbed to the cholera, which is a pestilence in the Capital right now. Mrs. Winterbottom, mistress of Aulich House and estates in Rannoch, died childless. Her husband, Captain Cecil Winterbottom, is the presumed heir to Aulich House and the Buchanan holdings in Rannoch.'"

"That damned Englishman has taken over our land. Sassenach squatter!" Lizzie spluttered, enraged all over again about their eviction.

"Aye, there's no justice, it seems." Her mother referred again to Kate's letter. "Winterbottom can't run the place without her, she says."

"I'm not surprised; it looked a bit run down when I went there two years ago," said Lizzie. "She hates the man, but she loves Rannoch, and, of course, it's not easy for her to get a good position as a housekeeper in Lewis."

"I didn't know about a family Bible. Och! It'll be grand to get my hands on it. Imagine, after all these years. Aunt Jennie must have thought me too young to be entrusted with it when I left Lewis."

CHAPTER FORTY

The Contents of the Kist

Ye sprightly youths quite flush with hope and spirit
Who think to storm the world by dint of merit

Jamie and Donnie both volunteered to make the trip to Rannoch, if they could get the time off. An argument ensued about who would get to go. Lizzie suggested they toss a coin to decide. She would have preferred to go herself, but Rob Roy had a slight fever, and Ma seemed to be coming down with the same thing.

Later that night, the twins came back from the Big Tree Bar. Ma and wee Robbie were asleep.

"What did you two decide?" she asked.

"We did like you said," Jamie started.

"But it went all wrong." Donnie tried to stop laughing and nudged his brother to behave, too. He went on. "The bartender tossed a sixpence, and it came down and rolled under the bar."

"That eejit, yer brother, tried tae get to it . . . covered in sawdust he was. Yon Peter Shanks came in; didn't see our Donnie and tripped over him." They were slapping each other in merriment.

"Sssh, ye'll waken the wean," said Lizzie, but she smiled, waiting to hear more.

The attempt to whisper made the twins even more uproarious.

"He sprawls across the bar and spills about three beers," said Donnie.

"And the fight was on!" added his brother. "We slipped out the back door."

Lizzie had to laugh. "And who won the bet, Jamie?"

"We didn't wait to find out. That Shanks is a madman. No tellin' what he'd do."

"We decided, Lizzie, we're both goin'."

"All right," she said. "Can we all get some sleep now?"

* * *

Ma stayed in bed for a few days, insisting she was just tired, but Lizzie worried that now she might lose her mother. She had no obvious sickness but could someone die of a broken heart? Then again, her mother's heart had been broken and patched so many times, and she had survived. Lizzie believed, or hoped, Ma was invincible.

Glad to have the twins gone, she could devote her energy to nursing Ma and wee Rob back to health.

"Are you any better, Ma?" Her mother was sitting quietly by the fire.

"Aye. But I'm tired tonight, just a bit light-headed. A good night's sleep will set me straight. So much happening in such a short time, it's hard for an old woman to keep up."

The next morning, Sunday, she asked Lizzie to sit on the bed. She had something to say. "It's time for you to take the contents of my kist."

"Ma. What do you mean? Are you ill?"

"Just tired, Lizzie, just tired."

"Oh, Ma."

"Go on, Lizzie, here's the key." She took off the fine chain she always wore round her neck. "I want to get some sleep."

Lizzie rummaged through the kist's treasures—bits and pieces of hand-tatted lace, baby shoes, and her mother's favourite wool dress. Wrapped in a piece of tartan was a portrait of a man in military attire, standing with a young woman who resembled Ma. At the bottom of the chest, Lizzie found a cigar box with three guineas in it, and a bundle of folded papers identified with each child's name, date of birth, and date of death. When unfolded, the papers revealed either a golden or a reddish lock of hair.

And then there was the book collection. When she picked up *Tales from Shakespeare*, a dozen or more sheets of fine writing paper fell from between the pages: letters to 'Flora' from 'C.B'—Charlie Buchanan, of course. The contents were innocent enough. Comments about books he had read, trips taken, newsy items about the family and staff at the big house, and requests for news of Flora's children. They always ended with warmest regards for her mother's well-being and a comment referring to the contents: "I trust this helps you through this poor harvest season."

Or: "Another child is a blessing, but I'm sure this will help your strained circumstances."

There were dozens of similar notes. The laird had been sending Mother money for years in Rannoch. But why? Mother had been very secretive about it. Was it shame? Fear? Something else? Lizzie decided to approach her mother with the question. There is nothing worse than unfinished business when a parent passes on.

What a thought. Ma couldn't die. Not now. Ma was just weary. Who wouldn't be, after all she'd been through.

Robbie woke crying. She hurried to the other room to attend to him before he disturbed her mother. But her mother had awakened and was comforting the wee lad.

"Ma, whose picture is that in the kist—the man? The woman must be Granny; she looks just like you."

"Aye. Everybody said that. But I never saw her. She died birthing me." Was that a note of guilt in her voice?

Rob Roy sat in the bed contentedly by his grandmother's side. He'd sit there hypnotized for hours listening to a story, even when he couldn't possibly understand it.

"And the man? Your father? Ma, it looks just like the picture of Colonel Buchanan that I saw the day I was at the big house."

"It does, doesn't it?" Ma hung her head.

So that was it after all. Just as so many had suspected, Ma was the colonel's love child.

"I showed the laird that picture one day." Ma's eyes looked off to the side, remembering. "It did give him quite a start. But he swore to me it wasn't him."

"How could you believe him?" Lizzie was losing patience.

"Well, my father was a Buchanan from Lennox; that I knew. I always believed . . . the MacKays believed, and the colonel confirmed, that Papa was just a clansman, not a close relation to the chief's family. The physical resemblance was a throwback to a past generation maybe . . ."

"Ma!" Lizzie was incredulous.

"You may think me naïve, Lizzie, and God knows maybe I am. I can't believe a father would treat his daughter as a servant. The laird did right by his flock . . ."

"But not by you. Why would his wife and daughter be so resentful of you? Och! It all makes sense . . ." She stopped when her mother started to weep.

"I'm sorry Ma, but if we are Buchanans, have we no claim? Mary is gone. Can that Sassenach be the true heir to Rannoch? What about the birth certificate Charlie has in Canada?"

"See there, Lizzie. If my father was Charlie Buchanan, wouldn't it say so on the certificate, and would Kate not have seen his name there?"

"Maybe. Maybe not. There are birth certificates that don't bear the father's name—for obvious reasons."

"And why would Murdoch MacKay tell me all those stories about my father?"

"I don't know about Murdoch. But I do see why you'd believe what he said."

"He wouldn't lie, Lizzie."

Lizzie was perplexed. It was a mystery. No doubt about it.

Lizzie's mind raced, "Ma, would there not be a record in the parish church in Stornoway?"

Her mother explained through her sobs, "I hoped you wouldn't ask, Lizzie, for if there ever was a record of my birth, it was destroyed in the fire. The Free Kirk burned in 1850. Uncle Archie told me about it on his trip south to Lanarkshire when you and Charlie were about ten. I'm so sorry, Lizzie"

* * *

The twins arrived bursting with tales of Rannoch and reunions with old friends.

"The air here stinks. I can't believe we ever got accustomed to it." Jamie screwed his face up in disgust.

"The air is so clean and fresh, and the quiet hills and moors were hard to leave. Rannoch is our home. We have to get back there before this place buries any more of our family," Donnie said. "Ma, ye wouldn't believe yon laird, paradin' round in a kilt like he's a Scot."

Jamie laughed. "His bony backside barely holds it up. They had to bring a doctor in from London to treat him where he cut his leg so bad when the dirk in his sock got loose on his skinny legs and skidded givin' him a deep cut in his calf."

"What do ye suppose he wears under that kilt, Jamie?"

"Probably some silk knickers from Paris . . ."

"Enough about the Sassenach," said Lizzie "What did Kate have for Ma?"

They dug an object, carefully wrapped in a plaidie, out of their duffle bag.

"Ma, you're a Buchanan. Mary's dead, no child. We are the natural heirs to Rannoch. Ma, we should be living there, not here," said Donnie.

"What are you talking about?" Lizzie said, reluctant to re-open that touchy subject after the last few days of discussing it with Ma.

"Kate Mackay told us the whole story. Open it," said Donnie, pushing the green leather-bound family Bible at Ma.

Lizzie leaned over her mother's shoulder to read the mysterious geneal-ogy on the flyleaf of the precious book. She scanned the many entries of generations of "Buchanans" born in Lennox—down to the last one:

James and Charles Buchanan, twin boys, born September Eleven in the year of our Lord 1790. In Lennox, Scotland.

James Buchanan married Elizabeth MacDonald tenth of November in the year of our Lord 1815.

Ma's father? It had to be.

"Twins!" Lizzie and her mother gasped the word out at the same moment.

"Just so," said Jamie. "Kate MacKay's mother knew all about the Buchanan brothers. She kept our grandfather's identity secret till close to her death."

"Aye. If she'd told someone before Charlie Buchanan died, it wouldn't have been so easy for him to leave his holdings to his own lineage exclusively."

"Aye, Lizzie, ye have a way wi' words. What yer sister means is, he couldn't have left it to the high and mighty Mary," Donnie said, nudging his brother.

"Och! I understood her," Jamie said. "In other words, Ma could have inherited."

"Yer aunt let you go to the mainland with Charlie because she believed he would do right by his brother's child. Treat you like his own," Lizzie said.

"He didn't though, did he?" Donnie's eyes sparked with indignation.

"I can't believe Charlie Buchanan would . . ." Ma's voice trailed off.

"I believe it," Lizzie said as the full portent of the news began to dawn on her. "He thought only about himself. His wife and his stuck-up daughter knew, too. They kept that secret from Ma—no wonder they hated her." Lizzie remembered the bitter conversation she had overheard at the mansion.

"He even let people think I was his illegitimate bairn . . ." Lizzie gaped at her mother. Flora knew all the gossip!

"Charlie Buchanan got too greedy. He didn't want to share what rightfully belonged to his twin," said Jamie.

"How could ye treat yer kin that way?" Donnie said.

Lizzie watched her brothers as they took turns dandling Rob Roy on their laps and wondered, too.

The story unfolded well into the evening, a more fascinating tale than any Ma could have produced out of the novels in her kist—their own story.

Donnie began. "James and Charles Buchanan left Lennox to go to the wars in Europe . . . as young men. Like most Highlanders they spent their fighting days on the front. James was injured at the Battle of Waterloo and spent time in hospital. There and on the battlefield he'd seen enough Scots dying for a cause they hardly cared about and felt the call of his Island home. They quietly welcomed him back in Stornoway as a hero, then sealed their lips about his wherabouts, because, of course, he was hounded as a deserter."

Jamie jumped in. "His parents thought James was dead, and he let them believe that, thinking they might feel he had dishonoured the fam—"

"But he hadn't," Lizzie burst out. "He'd followed his conscience. And it's what he truly believed. We all know it. Scottish blood is shed first in their wars. Some of the glens were emptied of young men in those days." Lizzie repeated her father's words, eager to defend her newfound ancestor.

"Aye, Lizzie. You're right, of course." Jamie went quietly thoughtful.

Donnie picked up the story. "The Buchanans in Lennox near Loch Lomond, had left their considerable wealth to their sons, James and Charles. James being primary heir to the estates and titles of the Buchanans made it way more complicated."

"Anyway, James chose to allow his brother to inherit but only on one condition, which he spelled out in a codicil to be attached to Charlie's will before Charlie left to marry Isobel Menzies in 1824 when he took our mother and Kate Mackay with him to the mainland," said Donnie.

"What is that? What is a codicil?" Her mother had not said a word since the Bible had been placed in her hand. She sat fondling it as though her contact with the ancient book united her with her broken and scattered forebears.

Lizzie explained, "To the best of my understanding, a codicil is an addition to a will to explain or change something in it."

"Where is it, then?" her mother asked.

Jamie said sadly, "Kate Mackay searched her mother's croft but couldn't find it."

Lizzie felt the joy and hope seeping out of the room.

Donnie said, "But why else would the Buchanan family Bible be passed along to Ma? It's the most precious possession, after the land, that a parent leaves to a child. Think of it. THE LAND! This means Ma had to be heritor to the Rannoch land. Surely her claim supersedes some Englishman who simply married into the family."

"The Bible doesn't mention Ma by name." Lizzie felt disgust and rekindled anger. "We're no better off than we were before."

"Aye, my mother would have added my name if she'd lived," Ma said. "But I know who I am. Finally I know the pieces of my story that always mystified me." She held the book tightly to her chest.

"But, Ma, without your name appearing somewhere, there's no other confirmation." Lizzie said, hating to deflate her mother.

"Aye, Lizzie's right. We need the baptismal record. Do ye think Charlie would have held on to it all these years?" said Jamie.

"Fat lot of good it'll do us in Canada, anyway." Donnie slumped into the chair with a defeated look.

"Our Charlie probably doesn't even know its significance." Lizzie thought it useless to discuss it further, and began to set the table for dinner. The group fell silent.

After they ate, Jamie found a half-empty bottle of whisky and poured a soupçon in glasses for the women and a hearty dram for him and his brother. Lizzie gulped the bitter liquid down to numb her disappointment.

Lizzie and Ma trooped off to bed and left the twins arguing about their future. Tomorrow was a workday.

CHAPTER FORTY-ONE

Across the Tracks

'Alas! How oft in haughty mood,
God's creatures they oppress!
Or else, neglecting a' that's guid,
They riot in excess

ummer in Whifflet meant that the muck in the street stunk more than usual. Potato peelings and other household garbage, mixed with the contents of chamber pots, stagnated on the road most days or coursed slowly down the sheugh when rain or the buckets of dirty water ejected from the houses turned it into a runnel. Diligent housewives swept, scrubbed, mopped, and dusted in a losing battle to eradicate the foul dirt that accumulated in the crowded one- and two-room houses. Lizzie would always be an outsider. Her refined accent and her education had always been resented by these women who had little or no schooling. Lizzie made no effort to make friends. What would be the point; she could never imagine spending the rest of her life here.

Though only three, Rob Roy loved to be outdoors with pals his age, but Lizzie and her mother worried about him constantly and one or the other kept an eye on him. Lizzie never could resign herself to raising her son in this village. She had admonished Rob Roy often enough about playing near the cart wheels or the privy, the sheugh, and the filthy streets, but of course he was accustomed to dirt and bad smells. He always followed

287

the other boys into whatever adventures and devilment they found to amuse themselves.

Out in the street, fighting and cursing usually filled the air after dark. But on this dry, overcast day the social interaction was strangely subdued. Neighbours, mostly women, and a few old men who weren't at the pit, stood around in groups in deep discussion, casting frequent glances at the door of number eight. Lizzie overheard their conversation when she put Rob Roy out to play. A neighbour's child had been ill, and the local women feared an epidemic.

The boy must have died for there to be this much curiosity.

"Do ye think he's gone, Sadie?"

"Och aye! That wean's had the fever on an' off for weeks now."

"Did he get the spots on his belly?"

"Ou-aye! An' the diarrhoea. Granny Wilson says it's the typhoid."

"Oh, well, that's bad then."

"Did that wifey no' lose other bairns wi' the fever?"

"She lost one wi' cholera. Her second bairn was born dead."

"Do ye tell me?"

"Ou-aye! It was all the talk at the time. Must've been a dozen folks died that summer. Mostly weans. Do ye no' remember? Must have been before ye came over frae the old country."

"It was two wee boys then, too, wis it no'?"

"Ou-aye! It's a' boys we lost. Cholera took them. Hard to keep the wee boys out o' the muck. They're ower there playin' around that privy. Ye'd think the stink would chase them awa'."

"If I've told my man once I've told him a hundred times, we were better off in Ireland. We didnae have much, but at least ye could breathe the air."

"Ou-aye! Too many people in one room. Too many families sharin' the privies. I widnae use them or let the weans use them, so I'm just about bow-legged carrying out chamber pots and cleaning up filth, and the house smells like a midden anyway."

Lizzie stood on the step and silently prayed, *please, God, get us out of this place*. She came back indoors, dragging Rob Roy. "Ma, it's been almost a year since we started trying to trace Charlie and Jock."

"Aye. And all the while old Freezy-arse is camped on our property," Jamie said.

* * *

"Good morning, Lizzie." Miss Ferguson smiled her usual greeting. "It'll be so good to have you here on Mondays from now on. Monday's when we sort the mail from London and abroad. Here, you start with this batch from the continent."

Lizzie arranged the letters, mostly from soldiers stationed abroad. Their sweethearts and mothers would be asking for these as soon the post office opened. When she finished the sorting, Miss Ferguson said, "Lizzie. You can take this."

"What is it?" Lizzie scanned the manila envelope from Ottawa, Canada.

"It's for your mother. Annie usually picks them up."

"What? Lizzie caught her breath. "How long have these been arriving?"

"I didn't always notice. Annie sorted the transatlantic mail when she was here. I think they came about every other month or so. Why? Did your mother not tell you?"

Lizzie couldn't answer. What did it mean?

"May I take this to my mother?"

"Of course, Lizzie. Can't it wait till dinnertime? I can spare you then."

"No. No. I have to go." Lizzie, vaguely aware of Miss Ferguson's curiosity, didn't want to answer any questions. Had Charlie finally received one of the letters she had scattered around North America? She had to know what the envelope from Canada contained. The fact that this was not the first reply puzzled her.

"Hurry back . . ." But she was out of the door and didn't hear the rest.

* * *

Lizzie burst into the house yelling. "Ma. Ma!"

"Hush, Lizzie, your brothers are sleeping. What happened?"

Speechless, Lizzie waved the letter in front of her mother's face. Ma took it and read aloud the postmark. "Ottawa." She sank into her chair and ripped open the envelope. After a few seconds, which seemed like hours to Lizzie, she heard her mother's sob and muffled words. "Charlie. It's oor Charlie."

She unfolded the single sheet of paper. Brightly coloured bank notes tumbled to the floor.

Ma seemed to have lost the power of speech. Lizzie grabbed the letter and moved quickly to the window to read. Although Ma had already read it, Lizzie read aloud:

"Dear Mother,

"Please respond as soon as possible. Or have Lizzie write to me. It has been over a year since you wrote. How is Pa?

"Lizzie must have had her second child by now.

"I will not send money this way again unless I hear from you. This is not like you. I'm afraid my letters are going amissing.

"I sincerely hope you are all well.

"Your Loving Son,

"Charles.

"P. S. Helene and I had a son this year. We call him Charles MacDonald MacGregor. A fine Highland name. He has the lungs of a piper."

Jamie and Donald stood in the doorway, rubbing sleep out of their eyes.

"A letter from Charlie." Lizzie heard her own words like a voice crying in the wilderness.

"We heard," said the twins.

Jamie bent to retrieve the money scattered on the floor.

"What's to be done?" Lizzie said. "Our sister has been intercepting these letters and keeping the money. Can you believe it?"

"Her husband must have put her up to this," said her mother.

"Maybe. He's been out of work for months, and they still live in that fancy house in Blairhill," said Jamie.

But Lizzie wondered if Annie was just as capable of treachery as her vile husband. The pieces began to fit. "Our Annie has some questions to answer."

Lizzie left the house abruptly with a scarf around her face to protect against the smoky, gritty air, and sped down Whifflet Street.

She should stop at the post office to explain to Miss Ferguson. Explain what? Maybe she'd wait to hear Annie's story. She turned the corner at Hozier Street and practically collided with the blacksmith, Davie Mills, coming out of the close, leading the horse Wullie used to ride in the parade.

"Mrs. Maclure. Awfy glad tae see ye." His heat-scorched face beamed in her direction. "Och! Ye havnae changed one iota from the bonnie young lass that arrived here aff the train . . . how mony years is it?"

"It's more than six years, Mr. Mills. Either your eyes are going bad, or you're getting the blarney in your old age."

The mare at his side whinnied and pawed the ground.

"Where are you aff tae in such a hurry?"

"I'm going to King Street to see our Annie," Lizzie said, an involuntary sigh escaping her lips.

"Ou-aye! Annie." He gave her a sympathetic smile. "Wid ye like a ride ower there? If ye don't mind ridin' in a cairt. I have tae make a delivery tae Bank Street; I'll be ready in twa shakes o' a lamb's tail."

"That would be a great service to me, Mr. Mills."

The sooner she completed this unpleasant mission, the better. She used the time to run into the post office. "Miss Ferguson, I have to take the afternoon off. I'm sorry. It's important family business."

Her boss nodded gravely. Lizzie was vaguely aware that Miss Ferguson now sensed the conflict and was drawing some conclusions, but was too well-mannered to pry.

"Oh, and Miss Ferguson, would your brother in Glasgow know a solicitor we could retain?"

"Gordon is a solicitor. But Lizzie, I don't know if I want him to get involved in a dispute between you and your sister. Annie was, after all, an employee of mine too."

"Oh no, miss. It's about another matter." Lizzie hesitated. Maybe there would be a conflict with Annie. Shanks would relish a fight. She couldn't think about that right now. "I'll be in early tomorrow."

In ten minutes, Davie had hitched old Bessie to the wagon. Lizzie climbed up and perched on the metal seat. The horse trotted down Hozier Street and turned right onto Wallace Street past St. Mary's Catholic Chapel. She settled down to an amble when they turned the corner onto Dundyvan Road.

Charlie . . . married . . . with a bairn . . . sending money to his mother . . . for years. How much? Had Annie stolen it all? There could be no other explanation. Annie never came to see them. Lizzie had always figured she considered them too lowly. But now there might be another reason.

Lizzie watched the landscape and tried to distract herself from her wild imaginings. Whifflet Farm was on the right, and farther down the cobblestone road the British Tube works spewed black smoke into the afternoon sky. Even the noxious fumes were overpowered by the stench of the slaughterhouse they were now passing. Poor old Bessie whinnied in sympathy.

They passed English Square. The square got its name from the skilled English workers that had been brought in from the ironworks in the Midlands. Not many English there anymore; the place had fallen into disrepair like all the rows. The housing was conveniently nestled between convergent railroad tracks on its north and south boundaries; to the east, a few yards away from the end of the row, was Dundyvan Iron and Steelworks. To the east, beyond the nearest pall of smoke, were the Eglinton Silica Brickworks and the Coatbridge Boilerworks. Nothing grew here except bow-legged children—not a tree, not a flower—nothing.

If they could reach Charlie; if they could prove their inheritance, perhaps her family could move from this dreary landscape.

Bessie pulled the wagon across uneven railroad tracks, shaking Lizzie precariously to the edge of her metal throne.

Did Charlie know where Jock was? Oh God! Jock could be married, too.

They passed the Presbyterian Church, with its fieldstone construction blackened by the grime that covered the buildings almost as soon as they were built. The road sloped down now to Bank Street.

"Just let me off at the corner," she said.

"Och, no, Mrs. Maclure. Ye'll ride in style. It's no' that much farther."

Lizzie settled back to enjoy the ride across busy Bank Street with its horse-drawn carriages and lively shops.

They crossed the Canal Bridge, and Davie pointed out the barges headed for Glasgow. He yelled a big "Hallo" to John Ferguson, a Dundyvan chap walking along the footpath, guiding a Clydesdale horse, which was pulling a wooden barge that sat low in the water, loaded with coal.

"Good day for a walk in the country," Davie called to him. John gave him a sardonic grin. Davie told Lizzie that John would walk the twelve miles to Glasgow today.

"Looks like that shoe's holdin' good fur him," he called.

"Ou-aye! It better hold up at the prices ye charge." John waved as he disappeared under the road bridge.

"That horse throws a shoe 'bout once a month," Davie told Lizzie.

The houses improved on this part of the road, and Lizzie quietly admired the pocket-handkerchief-sized gardens in front of the ground-floor homes. As they rode along tree-lined King Street, the houses became grander. Davie pulled up beside a prosperous looking, two-story sandstone house.

"Well, lass, here we are. Looks like Annie moved up in the world. Did she no'?"

He parked the wagon at the curb-side and helped Lizzie down to the ground. Lizzie, hesitant now about confronting her bad-tempered sister, made small talk.

"Look at those dahlias . . . and roses. I always wanted a garden. Nothin' wants tae grow in Whifflet."

"Och! Some day ye'll have a wee garden of yer own," Davie said.

Lizzie thought she caught a fleeting glimpse of dark familiar eyes darting from behind the swinging lace curtains.

She thanked Davie and walked slowly up the path, breathing in the exotic fragrance of roses in bloom. She thought she saw lace curtains move on some of the neighbouring windows, too. She reached the door and its shiny brass plate with "Peter Shanks" inscribed on it. The door opened almost before the echoing noise of the brass knocker ceased.

Annie leaned out past Lizzie, surveyed King Street up one side and down the other, and hissed between gritted teeth, "Get in here. What are ye trying to do?"

Lizzie stepped into the dark hallway. The place smelled of wax polish. Her sister bustled ahead of her into a parlour; dark velvet drapes framed the bay windows, and lace curtains covered the glass. The plush red carpeting had an intricate design; the mahogany sideboard was polished to a glasslike finish. It was the most elegant room Lizzie had seen since the Auld Laird's house in Rannoch.

"What are you trying to do?" Annie's question became vehement and loud, now that she was out of the earshot of nosy neighbours. Her eyes blazed; her full red face contorted with anger, and her white-knuckled hands left red welts as she grasped and ungrasped her chubby arms.

"Riding up to my front door on a blacksmith's cart. Have ye no sense of pro-pri-ety? Givin' the neighbours an eyeful. I am black affronted. No wonder I never have any of my family over here. Not one of ye knows how to act in so-cy-e-tee. What else can ye expect from folk that are content to live in a slum?"

Lizzie, who had not been offered a seat, pulled herself up to her full height and adjusted the shawl around her. "Where we live has not affected our integrity. I'll get straight to the point. Do you know something about our Charlie?"

"What should I know about him? He ran off after committing a crime. Lucky the new laird didn't chase us and . . ."

Lizzie thumped her fist on the shiny sideboard, rattling the display of china plates. "How do ye pay for all these fancy furnishings? Jamie says Peter Shanks has been laid off for months now."

"How dare you—"

"Where does the money come from Annie? When did you last hear from my brother?" Lizzie pulled off her shawl to dispel the heat she was creating with her anger and took a long step that put her very close to her sister. Annie cowered as though she expected to be hit.

"Och! Jist those stupid letters." Clearly she had guessed that Lizzie had received one of those "stupid letters." Her grin lent a sinister quality to this last remark. She seemed to stop herself, as if unsure what to say next or realized she had already said too much. "He's so spineless; he ran away from Scotland. Pshaw!"

"What letters did you get? What do ye know of Charlie? Tell me. Have ye heard from him?" Lizzie leaned toward her sister, barely resisting grabbing her by the shoulders and shaking her to speed up the story.

"It's not important. They're old news now."

"Do you still have them?"

"They might be around here somewhere . . . or maybe Peter threw them out." Annie shrugged her shoulders.

"Annie, unless you give them up, I'll search this house. I'll tear apart every room; I'll open every drawer."

To prove it, she marched over to the mahogany sideboard, the most likely place to store important papers, and opened the top drawer.

"Don't," Annie wailed, too late.

"What's this?"

Her eye was drawn to two delicate silver spoons among the neatly arranged silverware resting on green felt, baby spoons bearing the Buchanan crest:

Elizabeth Buchanan MacGregor
Born July 10 1843—her birth date.
Charles Buchanan MacGregor
Born July 10 1843—Charlie's birth date.
Ma's treasures.

"What does this mean?" Lizzie scrutinized her sister, who now looked truly frightened.

Annie started jabbering about Ma's kist. "It's not fair. She's leaving everything to you. I should have got something."

Lizzie regarded her sister with a stricken expression. She was a thief. The Highland code about trust between family members was unbreakable . . . her own sister, a common thief. Annie had stolen from the family, from their mother's kist. It was unconscionable. But she'd deal with that later; now desperate for news of Charlie she didn't care what Annie had stolen out of the kist. She wanted to hear about her brother. "THE LETTERS . . . NOW . . . before I turn you over to the authorities. Do you realize that intercepting the Royal Mail and posing as another for financial gain are serious crimes? You could go to jail for a very long time."

"What in hell is goin' on down there? Where's my breakfast, bitch?"

"It's him. You better leave."

Lizzie could see fear in her sister's eyes. She felt a fleeting sensation of pity.

"Did he put you up to this?" Lizzie asked.

"Och! You jist hate him because he chose me instead of you."

Her pity evaporated.

"You made a bargain with the devil, Annie. Maybe you're too stupid to know, but he understands the seriousness of this offense. Just keep the letters. I'd as soon have the constable come and look for them anyway. There's nothing I'd like to see better than Peter Shanks dragged out of here in handcuffs."

"You're a vindictive woman, Lizzie MacGregor. He had nothing to do with this. I only took what should have been my share. But I don't want you upsetting my husband. Here." Annie opened the other sideboard drawer, thrust a pile of letters in tattered, yellowed envelopes at Lizzie, and reverted suddenly to her old habit of nail biting. "Here, take the spoons . . . and here's some of the money."

Lizzie resisted her impulse to look at the letters and stuffed them and the spoons into her apron and tucked the end of it into her waistband.

"What money?" She needed to hear the confession from Annie. And maybe some reason for the theft besides treachery and greed. Though she couldn't imagine any mitigating circumstances.

"From Charlie, it wasn't much."

"Did you intercept any other letters?"

"No." But Annie wasn't even surprised at the question.

"Did you get any from anyone else?"

"Like who?"

"LIKE JOCK CAMPBELL?"

"Oh! That teuchter."

Lizzie took a delicate china vase from the sideboard, smashed it on the shiny wood floor, and reached for the second one of the pair.

A gruff, sleepy voice from upstairs yelled. "What the hell was that?"

"Stop it! I don't know. Yes, there were a couple of other letters, but I didn't even open them." Annie seemed to be offering this as some kind of defence.

"Where from?"

"I don't remember. Maybe Rannoch, a long time ago."

Lizzie felt herself getting light-headed. *Jock had tried to reach her before he escaped to Canada.*

"Maybe from abroad. I don't remember. I didn't keep them. Peter said . . ."

Lizzie scooped up the dozen or so manila envelopes and marched out of the living room. She almost collided with Peter Shanks in the hallway.

"What's going on here?" His bloodshot eyes opened wide when he realized who was brushing past him on her way to his front door.

Lizzie remembered Shanks was unemployed.

She snarled at him. "I think I just cut off your only source of income, Peter."

CHAPTER FORTY-TWO

Legal Advice

Wow, but your letter made me vauntie

When Donnie and Jamie came off the night shift, they came home to a house that smelled of ham and sausage cooking. Not the usual weekday fare. Lizzie hugged both of them.

"Sit down." She cracked half a dozen eggs into the sizzling grease.

"What happened?" Jamie said.

"What's that?" Donnie pointed to the heap of envelopes neatly stacked on the sideboard.

"Eat first." Lizzie hopped around smiling and ladling huge portions onto her brothers' plates.

"Ye got the letters from Annie then?" Jamie started to delve into his breakfast.

"What about the money? Did she have the money?"

"Better than that." Lizzie grinned. "Jock's with him in Ottawa."

"Hallelujah." They stood up and crushed Lizzie with a hug from both sides.

"We were up reading the letters till the leerie came by to put out the street lamps this morning." Her mother didn't sound tired.

"What else did he say, Ma?" said Donnie.

"The letters started in February '62. Your sister has spent all night arranging them in order. We've been trying to figure out why Charlie would keep sending money or even continuing to write if he didn't hear back from us."

Lizzie said. "His letters get shorter as time goes on. If Annie answered them, which she must have, she must have impersonated me or Ma."

"Who knows what Annie wrote to him," said Jamie. "The letters never stopped coming, ye say. So Annie's been pocketing this cash for years?"

"Aye. Probably jist thanked him for the money or asked for more. Bitch!" said Donnie.

"But our Annie must have stopped replying to them last year or didn't bother to tell him that Pa died . . . or that Lizzie's husband died," said Jamie.

"Maybe she didn't want to deal with telling Charlie that Pa had died," said Ma.

"Aye," said Lizzie, "she might have been afraid that news would bring Charlie over to Scotland."

"How did Jock ever find oor Charlie?" Donnie seemed to be thinking aloud.

Ma said, "We've been poring over the letters for clues. That one we can't answer. Charlie doesn't mention it. Lizzie's written a letter to Charlie and one to Jock."

"We do know that Jock met up with Charlie in Ottawa. They are in the fur trading business. Jock goes off for months into the wilderness . . . he never married . . ." Lizzie blushed.

"Och! We knew ye never stopped lovin' Jock," said Jamie. "Go on."

"Jock might have got a letter from Charlie before he left," Lizzie told them.

"But why would Jock not get word to us?" said Jamie.

"Maybe he did," Lizzie said. "Our dear sister has been kindly picking up the post for us for years. I believe it suited Shanks as well as Annie to have us continue to believe Jock was dead . . . and not just because telling the truth would mean cutting off the gravy train. The foundry accident and Jock's disappearance were on the same day, March 16. They have to be connected, but we don't know how."

"Lizzie, you're thinkin' Peter Shanks tried to kill Jock." Jamie sounded incredulous.

Lizzie nodded her head to her astounded brother. "Aye. That's exactly what I'm thinking. If he had anything to do with the accident, if he planned it to hurt Jock, he must be trembling in his boots to know Jock is alive."

"Jock must have known he was in grave danger," said Donnie. "It never made any sense that he ran off."

"He <u>was</u> in danger," her mother said. "I hope my lass isn't in danger."

"You mean Annie, Ma." Jamie said.

"Well, of course. She'll always be my bairn." Flora's voice trailed off into a private place.

"If we ever hear Jock's side of it . . ." Lizzie couldn't carry that train of thought further without getting caught up in overwhelming emotions.

Donnie thumbed through the envelopes. "What news of Charlie, Ma?"

"Oor Charlie is well. Och! It's just like I thought. He made a fine life for himself. Charlie has a factory and a store in Ottawa. He's married to a French Canadian girl called Helene—"

"I have to go to work now," Lizzie interrupted, suddenly realizing the time. "Keep those letters in order if ye read them." She put on her coat and headed for the door. "Oh, and Miss Ferguson says her brother Gordon is a solicitor. She was reluctant to recommend him at first. She thought we might be making trouble for Annie. I assured her we needed the solicitor for a different family matter. So don't you two go off and pick a fight with Annie or Shanks. Laying claim to Aulich house and the land comes first. I hope our Charlie kept that baptismal certificate. I've written to him and to Jock. It'll take them a while to get back to us." She wrapped the scarf around her face and hurried out the door to go to work.

* * *

It would take up to eight weeks for the long letter Lizzie had carefully composed to Charlie to reach him in Ottawa. Composing the letter had been a problem. How to tell him Pa had died? She settled for the simple announcement suggested by her mother, "Father passed away last winter." And though she hated to pressure Charlie about the baptismal certificate in this initial and poignant connection, they needed it immediately. She had to

301

give him some reason without bolstering his hopes. "We have learned that our mother may have some legitimate claim to Aulich house and the land in Rannoch. The birth certificate may support her entitlement."

Better to play it down in case the certificate had been lost or destroyed, in which case her brother would be devastated to be the culprit. Even if he still had it, how would he get it to Scotland? She told Charlie it was too risky to mail it. Maybe he'd know someone he could trust to hand-deliver it. Emigrants returned home sometimes.

Her letter to Jock had a "friendly" tone. How could she say what was in her heart? How much did he know about her life? Precious little, if the only source was Annie. Though she'd rather have told Jock in person about the baby their love had created, Ma insisted he should be told. How do you tell a man of the joy it brought to birth their child and the depth of despair felt without him by her side? Her emotions in turmoil . . . all these years . . . her dreams reaching for a way out of this place even while she raised her bairn. But never in her wildest imaginings a reconciliation.

"Lizzie, these letters are beautifully written and make me proud that I insisted on your education but you're wasting precious time," her mother had said. "Just say, 'You and I have a braw bairn called Rob Roy, born in August '63.'"

Lizzie reopened the sealed envelope, added that to the letter, and kissed the page.

* * *

Her mother read daily from her treasured Bible.

Lizzie said, "Ma, it's not as if you don't know every quotation, chapter and verse. Do you expect to find something different in <u>that</u> copy?"

Her mother smiled. "It just gladdens my heart to think of the people of my line who read this book. Here, Lizzie, it's as fine a volume as I have in my collection." She offered it to Lizzie for further admiration.

"Aye, I'm glad you have it, Ma."

Rob Roy came racing toward his mother at that instant and knocked the Bible on to the floor, splitting the back cover from the spine.

"What did ye do that for? Bad boy! Go to the other room." Flora stamped her foot in anger.

Rob Roy burst into tears and ran to the back of the house. Granny never yelled at him.

"Sorry, Ma." Lizzie bent to pick up the pieces.

Her mother went to look for the boy. She returned moments later, wiping his face, which had already turned to a smile.

Lizzie fumbled with the damaged book. She picked the severed cover off the floor. A scrap of yellowed paper with a note scrawled on it stuck to the inside of the back binding. Lizzie carefully pried it loose.

"Ma, look. What's this?"

But she'd already guessed what it was. She carefully unfolded the fragile, yellowed scrap and read:

"'Memorandum: July twenty-four, year of our Lord 1820.

"'I, James Buchanan of Lennox, being of sound mind, do hereby relinquish my claim to the estate of my father, Alexander Buchanan of Lennox, and bestow all assets on my brother Charles Buchanan to manage. Charles is determined to buy Scottish land with this inheritance, and his stated and sworn intention to me this day is to keep said land for present and future heirs of the Buchanan blood line.'

"And it is signed by James and Charles Buchanan and witnessed by the Reverend Angus Macleod. Ma, with this 'memorandum' what more proof could we possibly need? That English husband of Mary's has no rights to our land."

She relished the sound rolling off her tongue: "our land."

"Our land. Rannoch," she repeated.

Rob Roy started jumping up and down on the bed, sensing his mother's excitement. "Rannoch Moo."

Lizzie laughed, picked him up, and swung him around the room.

* * *

Granny Wilson took care of Rob Roy while Lizzie and her mother went to Glasgow in the train. Lizzie had the Buchanan family Bible, the memorandum, and a list of questions to ask Gordon Ferguson of Ferguson, Ferguson, and Milne Solicitors, Sauchiehall Street, Glasgow.

It took a whole day. They arrived home weary but excited. Jamie and Donnie sat by the fire with wee Rob running between them, being picked up to the ceiling by one uncle then the other.

"Here's a cuppa tea, Ma. And we saved you both some sausages." Jamie put the food in front of Lizzie, who hadn't eaten all day.

She gulped down the food, aware of her brothers hovering over her for news. "Mr. Ferguson says the first order of business is to send an agent to Edinburgh to find out if Colonel Buchanan had a will."

"Then we will know what he meant to do with the land?" Jamie asked. Her brothers fired a question each time she took a breath to refer to the lengthy notes on her lap.

"He called it a 'testament.' It would contain an inventory of the laird's property," said Lizzie.

"Does that include the house and the land?" asked Donald.

"Mr. Ferguson says that land is not always mentioned in testaments, unless there is a will spelling out 'dispositions and settlements to include heritable property.'"

"So that English bastard is squatting on land that is rightfully Ma's?" Donnie said.

"Aye. Chances are he doesn't even know anything about Ma. The first thing to find out is how Mary laid claim to the property, which is a big question, if in fact she even bothered to go through any formal process. Then we need to know, did Mary die intestate, without a will, or did she leave everything in 'fee simple' to her heirs . . . in this case Winterbottom?"

"Oh, no," said Donnie. "I've a feeling that 'fee simple,' whatever that means, doesn't make things simple for us."

"If we can prove Ma's inheritance, Mary's husband's claim would be null and void," said Lizzie.

"Thank the Lord for that," Ma said. "When the solicitor locates Charlie Buchanan's papers, we can begin to make our claim. We showed him the document. He grabbed it out of Lizzie's hand in his excitement. He told us that the 'memorandum' is actually the codicil. It is an extra part of a will that was dictated to someone. My poor father must have been too weak to—"

"Aye, Ma, but remember the solicitor said that without your baptismal certificate, it would be difficult to prove anything," said Lizzie.

"Ye know," her mother said, as though talking to herself, "Now that I think on it, I believe that <u>was</u> Charlie Buchanan's handwriting."

"Where, Ma?"

"On the memorandum."

"Ma, doesn't it seem strange to think he was your uncle?" said Jamie. "Not much Highland loyalty there, eh? Comparing how he lived and how we did."

"I'd always thought he sent what he could to help us, that more would have made Isobel even more suspicious. I was more of a threat to her than I could have imagined. I think Isobel Menzies would have run us off if she'd known who I was, especially after all her boy bairns died young. Colonel Buchanan knew about the gossip that some of the cottars and the gentry indulged in about my being a child he wouldn't claim, but he put up with it rather than divulge that his twin had survived the war and that I was James's daughter. He lied and stole what rightfully belonged to my father . . ."

Lizzie saw that the truth, and the enormity of the injustice done to her mother, was slowly sinking in.

"What about Kate MacKay?" asked Jamie.

Lizzie said, "Ferguson said the agent would locate her and get her testimony, but since Kate had not been aware of the identity of Ma's father at the time, she'd just be repeating the words of a dying old woman, her mother. Written documentation is better than word of mouth in these cases. It's not easy to challenge the landed gentry."

Her mother laughed. "Aye. Yon Mr. Ferguson was none too sure about even taking on our case till Lizzie laid out all the facts before him. He says our Lizzie could have been a solicitor or even an advocate. Can ye no see Lizzie with one of those gray wigs, arguing the case?"

Her brothers looked at her, not smiling.

"Aye. She'd do fine," said Jamie.

"How will we pay Ferguson?" Donnie asked.

"We took the Canadian money to the Clydesdale Bank."

"And?" said the twins.

"We got twenty pounds!"

"Twenty! I have tae work the best part o' a year tae make that much," said Donnie. "I wonder how much of our money Shanks has been spending in the pub."

"We gave Mr. Ferguson two pounds ten shillings as a retainer," said her mother.

Lizzie was thrilled to hear her mother so buoyed by the news. The woman who seemed to be on her deathbed a month ago had snapped back to the mother she remembered in Rannoch.

* * *

Every Monday Lizzie arrived at the post office before Miss Ferguson and sorted the international mail. In her spare time, Lizzie searched the empty bins for one she might have missed.

Seeing her disappointed expression, the postmistress said, "Uh-oh. No letter yet. Sorry, Lizzie."

Miss Ferguson was fully aware of the intercepted letters now, and the MacGregors' quest to establish their claim. It seemed silly to keep it from her, since she had guessed so much already.

"Lizzie, I hate to tell you this. It's October now . . . of course, there is still time for a letter that is in transit from Canada, but in a month that mail stops—"

"Stops? Why?"

"The St. Lawrence River freezes over. Shipping ceases in November until the spring thaw."

Lizzie felt the blood drain from her face.

* * *

Two weeks later, an official-looking envelope from the solicitor arrived. She had to wait till she got home in the evening to read it. After several readings she gave it to her mother to decipher. Was this good news or bad?

Finally they thought they understood it, at least enough to explain to the twins.

While the boys ate their dinner, Lizzie told them that the solicitor's agent had found the laird's testament at the Court of Sessions in Edinburgh.

They both yelled their approval and slapped each other on the back.

"Just wait a wee minute," Lizzie cautioned. "It's not so simple. There was no sasine, no document spelling out the disposition of the property. Mr. Ferguson says there might never have been one. Where there is an apparent heir, they simply need to apply for a charter of transfer, in matters of inherited land. The agent has inquired in Rannoch, in Perth, and in Edinburgh and can find no record of this. It doesn't exist."

"So Miss Mary just took over as her due." Her mother's voice rang with sarcasm. "The Menzies overlord in Rannoch could simply give his approval to what he believed to be the normal course of succession. Mr. Ferguson said that Mary Buchanan would have been presumed to be what he called 'the heir general,' with a right to both the heritable and moveable property of her father."

Lizzie explained. "Ma, on the other hand, would be 'the heir of provision,' who is one who succeeds by virtue of the terms of a settlement or some express provision. In this case, the codicil."

"What about Winterbottom?" asked Donnie.

Lizzie closed her eyes and shook her head. "We could have a problem there. Seems he's got wind of what's going on. Someone probably told him about the agent snooping around. He is taking steps to claim the estate as his. Mr. Ferguson says if Winterbottom's claim is not challenged, and if he has something to prove what Mary's wishes were, he could take it to probate."

"But we have the codicil," said Jamie. "It's clear what the Buchanan brothers agreed to."

"But we don't have the baptismal certificate," said Lizzie. "It ties together all the pieces, and if it doesn't come in the next few weeks our cause is lost."

The crackling fire was the only sound that filled the room as they sat, helpless again in the hand of fate. Even Rob Roy seemed to know to play quietly and leave them alone.

* * *

The letter from Charlie that arrived in November dated October 1867 compounded their misery.

My Dear Family,

I understand from Lizzie that you feel some urgency in the Rannoch matter. Why so mysterious? I cannot come to Scotland right now, I am afraid. To return to Ottawa in the winter is impossible and I must be here in February when Helene expects the baby.

Furthermore the business requires my attention right now as my partner, Jock MacGregor, now a famed backwoodsman, has been held up in Hudson Bay.

Yes. I did save the birth certificate Andy gave me prior to my hasty departure. I thought it would make a beautiful memento that her wayward son could present her with in person someday.

I was deeply saddened about our dear father. I trust James and Donald are taking over the reins of the family.

My dearest regards to Mother and all of you.

Charles Buchanan MacGregor

The irony of it was that Charlie had saved the baptismal certificate simply because his mother might like to have it one day as a memento. MEMENTO! He never realized, of course, that the "James Buchanan" named in the certificate was a brother to the colonel, no less their own grandfather and true heir to the Buchanan legacy.

Part Five

Vindication

CHAPTER FORTY-THREE

The Wanderer Returns

'So, may Old Scotia's darling hope,
Your little angel band,
Spring, like their fathers up to prop
Their honour'd native land!

On a bitterly cold November night, Lizzie anticipated Hogmanay 1866, a few weeks hence, with a heavy heart. After twelve tumultuous months, there seemed to be very little to celebrate going in to the New Year of 1867.

"Ma, listen to this. Mr. Ferguson says Captain Winterbottom is filing his claim. Seems all he has to do is convene a meeting of the local landowners. The superior of the land, the overlord, in this case is Sir Robert at Castle Menzies. If Sir Robert issues him a "clare constant," which if I remember my Latin means 'it clearly appears,' he is presumed the owner. Ma this is really bad news, he could be presented with a charter from the feudal superior transferring the title to him.

"Mr. Ferguson asks again about the baptismal certificate in this letter. If we could have presented it to Sir Robert, he'd have had no choice but to give you the charter. Winterbottom is meeting with him at the castle at Christmas."

Her mother wept, covering her face with her apron.

Rob Roy crept up on her lap, but the comfort he offered only caused Ma to burst into copious tears. Lizzie took her son from her mother.

"Granny is sad. She'll be all right in a wee while."

"Rannoch Moor," he said.

Lizzie wondered whether he was trying to cheer his Granny by mentioning the fabled place, or because he understood what he had heard his family talking about for years and realized the dream had darkened. She stifled her own sobs.

* * *

Business was even more brisk at the post office. People exchanged letters at this time of year. In anticipation of Hogmanay and Ne'erday, thoughts flew to loved ones.

Lizzie dragged herself up the hill after work. She saw Rob Roy racing down to meet her.

"Ma, I saw a cowboy," he said.

"That's nice. Did he have on a big hat?"

"Ou-aye! He has long hair and a leather jacket with fur INSIDE and brown boots." It always amused Lizzie that her wee boy, only four years old, sounded so grown-up, like a wee man. . . and like his uncles he loved to tell yarns.

"Did he have spurs on his boots?"

"No, Ma," he sounded disgusted. "I'm not making it up. He said the jacket was beaver skin. An Indian gave it to him. He came to our house. He's talking to Gra—"

She grabbed her son by the hand, gathered her long skirt in the other, and dashed the rest of the way to number twelve. Neighbours stood on the pavement, slack-jawed.

"Ye've got company," one said.

"Did you see him?" her companion asked. "All the weans were runnin' after him. He must be a real American. Wis that a bearskin he wis wearin'?"

"Naw! The wee boy says it's beaver. That's what we could use here tae keep warm."

There he was, leaning against the doorjamb, happed in furs; his broad grin quivered slightly, and his eyes misted over. "Lizzie . . ." he choked before he could say more and held the door open, gesturing for her to go in to allow them to retreat from the prying eyes.

He shut the door behind them and gathered her in his arms. The smell of leather and fur couldn't camouflage the tang of his body, the incense that blessed her dreams, the smell of Jock MacGregor.

She still hadn't uttered a word, afraid it might be just another dream. Then he kissed her. She touched his shoulders, his face, and reached towards his hair. She ripped off the wide-brimmed hat and grasped with her trembling hands his red-gold locks, bleached near blond by the sun in a foreign clime. She pulled his head away from her to take another look at him.

"You came back . . . how?"

"It's a long story, Darlin'. But you've got me here for a good long time. There is no way I can get back till the spring. That is, if I . . ."

Ma coughed. They turned towards her, coming out of their trance.

"I don't know how long since you ate, but there's Scotch broth for supper and a place at the table for ye. Where's your luggage?"

"I left it down the street at my auntie's. She told me Wullie died. She's not over it. She cried the whole time I was there. Seeing me brought it all back. Are you all right, Lizzie?"

"Yes." She didn't mean to sound so vehement, but at this moment memories of Wullie were dim and distant.

"Jock, this is Rob Roy."

"Aye. How are ye, Robbie?"

"Very well, sir." The boy stood beside his grandmother, eyes fixed on this amazing apparition that had appeared in their living room.

Lizzie hid her grin. It seemed Rob Roy didn't quite know how to address a "cowboy."

"I'll talk to him later," she told Ma.

"Aye. Please do. I cannae wait tae play with my son. We'll tell him together."

"You know?" Lizzie said.

"I got your letter, of course, but one look at him..." Jock choked on the words.

"You have a boy?" said Rob.

"Aye. A fine strong boy with red hair and . . ."

"Oh." Rob sounded disappointed.

If he wondered why his mother and this stranger stood holding hands and hugging each other, he said nothing.

* * *

By the time the twins burst into the room from the day shift, Jock's presence was no secret. Lizzie wondered if everybody in Coatbridge knew.

"Where is he?" they asked in chorus.

"Over at his auntie's. He'll be back for supper," her mother said, feigning nonchalance.

"Did he bring the certificate?" Jamie asked.

"I don't know," said Lizzie. "I didn't ask."

"Lizzie, where's yer head, lassie?" said Donnie.

Rob Roy grabbed his Uncle Donnie's pant leg. "He's a great big man with a furry coat. He's got a boy with hair like mine."

"Och! Lizzie, did ye no tell the boy?" said Jamie.

"Wheesht," said Ma. "Let them do it in their own time."

The buzz out in the street had started again just before they heard a rap at the door. Lizzie sprang out of her seat to open it. She pulled Jock through the door and kissed him before her brothers got the chance to monopolize him.

"Enough," cried the impatient pair. "Time for that later."

"Hello, lads. It's awfy good tae see ye." Jock shook hands with them. Rob stood next to his uncles, waiting his turn, apparently expecting to be treated like the other men. His father gravely shook his hand and held it longer than the others. At the table Jock fielded questions from all of them. Lizzie wanted to know why he disappeared without a word.

He groaned. "Did Paddy not tell ye?"

"Paddy was killed in a foundry explosion. Jock, we thought it was you. I thought ye were dead." Tears sprang to her eyes.

Jock stared at her incredulously. "Paddy Riley's dead? Then you didn't get the letter."

"Aye, Jock," said her mother. "We buried Paddy, thinking it was you. Then her father and I talked Lizzie into marrying Wullie. We didn't know.

314

We thought it was for the best. Och! He loved her, as ye know, and he was willing to give the lad a name. Lizzie moped for months. We were afraid for the bairn."

"It's not your fault. I understand. It's all about survival here. Ye did what ye had to do." He patted Lizzie's mother on her drooping shoulder and left his arm there while she sobbed quietly, then led her to her chair by the fire. He gave Lizzie a wretched look. "Ye warned me about Shanks, but I had to take the bull by the horns and confront him. When he found that threatening me might not work, he swore he'd lay off all the MacGregors and turn us out."

"So that's why you left," said Donnie. "He'd have fired all of us. We'd have been out on the street."

"There's more to it," said Jock. "He said something about Lizzie." In an aside to Lizzie, Jock said, "Did that filthy lecher ever put a hand on you?"

"Aye, he tried to . . ."

"Thought so. He made it sound like you were willing, and I punched him in the mouth. He began to yell about how he would kill me. 'I'll roast ye alive,' were his exact words, and he came after me with an iron rod. Paddy Riley stepped between us and took a blow to the head that knocked him down. Shanks backed off then. I think he thought he killed the man, but he'd just stunned him. But Paddy was still thinking straighter than I was; I wanted to go after him, but Paddy stopped me."

Jock got quiet for a moment, likely thinking about his pal.

"Then what happened?" Lizzie asked.

"Paddy said I should disappear for a month or two till Shanks cooled down. 'Ah'll work the ramp,' he says. 'I'll tell your family,' Paddy says. 'My lass would never understand.' I says. That's when I gave him the note for you. I thought I could come back and get you. I was on the train pulling out of Whifflet when a heard a blast. Didn't think too much about it at the time."

"Did ye no' hear the siren?" asked Jamie.

"Och! If I did, I didn't put two and two together."

"Wait," Lizzie blew the curl out of her eyes. "You wrote your mother from Rannoch. Didn't she tell you about the explosion? Didn't she tell you we thought you were dead?"

"No. All she said was how glad she was that I was still alive. I took it for a mother's concern; I didn't know she really thought I was dead."

"Ye went to Rannoch for a while?" said Jamie.

"I didn't fare much better there. I spent some time living in your old croft, looking around the area for some way to stay, maybe in a neighbouring landowner's employ. Andy warned me MacNab was coming for me . . . then I heard from my mother that Lizzie was married." He bowed his head.

"Oh." Lizzie's groan spoke volumes.

Jock put his arm around her trembling shoulders and guided her into the other room.

"Oh, Jock, how could things have gone so terribly wrong?"

"Lizzie, ye know I couldn't leave you. You were my heart. Shanks threatened to kill me and make everyone I love suffer I think he might have carried out his threat, only it wasn't me he killed but Paddy Riley. I'll never be able to prove it, but I believe that explosion was meant for me. Where is the bastard now? He should be brought to justice."

"He's married to our Annie."

"Wha . . .?"

"Aye. Maybe that's justice enough."

"Did ye not get my other letters?" he asked.

"Please don't tell me you wrote."

He looked at her with a quizzical expression.

"Aye, ye did." Lizzie was now sure it was more of Annie's handiwork. "She intercepted all the letters from Charlie. She must have started with yours. No, Jock, I never got any letter from you."

"I sent two: one as soon as I got to Rannoch to let you know where I was, and one after I heard from my mother that you were married. Glad you didn't see that one. I was bereft to think I'd lost you, and I just couldn't understand why."

Lizzie wept with great gulping sobs into his shoulder while he stroked her head.

* * *

Late into the night a second shovel-full of coal had been heaped on the fire. They'd each partaken of a dram or two of the bottle of Glenlivit Jock had brought as a gift. They sat around with Jock in the position of honour, in Pa's chair. He continued to tell his tale to the rapt audience.

Lizzie learned that her brother and Jock ran a substantial and apparently profitable trading warehouse in Ottawa. Charlie had a home nearby. Jamie asked about opportunities for men like him and his twin, and Jock encouraged them to give it some consideration. "Nothin' yer brother would like better than to have you two as part of his enterprise. Charlie has the Midas touch when it comes to business."

"Huntin' and fishin' and no game warden chasing ye off like a criminal. Trekking in the wilderness . . ." Jamie's eyes shone.

"Charlie has built a house that looks so much like Aulich mansion that I have to hector him about it."

"Speaking of Aulich House, did Charlie say anything about an important document he has?" said Jamie.

"Aye, I'm his emissary, so to speak." Jock reached into his jacket, pulled out a manila envelope, and with a flourish presented it to Lizzie's mother.

"Jock, we must take this to the lawyer in Glasgow right away, and hope we are in time to stop Winterbottom," said Lizzie.

"We didn't know about Winterbottom," said Jock. "How does he get mixed up in this?"

Lizzie and her brothers took turns telling Jock the convoluted story about their mother's inheritance.

"Charlie knew you had to have this paper soon, by the tone of your letter. Charlie wants a long letter with details. When I returned from the wilderness he persuaded me to deliver it. An invitation to see my future wife and son? Of course I was coming."

"You have a wife?" asked wee Rob, who'd dozed on and off all evening in the box bed near the fire.

"I will soon," said Jock.

"Is she in Canada?"

"She's right here." Jock put his arm around Lizzie.

She watched Rob's innocent eyes open wide.

"My mother is your wife."

"Aye. If she'll have me."

"Will you have him, Ma?"

"I will," said Lizzie.

"Then you'll be my father?"

"Aye, son."

Rob's wide smile developed into a yawn and he was soon fast asleep.

CHAPTER FORTY-FOUR

Glasgow Town

'He bids you mind, amid your thoughtless rattle,
That the first blow is ever half the battle

O n their way to the train the next morning, Lizzie insisted they stop at the police station to report what they knew and what they suspected about Peter Shanks and the foundry accident.

"Och, it's over now and we're together, Darlin'." Jock sounded more forgiving than she felt.

"It was an evil deed that was done and the man responsible is still lording it around here." She wanted Shanks punished.

Constable Graham, after he got over the shock of recognizing Jock, was very interested in their story. His sister's son had been one of the blast furnace men who died on that fateful day. His full report would be on the sheriff's desk that afternoon.

"He'll be in jail before nightfall if just for his own protection. If this gets out before I can arrest him, the bastard's life won't be worth tuppence. Excuse me, Mrs. Maclure."

* * *

Despite a light snow shower, Lizzie and Jock walked the short distance downhill from the Buchanan Street train station in Glasgow to Argyll Street, the hub of the city's business district. The snow melted as soon as it landed.

319

Jock held Lizzie's arm to steady her; Lizzie's eyes were on everything else but the slushy pavement. Women with the ubiquitous black shawls wrapped around their heads and shoulders, weighed down with heavy bags or baskets, scurried across the slippery streets on their daily round of shopping. Dirty children dodged horses and carts and piles of manure and suffered the curses of carters who seemed to think they owned the highway.

Gentlemen in frock coats guided ladies in awkward crinolines across Buchanan Street. The women held their skirts out of the mud and balanced umbrellas over their ornate hats. They provided the only splash of colour in the gray city. Lizzie admired the latest fashions displayed in shop windows.

Jock hurried her along. "We'll come back later."

As Lizzie and Jock walked by, the street theatre seemed to freeze, while one and all ogled her handsome escort, sporting attire that clearly came from the colonies. Jock seemed unaware.

Lizzie said, "You're causing quite a stir."

They found the door with the brass plaque that identified Ferguson's imposing office building as one of many elegant stone edifices on Argyll Street. Glasgow hummed with the construction of fine buildings.

The law clerk ushered them into the solicitor's grand office with the imposing desk of mahogany wood placed centrally, and the aging barrister seated behind it. Lizzie introduced Jock as her husband-to-be.

"You folks are no seein' Glasgow at its best on a day like this." Lizzie smiled at the familiarity of his colloquial accent, which had taken her by surprise at their first meeting. So many educated people acquired English accents, apparently thinking it made them sound smarter. Not Gordon Ferguson, a plain middle-aged man with an expansive midriff and a florid complexion that suggested he enjoyed his share of food and drink. Mr. Ferguson returned her smile.

Lizzie produced the document eager to get to the business at hand.

"So what do ye have for me?" Mr. Ferguson said.

He scrutinized it for several moments while Lizzie sat on the edge of her chair.

Ferguson let out an un-gentlemanly guffaw. "We have the bastard cornered." He thumped his fist on the desk. "Oh excuse me, ma'am. But this is grand, jist grand. Landed gentry ye'll be, by Jove. Fine work. Fine work."

Lizzie heard a bell ring in the distance, and a bespectacled clerk appeared. Ferguson must have a button on the floor he pushed with his foot to summon people.

"Yes, sir? Good-day, ma'am . . . sir."

"Here, Carmichael, get this over to the sheriff's court and tell them we need a writ of possession immediately for Flora MacGregor in the Rannoch land matter. They know what I need; I've talked to them. Tell them whatever you have to tell them . . . say it's a matter of life and death . . . get that nest of simpering idiots movin' and don't come back without it."

"Yes, sir."

Ferguson's manner softened as he turned to his clients. His voice modulated into a conspiratorial tone, barely above a whisper. "Sir Robert and his kin never expected to lose any of Rannoch to an incomer, not even a Scot of some stature like Charles Buchanan. But he has seen the agreement entered into by the colonel and Sir Robert's ne'er-do-weel cousin Archie. And, of course, had it examined by his legal advisors. Archibald Menzies gave up the land to cover his debts, and that's a fact. The old boy has resigned himself that he cannot annex that part of the Menzies holdings back into the fold that was lost by the black sheep of the family, so to speak."

He took a moment to chuckle at his own pun.

"Nor do any of the Menzies relatives have a claim that would negate your own. The Menzies rule the roost in that part of the Highlands, as ye know.

"Sir Robert Menzies is holding off this Captain Winterbottom as long as he can. Having Rannoch fall into <u>his</u> hands is unconscionable. None of the landowners there, including Sir Robert, has any pity for the Sassenach. Seems Winterbottom has taken a leaf out of old Archie Menzies' book. He's a drunkard and a gambler. Not that I mind a wee dram myself sometimes, but ye have to attend to business. The man never draws a sober breath, they say."

He took a moment to rearrange his ink blotter and inkwell on his already immaculate desktop.

"I told ye Ferguson would earn his fee. Aye! And give ye the kind of support ye needed? Aye, that we did, for it's an excellent outcome for yer family. The sheriff's officer will bring the writs to serve on that damned usurper, and you will get your own copies. It gladdens my heart to see a wee corner of Scotland saved for our own folk."

Lizzie heard a bell off in the distance again. This time it heralded a white-aproned, apple-cheeked young woman bearing a silver tea service.

"The scones are still warm, Mr. Ferguson. Jist the way ye like them."

"Ou-aye! Agnes, ye'll make some man a guid wife."

"Mr. Ferguson," she scolded with a simpering smile as she served the tea.

They had finished their tea when the breathless clerk burst into the room, quaking. "The judge was finished for the day. They promised to get it from him first thing in the morning."

He left quickly, before Ferguson could take out his ire on him.

He frowned and scratched his head. "I'm sorry, lass. The papers will be ready tomorrow."

"Tomorrow!" Lizzie let out a disappointed cry.

"I'm so sorry, Mrs. Maclure. I really am, but I'm afraid it's out of my control at the moment. Would ye not enjoy an overnight in the city?"

Lizzie looked at Jock, who grinned like a fool.

Mr Ferguson continued, "If you can stay in town tonight, my driver will take you to the the Bedford Hotel in St George's Place. Excellent lodgings. By morning I'll surely have the appropriate papers. Mr. MacGregor, there is a fine restaurant not one hundred yards from here. Take your affianced out for an elegant lunch."

"Thank you, Mr. Ferguson, but Lizzie and I would like to walk. We need to make a few purchases. We'll hire a carriage when we've finished."

Lizzie appraised her sophisticated escort, certainly not the blushing boy she used to know, and was answered by a wide grin.

* * *

The hotel manager stared at Jock when he asked for adjoining rooms for them. Was he suspicious of their intentions, or just curious about Jock's attire? People in Glasgow, on the streets, in the shops where he bought her "trousseau," and in the tearoom where they lunched, gawked. Lizzie covered her grin with her hand, newly gloved in white kid, when the ladies stared,

nudged, and gossiped. She felt sure they were jealous, for Jock with his bur-
nished skin and brawny physique developed by canoeing for weeks in the
Canadian wilds, was as fine a figure of a man as any to be seen in Scotland.
He exuded confidence.

"Certainly, sir." The hotel manager snapped his fingers, and three red-
uniformed boys appeared to load the boxes from the finest stores in Glasgow onto their brass trolleys.

They showed Lizzie to her room first. The enormous bed, the brocade
curtains, and the roaring fire dominated the room. She could see towels
draped over brass racks and a giant tub in the adjacent water closet.

Lizzie gave the boy a sixpence, and he left to open the adjoining room
for Jock. She flounced onto the feather bed.

* * *

Lizzie awoke to a persistent hammering. She shook her head and
inspected her darkened environment. Rain battered her window. There was
no way to know the time of day. She cast her eyes down to the bottom of
the bed. She wore her new soft leather boots, still laced. She felt the pinched
waistband the of the green velvet dress. Its voluminous skirt spread across
the bed. She'd tried to convince Jock it was too fancy and not practical in
Coatbridge. She raised her hands to touch the matching bonnet still on
her head and pulled the ribbon to untie it. A cursory inspection of the
elegant creation in the dim light revealed its feathers and ribbons intact and
its straw brim uncrushed. Relieved she hadn't damaged it, she turned her
befuddled mind to where she was and what time it was.

The knocking began again.

Jock!

It must be Jock. She bounced out of bed and flew to the door. He stood
there, water pouring off the brim of his hat.

"Lizzie, I thought you'd run off." He grinned.

She reached out the door, grabbed his wet sleeve, and pulled him into
the room.

"Where have you been?" she asked.

"I went out to buy you something."

"Jock, you've been buying me things all day."

"Not like this."

"What?"

"It's a secret. Later."

He hung his hat on a peg, dripped his way across the carpeted entryway into the bathroom, and draped his jacket over the towel rail.

She followed him, kissed him hungrily, oblivious to her surroundings. He disentangled himself from her arms and dropped his remaining clothes onto the tiled floor.

He stood naked, fumbling with the tiny buttons on her bodice. She moaned and breathed deeply, impatiently trying to help him and popping several buttons in the clumsy effort.

She began to laugh. He regarded her inquiringly, a smile playing around his lips, willing to enjoy the joke if she would share it.

"I hope you don't have to answer to Uncle Archie about this," she sputtered.

"Ah, yes! Suspicious old Uncle Archie. Protecting his innocent niece against the wild Highlander . . . . . And did you take a bit tumble too, lad?" Jock said in a perfect impersonation of Archie's Island lilt and scowl. "Best be on your way. Ye've done all the helpin' ye're goin' to do this day." He pushed her ahead of him into the bedroom towards the fireplace and began to kiss her neck. "Get you inside, gurrl."

Remembering the youthful embarrassment, they made mock apologies to Uncle Archie for the liberties they were taking with each other's aroused bodies.

"And what have you been up to, lad? Not takin' advantage of my niece, are ye?" Jock scowled.

"Hope Uncle Archie is enjoying the joke from whatever corner of heaven he is croftin' in," she mused. "Och! No, Uncle Archie, this nice man has just been showing me around Glasgow . . . and this big four-poster bed." She pushed him off balance, and they landed in a heap on the feather mattress.

"Whoops." Her bodice burst open, exposing one breast and an erect pink nipple.

"Lass, ye need to sew those buttons on wi' steel thread."

Their laughter softened into murmurings. The years fell away. They were ageless, and time meant nothing. The passion in Whifflet Park, the passion in her dreams, the passion she carried in the very deepest part of her soul exploded to the surface in the arms of this man, still alive and here and wanting her just as much as she wanted him.

In the glimmer from the firelight she watched the back of his beloved head and felt his lips nuzzling her breast. The tingle spread to her thighs. She writhed and moaned, guiding him to the centre of her desire.

He pushed her petticoats up over her waist and entered her. Her deep sigh told him she was ready for him. She moved her hips to accommodate him and began thrusting towards him. The sudden, intense orgasm forced a soft moaning that rose to a crescendo that met and matched her lover's cries of joy.

* * *

She awoke alone in the bed to the sound of water splashing in the other room, Jock taking a bath.

"Get dressed, Darlin'. I'm starved," he called out.

"What time is it anyway?" she said.

"Past seven in the evening."

* * *

The carriage took them to an intimate dining room. The Maitre d' gave her man a conspiratorial look and led them to a quiet alcove.

"He knew you were coming," said Lizzie. Her companion, who gave every appearance of being a rustic voyageur, had nevertheless attained much refinement along the way. She felt pampered.

The continental meal of turtle soup and French bread was followed by sweetbreads in cream sauce. Their discreet, efficient waiter served them coffee from a silver pot and a selection of shortbread, meringues filled with sweet cream, and lemon cake from a china cake stand.

Lizzie sipped the white French wine; she allowed it was on a par with her mother's elderberry wine. They reminisced about the Hogmanay in

Rannoch when their mothers set out the Highland feast. She told him that was the night when she became aware of her love for him.

"It's almost as though I can still hear the bagpipes," said Lizzie. "Wait. I do hear bagpipes."

The sound came closer. A piper soon came into view at the door of the establishment, playing "Comin' Thru the Rye."

She sang softly, "Gin a body meet a body, comin' thru the rye."

The piper came right up to their table and stopped playing. He stood there with a silly grin on his face. She glanced towards Jock. He had disappeared. She looked down to see him kneeling beside her, opening a blue leather box.

"Wha—?"

"I've waited and dreamed about this moment. I wanted it to be special. Will ye marry me, Lizzie?"

"Of course I will." Tears sprung to her eyes. "Ye knew I would."

"This evening was part of the dream I held." He fastened the sparkling pendant around her neck.

"What a beautiful thing." She couldn't come up with adequate words.

"It's a blue-green emerald to match your eyes."

⁕ ⁕ ⁕

At the law office next day, Mr. Ferguson had some good news and some bad.

"Sir Robert sent me word that the weather up there is awfy bad. It may not be a good idea to take the ladies into Rannoch till there's a bit of a thaw, Mr. MacGregor."

Lizzie was crestfallen. "Mr. Ferguson, I grew up in the Highlands. A wee bit snow can't stop me."

"But what about yer mother?" he said. "She should be there to take possession."

Yes, Mother. Maybe they'd have to cool their heels. Perhaps it was for the best. Mother needed to make some preparations. Pack up some things. A lot of the pathetic plenishings that had supported their subsistence could be thrown out. Ma still needed to place a monument on Pa's grave. The

326

twins would have to decide if they would go to Rannoch or stay. Or maybe they had other plans.

Ferguson's voice reached her through her contemplation. "The good news is that Sir Robert is encouraging Winterbottom to believe he has no need to take the case to probate. He can't do that indefinitely, so I have taken the liberty of making duplicates of the writs of eviction to be sent by rail. My agent in Perth will serve them on Winterbottom. With any luck he will be gone before you get there."

Lizzie's mind raced. "The house needs to be attended to. When you answer Sir Robert, would you ask him to install Miss MacKay as caretaker until we arrive?"

"I'll do that this very day."

"My family is indebted to you, sir." Lizzie reached into her reticule and pulled out an envelope.

"This is the fee we agreed upon." She gave him the last of the money from Charlie.

"Is there something else we can do for you, lass?"

"Oh. I was just thinking: Wouldn't it be grand if we could tell Charlie?"

"Ye mean yer brother in Canada?"

"Yes," Jock answered, "He's my business partner."

"Ou-aye! Well, ye're in luck. There's a new telegraph office opened jist down the road. They jist hooked up that transatlantic cable this September. Ye can telegraph to Canada and America now. It's no bother at a' to send Charlie the news." Mr. Ferguson seemed proud of himself to be so acquainted with the latest in modern paraphernalia.

* * *

They stopped at the telegraph office on their way to the station and carefully drafted a short message: "Birth certificate final piece of puzzle. Thank you. Stop. Claiming Aulich for our family in the spring. Stop. Letter on way with details," their wire said. Lizzie was eager to share their news with the family.

* * *

A return telegram was delivered to the door in Whifflet within a week: "Great. Stop. When will Jock return?"

Here was a topic they had avoided; but they could no longer do so.

The family sat around a blazing fire after supper.

Jock laid out his thoughts. "I know Charlie needs me. But he'll understand if I elect to stay in Rannoch with his sister. And that is my wish."

Lizzie looked at him with pride and adoration, then blushed when she realized everyone was watching her reaction.

Jamie surprised them when he said, "Donald and I have been talking this over. He wants tae go live in Rannoch, but I'd like tae join oor Charlie."

Lizzie knew this must have been a heart-wrenching decision for them to reach. They had always been inseparable.

The silence weighed heavily in the room for several minutes, finally broken by Jock.

"We'll cable Charlie. It means we'll have to go to Glasgow again . . . if that's all right with Lizzie." She could barely disguise her amusement.

Lizzie and Jock took another trip to Glasgow to wire her brother to tell them about their intended marriage and that Jamie would be coming to join him. It was a good excuse to spend a night or two in their favourite hotel. Privacy in the two-room house was nonexistent.

They stayed for three days until Charlie's reply arrived at the telegraph office. "Congratulations. Send me a MacGregor."

* * *

Following a jubilant Hogmanay of '67, the family became restless to move and hoped for an early spring. The matter of Lizzie and Jock's marriage occupied them for a few weeks and Flora, the twins, Rob Roy and the happy couple took the train to Glasgow in early February to legalize their union. Jock arranged for rooms at the hotel for all of them. The lads were a bit overwhelmed and found a friendly pub to pass away the evening while Jock took his new wife, his mother-in-law and his doting son to dinner.

Back in Whifflet, Wee Robbie paraded his father around to his pals and up to Whifflet Park with the football his father bought him.

Finally, at the end of March, the weather seemed mild enough to take the trip to Rannoch.

The lads spent a last night at The Big Tree Bar and came home the worse for wear. They had to say goodbyes to men they'd worked with for six or more years, then they stayed till closing time talking to Jock about Canada.

* * *

On a bonnie spring day they took their leave of Whifflet. Jamie and Donnie decided to take their goodbyes with each other in Rannoch instead of this unhappy place. Jamie said he wanted to see Rannoch one more time.

Lizzie felt the sadness of her brothers. In her mind, she thought, they'll never see each other again.

Then Jock said, "You can come back to Scotland any time, Jamie. The steamers are getting faster every year." This seemed to cheer the twins. "Charlie will need you to take my place. It's a job you'll love and the pay's no bad either" He placed his arm around Lizzie. "Anyway, we'll see you again over there before long. I want Lizzie to see Canada."

Of course, she thought, Jock had made the trip and returned. He would lead the way. She'd get to see Jamie and Charlie and her new sister-in-law and her little niece or nephew. Everything seemed possible.

On the last morning, before they left, they put their meagre belongings outside and watched them disappear into the small, dark caves. Maybe they would brighten someone's day.

All their precious books and documents and mementos got packed in Lizzie and Fiona's kists.

CHAPTER FORTY-FIVE

Aulich House

March 1867

Ye ugly, creepin', blastit wonner,
Detested, shunn'd by saunt an' sinner!
How dare ye set your fit upon her,
Sae fine a lady?

Lizzie knew they were a strange-looking troupe. People stared at them in the train and at every station on the journey from Whifflet to Pitlochry.

Ma wore the new clothes Lizzie had bought her in Glasgow; the twins had only their pit clothes, scrubbed and patched; wee Rob had a new wool coat, cap, and mittens; Lizzie wore her green velvet dress with a hand muff to match and a warm black wool cloak to guard against the chill of the journey.

Their belongings travelled in two leather, metal-strapped trunks bought for the trip.

Duncan MacNab, the weasel-faced factor with the shifty eyes, who'd unceremoniously kicked them out more than six years ago, met his new employers at Pitlochry station. On instructions from Sir Robert Menzies, Lizzie guessed, by the looks of the crest on the black polished door of the carriage. The over-lord no doubt, had ordered him to pick up Flora

MacDonald MacGregor in his four–wheeled coach. Lizzie watched the men of the family, including Wee Robbie, wide-eyed at the excellent vehicle.

MacNab seemed to recognize Flora as she alighted the first-class carriage. He led Ma to the stately black Brougham parked in the road with the matching pair of gray horses pawing the ground, eager to move on.

MacNab secured the two trunks on the rear rack, leaving Ma's kist sitting forlornly by the roadside.

"Put that inside, MacNab, it will fit under the seat." Ma said.

"Right away, Mrs. MacGregor." So he knows her, and he must have guessed who Lizzie and her brothers were, but she could see he wasn't sure about Jock.

He did seem to assume, though, that Jock had authority and deferred to him. "Like to sit up in the front, sir, with one of the other gentlemen," he gave a faintly distinguishable sneer while referring to her poorly dressed brothers as 'gentlemen,' "while I make the ladies comfortable in the carriage. With the side seats down there's room for four inside?"

The twins left off inspecting the Brougham to help Ma into the carriage and tried to console the squealing Rob, who wanted to ride up front.

"It's too cold for you," Jamie told him.

"The lady and I will ride up front." Jock told the bewildered MacNab. "Your other four passengers should be comfortable inside." His wink at Lizzie conveyed 'He doesn't know who I am.'

"Where will I sit, sir?" MacNab stared at Jock.

"Well now, in the colonies we sometimes jumped on the back and hung on for dear life. Give it a try, MacNab."

"Sit up here with me, lass." Jock indicated the platform that supported the driver's padded seat. Jock stepped up and straddled the jump seat and gave Lizzie a hand up. He wrapped both of them in a large plaid travel rug, creating a tent-like covering for protection from the elements, and for privacy. The factor, slack-jawed at such a display of intimacy, studied Jock, thought better of arguing with him, and scrambled up on top of the trunks at the rear.

The swaying of the carriage and the warmth of Jock's body lulled Lizzie to sleep. She dreamt she searched for lambs on Slios Minh and met Jock, who took her into his arms. She snuggled closer and awoke truly in her lover's arms. His steady gaze surveyed the familiar territory, a satisfied expression on his face.

MacNab's yell from the rear intruded into her bliss. ". . . from abroad are ye?" MacNab didn't bother to wait for an answer. Apparently this one-sided conversation had been going on for some time while Lizzie slept. "Ah weel, even some foreigner, American, Canadian, whatever ye are, would be better than what Miss Mary's husband's become. And maybe I'll start getting paid again." Lizzie glanced back to see MacNab perched precariously on the trunks clinging to the roof of the carriage.

"Isn't Miss Mary's husband gone?" Jock called back.

"Nah. Sheriff's officer warned him to vacate the premises, but he's hanging on. You'll have your hands full with him.

"Wastrel! Everything I bleed out o' that estate is lost at the gaming tables . . . or guzzled down yon Englishman's throat . . . fancy French wine he favours. Never saw that Sassenach drink a decent dram of whisky—ever. Creditors at the door every day, and him drunk as a lord. Drunk as a lord . . . that's a good one."

Lizzie felt Jock's hand deftly unbuttoning her bodice under cover of the rug.

"And I'm the one has to make excuses. 'The master's gone to London.' 'The master's ill.' 'The master's gone to visit the Duke of Argyll.' That's a good one. The Duke might enjoy a dram like any good Scotsman, but he's long since stopped entertaining that snivelling wastrel Sassenach, Cedric Winterbottom. Och! Maybe better times are ahead. Eh?"

Jock had released the last button, and her left breast tumbled into his cupped hand.

The west wind bore down on them with the promise of rain or even snow. MacNab's endless blathering lost any persuasiveness in the gale.

The horses trotted along the familiar path without guidance. Jock's hand found her erect nipple and squeezed. Her groaning disappeared into the blustery wind. He picked her up on his lap and pressed her body against his erection, writhing in rhythm to the swaying coach. He bunched her dress and petticoats around her waist and found the opening in her pantalets. He was not in a position to penetrate her as he desperately wanted. She felt his fingers move around her sex in ways he knew would bring her quickly to orgasm. She tightened her body, half-turning to cling to his jacket and offer her lips for his kiss. He placed his mouth over hers to quiet the sounds she began to make. She felt the bulge in his breeches still swollen and pressing against her buttocks.

"We'll have to take care . . . of the rest . . . of this operation in a different position," he whispered into her ear, the words punctuated by gulps of air as he tried to control his passion.

"If ye want my advice, ye'll clear the rest of the tenants squatting on this land and create a hunters' paradise, with grouse, red deer, salmon and trout," said MacNab when they had turned into the shelter of Schiehallion.

"Bastard." Lizzie hissed.

MacNab, perhaps startled by the disembodied voice, or dislodged by the quick turn Jock made, fell off the coach.

Jock slowed and stopped. "Better sit up here. You'll never make a frontiersman."

MacNab, apparently unhurt and still talking, dusted of his pants and climbed up on Jock's side. "Gettin' close now. Before we get there, I just want to put ye wise to a few things."

"And what would those be, Mr. MacNab?" Lizzie asked from under the cover of the rug.

Missing her sarcasm, he said. "Oh ye're awake, madam. Did ye have a good ride?"

Jock pinched her backside. "Tell the man how good it was, Lizzie."

She dug her elbow into his belly.

MacNab was oblivious; apparently focused on impressing his new employers. "Yer mother needs to know, madam, that the Sassenach has let yon lot of useless crofters, that escaped the '59 clearance, stay on. Sheer laziness on his part. Doesn't know a freeloader from a lord, that one. Probably the upstart son of some English tradesman himself. Give me a free hand to clear out the rest of the riffraff, and I'll show ye how a good factor can make the place profitable. Rich men from all over the continent and from England would pay well to hunt around these bonnie hills and fish the sparkling loch—and," he chuckled, "they tip well."

Lizzie ignored him, lost in the joy of seeing again the familiar moors and hills. "Rannoch," she whispered. "Rannoch." Hallowed ground. In the gloaming she could make out the white-topped cone of Schiehallion against the setting sun, piercing the pink-tinged gray clouds of evening. Soon it would be dark. The end of another day in Rannoch.

Jock nuzzled her hair.

The matching pair of grays trotted up the hill, eager to reach their stable. They pulled the coach past the high stone wall. Lizzie could barely see down Aulich Hill to Loch Rannoch now that the darkness had deepened. But she knew what was there, and tomorrow she could view her glen—and walk on the moors and sing her songs. And the next day, and the next.

She straightened her skirts into some semblance of propriety and retied the ribbon on her bonnet. "We're home," she whispered into Jock's ear, barely trusting her voice to carry the simple, ardent words.

* * *

MacNab preceded them into the grand hallway.

"Miss MacKay!" His voice echoed back from the bare walls. "He should have got rid of yon old biddy," he confided to Lizzie, "but Sir Robert insisted Captain Winterbottom needed her around to 'keep the servants in line.'"

"Kate MacKay," he bellowed. "Where is she? It's none of my business, sir, but if you ask me you'd do well to fire that old teuchter."

* * *

The old woman hobbled to the entrance from somewhere in the bowels of the almost-empty house. "I hear ye. I hear ye." She peered at Lizzie, Jock, and Flora with a jaundiced eye. "Who have ye here, MacNab? Ye know the master doesnae want visitors."

"This is your new . . . uh . . . new laird and . . . uh . . . the mistress of the house." He didn't pretend to understand the relationships among his passengers, and nobody offered to explain to him.

Miss MacKay came closer to peer into their faces. "Flora?" she said to Lizzie. "It is Flora MacDonald, is it not?"

"I'm her daughter—Lizzie. Ma's here." Lizzie reached for her mother's arm and gently drew her towards them.

When she got within Kate's vision, the housekeeper drew her cousin into an embrace. "Thank God! I don't see so well any more. Florry, Florry! I was afraid ye'd gone to yer just reward . . . like everyone else I've known. Ye made it safely home. Ye're well then?" She inspected Lizzie's mother closely. "Of course ye are. Aye, of course ye are. Come away ben, I have a fire going in the parlour. There's a cup of tea will be ready in a minute and some of my Dundee cake, Florry, I know it's yer favourite" And to MacNab: "Go tell the master the company is here."

She gave the incredulous MacNab a nod of her head that showed who was in charge here now. "Aye, MacNab, your bonnie fiefdom is coming apart. Ye're not in control of Rannoch now."

His eyes widened as he backed out of the door, cap in hand, and turned tail to get Winterbottom.

* * *

What she had to do tonight made Lizzie feel very anxious. She had anticipated this day for months, ever since she learned her mother was heir to Aulich House and the land. The idea of ejecting anyone from what they considered their own home brought back awful memories. Revenge was bittersweet. Thank God, Jock was with her to give her courage.

"Miss MacKay. Och! I'm so glad you're still here," said Lizzie.

"And where would I be? I'm not dead yet, as ye might know. I wasnae too old to travel to Stornoway and back for an important bible. If the mission is important, call for Kate MacKay."

They all laughed at the old lady's humour.

"So I'm here, and if I understand your undertaking correctly, I have not lived these last years in vain, for you have come to claim your inheritance, I'm told. That foolish nephew of mine was supposed to give the important envelope into your hand, Florry, and he gave it to one of your lads instead."

Kate MacKay had certainly aged, but she still had her wits about her.

Flora said, "My son Charlie carried it all the way to Canada . . . it's a long story. I'll tell it to ye by and by."

"He never reads his mail," Katie continued, nodding her head up the massive curving stairway, indicating her employer. "I told him about the eviction notice and who would be coming to live here. But did he listen?" She snorted in disgust. "I'll warn ye. It might not be easy to remove him. He either does not or will not understand."

They heard him cursing for several minutes before he appeared at the door on the arm of the frightened MacNab. Captain Cedric Winterbottom was almost comical in his ill-fitting kilt. His wraith-like appearance was accentuated by his unshaven, yellowed face. His bloodshot eyes bore through Flora. "You think you'll throw me out, do you, Highland bitch?" He lurched towards her.

Lizzie cried out, "Leave my mother alone," just as Jock and the twins stepped between the drunken man and his target.

"Who do you think you are? Coming here claiming to own this place . . . my place."

"It no longer belongs to you," Jock said.

"It NEVER belonged to you!" Lizzie couldn't hide the rage that escaped with the words.

"You have to leave today. You've been given ample warning, sir," said Jock.

"The letters I read to you—remember?" said Kate MacKay, her voice laced with sarcasm. "Maybe ye should have listened to a 'stupid old teuchter.'" Her harsh laugh ended with a snort. Lizzie could see Kate relished throwing his own words in his face.

"We are taking over occupancy of Aulich house this day," said Lizzie.

"I'll see you in hell first." He spat the words at her and gripped Mac-Nab's arm to steady himself.

"I've been in hell already because of the likes of you," Lizzie spat back.

"Who do you think you are? Mary's father, Colonel Buchanan, was young and foolish when he agreed to that memorandum. Probably under pressure from his pitiful deserter brother."

Lizzie thought, drunk or not, he certainly had his version of the story committed to memory.

"My father was a proud Highlander," said Lizzie's mother. "This, sir, is our native soil. We won't be needing any more opinions about our family from a land-grabbing Sassenach like yourself."

Lizzie pulled herself up to her full height and threatened to run him off herself.

"Sir." Jock's voice was quiet and tightly controlled as he held off the twins. "You will pack a bag with all you need for the night and leave immediately in the coach that awaits you at the door. Say no more if you have a desire to leave these premises with all tender parts of your physical anatomy intact. You may return in the morning for whatever else you think belongs to you."

"There's not much left to remove, Miss Lizzie," Kate said. "He's sold it all for drink and God knows what else."

"And you," Lizzie addressed the factor, who, evidently enjoying his bumbling laird's distress, had one hand partly covering a smirk while the other still supported the befuddled Winterbottom.

"Yes, madam?"

"You will return in the morning to receive your severance pay. We have no more need of your services."

MacNab raised his other hand to his mouth to cover either his facial expression or to hold back a retort. His lack of support unbalanced the captain who slowly slid to the floor. In his struggle to right himself, he got to his knees then onto all fours with his rear end higher so his kilt flew up over his waist.

"Scrape his lordship off the floor, MacNab, and tell him no real Scotsman would wear silk drawers under his kilt," said Donnie.

Jamie opened the great front door to facilitate Winterbottom and Mac-Nab's exit. Kate stood sentinel till they cleared the gate, then turned to face the MacGregors. Lizzie heard the Island woman's raucous laugh reverberating through the mansion.

Lizzie ushered Jock into the drawing room, where she removed her shoes and hose and invited him to do the same. Walking barefoot across the thick pile of the carpeting, she led him by the hand to the warmth of the blazing fire. They sat in awed silence for a while. Lizzie observed that the wonderful library had been left undisturbed. The piano still had its place of prominence.

"We're home, Jock." She nestled into his embrace. "Jock, remember when you said back in Whifflet that our son would have a better chance than we did?"

"Aye. But I never imagined this."

"Do ye remember what else ye said?"

"What did I say?"

"He'll have a guid hoose and the verra best of food and we'll read to him, send him to school and college . . . and we'll do the same for all his wee brothers and sisters."

"What are ye saying, Lizzie?"

"His wee brother or sister will be born in Rannoch in about seven months."

The End

Author Notes

But to conclude my lang epistle,
As my auld pen's worn to the gristle;

* * *

Rannoch

Loch Rannoch

* * *

MacGregors, referred to as the Children of the Mist, hid in the wilds of Rannoch Moor, a favourite place of refuge since 1488 when the Act of Council gave the Campbells legal right to hound and kill them. From Rannoch for forty-two years, under the leadership of Duncan MacGregor, they plundered and terrorized the area and continued to do so after Duncan's death.

In 1589, after a particularly heinous crime of revenge involving a head delivered on a platter to an enemy's wife, the name 'MacGregor' was proscribed (meaning they called themselves MacGregor under penalty of death).

In 1602, 500 MacGregors were triumphant over 800 hastily assembled Colquhouns and others (with the blessing of King James VI). After this the bloody retaliation against the MacGregors intensified, and they were 'legally' captured, killed, branded, and enslaved.

By 1775 the name was no longer proscribed and MacGregors lived peacefully with other clans on sparse land that became less and less able to sustain them. Some still remained in the Rannoch area.

* * *

I searched the northern shore of Loch Rannoch for signs of the Mac-Gregors having lived there into the 19th century. My curiosity sent me scrambling over an ancient stone dyke into a cemetery waist–high with brush and weeds where I found proof that there were indeed MacGregors in the mid-1800s who had left their bones under monuments bearing their names. Some were probably caught up in the infamous Highland Clearances and cruelly ejected from the land they had fought so hard to inhabit for centuries

* * *

The flight of the native people of the Highlands and Islands of Scotland occurred in a period extending over 300 years and particularly from the mid-18th to the mid-19th centuries. Tens of thousands were evicted from their traditional homeland without warning by 'legal' land owners who might have been former clan chiefs or usurpers given tracts of land at the whim of English Kings.

Thousands trekked to the coast to be shipped unceremoniously in "coffin boats" to the Americas or Australia with or without the financial help of their former landlords. Others found their way to coastal regions or to the industrial Lowlands of Scotland or to England to compete for back-breaking work that paid meagre wages and offered deplorable housing.

* * *

Whifflet

* * *

The history of our grandmothers is rarely told, yet is a fascination for me. Mine are Scottish. When I was young, my mother took me to Whifflet to visit my grandparents who had lived their lives within the boundaries of that heavily industrialized village. Granny Milne lost four youngsters and Grandma Fox lost five sons (all my mother's brothers) from treatable childhood diseases. Granny said she buried one twin only to come home to find the other dead. Widowed at forty, she raised her remaining five; four reached adulthood. Other stories I gleaned from the gravestones at the Old Monkland Cemetery.

These hardy women were religious, one a staunch Presbyterian and the other a retired Salvation Army officer. They were teetotallers yet Granny shared with me, on occasion, a wee tot of whisky she saved for medicinal purposes only.

At the behest of the coal and iron-masters, the village of Whifflet in Lanarkshire, along with adjacent villages, was denied burgh status to prevent the passage of public health laws that would have hurt industry profits. In 1885 Whifflet finally became incorporated into the newly formed burgh of Coatbridge.

"The Wheeflet", as it was affectionately called by its loyal inhabitants, only began to improve in the mid-20th century, when mining and steel mills were in decline. The picture that appears on the cover of an early edition of George Orwell's 'The Road to Wigan Pier' is actually from a photo of the Rosehall Rows which were not pulled down till 1930.

Rosehall Rows, Whifflet.

* * *

Surrounded by a region steeped in the Presbyterian faith, Coatbridge has been called 'the most Catholic town' in Scotland, and reflects the same religious strife that infects the North of Ireland. Waves of Irish immigrants, many Catholic, swelled the force that worked alongside Scots with other migrants to tend the huge industrial machine that gave prosperity to the owners.

The Bairds, a father and seven sons, were local farmers who began coal-mining on their property and expanded to iron foundries to become the region's most prosperous coal and iron-masters. Dominant in the district, they garnered profits that allowed them to purchase huge land-holdings in Coatbridge and beyond. Their offspring attempted to buy or marry their way into the upper class. Young Abingdon Baird took the actress, Lily Langtree, as a lover and lived the high life, burning through £3 million (at 1870s prices) in seven years. He died, penniless, with 86 racehorses to his name.

My forebears tended the foundries and mines (one grandfather died at 50 with a "chest" problem and one great-uncle lost an arm in a foundry accident). In the 20th century they found their way out of that lifestyle with their instinct for business.

Alas, no racehorses.

About the Author

Joyce D'Auria, nee Milne was born and raised in Scotland. She graduated from Glasgow Royal Infirmary Nursing School then immigrated to the United States. After raising her daughter, Linda, she earned a Counselling degree at St. Lawrence University in New York and subsequently practiced as a therapist in Florida.

Joyce's humorous articles appeared regularly in The Scottish Banner, distributed to expats in USA, Canada and Australia. A compilation under the title *Lumpy Porridge and Other Scottish Memories* is available online at www.Joycethescottishwriter.com

Joyce lives in Florida with her husband Paul and two cats, Valentino and Caramella.

Glossary of Scottish Words

Ae, one
aglee, awry
Auld, old
Auld Kirk, in Scotland the established church
Auld Lang Syne, lit. old long since, long ago

bairn, child
banes bones
bine, wash-tub
birling, whirling around
black puddin', pudding of blood, oats, meat, etc. traditionally stuffed into
a sheep's stomach and boiled
bletherin', talking idly
blubberin', crying
bluid, blood
brae, hill-slope
braw, fine; handsome; good-looking
breeks, trousers
bunnet, cap
burn, stream
but and ben, kitchen and parlour; to go ben the house, to go into the parlour
byre, a cowshed

cairt, cart
cairted, carried
cas chrom, lit. crooked foot, kind of spade
cateran, cattle thief
chaunt, sing

cheek, impudence
clachan, a small village
clootie dumpling, a dumpling wrapped in cloth and boiled
coronach, dirge
cottar, cottager
croft; crofting, a small piece of arable land, esp. adjoining a dwelling; (verb)
farming a small area
crookit, bent
cuddy, horse

dominie, schoolmaster
dochter, daughter
dram, in Scotland, a drink of any size, usually whisky
dyke, a low dividing wall of stone

eejit, idiot

feart, afraid
frae, from

gaed, went
gang, go
gallivantin', gadding about
gawkit loon, foolish boy; blundering scallywag
gie, rather, very
girnin', crying
glen, a narrow valley with a stream, often with trees
Gleska, Glasgow
glaikit, daft

hap, wrap
heid, head
hielan'; Hielands, highland; the Highlands
Hogmanay, New Year Eve, a gift given on that day
howking, scoop out

jaicket, jacket
jotter, notebook

kale; kail, cabbage or the broth made with it
ken; kent, know; knew
kirk, church esp. church of Scotland
kist, a chest (often used by an girl to collect linens etc. for marriage.)

laddies, boys
leerie, lamplighter
linsey, cloth made of linen and wool
lug, carry

mair, more
mince, stew made with ground beef, onions etc.

nary, never
navvy, a labourer-originally a labourer on a navigation or canal

Orangeman, a member of the Protestant society, Loyal Orange Lodge
ower; owre, over

peenie, apron
plaidie, long piece of woolen cloth, usually tartan
plenishments, furnishings
purritch, porridge

roup, sell at public auction

sae, as
scone. (pronounce to rhyme with 'gone'), round or quadrant shaped plain cake
Scramble, Scottish tradition of throwing coins from the bride's carriage
sheugh, a trench or ditch
sich, such

siller, money
skelped, smacked
skreiching, shrieking
"Slainte mhath!" (Gaelic, pronounce-slahntchuh va) "Good health!"
Slios Garbh; Slios Minh, rough slope; smooth slope
sodger, soldier
sporran, (ornamented) leather pouch worn in front of a man's kilt
spurtle, a stick with which porridge, broth etc. are stirred

tattiebogle, ragamuffin
tacksman, the chief tenant
tatties, potatoes
teuchter, a Highlander; a country person
thon, that
toff, a person of a better class

uisge beatha, or usquebae or usquebaugh (Gaelic, water of life, pronounce-ooskibay), whisky

vauntie, pleased

wean, infant
wheen, several, a lot
wheech, a sudden sweeping movement
Wheesht!, Hush!

ye glaikit big tattiebogle, you stupid big ragamuffin
yin; yins, one; ones
yon, that

Printed in Great Britain
by Amazon.co.uk, Ltd.,
Marston Gate.